NOBODY'S SON
Winner of the Aurora Award

PASSION PLAY

Winner of the Aurora Award and the Arthur Ellis Award

"Dark and nastily believable . . . Sean Stewart [is] a talent to watch."
—William Gibson

"A terrific novel by an author whose talent is both obvious and subtle, a story that engages the imagination and, even better, leaves echoes after the book has been shelved . . . A new voice as distinctive as any in SF."
—Robert Charles Wilson

"Both entertaining and cautionary, *Passion Play* is a wonderful debut novel from a talented new voice."
—Charles De Lint

"A fine novel, in the grand tradition of the SF thriller . . . A very exciting debut."
—Kim Stanley Robinson,
author of *Blue Mars*

"The best piece of Canadian SF since *The Handmaid's Tale* . . . It establishes Stewart beyond doubt as a writer to watch."
—Horizons SF

"A novel so subtle and layered with meaning, that works on so many levels at once, simply has no business being this compulsively readable. *Passion Play* is one of the best first novels I've ever read."
—Spider Robinson,
author of *The Callahan Touch*

"Succeeds both as science fiction and a mystery . . . [A] fast-paced and thoughtful debut."
—Publishers Weekly

Ace Books by Sean Stewart

PASSION PLAY
NOBODY'S SON
RESURRECTION MAN
CLOUDS END
THE NIGHT WATCH

Now available in hardcover from Ace Books
MOCKINGBIRD

THE NIGHT WATCH

Sean Stewart

ACE BOOKS, NEW YORK

This Ace Book contains the complete text of the original hardcover edition. It has been completely reset in a typeface designed for easy reading, and was printed from new film.

THE NIGHT WATCH

An Ace Book / published by arrangement with the author

PRINTING HISTORY
Ace hardcover edition / November 1997
Ace mass-market edition / September 1998

All rights reserved.
Copyright © 1997 by Sean Stewart.
Cover art by Tara McGovern-Benson.
This book may not be reproduced in whole or in part,
by mimeograph or any other means, without permission.
For information address:
The Berkley Publishing Group, a member of Penguin Putnam Inc.,
200 Madison Avenue, New York, NY 10016.

The Penguin Putnam Inc. World Wide Web site address is
http://www.penguinputnam.com

Check out the Ace Science Fiction/Fantasy
newsletter, and much more at Club PPI!

ISBN: 0-441-00554-3

ACE®
Ace Books are published by
The Berkley Publishing Group, a member of Penguin Putnam Inc.,
200 Madison Avenue, New York, NY 10016.
ACE and the "A" design are trademarks
belonging to Charter Communications, Inc.

PRINTED IN THE UNITED STATES OF AMERICA

10 9 8 7 6 5 4 3 2 1

THE NIGHT WATCH

CHAPTER 1

Three days ago Emily Thompson had been Southside's heir apparent. Every soldier in the city had been hers to command. Now the guards outside her door were the only people she had seen since her arrest. They weren't supposed to talk to her. She didn't try to make them. The last thing she wanted was to make some innocent bear her grandfather's anger.

It was six in the morning, March 21, 2074. Not yet dawn. Snowflakes drifted down out of a dark sky into the lamplight beyond Emily's window. Magic comes like this, she realized. At first it barely exists. At first you only see snow in the air; it disappears the instant it touches the ground, or your coat. You never notice the exact moment it starts to endure, a drift of white dust on a sidewalk, or along a tree branch. You go to bed with flakes still falling; when you wake up in the morning the snow is *everywhere*. Everything else has disappeared. Paths and roads have been erased, signs are buried or hard to read. Even the trees look different and strange. The old landmarks are covered or lost, and the world you thought you knew is gone.

Now I understand why Grandfather took the name Winter, Emily thought.

Magic had started falling at the end of World War II, invisible at first, then gradually more obvious. By the time Emily's grandfather was a child, in the 1970's, little drifts of it were building into monsters or miracles often enough to make it clear that a great change was coming. The climate of the world was shifting away from the light of reason into a dusk where dreams put on flesh and the hungers of flesh. Finally, late in the winter of 2004, the rational, scientific world was entirely covered, as lost to memory as summer is in the cold grey days of December. That year, many things that had slept through the age of reason finally woke up. Forests woke up. Buildings woke up. Gods and ghosts and demons woke up everywhere.

When Emily's grandfather was young, he was by far the most powerful angel in his home town of Edmonton. (*Angel*—that's what they called those who felt the magic most deeply back then). Edmonton was a boiler-room of a town, nearly a million people settled on the Canadian prairie one hundred thirty miles east of the Rocky Mountains. They knew something about winter there. In 2004, it was Emily's grandfather who had managed to salvage part of the city, pinning the newly awakened ghosts and demons on the north side of the river that ran through town. On the Southside, there was hardly a trace of magic. Nobody knew how Winter had done that, and he never spoke of it, even to Emily, who was his heir.

That was before he had hit her and put her under house arrest, of course. That was before her inheritance had begun to melt away like a snowflake in her hand.

She heard David Oliver's voice in the corridor, speaking quietly to her guards. Then a soft knock. "Miss Thompson?"

"Jailers don't have to knock, David."

Major Oliver let himself in. "Good morning, Miss Thompson." He was in his early forties and lean, not blocky with muscle like most of her soldiers. His fatigues were always wrinkled and rumpled, his face always clouded with little lines of worry and calculation. Emily thought him the best analyst in Intelligence. He and his computer familiar together made up an exquisitely sophisticated instrument for reading people.

"Business or pleasure, Major Oliver?"

He sat down. "I'm not here to interrogate you, Emily. If that's what you mean by business."

"Thank God." For the last two days Emily had been haunted by the vision of herself strapped to a table with an IV drip in her arm while David slowly and carefully and sadly stripped her soul bare for her grandfather to examine.

"I came to see that you were doing . . . as well as could be expected," David said. "Is there anything you need?"

"To know whether Grandfather is going to have me killed."

"I don't know."

"Guess, David."

He gave her a small smile. "Emily, come on now. Even my guesses are classified."

"I don't think he'll have me killed. All I did was build a fire. I made a little offering, I don't even know why. I didn't know it was wrong."

"Yes you did."

Emily colored. "Okay, I knew he wouldn't like it, but I didn't know why. But it couldn't possibly be worth killing me for. Mind you, I wouldn't have thought he would hit me, either." Emily studied her bruised face in the mirror over her dresser. If her grandfather had taught her one thing it was this: to see a thing for what it was. There was still a dark purple ring near the orbit of her eye, but under that, on her cheek, the bruise was turning brown. In a few days it would yellow and fade. None of the Southside soldiers she commanded would think much of such a shiner. A lot of them had been knocked around by family, too. They had lived.

She would live.

"I just hate the worrying, David. It's such a waste of energy. In three days we have this envoy coming from Chinatown and you and I should be working on that. I try to focus on it but I can't. I keep imagining one of those guards will take me outside and make me kneel in the snow and shoot me in the back of the head. It breaks my concentration."

"I think Winter is coming to see you this morning," David said.

"Ah. So that's why you're here. Advance warning. Why you, though? Why not Claire? Why hasn't she been here?"

"Your governess has been reassigned," Major Oliver said. He paused. "Winter is a hard man, Emily. He's had to be. But he is fair. I really believe that."

"We all do," Emily said.

Quiet as David was, her room felt infinitely more empty when he had gone.

Come on, girlchick, Emily thought. Enough brooding. Enough feeling sorry for yourself.

Still dawn had not come. Emily ordered the lights off in her room and lit seven devotional candles and placed them on her votary. Burning, they gave off a bittersweet smell of incense. Their seven flames she saw doubled in her mirror and redoubled in her dark window. She prayed: forgive us our trespasses, as we forgive those who trespass against us. She prayed to Christ, who had redeemed the world with his own blood, and to Blessed Mary, the Theotokos, the Mother of God. She prayed for strength, and then, more honestly, for deliverance.

When she was done she sat straddling a chair, looking out her window. It was still snowing. You could not tell it was almost dawn. You could not tell that day would ever break again. The snow fell and fell, sliding forever into the floodlights from the surrounding blackness. Emily moved her chair closer to the window and watched it come; the million flakes of snow birthing from that black night, sliding white and lost and windborne, like souls from that outer dark.

It was her angel's fault she was in this fix.

Emily thought she had a touch of her grandfather's gift. There was a voice inside her that was not her own. It knew things she did not know. She trusted it completely and wished she didn't. She was a very practical young woman and didn't like the thought of having something magical inside her. An angel was dangerous and unpredictable, the sort of thing that got you into trouble.

Which in fact it had. It was her angel who led her to the High Level Bridge, the only bridge still standing that connected the Southside to the North. If Emily's governess had been there, she would have held her back. "Destiny doesn't exalt people," Claire would have said. "It just uses them." Claire was only half human, the child of a mortal man and the white hawk demon called The Harrier. She knew a thing or two about destiny. She would have known better than to let Emily follow her angel's voice. But Emily was twenty, a big girl now, and her governess wasn't always around to keep her out of trouble.

Emily's angel had led her to a little hollow under the Bridge, where the roadway first lifted itself clear of the river valley. There, under a lace of iron girders, Emily found a cross drawn in the snow, its edges blurred with drift. Bird tracks were everywhere around it, scratched in the snow like the letters of a language Emily could not read. Beside the cross a little sacrificial fire had been laid but left unlit: a crude pile of dried bark and pine needles, twigs and other tinder.

Southsiders burned ritual fires for their dead, and Emily knew at once this was meant to be a funerary pyre. She hunkered down in the snow and looked more closely. Resting on top of the kindling she saw a bone button and an old brown bootlace that filled her with inexplicable dread. She backed away, turned, and ran gasping in the freezing air all the way to the Tory Building. When she walked into the family's private apartments she saw Winter's boots beside hers on the mat. The right one was missing its lace. One button was gone from her grandfather's old greatcoat.

Emily searched the town records. Four children had died that winter: one crib death, one harvest accident outside the city proper, one from pneumonia, one from abuse. Nothing to connect any of them to the Bridge. But from the day Emily saw the snowy cross, a dead boy came to haunt her dreams, a cast-off child, shivering with cold.

There was a certain thing Winter had commanded to be

done with each child born on the Southside. When the child could walk well, some time between eighteen months and two years of age, it was taken to the top of the High Level Bridge and released, to see whether it would be "called over" to the North Side. Emily had never heard of a child choosing to run from its parents and dash across the Bridge. She had always assumed this was a purely ritual exercise, like circumcising infant boys, or singing the interminable Pascha mass, or reciting the Akathista to the glory of the Theotokos, the Blessed Mary, on the last Friday of Lent. Now, though, she wondered if once upon a time there had been a child, a little boy, who had been called down the long path onto the Bridge and across the river.

She denied the angel in her for days, then weeks. But every night the little dead boy came into her dreams and at last she broke down, hardly knowing what she did, and stole out to the Bridge with a pile of Winter's cast-off clothes to make a funerary pyre. To exorcise that shivering ghost.

Winter caught her doing it. That was when he hit her.

It was nine in the morning when her grandfather finally came to see her. Emily was sitting on the edge of her bed, nursing a cup of hot chicory. Winter stood in the doorway to her room. His eyes were the old grey of weathered wood, of December skies. He gave her the dignity of keeping his distance. Grim and careful and accountable, he required himself to study her bruised face. "May I come in?" he said. She nodded, heart hammering.

lighter, said her angel's secret voice.

"Please," Emily said. "My own company bores me. I agree with myself too much."

"That's a good problem to have." Her grandfather sat down.

"Where's Claire?" Emily asked.

"Reassigned."

"That isn't fair to her. What I did wasn't her fault."

"Fair is none of my concern," Winter said.

wait

wait

"Where did you send her?"

"She has joined our squad of peacekeepers in Chinatown," Winter said.

Emily started. Chinatown was a section of the city of
Vancouver, five hundred miles away, over the Rocky Mountains. "You really did want her out of the way."

"Claire's loyalties are to you, Emily. Not to Southside."

"Not to you, you mean."

lighter

"Claire is less sentimental than you," Winter said. "She
will take her fall from grace in stride."

"True. Any disaster tends to gratify her rather gloomy
view of life." Emily almost smiled. "But she still won't
like being that far away. You forget she loves me."

Winter said, "Not for an instant."

A moment's pause.

Winter was sad, and weary, Emily thought, but not hardened; there was not the steel behind his eyes she would have
expected if he meant to have her killed. She could have cried
with gratitude and relief.

It was entirely Emily's fault that Claire had any place to
go to in Vancouver. Travelling large distances overland was
still impractical; the world was too full of monsters and
bandits and pocket gods and Powers. But the Southside had
been in regular radio contact with people in Vancouver for
almost ten years. Apparently there were several islands of
humanity remaining where the Greater Vancouver Regional
District had been; perhaps eighty thousand souls left of the
two million who had lived there before the Dream of 2004.
Half of these people were in Chinatown.

Five years ago, having put several airplanes in good
working condition, Chinatown had sent a delegation to the
Southside. One of its members, Raining Chiu, had even
fallen in love and married a Southsider, remaining behind
when the rest of her people returned to Vancouver. Eventually Raining and her husband had split up and she had
returned to Chinatown with their daughter, but from conversations with her before she left, Emily had gathered that
Chinatown was increasingly besieged. Growing friction

between several factions had led to gang wars. Reports of demons, spirits, restless ghosts, and nightmares were increasing. Worst of all, monsters that once had been content to prowl Vancouver's Downtown had begun to spill out, pressing harder and harder against Chinatown's borders, just as a thousand years before the Mongols had pushed against the borders of old China itself.

For many years Southsiders had been hiring themselves out as soldiers, which not only sent a supply of needed trade goods back, but also reduced the number of mouths to feed from the meager produce of the short prairie summer. Emily had suggested to the Mandarins of Chinatown that a squad of Southside's best would be a perfect solution to their problems. They were more than a match for the horrors from Vancouver's Downtown, and because they were unaligned with any Chinatown faction, gang, or Power, they would make excellent policemen and tax collectors. The Mandarins had been slow to buy into Emily's idea, but after an ugly incident when three roving monsters from Downtown had slaughtered two whole families before they could be stopped, the Mandarinate agreed. On February 19, exactly a month before Emily's arrest, one hundred Southside soldiers arrived in Vancouver by transport plane and set up a barracks on the outskirts of Chinatown. Now Chinatown was sending a new delegation to discuss their deployment. This was the meeting David Oliver and Emily had been preparing for before her arrest.

Sending Claire to join a garrison that would not have existed without his granddaughter's efforts was an irony Emily was pretty sure Winter had intended.

Winter leaned back in his chair, crossing one booted foot across his knee, old eyes narrowing. Crow's-feet like streambeds on the gaunt prairies of his face. Emily had never understood what an honor his attention was. He was a man to whom friendship came easily, but respect came hard. How arrogant she had been, to take his respect for granted.

"Grandfather, how bad was the thing I did?"

"I don't know." He reached out to her, his skin tough

and his touch gentle on her bruised cheek, like the brush of wheat stalks bending in the wind. "You burned an offering for a little dead boy, didn't you?"

"How did you know!"

"Because I killed him," Winter said.

"Oh my God."

"Finish that cup of chicory," her grandfather said. "Let's go outside."

Emerging from the Tory Building, Emily and Winter walked along Saskatchewan Drive, past the university campus and the fine river valley homes where their important advisors and landholders lived. Winter dismissed his personal bodyguard. From long familiarity, Emily could pick out the perimeter pickets watching their progress: the man on Tory's sentinel platform; the woman ambling a block ahead of them; the occasional soldier on routine patrol, informed by Security via multiplex transmission that Southside's chieftain was taking the heir apparent for a stroll through the neighborhood.

It was a sunny March day in the season Emily always thought of as Melt. The temperature had climbed a few degrees above freezing. Ice glistened wetly on the sidewalk.

listen

Winter's hood was down. He drank in the mild air and the sunshine. "Do you know what an angel is? Not the religious kind you're so keen on, but what they used to be, back before 2004?"

"More or less."

"A person with a talent for magic. Someone who could do impossible things, extraordinary things. I was one. You probably knew that, or guessed it." His long, slow strides were sure on the icy sidewalk. "The magic had been rising since the end of World War Two. Everyone saw that we must drown in it at last. Like many angels, it was given to me to see something of the future, of what would happen after the magic washed the old world away.

"The angels were disappearing very quickly in those years. Men I knew, of great power and influence. Women too. Some fled, some hid. Some were killed by crazy people.

But most of them just . . . stopped being human. They let the magic take them and turn them into something else. I saw a fellow dissolve, day by day, over the summer of 1998. A friend of mine who loved the wind too deeply, and was lost in it. Was he dead? Alive? Something in between? Were the angels who left their humanity behind happier in their new avatars? I didn't know.'' Winter slowed and stopped. ''But I knew they were deserters.'' He looked shrewdly at Emily. ''I do not call them fools, you understand. Your angel's voice feels so right; and you know, deep down inside, that it speaks a truth deeper than right or wrong.''

Emily looked away uncomfortably.

listen

Winter walked on. ''But that's a terrible kind of pride. That puts your soul ahead of your community. I was not a deserter. Not then. Not now. My angel had shown me much of what was to come. But that same angel made me vulnerable to the magic. I knew he would carry me away, to safety or damnation, long before the magic rolled over my fellows. So I cut my angel out and cast him from me.''

A magpie flapped heavily from the wooded river valley and came to land on the branch of a bare-limbed maple just ahead of them. Greedily it eyed their foil jackets and squawked. ''Pretty pretty shiny shiny,'' Emily said. ''Look at it size us up. If it had two friends, I believe it would try to fly off with us.''

Her grandfather laughed. ''Magpies don't have friends. Accomplices, possibly. Friends, never. I used to be a bird watcher, you know.''

''Hm.'' Emily could remember scores of times when her grandfather had demanded her attention, pointing out sparrows or finches, chickadees, crows, cedar waxwings, titmice, pigeons and grouse and woodcock and quail; the snowy owl that stooped like an omen over the south end of the Bridge. Really, we are a principality of birds—North Side as well as South, she thought. All the famous demons of the North Side were birds: ominous Magpie, the seductive Meadowlark and philandering Woodpecker of folktales, and of course Claire's demon mother, the white hawk goddess men called The Harrier.

"When I was young, in the seventies and eighties, this city was ten times as populous," Winter said. "Twice as many cars as people. We were the lords of creation then. We produced more food than we could eat. Imported delicacies from all over the world. Strawberries in January, if you wanted. The outside world made no difference to us." He stopped again to look at Emily. "You understand? We heated our houses in winter and cooled them in summer and the seasons went away. We turned the lights on after dark and the sun ceased to matter. Inside the greater world, we had managed to create another little world, a human world. One so complete we almost forgot the other one existed. Where the seasons and the weather and the cold are in your vision of the world, we had, oh, politics. Fashion. Sports. Human things.

"Now, precious few animals could ever live in the city. You might see a deer once a year, if you lived down by the river valley. Maybe a raccoon, or a beaver along Whitemud Creek. But that was it. But birds, now—" Winter studied the magpie. "What always fascinated me about birds was the way they lived half in and half out of things. Roosting on office buildings. Raiding people's gardens. Straddled across two worlds, the human one and the greater one beyond. Like angels, you see?" He turned away from her. "But sooner or later, Emily, you have to choose."

more

"The little boy."

"Hm. Yes." Her grandfather strode on. "So I cut him out. The angel in me. I took a bottle of whiskey and my grandfather's old shaving razor and I went down to the Bridge late one night. It was a few days after the Dream of 2004 hit us. Traffic had stopped coming from the North Side. A deep ice fog had settled over that end of the Bridge. Nothing that went over came back. The sky was so clear that particular night. Hard cold coming, I thought. That sky so clear and deep. Stars falling through it like snowflakes.

"There were Powers pressing on me all the time in those

days. That was the nature of the magic, you see. To run into any little crack you might have and then freeze there, like frost splitting a sidewalk.'' They came to the end of Saskatchewan Drive, passed through the gate, and stepped over the train tracks beyond. In another minute they were at the head of the High Level Bridge, just where the road started its long slide down from 109th Street to the bridge proper.

Winter pointed at a snowbank only steps away from where Emily's angel had shown her the snowy cross. ''I did it right there. Drank four-fifths of the whiskey by way of anesthetic, and used another few shots on the razor. It was just after moonrise when I stripped off my coat and shirt. It was early in March, this same time of year. Between the fear and the magic and the cold, the skin on my chest and back was so puckered with goose bumps you could have sanded wood with it. Then I laid my belly open with the razor, and dragged my angel out.''

listen

''He didn't want to come, but I was bleeding like a stuck pig, so I yanked him out by the foot and then pinned him under one leg. There was a lot of magic in this, of course. That was the time it was. And I was young then, and counted strong, even among the angels of my day. I splashed the rest of the whiskey on the cut, screaming and swearing between my teeth, and then I packed the wound with snow. The cold was more terrible than you can imagine.''

The man hunched and shivering, his blood pouring onto the moonlit snow. His angel made flesh as a little boy, trapped under his leg.

balance

''You took him over the Bridge,'' Emily said. Her grandfather did not speak. ''That was the Deal you made with the North Side to leave the Southside alone. You cut out your angel and sacrificed him to the dark Powers across the river.''

''I chose to cast my magic from me, so that people— decent, ordinary people—might live, and not be drowned under the magic's tide. I made a sacrifice.''

"And all the other children that we take down to the Bridge, they are part of the Deal, too."

Winter shrugged. "You can't understand what the world was like. Would still be like, if not for that bargain. The magic can be beautiful, Emily, and it can be true. But it is also mad, as mad as fire. It has no rules."

Emily said, "Has there ever been a child really called over to the North Side?"

"Twelve."

calmer—"Oh my God"—**calmer** "I thought it was just a ritual," Emily said. "Twelve little kids. That's a lot." One for each of Christ's disciples. "That's too many."

"The greatest good for the greatest number. The arithmetic isn't difficult." Winter waved back at Southside: eighty thousand souls. "It's the angels who are called, Emily. The ones with a touch of magic in them, the ones who would end up on the North Side anyway, sooner or later. They have a role to play there, or so I choose to believe. They too serve our community."

Called, Emily thought. As if those children walked across the Bridge and were gathered up into the arms of someone waiting there. Southside's changelings, returned to their proper homes. What a lie. She felt hot with shame for her own ignorance. How many, many people there were who must have known the families of those missing children. And she had known nothing. She should have known. She should have been able to tell.

She imagined the children walking across the Bridge into the cold and no one waiting and the children lost, crying for their parents, and dying there. And their bodies, together at the north end of the Bridge. Twelve of them. And her life built on their bones.

Winter said, "You know I carry every one of them."

"I know."

Her grandfather studied her face. "I would fear for your heart if you were not appalled. It is an appalling price. A terrible price. But the lowest price I could pay."

balance
balance

"I wonder if that's what Herod said when he ordered the slaughter of the innocents."

"Don't give me that pious crap, Emily. This is too important. Don't you see, girlchick? It was my little boy you made the offering to. My angel. You've gone and spliced the connection that I cut, all those years ago. You little fool." Winter grimaced. "I felt it the moment it happened. Long before I got down to the pyre beneath the Bridge. In one instant, everything I had made had been undone. Those twelve children, wasted. I could feel my angel again. Not inside me, not yet. But I could feel him stir, and start coming for me like a hound on a trail. He won't rest until we're together again. So I believe. And the Deal will be undone, and the Powers of the North Side will come sweeping over the Bridge, and the fate we were spared seventy years ago in the Dream will take us after all.

"I am one hundred and thirteen years old, Emily. The Deal has held time back from me—but it has been so many years with the frost running through that crack in my middle. And then to feel suddenly that a stupid girl had wasted all my work . . ." He reached out to touch her bruised cheek. "Well."

"I'll live."

He looked at her. "You too are an angel, Emily. In your own way. And being an angel, you have come, as my heir must, to this terrible secret. That is right and proper. You are the blood of my blood, and you are the one who will keep the city when I am gone."

closer

balance

Water dripped and trickled around them, creeping always downward in its blind search for the river valley.

no

no

"Do you see, Emily? The Deal has passed to you. You have grown into your power now, and also into your responsibility. This time it is you who must"—**no!**—"cut the angel from yourself. It will be easier for you than it was for me. I'll make sure of that." He took her hand and she flinched. "A delegation is coming from Vancouver this week to discuss the deployment of our troops there. Your first major policy initiative. You should be proud. We will entertain them for the Feast of the Annunciation," Winter said. "After that business is finished, you and I will do what must be done for the good of the Southside."

no

"You made a deal with the devil, Grandfather. I won't let you cut me open to keep the bargain."

"What do you suggest I do, Emily? Deliberately sacrifice a real human child? The North Side might accept that. Would you really take a little boy or girl from one of your people to save the ghost that lives in you? Did I bring you up to be such a coward?"

Emily's eyes stung. "You don't believe that."

"I know the pain is great," Winter said. "I know the loss is hard. But this is a needful thing, Emily. And I am not asking your permission."

CHAPTER 2

Emily's banished governess, Claire, was in Vancouver. To be precise, she was standing in the gym of the Hong Hsing Athletic Club in Chinatown. The captain in charge of South-side's mercenary troops had chosen her, as the person with by far the least combat training in his company, to demonstrate the value of his soldiers to Water Spider, Chinatown's Honorable Minister for Borders. Jen, Water Spider's bodyguard, would spar with her. Jen was not afraid. Fear was not one of his problems. Then again, neither was stupidity. He was not inclined to underestimate Claire.

It took about ten seconds for the white devil to fake Jen out, distract him with an agonizing pop to the pressure point in his elbow, and then smash him with a snap-kick to the head. He couldn't remember the time between the kick to his head and finding himself gasping with his face pressed into the mat. Judging from the way his whole body was ringing, he hadn't just fallen after the kick. Probably she had slammed him down with a hip throw. Shoulder throw, maybe.

Fuck.

There were three great Powers in Chinatown: Double Monkey, that sneakiest of gods, the Lady in the Garden, and the Dragon. The Dragon was a ferocious Power and the Hong Hsing Athletic Club was the heart of his turf. Jen could feel the eyes of all the Dragon's bully boys on him.

They were lounging against the gym walls, well back from the Southsiders, watching him get the shit pounded out of him by a skinny white lady.

Fuck.

So this was the least dangerous Snow, eh? Not even a soldier. Only as much combat training as they deemed necessary for a little light bodyguard work. Jen blinked the sweat out of his eyes and turned his head just enough to look at her. She stood waiting on the mat. Gangly. A little uncomfortable, even. Not at home in a gym.

Buddha's balls.

The watching Snows clapped and whistled. "Oh, baby, that's gotta *hurt!*" "She shoots, she scores!" "Way to go, Grandma!" "Count one for the governess!"

"Good work, Claire." Jen heard the Southsider captain clap lazily. Clap. Clap. Clap. Big-nose bastard.

Jen touched his face where she had kicked him. "It will be embarrassing, this foot-shaped bruise. Size eight," he said. "Maybe nine."

The Snows laughed. "Nine," Claire said.

Jen's opponent held out her hand to help him up. She was much older than the enlisted men. Middle to late thirties, Jen guessed; not much younger than his mother. Tall and ropy. Small breasts that sagged under her shirt. Her skin was cold to the touch and white. Not white like the other Southsiders were white, but *white;* the color of thick frost on a window. Her eyes were the color of melting ice cubes and her hair was white as dice. Her pants and tank top were also white. Unlucky.

Jen's mouth was full of blood.

Be fire. Be fire.

He hopped back onto his feet, ignoring her offer of help. His scarlet shirt and pants fluttered like licks of flame. "Not bad. For a girl."

Claire reached out and tapped him, ever so lightly, on his bruised jaw. "Woman."

He was standing now. Better. But he was still empty inside, hollow as a reed, the impact of the blow still humming in his bones. On a chain around his neck he wore a lucky

charm, the leg bone of his grandfather's cat. He touched it
and took in a deep breath, pulling the air down to *dan tien*,
to fan the fire there. His center became heavier, filling with
chi. Warm energy broke freshly from the coals in *dan tien*,
creeping out to his limbs. His limp fingers curled imperceptibly as he let the *chi* build in his palms. He was no longer
so empty inside. The buzzing faded.

Jen ignored the fucking Hong Hsing Athletic Club thugs
and looked back to his master, standing on the sidelines.
Water Spider's hair, just touched with dignified grey, was
immaculately bound and pinned; his lean face was calm as
a mountain lake. Why shouldn't it be?—it wasn't him the
Snow was pounding into cat shit. Jen's master returned his
glance, and gave a measured nod.

Jen swallowed his own blood and grinned at Claire.
"Again? Double or nothing?"

The Southside captain nodded to Claire. She assumed a
fighting stance, carrying most of her weight on her back leg,
her front leg empty, toe just touching the ground. Ready
with a kick, should the opportunity to use her superior reach
reveal itself. "You are a good fighter," Jen said. "Very
good. But ugly. There is no elegance in your stance. No
detail."

"True—but I don't have a footprint on my face."

"Not yet." Jen darted in, two quick shuffle steps, just to
watch her move. He had his nimbleness back now. Wary as
a bird. They circled, rocking and watching. Be fire, he told
himself. Bend like flame. Break and split, burn and creep.
Hands and feet quick, quick as a cat. Quick as little fish.

She tracked him, words and numbers streaming down her
melting-ice eyes. Fucking Snows and their computer familiars and heads-up display contact lenses.

She would crush him, of course, this governess who
wasn't even a soldier. A blind man could see that. Water
Spider could see it too. Clearly that wasn't the point. Jen
wished he knew what the point was. He swallowed a little
more blood, and pushed on his front teeth with his tongue.
He didn't think any of them were loose.

No doubt Water Spider had his reasons.

They rocked and circled. Jen wondered if the better fighters would have hit him so hard. Probably not. More control.
Fuck. Claire's white calves and arms were shockingly defined. "Wouldn't want to take you to bed." He shook his
head, considering. "Hurt myself." The Snows laughed behind Claire's back.

"I'd save you the trouble," she said.

She towered over him, tall as a crane. He was a small
fighter, short and blocky and explosive. He fought the Wing
Chun style, lots of speed and power, lots of short force, lots
of joint locks and throws. Infighting. But this Claire was a
white devil: balance like a snow leopard, limbs like whip-
steel. Words and numbers and shapes hissed in tiny lines of
pale blue fire across her eyes.

"You have a very cold luck around you. You know that?
Brr. Your friends here: just a bunch of big muscle round-
eyes. But you! Cold luck. Cold cold luck." Jen clicked his
tongue against his teeth. "And so white! All Snows are
white, but you! Did someone bleach you as a baby?"

Claire smiled. It was a singularly warmthless smile. "I
got my looks from my mother," she said. Her foot jumped
out like a jackhammer.

Jen dodged and feinted. "You used to be the princess's
bodyguard."

"Governess. And Emily is no princess. How did you
know that?"

Jen smirked. "I wonder how you failed, to lose your place
of honor and get sent out here?"

She slapped his leading hand away. Her left leg flashed
out in a fast kick. It was only meant to be a feint, but Jen
barely jumped back in time. He dropped to the floor and
sprang in to sweep her feet out from under her—but she
was already in the air, not just jumping above his sweep-
kick, but driving with her other foot for his chest. He threw
up an arm to block. She took the force of his block as a
momentum gate, spun, and drove a back-knuckle strike into
his solar plexus.

Air exploded out of him and he toppled over like a
chopped reed, diaphragm in spasms.

Claire jerked him up off the mat and held him for a moment by his collar. "Mind your manners," she said. Then she dropped him and walked back to the other Snows.

The Southside captain held his hands out to Water Spider. "It's not your boy's fault. You can't compete without a familiar. Everyone in the squad has been wired up for at least eight years. That's eight years of absolute optimization: muscle mass, respiration, heart and lung capacity, reflex arcs—everything. Every strike, every block, every throw. We barely have to pay attention. If she had to, Claire's body could replay exactly what your man did in the last two falls. And she's spent less time in combat training than any of my regulars."

Jen's face burned. The fucker was embarrassed for him! Fucking big-nose cat-cunt licker.

Water Spider said, "How interesting." He looked at his bodyguard. "Jen?"

By the Buddha's three rotting testicles! Jen moaned inside. He sucked another breath through his clenched teeth, and grinned at Claire. "One more? Double or nothing?"

"This is pointless," Claire said.

The Southsider captain spoke softly. "There is no shame in losing, sir. Not when you are outgunned."

Water Spider's face was as distant as clouds.

Jen rubbed his aching stomach. "Please, Captain: I am my lord's personal attendant. Your Claire has already failed at such a job. How can I pass up a chance to learn from her?"

Claire turned and walked back onto the mat.

"Claire, I have not authorized—"

Her pale eyes locked on Jen like gun sights. "Let's go."

Jen bowed to Water Spider, and then to Claire. Halfway up from the bow, he raised his head and spat in her face.

Even when she hissed and raised her hands he didn't underestimate her. He drove in with a high kick, giving her something to block on pure reflex, following immediately with a fast back-knuckle strike to the face. At the last instant he opened his hand, turning the back-knuckle into a ringing back-handed slap, and then dodged back out of range. The sound of the slap echoed from the gym walls in the shocked silence that followed.

Somewhere in the background a couple of the Dragon's fighters jeered and whistled. The stupid fucks had some ideas about honor and fair play and no doubt were embarrassed that anyone from their city, even a thug like Jen, should have spat in the Southsider's face instead of getting his ass whipped with dignity. Fuck 'em. Jen admired his handprint on Claire's white cheek.

The Southside captain shook his head. "You dirty little shit."

Water Spider said, "Is there a problem, Commander?"

"Problem! You saw what the little bastard did."

"Three weeks ago a minotaur came out of the slums and ripped the arms off an old man behind his house on Carrall Street and drank his blood." Water Spider glanced at Jen, who stood piously at attention. "Perhaps you and your usual enemies have a set of rules worked out for your encounters, Commander. Alas, we have managed to arrange no such niceties with our demons, or with the monsters that come from Downtown. We expect any fighting to be . . . no holds barred."

The Snows' captain, a chunky man in his early forties who could no doubt bench press Jen for hours, eyed them both. His anger rapidly faded to something like contempt.

Jen said, "There is no dishonor in serving well."

Claire wiped the spit off her face. Blood trickled from a split lip, shocking against her eerie snow-white skin. Lines like veins of frost flowered and faded across her melt-water eyes. "Go again, little man? Double or nothing."

Water Spider nodded.

Jen fought to hide his shock. Had he failed somehow? Could Water Spider have expected him to beat the Snow? Was he being punished for his weakness? Was he now expendable?

He touched his lucky amulet. Flame can't be broken, he told himself. Smoke can't be held. Be fire. Be fire. "Let's go," he said. He still couldn't seem to get his breath back and his right leg was shaking. Every Southsider would know

it. They all knew he was inferior. They had known that from
the beginning. But now they knew he was afraid. He yelled
and leapt to the attack.

Seconds later he was flat on the mat with Claire's knee
in his chest. Fireworks burst and faded before his eyes.
Slowly and deliberately she took his cat-bone charm between the fingers of her left hand and snapped it in half.

Jen screamed, grabbing for the broken amulet. She held
the halves up and then snapped them in two again. Then she
let the pieces drop on his chest. "You broke my luck, you
bitch!" He swore vilely in Cantonese. The collar of his scarlet shirt was grainy with bone dust. "Well? Are you done?
Or do you want to break more bones?"

She took her knee off his chest. "I'm done."

Later that afternoon, Jen limped stiffly over to his master,
who sat enjoying the classical garden at the heart of Government House. "Old man!" Water Spider called. "Please,
venerable sir, won't you join me on this bench?"

Jen scowled. "May your penis fall away and be carried
off by cats." He had rubbed his skin red with Tiger Balm
liniment, but even so, his bones still seemed to creak like
bamboo wind chimes at every step.

"Sit," Water Spider said, unoffended. "Let your mind
find tranquillity."

"But—"

"And your mouth find silence."

Jen shut up.

Like a closed fist, the garden held yin and yang within
itself. Wind and rain-carved sculptures of Lake Tai lime-
stone were balanced against crooked pines, a harmony of
living and unliving. The broad flatness of the central pond
was interrupted by a jutting rocky island in its midst.
Though scarcely twenty paces in diameter, this island was
bored through with caves and grottoes underneath. A black-
crowned night heron, smaller and more furtive than the great
blue herons that usually graced the gardens of Government
House, lurked at the island's edge, watching Jen and his
master.

"I wish to give up my post," Jen said.

"Request denied."

"Why? Why gamble on me? Surely you can see that any Snow would make a better bodyguard."

"True."

"So do it. You would be a fool not to throw away an old card for a better one."

Overhead, small white clouds quarrelled in the afternoon sky. Water Spider said, "My father once told me of a wise saying of his time: 'Own property, but lease cars.' "

"What?"

"The Snows I can only lease, Jen. In this case, I prefer to own."

"Honor is everything to the Southsiders. They would rather die in your service than break their contracts."

"Mm. I could find one to die for me, no doubt. But would one be shamed for me?" Water Spider looked shrewdly at Jen, who flushed under his eyes. "Now that's a different question, eh?"

Jen grunted. Trying not to whimper, he lowered himself to the tiles at the edge of the pond. The heron watched him impassively from one yellow-ringed eye. Jen made a face at it.

Little suns were radiating from the patches of Tiger Balm smeared on Jen's body. I should have just bathed in it, he thought morosely. "So why don't we use familiars ourselves? There must be something we could trade to the Snows for them." He winced, rubbing moodily at the burning point under his rib cage where Claire's back-knuckle strike had taken him. "A single one of these Snows could demolish the Shrouded Ones without breaking a sweat."

"You speak of things you do not understand," Water Spider snapped. Jen looked up, surprised. "The Shrouded Ones are a mystery you do not grasp." Water Spider gazed into the darkness of the pond. "When I was a boy, I used to play with a little girl who lived at the end of our street. Her name was Mai. We would climb trees together, or pretend to be robbers or ghost-catchers.

"Then one day Mai didn't come out to play. I saw that

a shadow had fallen on her house. There is no better word. Even in the brightest sunshine, darkness clung to it. The next day there was a gargoyle on the roof, perfectly still, hunched over the living-room window. The next day another. By the end of the week, there were four of them. At night you could hear them whispering. Now the house was always dark, wrapped in shadows even at noon.

"We all stayed on the other side of the street, of course. We tried not to go down that way. But at the end of the week, because Mai was my friend, I went to stare at her house from behind a neighbor's hedge. I saw Mai and her mother looking out from a window on the second floor. Mai with her little face pressed up against the glass. Her mother grabbing her by the shoulder. Watching.

"I ran home crying to my father. All that week he had been very deep in his wine, but he had just awakened from a long sleep when I returned, and I told him about my friend Mai. I had told him before, of course, but he had not remembered. He looked at me for a long time, and then he asked if he should save them. I said of course he should. I said that just because Mai had no daddy, that was no reason she should die.

"He gave me a curious look, and then he did a very strange thing. He took a long hot bath, and when he came out of the bathroom I saw that he had shaved as well. He put on his finest clothes, and belted on this," Water Spider said, tapping the ancient and beautiful sword he carried at his side. "I asked him where he was going. He said he had to ask a favor of some people he had known once, long before.

"Midnight had swallowed Mai's house by the time he returned. With him came a small man he did not introduce. This man frightened me greatly, for he was dressed all in white. He did not speak, and his eyes were like a road that no longer has a destination. He walked up the path to Mai's house, and knocked. Gargoyles boiled up around him like leaves tossed by a storm, but they did not touch him. He passed inside. Some time later he returned with Mai and her mother.

"As soon as they left the shadow of the house, the mother gave a great cry and fell to the ground. Two thin snakes slid from the pupils of her eyes, and another one, much greater, poured from her mouth, coiling around Mai. Then, I heard the voice of the man in white, for he gave a great cry, and grabbing the large snake around the neck he thrust it into his mouth and devoured it. The first of the small snakes he crushed beneath his foot, but the other slid into Mai through her screaming mouth. It took many months for Hsieh Wen the herbalist to cleanse her of it, and she went blind from the potions he gave her."

Jen's mouth was dry. "The mother was dead?"

"Worse."

"And Mai?"

"That I do not know," Water Spider said softly. "I have not seen her in many years. I heard once that she had gone to serve the Lady in the Garden, but I do not know if that was true. It was many months before she could come out to play with me again. When she did, she could not see, and I was a boy of great energy. In this I betrayed her, for I was impatient, and her white eyes scared me."

"If it hadn't been for you, she would never have lived at all."

Water Spider looked deeply into the water. "To do what is right and honorable is small credit to a man. We expect it. A lifetime of accomplishment does not excuse the moment's cowardice. A hero who betrays a friend is worse than the fleeing coward; for he knows full well what he does." A light breeze passed through the branches of the plum trees that bordered the pond, shaking down a scatter of blossoms to float on the water's surface. Water Spider said, "Do you think one of your Snows could have gone into that shadowed house?"

"Mm."

"We are like the T'ang: barbarians pushing always on our borders, petty squabbles weakening us from within. We need a strong Emperor, but the throne sits empty." Water Spider opened his hands and allowed himself a small smile. "We poor bureaucrats do what we can. The barbarians from

Downtown are much like men. Distorted, deformed, grotesque—but men just the same. Yes, the Snows will beat
them back. But there are worse things than those poor mock-
eries of men, Jen, and older.''

"Mm," Jen said again. He never knew what to say when
Water Spider got mystical on him.

"I did not think it was a good idea to bring the Southsiders here when we voted in Council on it, and I do not
think it a good idea now," Water Spider said. "I worry that
the Double Monkey will cheat them and the Dragon will
want to fight them and the Lady in the Garden will find
them . . . unaesthetic." He opened his hands. "But they are
here and we must accept that. We are sending a delegation
to the Southside to report on the progress of this venture.
Each of the Powers will be represented, and of course Li
Bing will go to speak for the Mandarinate. Her daughter, Li
Mei, works in my Ministry. I think I will send her along
too. I would like a pair of eyes there."

Water Spider paused. "Hm. It occurs to me that it would
be polite to invite someone from Cedar House as well."
Cedar House was several miles to the east, just where Chinatown was walled off by the great Forest that had swept
over much of Vancouver in 2004. The family that dwelt in
Cedar House had a special relationship with the wood.
While the brooding Forest was not precisely one of the Powers of Chinatown, Water Spider felt it politic to keep on its
good side. "Jen, I have an errand for you. Go to the east
end and find a friend or relative who will take an invitation
to Cedar House. Do not venture under the trees yourself, of
course."

"No fucking fear there," Jen said. He would rather go
ten more rounds with the white devil Claire than set foot in
the gloomy Forest that had swallowed a million people during the Dream and never let them loose. "Should I wait for
a reply?"

"Oh no, nobody will come," Water Spider said. "Raining Chiu was on the last delegation. Do you not know this
story? I suppose you were still busy robbing wine stores and
beating people up back then. The daughter of Cedar House

went to the Southside five years ago, met a man there and
married him and had a child by him, too. Their marriage
fell apart and she has since returned home with her daughter.
I think it unlikely she will choose to go back to that white
cold hell. But it is polite to ask.''

"So all I have to do is give the message to someone who
will take it to Cedar House?''

"Exactly.''

Jen's bones and muscles creaked and whined at the
thought of having to get up and run errands. "Master? Why
did you bid me go the extra round with Claire-the-bitch?
You must have known what would happen.''

"I wanted you to know just what they are, these Snows,''
Water Spider said. "I want you to understand their
strengths. Because I fear that one day I will need you to kill
one for me.''

Soon Jen left on his errand and Water Spider returned to
the offices of his Ministry within Government House. Only
then did the black-crowned heron who had been watching
them from the pond shake out his blue wings and climb into
the sky, beating over the red walls of Government House
and across the street, to drop down into the Lady's Garden
there.

In this place was beauty beyond the skill of painters to
depict, for here dwelt the elegant Lady who was one of the
three great Powers of Chinatown. A time was swiftly approaching when Chinatown would change utterly, and the
Lady, like cunning Double Monkey and the mighty Dragon,
had many eyes hidden in the eaves of Government House.
Of all that Water Spider had said, her servant the heron told
her, and of many other things beside. "Soon or never,'' the
heron said. "If you want to fill the Emperor's throne, soon
or never.''

"Soon, I think.'' The Lady stroked her servant's black
head-feathers. "Even if Chinatown survives, the Powers are
dwindling. It would be good to have an Emperor on the
throne when we fade away at last.''

"The Lady is eternal,'' the heron said stoutly.

"Nothing lives forever, not even gods," she said gently. "For all his strength, the Dragon cannot best Death. For all his cunning, Double Monkey cannot cheat him. Shall I last when they pass away? No. Our part in the world is ending. We have just a little time, a breath, to leave all in harmony for the coming dawn."

"The Dragon does not care about harmony. Harmony is not the Double Monkey's love."

The Lady smiled. "They will serve it nonetheless. It is my role to make it so."

The heron fluffed and preened and stepped nervously from one foot to the other. "And do you then see who must be Emperor?" he asked. "I have studied all of Chinatown's noble men, all our finest ladies. I cannot see one of Imperial quality."

The Lady's smile broadened. "Perhaps you should not look at fine ladies or noble men," she said. But who she meant to put on Chinatown's throne, she would not say.

CHAPTER 3

The young woman who offered to carry Jen's message to
Cedar House was named Wire. She and Raining had been
friends since they were girls, and Wire was quite sure Raining ought to go back across the Rocky Mountains and patch
things up with Nick, the Southside man she had married.
Wire could just imagine Raining, left to her own devices,
settling for a lonely, loveless life; she had always had a taste
for bitter things, an eye for shadows. Wire, more sensibly,
liked her stories to have happy endings.

Wire lived a couple of miles from Government House on
the southern edge of Chinatown, right against the Forest.
From her balcony she could just touch the petals of the
blossoming cherry tree that stood between the human world
of her apartment and the copse of birch and poplar that
formed the outskirts of Raining's wood. Jen had come too
late in the afternoon for Wire to set out that day. Welcome
as she usually was in the Forest, she would never go there
after dark, not without Raining. So she paced around her
apartment making plans and sandwiches for the next day's
journey. She meant to get to bed early and start out at dawn,
but boredom drove her out of her apartment that evening to
visit friends. What with a cup of one thing and a bowl of
another, she didn't get back until after midnight, and she
slept in, snoring gently, until well after sunrise.

When she finally woke it was at the touch of a god's eyes.

He was sitting in the cherry tree beyond her balcony, clad in the body of a red-crested woodpecker, his powerful head thrust back, his beak open and laughing. She knew he was a god because of the way the skin crawled on her back, the weight of his black eyes, and the way the air smelled of lightning and peaches.

With a hop and a rustle the god was gone, leaving only quivering branches behind. Wire made a brief devotion to him and sat up in bed, wondering why he had been watching her.

You never could tell what gods were up to.

It was a promising morning. To the north, mist coiled on the lower slopes of the mountains. To the west, early sunshine glinted on the waters of False Creek and English Bay. South lay the Forest, its dark heart of pine and cedar wrapped in gloom. Wire wasn't much looking forward to hiking in there; she would definitely have to choose her charms with care. Of course, it might not be necessary to have extra luck on her side. Maybe Raining would be easy to persuade. Maybe she would say, Wire, you are quite right. I see that now. Of course I should return to the Southside and put my marriage back together. Thank you so much for showing me my mistake.

Wire laughed and headed for the shower.

After shower and breakfast came the difficult task of choosing the right clothes for her journey. Wire dithered for some minutes, then closed her eyes and picked something at random, promising herself to wear whatever she grabbed. She came up with a charcoal vest she had been in love with a year ago, but was tired of now. She stuffed it back in the closet. Finally, forbidding herself to question the impulse, she pulled out a deep blue rayon skirt, shrugged into a matching shirt, and gathered her long black hair into a ponytail.

Why would a god be interested in her? Of course, there had always been plenty of gods of the sort who hung around peering in women's bedroom windows, if stories were true. Wire was twenty-seven years old, with a body that pleased both her and the men of her acquaintance. Perhaps that was all the god was interested in. An alarming thought. The affections of gods were hard to avoid, and sometimes dangerous.

She pushed that worry aside for later and stood before her cedar treasure chest, wondering what to take as a good luck charm. Her wisdom teeth in their little bone box? Not quite right. A vial of crushed poppy dust? A pierced silver dollar dangling from a red cord? With a smile she picked up the little fluted seashell with the god inside that she had found on the beach when she was four, and held it to her ear. But the shell was silent; the little humming god was gone.

Wire felt crushed. Her oldest, dearest charm was just a shell, now; an empty bone house where some sea creature once had lived. No luck to anyone anymore. "Well, damn," she said. Her eyes teared a little and she wiped them with her hand.

It wasn't as if there had always been magic in the world. Raining's father told her once that there was hardly any magic from the 1600's to World War II. When it started coming back, people had been scared of it. For years nobody believed in the golems that had manifested themselves in the concentration camps at Treblinka and Dachau, until the number of confirmed witnesses was too great, and the first minotaurs began appearing in America. Wire supposed it would have been terrifying to live then, with the magic creeping a little higher every year like the high-water mark of an endlessly rising tide, until the Dream, when Powers all over the world began to wake.

But that was Wire's world. And if it had been a desperate thing to feel the magic rise until the world you knew was drowning in it, was there not a different bitterness to living in an age when the magic was draining away? To watch the spirits leaching from their temples, one by one? To lift a shell that once a god had filled, and find it empty? Because that was what was happening, Wire was sure of it.

Not many people here believed her yet, but that was because they didn't look. They just wanted to wear their charms, hoard their luck, and get on with the day. Well, they would see. In a few more years the world would be so empty that even her busy fellows would notice the silence.

Sadly Wire put back the shell.

Next she picked up a gold locket Raining had given her, with Wire's portrait etched on a piece of ivory. Raining hadn't made it an especially flattering portrait: a profile, in cameo style, of Wire in middle age. Her hair was pulled back into an unattractive bun. The line of her jaw had begun to blur with fat. Wire had never found it a very lucky charm. The days she wore it she often felt sadder than usual, and more uncertain.

She straightened and hung the locket around her neck. This day, of all days, she couldn't afford to lose faith in Raining's friendship. She pulled on her chunky black ankle boots and did up their lucky red laces, then grabbed her wool over-cape, in case it was drippy in the wood. She touched the locket with her fingertips, and said a quick travelling prayer.

The path to Cedar House never went the same way twice. Sometimes, for a friend like Wire, it was a few quick minutes trotting through a pleasant birchwood to reach Raining's house; other times, or for less welcome visitors, the way could wind for hours, or even days, through gloomy chambers of pine and red cedar and western hemlock. Wire grinned to herself, remembering Raining's birthdays when they were girls: how Wire would step from the meadow onto what looked like a path snaking deep into the wood, only to find her foot falling into the parlor of Cedar House, and Raining waiting there for her, all greedy eyes and fingers.

Today the path went on and on.

The first part was always the easiest, a pleasant track winding through a copse of birch and poplar trees. Wire stopped for lunch just before noon, squatting down with her back against a skinny birch. She unpacked a meal of cold fried bread and smoke-cured salmon and two of last year's apples, wrinkled and sweet.

By the time she stood up, wet low-lying clouds were moving in from the sea: flat drippy-looking things like damp cloth, thickening gradually into a sodden grey quilt. The sun smeared and dwindled, mumbling as he drifted away from her. A cold wind sprang up, stealing the sun's words and making Wire's head ache. Each time she put a leg forward, the wind slipped through the split in her cape. Unhappy birch leaves shivered overhead.

Turning a bend, Wire was startled by a narrow, deep channel with a stream running at the bottom of it. The water slid, cool and certain, under an old plank bridge and away between banks clotted with ferns. Wire stood for a moment on the bridge's back, looking down. A dense coldness rose from the stream. Toppled trees had sunk into him along his length; tongues of yellow and green moss licked and curled around them like slow flames.

Once when they were teenagers she and Raining had discovered this stream, and Wire had wondered out loud what it would be like to take him as a lover. It had seemed like an obvious question—sex was everywhere for her back then—but the comment had delighted Raining. Wire remembered the flush of pleasure she had felt, seeing the admiration in Raining's bird-bright eyes. Later, when Raining showed her the sketches she had drawn of the stream's smooth nakedness, Wire had shivered at how perfectly Raining understood her. How perfectly they understood one another.

Which was why they would be friends forever. Raining could hate her, or she could hate Raining; often had, for a minute or a day. That didn't change anything important. That didn't change the way you felt her breath inside your chest.

Shortly after Wire crossed the stream, the birchwood ended and the real Forest confronted her: a looming wood of mournful cedars and towering Douglas fir. She slowed, then stopped, reaching out to touch the last little birch. The light failed suddenly at the edge of the cedar wood; she could not see ten paces into its shadows. Raining had taken her through the cedars often enough, of course. But only a few times, in their rocky teenage years, had Wire had to

plunge into the dark wood alone. "Come on, Raining," she
said out loud. "Don't be like this."

The sky was grey and dreary. Birch leaves hissed and
trembled around her. A thin strand of rain touched her cheek
like a wet thread. The cedars creaked and sighed among
themselves in dark, restless voices.

Wire wished she could still hear the sun.

Ch-ch-ch-ch-chk! Wire jumped at the sound of a beak
drumming against wood. It was the woodpecker who had
been at her window. He sat high on the trunk of the last
birch tree. His head was cocked to watch her, and his bright
black eyes gleamed. His beak gaped, laughing.

Wire thought. Presently she dragged a small folding knife
out of her pocket and carefully cut a few black hairs from
her head. These she tied around the lowest branch of the
woodpecker's tree. They fluttered there like strands from a
broken spider web. She knelt to ask the Forest's blessing.
Mud and leafmold squelched beneath her knee. Then she
was up on her feet again, slapping the dirt off her skirt.
"Right," she said. She touched her locket once for luck,
and stepped inside.

Evergreens rose around her like the ruined walls of an
abandoned house. Old needles and darkness had choked off
any ground cover but ferns, with here and there an isolated
patch of salal or Oregon grape, or a sickly huckleberry bush.
Between the chambers of cedar and Douglas fir, a few thin
pines struggled for light, their trunks marked with trails of
crusted sap. The air was musty and damp and still.

The forest track shrank, pattering between the trees like
a small animal, pausing to hem and haw over every turn
and twist. Wire hadn't heard his busy little voice outside,
but here it seemed precious to her. The path paused; started
to the left; changed his mind and doubled back to wind
around an enormous cedar before hurrying off into the
gloom. Wire took a deep breath. "Ready or not, here I
come!"

And really, she was thinking crossly two hours later, it was
just like Raining to run into the wood and hide from her

problems. Wire stumbled over a root and swore. Up ahead,
the path paused and looked back, murmuring fretfully to
himself. Wire squatted down to rub her bruised toe. Her legs
felt heavy from too much walking and her head ached. It
was always dark under the cedar wood, but it was getting
darker.

A glint of distant light caught Wire's eye as she stood up.
She stared through the gloom. Just when she had decided
there was nothing there, she caught it again: a quick flash
of yellow lamplight breaking through the trees. Cedar
House. Relief rushed through her, even though she knew it
might yet take the path hours to find the house, or days. But
the house was there, and that was something.

Mind you, she never felt entirely safe in Raining's home.
Many times Wire had been sleeping over and wakened from
strange dreams to find no roof above her, but her bed lying
under a canopy of dark branches. Overhead, a burning moon
adrift in pewter-colored clouds, or a handful of glimmering
stars.

Once, creeping out of Raining's room to use the bathroom
in the dead of night, she had opened the door to find the
hallway gone, and in its place only a narrow path between
dark trees. She had stayed on the threshold for the longest
time, rocking back and forth so her bare toes touched the
dirt, staring at the distant flicker of the night-light in the
bathroom, trying to work up the courage to walk there. She
had closed the bedroom door and waited in the dark until
her bladder forced her to try again. This time the hallway
was back and the bathroom only a few steps away. She peed
in messy haste and ran back to Raining's room as if all the
gods in hell were after her. She jumped into bed to lie cow-
ering next to Raining's small warm body for what seemed
like hours. When she fell asleep at last, the cries of owls
followed her into her dreams.

Still, better to be in Cedar House than out here in the
Forest, lost and alone.

Wire dug a flashlight out of her skirt pocket. Her hands
were shaking. She tabbed it on, wincing at the sudden glare.
The path jumped, every root and jutting rock stark in the

harsh light. Green moss smoldered down tree trunks and crawled over stumps, or hung in dull yellow strings where it had died. Beyond the edges of her light, the darkness was absolute.

She forced herself to walk on.

Once, when they were young, Raining had left her in the Forest. They were supposed to be playing hide and seek and Raining got mad because Wire ran too fast and always managed to reach home base without being tagged. So one time Wire dashed back to home base but there was no Raining there, just dust and dim light, and the gloomy cedars creaking overhead. She panicked and ran off the path, crashing through the wood until they found her an hour later, slumped against a tree and bawling her head off. Raining told her it was her own fault for leaving the path.

Wire remembered that.

The evening wind came up, making the big cedars creak and groan. She went faster. The beam from her flashlight jumped and jerked. She was right on the heels of the little path now, running him down so he only stayed a step or two ahead. She had to stumble and twist to follow him between the trees.

A big branch lashed out and slapped her in the face.

"Shit!" Wire wiped her mouth on the back of her hand, spitting out the taste of wet bark. She ran on, her breath ragged. Her whole mouth was tingling and salty with blood. She could feel her lip getting fat. Her footfalls thumped heavily into the muffled ground. She felt the darkness thicken and contract, waking up and turning its attention on her. She sprang forward.

The startled path broke away and bolted into the Forest, leaving her. Twigs cracked and ferns rustled in his wake, and then fell silent. Wire swung her flashlight around, stabbing at the darkness. She was alone.

She swung the flashlight around more slowly. Her shaking hands made nervous shadows. No sign of the path.

All right. Think.

Her batteries would last for days, if need be. There was plenty of water in the little streams that crisscrossed the wood. All she had to do was find one and follow it down to the sea. She could wait for morning, if necessary.

Except nobody got out of the Forest. Not if it didn't want them to. She was trapped.

"Please, Rain," she whispered. "Don't leave me here."

CHAPTER 4

"I would never do that," said a voice from the darkness. "Though I can see why you might be worried. I'm in the habit of leaving people lately, aren't I?"

"Raining!" Wire cried, spinning around. "Rain! You—you came for me. About goddam time, too." She swung the flashlight beam toward Raining's voice and caught a glimpse of her shoulder through a screen of branches. With the path gone, Wire had to push her way through a thicket of pine boughs. "I was on the path twelve hours, Rain. Until he bolted."

"How much of you could he be expected to stand?" Raining said, but she pulled Wire close and hugged her. Raining had never been cuddlesome; even as a baby she had squirmed away from doting grown-ups. Wire, who was incurably given to spontaneous hugging, backslapping, hand-taking, shoulder-grabbing, and hair-tousling, knew Raining's flinch better than anyone. But Raining was not drawing away now. In the dripping darkness she hugged Wire fiercely and would not let her go. Wire was glad of her, and the warmth of her.

"You're shivering," Raining said, stepping back at last. "Let's take you home and get a nice hot cup of tea in you."

Wire shone the flashlight around, still tightly gripping Raining's hand. "Are you sure you can find your way back?"

Raining laughed. "It's my forest," she said.

On the morning the Forest had awakened and spilled across much of Greater Vancouver, Raining's great-grandmother, Jackie Chiu, had been a student at the University of British Columbia. Seeing that the road out from campus had been overwhelmed by trees, she had abandoned her car and plunged into the newly conscious wood on foot. All the works of man had been consumed within. Roads had been swallowed, old trails obliterated. Telephone poles thrust out branches and burst into leaf. Vines and creepers wound around houses and pulled them down, doing in hours the work of a hundred years.

Three days later, scratched and gaunt and bitten, Jackie Chiu had emerged delirious at the edge of False Creek, passing by the ruins of the Science Museum and wandering onto the Skytrain platform that marked the edge of the wood. Afterward she said, "You keep walking for what you love." In the seventy years that had passed since, she was still the only person to have passed all the way through the Forest alive, and human.

Her love bit into the wood like a nail driven into an oak. The Forest grew around her as it awoke, and she in turn lost a part of herself beneath the trees. The Forest let one house only remain inside its borders. This it gave to Jackie Chiu, and it was here she brought her family. Her daughter, Mouse, and granddaughter, Bell, and great-granddaughter, Raining, were raised inside the wood, and did service to it; and the wood watched over them in turn.

So it really was Raining's forest, in a way. As if to prove it, the path which had led Wire aimlessly through the wood for a whole day before abandoning her appeared under Raining's feet. They set out. Within a few steps they could see the lights flickering in the windows of Cedar House, and moments later they were opening the back door, tracking in mud and a smell of moldering pine needles.

Wire jumped at the threshold and gave a little yelp as a bird flapped right by her ear. It was the woodpecker. In the light that spilled from the kitchen she could see him beating into the night. She wondered again why he was following her; and wondered, too, what it would be like to sleep with a god.

"Wire's here!" shouted Lark, Raining's three-year-old daughter. She bounced off the couch and ran across the room, ponytail flying. Wire couldn't help smiling back into her grinning upturned face.

Wire took off her felted cloak and hung it on a peg in the entry hall next to Raining's. Lark bounced solemnly in place. "You're all wet."

Wire rubbed her mouth, testing the puffy edges of her split lip. "I'm aware of that."

Raining's mother, Bell, came down the stairs and into the parlor room. Bell had been born when the Forest's power was greatest, and she carried its mark more deeply than her daughter. She reminded Wire of a birch tree. She was even thinner than Raining, and much taller. Her skin was a pale, almost silvery white, and her black hair was shot with highlights of forest green. Despite her odd appearance, there was nobody more warmly human than Bell, and Wire had often wished she and Raining could have swapped moms. "Wire! Hello, dear. You look like you could use a hot bath and a cup of tea after."

Wire wasn't sure if this was pure kindness or an oblique hint that her long day's trek had left her smelly. Whatever the reason, hot water seemed an excellent idea. By the time she got out of the tub and wrapped up in a borrowed robe, Bell had tea waiting for her. Wire settled into the rocking chair beside the wood stove and put her hands around the hot mug with a sigh of pure bliss. Curls of steam drifted up from the tea, smelling of blackberries; weak competition at best for the wet wool aroma of her socks drying on the cast-iron stove top.

Raining had painted beautiful ivy borders around the top and bottom of Wire's cup. She had hand-painted most of the cups and plates in Cedar House, and there were plenty of other traces of her handiwork about. The teapot had been embellished with a cantankerous blue and whiskered catfish, the front door appeared to be swathed in brambles, and dozens and dozens of birds quarrelled, perched, and fluttered on the kitchen and living-room walls, painted just below the ceiling.

Raining was wearing jade-green pants and a black sweatshirt with red calligraphy painted on it. Raining had once told Wire that a painter never dressed by accident, however casual she might look, and Wire wondered what this outfit was supposed to communicate. How relaxed she was, as if she didn't know how deeply she had buried herself in the wood? Or maybe, a mother now and running from a broken marriage, she didn't choose her clothes quite so carefully at twenty-eight as she had at eighteen.

"You know, Wire, with your hair slicked down and that flowered robe, you look like one of those tall Pre-Raphaelite heroines by Morris, or Rackham," Raining said. "A damp Lady of the Lake, standing in the drizzle with a rusting Excalibur and thinking, 'Now where is that idiot Arthur?' "

Wire laughed. Once, at Wire's request, Raining had asked her mysterious Companion to Art to show a portrait of herself. Instantly its display screen had filled with a color plate from *Birds of the North-Western Americas,* 1881, written and illustrated by Tristam Flattery, F.R.S., and showing a black-crested bird with dark blue wings and body, kindled to sapphire by a shaft of morning sun. Under the plate ran a brief caption:

> *Like all members of the Corvidae, Steller's jay (Cyanocitta stelleri) is clever, craven, and frequently obnoxious. An indifferent mimic, but dedicated thief, its personality is more marked than pleasant. Cunning and occasionally bold, it is far more volatile than the calmer gray jay (Perisoreus canadensis), and seems clearly to exhibit pride, mirth, and even vengefulness. Its call is a raucous chak! chak!*

Wire had thought she was going to die laughing, and from that point on nursed a deep respect for the Companion.

Truly Raining was a jay of a woman, all rags and feathers and elbows and eyes; beady black Chinese eyes that were always watching, watching, watching. Raining had the most inquisitive fingers Wire had ever seen, with the possible exception of her husband, Nick. They had been well-matched in that. But his hands were patient and relentless, where Raining's were smarter and more nervous.

Taking a sip of tea, Wire leaned forward to get a little closer to the stove. Her toes wiggled in front of its hot glass face.

"Oo, yich," Lark said. She had spotted a centipede rippling its way across the living-room floor and now squatted over it, watching intently. On her face she wore an expression of acute absorption so clearly one of her father's that Wire glanced instantly at Raining, and saw the weeping ghost in her eyes before she could blink it away.

"My little scientist," Raining said.

Wire sat, sipping her tea.

"So. You came to lecture me."

"What?"

"Your dress," Raining said. "You always wear Sensible Blue when you want to Make Me See Reason."

"I do not!"

"You are so obvious, Wire. Sometimes I swear I can hear your toenails growing. Let me save you some time," Raining said. "The long-awaited squad of Southside soldiers has arrived at last, and there is to be a delegation sent to discuss their deployment. You are trying to get me to join it—not because you care about politics, but because you think I should patch things up with Nick." She glanced over at Wire. "Am I more or less right?"

"More or less. It's not just my idea, though. There's an invitation from the Mandarins."

"Thank you a thousand times for your trouble," Raining said. "Alas, I must decline."

"Don't get polite with me, Rain."

"I thought you'd find it a refreshing change."

Wire drank the last of her tea. "I think you're scared. I think you don't have the guts to act like a grown-up and stick it out."

"You have no idea, Wire." Raining's voice was low and

very quiet; not like her at all. "You have no idea what happened on the Southside."

"I know you loved him enough to leave the Forest, once. That kind of love doesn't just go away."

Bell poked her head in from the kitchen. "Bath time, Lark!"

Lark, sulking, allowed herself to be led off for her bath, and Raining took out her easel. By the time Lark returned with clean teeth and frog-green pajamas, Raining had dragged out her tackle box full of paints and hung two bright candles overhead from hooks screwed into the living-room ceiling. At one point Raining's great-grandfather had dragged a generator into the wood, but it was forever breaking down. The Forest didn't care for things that were too overtly technological. The candles were a compromise, made from lengths of bright-burning fibrous butane, dipped in a beeswax medium for greater sylvan authenticity.

Lark flopped onto the couch and lay on her tummy playing with the Companion. "Horses," she murmured. Wire watched her study the paintings of horses that came up on the screen: Matisse, Daumier, something Greek, something Chinese with seven feisty-looking stallions.

"These are pretty," Wire said, looking over Lark's shoulder at the next picture, a painting of three adult horses and two colts under an oak tree. An impossibly golden, cloud-quarrelled sky was spread above them.

Raining glanced over. "George Stubbs," she said briefly. " 'Mares and Foals in a Landscape.' " She studied the paints arranged in little jars before her, then slowly opened one that Wire had rarely seen her touch, the zinc white Nick had mixed for her in Southside. No emotion showed in Raining's face, but Wire could see it in her fingers, tightening around the paint pot's lid. An unlucky color, white. The color of death.

"Stubbs's perspectives are bad and his skies just pretty gauze, but his horses are excellent," Raining said. "Look at the bones in their lower legs." Quickly now she opened up the other jars and mixed her colors, scooping out chunks of paint and cutting them together with her palette knife.

"That's where his real passion lay. Those great haunches and hooves, so much more real than the ground they're standing on!"

"Cats," Lark said pointedly. Obligingly the Companion made the Stubbs disappear, to be replaced by something Egyptian.

Raining painted.

"Landscape, now. There's a very deep art in landscape," Raining said. She worked quickly. First, two large color masses, hard cobalt-blue for the sky, dirty white for the snowy ground. Then a silvery object: trapezoidal front, upright rectangle, longer sideways rectangle. A truck, the shape suddenly obvious. Circles below for tires. It was always a miracle to Wire how Raining could bring a world into being under her hands. "What's wrong with Stubbs is that his work is fake."

"You mean it's not realistic?"

"I mean it's a lie."

Raining rummaged in a drawer and returned with a sheaf of sketches and photographs of the Southside. Landscapes in color and black-and-white, half-drawn portraits, architectural studies, pictures of trees and machines. With a small cry of triumph she found a photo of one of Nick's many reclamation projects, an '02 Chevy pickup scarred with rust. "Never paint without references," she said. "Painting is about the particular. Not the lazy half-things we imagine, but real objects, real places. Real people. Truth."

Raining let her hand wait, and then dart in again. A few quick vertical strokes, brown up close, blue in the distance— barren trees, brittle with cold. Behind them, the pale white light of an early spring sun. She cut a bit of sky-blue into her white ground paint with her palette knife, then added a drop of glistening linseed oil, thinning the color. She cleaned her brush in a pot of turpentine, dipped it in the new paint, and applied it to the canvas, laying down a long blue shadow to stretch out from the truck.

Wire would never have believed in blue shadows before she went to Southside to help Raining prepare for her wedding. Now she remembered them, and the sparkle of ice-crystals in the freezing air, fired by the slanting sunlight, unbearably bright. The sting in your nose when you tried to breathe with your mouth closed. The squeak of dry snow underfoot.

"If you look at the landscapes of Constable, for instance, you will see the utter opposite. He has such a profound respect for his subject. Such a single-minded determination to witness what is. But that doesn't mean only realists are telling the truth. Look at Turner's seascapes, or the trees of Ma Yuan. Those show both the substance and the spirit, as Ching Hao says."

Raining filled out the bitter landscape: the cold light, the sky hard blue overhead, milky at the edges. She cleaned her wide brushes. "Because in painting, truth is the only thing that matters."

With a finer brush now, her hand moved in again. Somehow, with a stroke or two of paint, a dab here and there, the landscape changed. The pale sun warmed. Using her precious 00 brush, Raining etched tiny strokes of silver and azure, and—Wire didn't understand how this worked—yellow and orange to make the snowfield scintillate with a pale, luminous blue. Again and again, Raining's hand went darting back to her palette, dipping the brush in almost haphazardly, careful not to blend her paints too much, so that every brush stroke held a different color. She painted powdery snow caught in the truck's tire treads, and sunlight burning around bare branches.

She spent the most time on the truck windows, making them glitter with white frost. Utterly opaque. The driver barely a shape, an unseen darkness behind. At the bottom of the front window, on the driver's side, a tiny clear patch, the work of the defroster. Behind it, only the darkness of a suggested shape, and a single flesh tone: perhaps the half-glimpsed edge of a heavy hand.

"What are you doing?" Wire asked.

"I don't know," Raining said.

On the couch Lark's small black head, propped between her hands, slipped a little closer to the Companion as she stared blearily at a picture of ladies and gentlemen in late nineteenth-century dress, calmly taking tea with a tiger in their midst.

Bell peeked into the room, asking if they wanted more tea. Raining glanced around. "Mom? What's the most important thing in a husband?"

"He has to laugh at your jokes," Bell said.

Raining nodded. "Yes. That's what I thought too. Just checking."

Bell left. Raining painted, touching smaller and smaller color shapes onto the large masses she had started with. She painted the new damp in the air, the pine boughs heavy with snow. She put down her brush; picked it up; put it down quickly in the turpentine and started to clean up. "Don't think too much," she muttered.

She looked at her daughter. Lark's cheek now lay against the Companion. Her eyes were closed and her mouth was open in the unselfconscious sleep of a child. "I hate being a mother," Raining said.

"Rain!"

"Nick and I used to say, 'How do single parents cope?' Just like that. So smug. Well, the answer is, they don't. I don't, anyway. Not most days. I sing songs with her and I tell her stories and we draw pictures together, and I love her more than breath. And the minute my energy flags, the smothering boredom comes down again and I wish to God I could be free of her."

"You are not a bad mother," Wire said. "You love Lark. I know that."

"Yeah, well. I loved Nick too," Raining said. "I'm twenty-eight years old, Wire. I'm not a girl anymore. This is not pretend. This is my life, my real life. It's not the study, it's the painting. And I made it all myself."

Raining knelt by the couch, bending over Lark, touching her cheek with a hand strangely hesitant, as if she were unworthy of her daughter. She said, "Do you know what they do with children on the Southside, Wire? They sacrifice them. They take each one out onto the High Level Bridge when it is old enough to walk and turn it loose. Most run back to their parents. Some start forward for a few steps and then turn back. And sometimes, in a very few cases, they keep walking. They toddle and slip and fall and pick themselves up again, and keep walking north, while their mothers and fathers watch. Until they cross over the Bridge to the North Side, where the spirits are. And they never come back.''

Wire looked from Raining to Lark and back again, horrified.

''Nick promised me he wouldn't bring Lark to the Bridge, but he did. One autumn day he offered to take her for the afternoon so I could have time to paint. I jumped at the chance, I was so bored of being with her, so desperate to get away, to paint, to have time to myself. He took her to the Bridge while I was working.

''When he told me what he had done, I had waking nightmares about it constantly. I'd be sitting in a chair with a cup of chicory, talking or sketching—and then suddenly I would see her, falling in the snow and laughing like she does, and scrambling up, and walking away across the Bridge forever.''

Wire could not speak.

''But you're right,'' Raining said. ''I should go back.''

''Go back!'' Wire cried.

Raining put down her brushes and collapsed into the big armchair, flicking a centipede off its right arm. ''I haven't painted worth a damn since coming home.''

''You can't go back to that son of a bitch to improve your painting, Rain! You can't trust Lark with him!''

''It's not that my technique has decayed. It's me,'' Raining said. ''If I didn't love him anymore, that would be one thing. I could walk away from that like a finished canvas.''

''I won't let you go back,'' Wire said. ''If what you say is true, the Southsiders are barbarians. Cannibals! Nick most of all.''

''Didn't you come in on the other side of this argument?''

''Don't change the subject!''

''—She said, changing the subject.'' A characteristic Raining smile, thin and sharp. ''Don't feel too sorry for me.

I squeezed two drops of blood out of Nick for every one of mine that hit the floor.''

Wire winced. ''That, I believe.'' And then, ''Are you really going to go back?''

''There is no borscht worth eating in Chinatown,'' Raining said. ''Or pierogies, no good pierogies either. So you see, I really ought to go.''

''And you love him.'' Wire threw up her hands. ''For once I get you to listen to me, and then I wish I hadn't.''

''You know,'' Raining said, ''if Nick and I do get together again, then everything was wasted. The tears and screams and fights, the guilt. The loneliness. Everything I put Lark and Nick through was for nothing. What do I say when I see him, Wire? 'Hi honey—I'm home! Did you miss me?' We don't think so.''

''Bark like a dog,'' Wire said.

''What?''

''Whenever I'm really in trouble and I don't know what to say, I bark like a dog. It throws people off.''

Raining laughed. ''I'll have to remember that.'' She walked over to the couch and picked up her daughter. Lark woke at once, fuddled, blinking around the living room with solemn eyes and wondering where her bedroom had gone. She squinted at the new painting. ''What's this?''

Raining held her, and they stood for a moment together, two sleek black heads studying the painting of the snowy landscape; the hard blue sky; the truck, its windows blind with frost.

''Your father,'' Raining said.

Much later that night, Raining sat at the workbench in her stone-flagged studio just down the corridor from the living room. Everyone else had gone to sleep.

She was drawing Nick's face on the screen of the Companion, working by the light of two butane candles. It had been just over a year since she had left him, but she had not forgotten his face, oh no. She studied his head. Even before she had left him, baldness had started to creep up his forehead in two ovals, like a truck window defrosting. She admired the plates and bones of his skull. Their rough geometry. She pushed and pulled her tonal values, erasing out highlights and filling in tiny shadows all the way down to his hard eyebrow ridges, not beautiful but such a pleasure to model, their familiar masses alive under her stylus as if she were modelling his head out of clay.

Not a bad likeness.

"Say something. Hey? We're not even fighting."

Nick's mouthless face regarded her until she looked away and put down the Companion. Which is how he had always answered her ironies.

Raining saved the drawing of Nick. She held the Companion in her lap. Once it had been little more than a machine, a computer device her father had bought in an art shop in Chinatown for her fourth birthday. The Forest had gotten into it, though; it was something different now, a place where her art and the Forest's magic met and spoke. "Mirror, mirror, on my knee/ Does he feel the same as me?"

Its screen cleared, and then filled with Edvard Munch's "Night by the Oslo Fjord." The distant island, the empty moonlight. The tiny figure on the embankment.

The wide dark water, green and black.

Some time later Raining put down the Companion. She found her copper candle-snuffer, and gravely extinguished the candles, one, two. She stood and pushed the window above her workbench open a crack. A damp cold eddied into the room, smelling of mud, brush, wet cedar needles, cold dirt, cold water, decay. The Forest was full of the sounds of wind and running water and other things not human, which are the same as silence. She listened to it for a long time.

Then she went upstairs and began to pack for her trip to the Southside.

CHAPTER 5

It was Friday, March 24, 2074; three hours before the great banquet that would celebrate the Eve of the Feast of the Annunciation. Nick Terleski was standing at the rail of the High Level Bridge. It had thawed that morning, but now in the late afternoon it was getting cold again. The lively spring light had leached away, leaving behind the cold colors Nick had never noticed until he saw them through Raining's eyes. The heavy brown river. The blue shadows. The quiet snow.

Five years before, at the height of their courtship, they walked in the snowy river valley. "So you don't trust men," Raining said, laughing, "because most men are fools. And I know you don't trust women—"

Nick smiled. "Too clever for their own good."

"Animals?"

"Too dumb."

"Machines?"

He thought about that. "They break down."

"So what do you trust?" Laughter in her eyes and utterly desirable.

He thought for a long time. "The cold," he said.

And watched her smile gutter like a candle and go out. Her breath smoked in the freezing air of his homeland. "That's not enough, love."

How could he say, It's all I know.

Now, five years later, the cold was all he had left. Nick

rocked back and forth, rolling his weight across his feet to press the feeling back into them. After a while he changed to kicking at the sidewalk with his numb toes. He should have worn his foil parka. The cold stung his ears, and his thick fingers had begun to stiffen, like wet snow hardening. Tightness was creeping over his face like a skin of ice forming on a pond.

Raining was back on the Southside. She had come with a delegation from Chinatown. He would see her at the banquet tonight.

The news had slipped like a key into Nick's back that morning and wound him up, tightening all the springs in his chest and limbs, driving him out to pace through a world of puddled melt-water and pale March sunshine. He had thought of volunteering for the platoon sent to Chinatown, just to be near Raining and Lark, but had pushed the thought away. Now they had come here.

A toy soldier. She had called him that, once.

—Called you a lot worse things than that, too, Magpie remarked.

Magpie was Nick's familiar. A familiar was a cross between a computer program, a notebook, and a servant. Most Southsiders wore them. Early work in artificial intelligence had focused on making expert systems, programs which were designed to make the knowledge of accomplished individuals widely available. Two early examples were the development of computer programs that could play chess, or diagnose illnesses. As neural-net modelling evolved and computer systems became more responsive to their environment, a lab at the University of Alberta worked out a design for a personal expert system, an expert at being *you*. It paid attention where you paid attention, and remembered the things you needed to remember. If you were a salesman, your familiar would memorize street directions, remember the names of your clients and their children, their past ordering history, their cocktail preferences.

After 2004, familiars became more powerful and more subtle. Some never amounted to more than dumb subroutines in the computer gel-pak most Southsiders wore around

their waists. But some familiars developed genuine person-
alities. Magpie, besides being chock full of salvage lore, site
maps, and Merck Index figures on everything from the melting point of potassium to the range of carbon content in
stainless steel, had more than just a personality. Though
Nick never would have said it out loud, he was perfectly
certain Magpie also had a soul.

—Mindless robot. She definitely called you a mindless
robot on more than one occasion, Magpie reflected. Raining
had a good selection of Chinese names too. I took the liberty
of getting them translated. Remember that thing she used to
say when you made cabbage rolls for dinner? It turns out—

—Fuck off.

The tiny letters printing out on Nick's contact lenses
dimmed as Magpie paused.

—You can't run from what you have made, she said.

Down below the Bridge, the ice was breaking up. It had
started two days ago, creaking and shuddering, and finally
tearing apart so you could see the North Saskatchewan
again. Chunks and floes of ice still clogged the channel,
crashing and grinding together, jamming up around the
bridge foundations or spinning ponderously downstream.

The last six months Nick and Raining had been together
had ground him down, had stripped his threads. The fights
and reconciliations, the sex and the tears, hammering down
one after another, leaving him blank and stupid with exhaustion. His whole body remembered that terrible weariness.

—We can never go back.

—Never is a long time, Magpie said.

—Some things are stones, Nick said. A man's a fool who
doesn't know that. Some things are broken and can't be
fixed.

—A fool is a man too proud to try, Magpie said. And
Raining aside, there is Lark to consider.

—What have I got to give her? What my father gave me?

Nick rocked forward, elbows resting on the bridge rail,
chin resting on his fists. White scars on his hands stood out
in the cold, reminders of a dozen stupid mistakes: a careless

weld, a jammed fan belt, moments of inattention with hacksaws and battery acid and the sapper's screwjack he wore on his belt. Under his nails, black crescents of oil that never washed clean. They were hard hands. Meaty, heavily muscled, big-knuckled, blunt-fingered. His father's hands: he knew them well, oh yes.

—She'll be better off with her mother, Nick said.

—What's best for her doesn't matter.

—What?

—You are Lark's father, Magpie said. It doesn't matter whether she would be better off without you. Your duty is to be with her. To fail her as a parent, if that's all you can do.

Nick thought.

—That's toy soldier talk, you know. Duty. Responsibility. Raining would hate that.

—Who gives a damn what Raining likes? If she only needed what she liked, she would never have married you in the first place.

Nick allowed a smile.

—This is true.

—You didn't think it was a noble deed not to follow them to Vancouver, did you? Some sort of stoic sacrifice?

—I was trying to do the right thing.

—You were a coward.

"Fuck off!" Nick said out loud. He rocked back and forth, his heels grinding in the hardening snow. His breath smoked in the twilight. Ice-floes crashed together down below. Like spring-addled rams in rut, Nick thought. Brainless head-butting bastards.

He would see Raining tonight. Oh, God, how he loved her still.

The whole south side of Edmonton's river valley had once been a series of pleasant parks: the Devonian Gardens, Emily Murphy, Mayfair, and so on. Of these, Mayfair Park was the largest and most central to the life of the city. Its greatest attraction was the small lake in its midst. In summer there were paddleboats; in winter, skating.

In the strange and dangerous times after '04, when out-landers were to be given neither offense nor an opening, Winter's priorities were to make his guests feel both welcome and vulnerable. A set of four chalets, designed for comfort and appointed with a battery of surveillance equipment, had been built at the edge of Mayfair Lake to house visitors. On the small island in the middle of the lake, he had built the Visitors Pavilion, a gorgeous, welcoming conference building of tall, polished wooden ceilings and enormous triple-paned windows to let the daylight in: charmingly picturesque, and militarily indefensible.

Here, as the Eve of the Feast of the Annunciation turned colder by the hour, the dignitaries of Southside and Vancouver met, and mingled. The splendor of the Annunciation was magnified, but the milk and meatless fast of Lent kept, by a sumptuous smorgasbord loaded with tureens of borscht and potato soup, platters of snow-cured goldeye and pickerel, french fries, boiled wheat and honey for the children, bowls of sauerkraut and potato salad, loaves of eggless rye flatbread, endless trays of meatless cabbage rolls, perogies, scalloped beets (a Southside delicacy), parsnip fingers, turnips carved into fancy shapes, jars of honey and pots of searing horseradish and heaps of sweets: raspberry crumbles, crispy finger-kuchen sticky with chokecherry syrup, baked-icing figurines, bricks of toffee, and sugar-crackers to be spread with fragrant rhubarb jam. In short, it was a vast, friendly, generous feast—smelling pungently of beets, sauerkraut, and rhubarb—guaranteed to make the esteemed visitors from Chinatown feel not only welcomed, but uncomfortable, and acutely out of place.

Had the food been modelled in clay and left unpainted, Nick could not have wanted it less. His stomach was a knot. His dress uniform was stiff and uncomfortable.

A toy soldier.

He hadn't worn the dress uniform since finishing his mandatory three years service, but it was one of only two pieces of formal clothing he owned. The other was the suit he had been married in. He hadn't had the courage to wear that.

—**92** In disgust, Magpie was posting his heart rate in huge numbers on his right contact lens. Normally he ran from 68 to 72 beats per minute.

Raining entered the Pavilion.

—**115**

Meanwhile, at one end of the head table Li Mei, Water Spider's aide, sat making small talk with Emily Thompson, Southside's heir. As well as being Water Spider's eyes and ears here, Li Mei was the daughter of Li Bing, Chinatown's chief diplomat to the Southside. She had been raised in a cultured environment; to her eyes the Visitors Pavilion was filled with the same tasteless barrack-room utilitarianism that permeated the Snows' lives, from their graceless homes to their appalling clothes. Their idea of dressing formally here was to pin extra medals on their combat fatigues.

"Have you given any further thought to purchasing the technology we discussed last time?" Emily Thompson said. Which was curious, for on the two previous trips Li Mei had made with her mother to this cold white city, she and Emily Thompson had never had such a conversation, and she was quite sure the Southsider knew it.

Her mother always said, "When in doubt, smile." Li Mei smiled back at the young woman who stood to inherit this depressing kingdom.

Li Mei had dressed for the banquet in a shawl-cut burgundy jacket over a fitted blouse, its sleeves peeled back and pinned over the jacket cuffs with garnet cuff-pins. A narrow gold belt defined her waist. Below this she wore an ankle-length cross-pleated skirt, and black cloth boots with gold buckles. A mother-of-pearl clasp defined the part in her hair, and she wore that perfume called Sunset On Red Water.

In contrast, Emily Thompson was roughly the shape and color of a peeled potato, almost offensively drab in a white jumpsuit with grey piping. The red scarf she wore around her head made her look as if she were about to sort through a pile of cabbages. Her only piece of jewelry was a hideously clunky crucifix, enamelled and inlaid with garnets and amethysts, which she wore on a gold chain around her neck.

"Not only are our surveillance devices excellent in themselves," Emily continued deliberately, "but they come with an AI monitor capable of very subtle key-word sensitivity. The sentry-familiar never goes to sleep, never gets bored. Always watching. Always listening." Emily's eyes flicked to a guard who stood a few meters away at an easy parade rest.

Tension fluttered in Li Mei's stomach.

"My governess has been assigned to the garrison in your city," Emily Thompson remarked. "A couple of my grandfather's personal guards are watching over me just now."

Always watching. Always listening.

Li Mei glanced at the guard. "I see." Emily was being watched by her own people.

She knew at once she should not have spoken. Her mother would not have done that; her mother would have waited, showing no understanding. Withholding commitment. Whereas she had already entered into a kind of collusion with this dumpy Emily Thompson by joining her cloaked conversation. This was what Emily Thompson wanted; but this was not necessarily in Chinatown's best interest.

Her mother always told Li Mei there were four kinds of dragons. Yellow dragons, whose direction was southeast and whose metal was sulphur, whose aspect was splendor and who attacked through pride. Red dragons, whose direction was northwest and whose metal was mercury, whose aspect was brilliant and who attacked through inconstancy. Black dragons, whose direction was southwest and whose metal was iron, whose aspect was power and who attacked through force. And white dragons, whose direction was northeast and whose metal was silver, whose aspect was death and who attacked through fear.

Li Mei wondered which kind of dragon Emily Thompson was.

"I would very much like to visit the Vancouver Islands," the Southsider said.

Now? Li Mei worried. Or some other time? No—now, surely. That was the point of drawing attention to the fact that she was under surveillance by her own people.

"We could go together," Emily suggested.

Oh no! What kind of overture was the dumpling woman making? "That, ah, that would be difficult," Li Mei said.

How did she find herself in this terrible situation! She should have stayed in her office in the Ministry of Borders; it was small but she could do that job, she understood the rustle of paper. She should have made an excuse to Water Spider and declined to come on this trip.

Li Mei tried to compose herself. "We take our relationship with the Southside very seriously. In these worsening times your troops may be all that stands between Chinatown and destruction. Whatever my own impulses, I could never permit myself to do anything which might endanger the good of my people."

Emily Thompson sat slowly back in her chair. "Just as I must always put the good of my people first."

"Exactly."

The red Orthodox scarf wrapped old baba style around Emily's head framed her brown eyes. Words and numbers were pouring across them in tiny blue lines. Li Mei looked away. This aspect of dealing with the Snows still disturbed her, and Emily Thompson screened prodigious amounts of information, even by Southside standards. Li Mei did not like to feel the weight of all that calculation focused on her. Data, analysis, background, projection, measurement, measurement, measurement: the fierce relentless rhythms of calculation, projection, evaluation.

Emily said, " 'The Five Strategic Arts are measurements, estimates, analysis, balancing, and triumph.' "

The potato woman was a mind reader.

Li Mei allowed no expression. "You know Sun Tzu."

Emily said, "We are a soldiering people."

A new wash of information cascaded across Emily's contact lenses. Lines of Chinese characters flowed by. Were they from Sun Tzu's *The Art of War*? Could Emily Thompson read them? Were they being translated? Were they simply marginalia to an English translation?

Emily appeared to decide on her strategy. She said, "Tactically, I do not like our position in your city."

Li Mei remembered to hold her silence.

"At first we were merely to guard your borders, but now you have asked us to become the aggressor in your war, securing the no man's land between yourself and Downtown, where the barbarians live."

Li Mei said, "Is this problematic? I am afraid my knowledge of strategy is not profound."

Emily stared over the rim of her cup. Her eyes so rude, yet it was Li Mei who felt guilty, looking away. "Unlike your mother, who is attached to the Ministry of Foreign Affairs, your posting is in the Ministry of Borders. Your office is on the third floor of Water Spider's wing of Government House. Your window faces east. You entered the Ministry eight months and three weeks ago, posting excellent scores on your entrance exams, including first class commendations in geometry, deportment, and brushwork. Your Minister is the man in charge of coordinating the actions of our troops in Chinatown. If your knowledge of the situation is not profound, detailed, and specific, I would be forced to assume that either the Mandarinate is not, as claimed, based on merit, and that you got your post through your mother's influence; or that your Minister is a fool. I do not believe that Water Spider is a foolish man."

Li Mei covered her face by raising her cup of chicory. "This really is an excellent drink, on a cold day. I believe I will have another."

Water Spider and her mother had both told her how the Southside familiars could track your pulse rate and the dilation of your pupils to help their masters gauge your mood. She should not have complimented the dreadful chicory beverage. The apology was apparent. She should have demanded tea instead.

Too late.

Emily held her eyes. "On reflection, I believe the situation is tactically unsound. I am afraid I will have to ask Grandfather to recall our troops."

"Surely he will make that determination by himself!"

"It was my decision to send the troops. A mistake, as I now see. And Grandfather is about to owe me a very great

deal," Emily Thompson said. "He will do this, if I ask it
of him."

Emily Thompson was a black dragon. Li Mei saw that
now. She was of the north, and there was iron in her. With
delicate fingers Li Mei removed the garnet cuff-pin at her
left wrist, adjusted the crease of her blouse sleeve, folded it
back, and retacked it. "You are not serious."

"I have never been more serious in my life." The ghost
of a smile crossed Emily Thompson's face. "And remember, I have been raised as Southside's heir. It's been a serious life." They looked at one another. "Perhaps if I were
to visit your city," Emily said, "and examine the tactical
situation in person . . ."

And then Li Mei saw the beauty of Emily's trap.

For some reason, Winter's granddaughter desperately
wanted to leave the Southside. The threat was plain: if Li
Mei left her here, Emily would use her influence to withdraw the Southside troops, leaving Chinatown exposed to
the advance of the barbarians from Downtown.

Of course, they could try to replace the Southsiders. They
could go south, looking to woo fighting strength from the
Seattle Clans, but those were constantly busy warring
amongst themselves, and the troops they could provide
would be nowhere near Southside's caliber. The Southsiders
were the best trained, best equipped, smartest and most honorable mercenaries on the continent, and they were very
careful to maintain that standard.

It was unbearable that Chinatown, a culture infinitely
deeper and more sophisticated, should be forced to rely on
them—but when the horrors had started to boil out of Vancouver's Downtown, spilling up to Chinatown's very borders, they had been left with no choice.

Li Mei said, "I think you will make a very fine leader
for the Southside, one day."

Emily Thompson, dowdy with her scarf and crucifix,
smiled pleasantly and quoted Sun Tzu. " 'What if an op-
posing leader approaches with his multitudes whole and
ready? I say: Locate beforehand his deepest attachment and
then seize it. He will comply!' "

• • •

Several tables away, Magpie was screeching in Nick's ear.

—Do you think Raining has forgotten you have rounded shoulders and a little pot belly?

—Shut up.

—Then why bother standing stiff as a telephone pole? You have nothing to hide, Nick. She has already seen you at your worst.

—No, she hasn't.

Raining had not watched him set Lark down with her feet on the Bridge. Hadn't watched their baby daughter take a few tottering steps out along the snowy roadway, heading north. It had been a dry day, with the wind blowing. He remembered the whispering lines of snow, bending and flowing around her little boots.

He closed his eyes.

When he opened them again, Raining was closer, threading through the crowd with Wire beside her. She was clasping Lark's hand. Every now and then he glimpsed his daughter's shiny black hair.

When he thought about Raining, he never pictured her in the sober dresses of the last months of their marriage. During the long nights since she left, she had haunted his memory in the bright, japing clothes of their first few months' acquaintance: patchwork panels of shimmering synthetic silk, or magical wetlands dresses in dark greens and browns, running and rippled with rainbow colors, like rain-washed streets glittering with oil. Tonight she wore a scarlet jacket over a dark red dress, with gold embroidery around the hem.

—For luck, Magpie said.

—I know.

Then, through a gap in the crowd, Lark saw him, and shouted something, and pulled on Raining's hand.

—Lark remembers you!

Nick couldn't believe it.

Raining's head turned with a flick, bangs swinging, and the quick eyes there were still the same ones that had seen in him a man deeper than he had ever seen in himself. She stopped. At a word, Wire began to drift away. Raining came forward again, leading Lark by the hand.

—I don't know what to say. Any ideas?

—Knowing Raining? Magpie laughed, a dry little chuckle.

Nick grinned. His wife had rarely obliged him to start conversations. Only to end them.

"Daddy!" said Lark, denying either of them the chance to get in the first word. She bounced on the balls of her feet, grinning hugely. "When I was come last day in a helicopter! And Mommy and Wire, only we didn't crash." She shook her head. "*That* not a good idea."

Nick walked around his table and knelt so his face was level with hers. She did not hug him.

A whole year of her life gone, infinitely more precious than the year of his own life he had lost. Looking at her— so big now!—it all flooded back to him: the endless messes at the kitchen table, the temper tantrums, the times he had tickled her until she gasped, breathless from laughing. He remembered that the sound of her laughter was the most beautiful sound in the world.

And further back, a thousand conversations with Raining about how they would handle bedtime, what foods would be good for her—Raining couldn't believe in a diet without fish—how they were going to survive her habit of bouncing out of bed, brimming with good cheer, at five-twenty every morning.

And earlier, her babyhood: wondering whether she would be right- or left-handed, arguing over handling a teenager (Raining scared as hell; Nick convinced that Lark's sunny disposition would make it a nonissue). Sober, lengthy analyses of the color of her poop. "I've missed a lot," Nick said.

Raining nodded. "Yes. You have."

"You knew who I was," Nick said to Lark. He found he was grinning.

Lark bobbed her head. "Mommy painted a picture of you last day."

"She did?" Nick looked at his wife, suprised and touched.

Raining just looked surprised.

Wire scooped up a couple of juicy cabbage rolls from the smorgasbord. She had developed a weakness for them when she had come to the Southside to help with Raining's wedding. Delicious as they were, they were also wet and sloppy, making them difficult to eat with her eyes riveted on Raining and Nick.

Hm. Well, so much for them falling tearfully into each other's arms. Raining was stiff as a stick. It wasn't going to be easy for them to get back together.

Wire's thoughts surprised her. Only a few days before, she had been saying that Nick should never be forgiven. Considering how deeply Wire felt all her opinions, their habit of changing on her was a bit distressing. Still, the years had taught her that she could never be sure what she would be certain of next. She had noticed it first with men, who seemed to change from toads to princes and back again with alarming speed. Her mother was another person about whom she had at least six decided and unalterable opinions. Slithery: that's what life was.

But they loved one another, she was sure of that. And Nick was good for Raining. Of course, since when had Raining ever done what was good for her? Let alone what made her happy. Wire sighed, nibbling on a cabbage roll, and studied Raining's tense, unhappy face.

Winter, rising from his place at the head table, made a gracious speech to welcome the delegation from Vancouver, and presented Li Bing with a ceremonial gift, a beautiful white headscarf woven from rayon and shot through with silver threads. Li Mei watched as her mother flinched only for an instant, and then accepted the terrible gift with her usual, poised grace.

"Winter does know that white is the color of death," Emily remarked.

Li Mei looked at her, astonished. "Then . . . why?"

" 'Therefore, when opponents are comfortable, they should be troubled; when satisfied, they should be starved; when calm, they should be moved.' "

"But we are allies."

"Negotiation is a strategy as great as war. Grandfather would never surrender an edge."

Li Mei said, "Why are you telling me this?"

"I thought you deserved to know. I am asking much from you and your mother, Li Mei. I hate being in debt," said dumpy, cunning, fearsome Emily Thompson. "Balance is the prerequisite for triumph."

"I will be Lark's father," Nick said.

Between her parents, Lark stood on tiptoe, stretching out to grab a french fry from a nearby platter.

Raining shook her head. "We go back in three days. It's already arranged."

"I'll come with you." There. It was said. He would be with them both. Even though he knew that there would always be times when it wasn't good, when he and Raining would fight, when they would hurt one another. Raining would withdraw and anger would wad up in Nick's muscles and Lark would watch it all and learn from it, to her parents' shame.

But he had chosen Raining now, and Lark; chosen them as wholly as he could choose anything in this life. He would have to trust that they could all remember, however bitter things got, that their lives were bound together, now and always.

"We won't take you," Raining said.

"Then I'll hop on the next troop plane bound for Chinatown."

Raining cocked her head to one side, examining him. Once, the fact that she was smarter than he was had worried him. He had been very young, back then. "Li Bing could get Winter to confine you to Southside."

"If I can't fly, I'll walk." For the first time that evening, Nick's heart rate began to drop, turning over like the engine of a reliable car with a clear road ahead and a certain destination.

Raining looked at him in exasperation. "You would do it, wouldn't you?"

He smiled. "By John Walker's shiny black boots, I swear it."

Lark was looking dolefully at her naked french fry. Nick dragged a bowl of ketchup over. He watched her eat. "I owe her."

Slowly Raining nodded. "That kind of comment sounds wonderful in stories, you know. Deathless commitment. Love-you-forever. In real life it sounds scary."

"Life is scary," Nick said. "Not everything is about you."

"Two years ago one of Wire's cousins left her husband. He killed her for it."

"Raining, don't waste your breath. Not even the tiniest part of you believes that of me."

There was a tear on Raining's cheek. She ignored it. "You have a lot of reasons to hate me."

"I couldn't hate you, you dumb bitch!" His damn heart rate was climbing again—she could always do it to him if he gave her long enough. "There would be no *point* to that, Rain. It would be like hating the weather." For once, Raining looked surprised: a comical consternation on her face that made Nick laugh. His stomach unknotted and something in him said, *Oh, yes; another fight with Raining.* Now the strangeness was past, and for better or worse they were back on familiar ground.

People were beginning to stare. Nick ignored them. "You're not a person to me, Rain: you're a, a frontal system. Metal fatigue! Technical difficulties! Your bitchiness is like a bad smell in my air. What am I going to do—stop breathing?"

Raining held up her hands, blushing. "Enough!" she hissed, laughing. "Everyone is looking at you."

"I'm not concerned about my image," Nick growled, but he lowered his voice.

—Now that is true love, Magpie drawled.

"More ketchup," Lark said.

Nick fetched another bowl. "Um, I think—Oh, hey now, honey: don't just dip your fry in the ketchup and lick it off." Lark scowled. Nick found he had his hands on the child's arms. He took them off, glancing at her mother.

Raining smiled. "I had forgotten what I missed about you." Then, slowly, she shook her head. "But there's no going back. There is no going back."

"I'll keep walking after you."

"How good are your arches? You may be on your feet a while."

Nick looked at her until her bright black eyes flicked away. He said, "A wise woman I once knew told me that you have to keep walking for what you love."

Raining didn't answer for a long moment. Then she glanced over at Wire, who stood at the smorgasbord staring shamelessly at them. "Yip," Raining said. "Woof. And bow wow."

Wire just about peed herself laughing.

CHAPTER 6

Two hours later, Raining stood in the living room of one of
the diplomatic chalets. Nick had come to help put Lark to
bed. He had left about five minutes earlier, and Raining was
calculating how long it would take for Wire to come pounding on her door.

Two minutes for Nick to get back to the Visitors Pavilion.
Then give it five seconds for Wire to spot him, a minute
more for her to gulp down her current glass of blackberry
cordial (no alcohol during Lent), and excuse herself from
whatever man she was flirting with. Two minutes to trot
quickly over the bridge and around to the chalet to find out
why Nick wasn't spending the night in Raining's bed.
Which would make it just about—

The front door slid open. "Well?" Wire demanded.

Raining shook her head. "I should have married you."

"What went wrong?"

"Wrong? Nothing went wrong. Lark asked him to put her
to bed. He came, he helped, he went away. End of story."

"That's it?" Wire strode across the living room, licking
the remains of some sticky dessert from her fingers. "I don't
believe it. I was watching his face while you two were talking. He's still crazy about you."

"Crazy, yes. In love, I don't think so."

Wire flopped down on the big couch that faced the fire-
place. "Lark's in bed, I guess. Fire, please. Roof: clear.

Walls: clear above one meter. Lights down." The gas fire leapt obligingly into being, the lights went down, and the top of the chalet turned transparent.

Outside, snowy fields stretched to the black fringe of trees that edged the river. Overhead the sky was a fragile water-color black, the darkness much thinned by stars. "At night the sky is so much paler than the ground," Raining said. "I never noticed that until I tried to paint it."

Wire shivered. "Look at the trees: crab-backed old hags with curses hidden under their black coats. It's the cold that puts them out of temper, I suppose." She tugged Raining down onto the couch beside her and sat holding her arm, lacing her slightly sticky fingers with Raining's. "Were you horribly disappointed?"

"Lark kept asking and asking for him to come for bed-time. I knew it was a mistake as soon as I said yes. All the time we were walking over here she was pulling him by the hand. I was scared sick."

"Of what?"

"My knees were shaking so badly I couldn't stand still. I had to keep pacing once we were inside. This horrible clammy fear." Raining looked into the little gas fire. "I don't know. I don't know."

"Did you think he was going to hit you?"

"And then of course she wouldn't go to sleep right away. Kept popping up. 'I want another story'; 'I want a hug'; 'I want a glass of water, Mommy.' 'Can you fix my ponytail?' So there was this agonizing time while we waited for her to go to sleep. I knew Nick wouldn't talk about anything im-portant while she was awake. He passed on gossip about people I couldn't remember: Mrs. Mop-head had an affair with a gopher; Mr. Cabbage Roll took his pants off in church."

Wire giggled.

"I jumped around the room like I was scratching for worms, trying to think how I was going to get rid of him. And then, finally, the chalet told us Lark had gone to sleep . . . and Nick left! The bastard." Raining cackled. "No preg-nant pause, no prepared speech. Not even a goodnight kiss.

He just left. I'm to call tomorrow if Lark wants to go out to a park.''

"Smart man!" Wire said, impressed. "Well done, Nick. You were crushed, right?"

"Flattened," Raining said. "I am not, it has been observed, an easy woman to satisfy."

Wire laughed. "You never want to be satisfied. You want to be provoked. You two could put it back together if you would just stop talking, you know."

"If he were to reach out and touch my cheek," Raining said. Then she shrugged. "Or maybe I'd kill him."

An hour later Raining sat drawing in her room. The banquet was over. Wire had gone to bed in the next room. She and Raining had been quartered in the smallest chalet so the other envoys did not have to put up with Lark.

The room lights were bright near Raining, dim on the far side of the room where Lark lay asleep. The frame on the wall was showing an A.Y. Jackson she particularly loathed, with two other Group of Seven landscapes as the alternates. From her years in Southside she knew the desk monitors could pick up remote feeds from her Companion to Art, so she uploaded John Martin's "Sadak in Search of the Waters of Oblivion." Let the room's soothing, tranquillity-inducing algorithms choke on it.

After a brief and unsatisfying prowl, Raining lay back on the bed with her hands behind her head. Immediately the lights dimmed, and the bed, initially stiff and somewhat springy, began to soften, almost imperceptibly, into a pleasantly warm and supportive surface.

"Quit that," Raining growled. "I'm not ready to go to sleep yet."

So sorry.

Though the house was vocally equipped, the room printed its reply neatly on the wall, just to the left of the picture frame. Not wishing to disturb Lark, naturally. Raining noted that the wall had changed hues, tinting itself ever so faintly brown-gold, to harmonize with Martin's "Sadak."

"And bring the lights up," Raining added. "I don't want it soothing. I want it edgy."

I'm not very good at edgy.

"Troubled?"

Sorry.

"Melancholy?"

Regretfully, no.

"Belligerent?"

Definitely not. May I suggest 'Wistful'?

Raining grunted. "Look, why don't you just turn yourself off?"

Why don't you? the room answered, nettled.

Raining reminded herself that there was no point fighting with objects; they never knew when to give up. Instead she uploaded Francis Bacon's hideous screaming "Pope II" to the picture frame. Optimize that.

"Bed?" she murmured, sitting down again. "As for texture, what I really find relaxes me is Stippled."

Stippled? Confirm?

"Stippled."

Obediently the bed broke out in slow, bending goose bumps beneath her. It was rather like sitting on a thousand fingers. Odd.

She picked up the Companion and began to draw.

When Raining had turned seriously from pencil to paint at age twelve she found the same thing that made her drawings excellent made her first attempts at painting disastrous. She had trained her eye to be exquisitely sensitive to contour: she thought of objects in terms of their outlines. Unfortunately, paint did not take well to such handling.

Disgusted with her initial work, she had asked the Companion to teach her what was meant by the often-used phrase "painterly." It responded with great zeal, dragging her headlong into Hals's "Governesses of the Old Men's Home in Haarlem," Van Gogh's "The Yellow Cornfield," works by Cezanne and John Singer Sargent. . . .

It was devastating.

She didn't look at another Old Master for the next three

years. Instead, she went back to her strengths, and began painting birds. It was then that she fell in love with Audubon, with his meticulous attention to detail, the liveliness of his characterizations, and above all his not infrequent mistakes. Every artist needs a master she can admire, and occasionally exceed, and Audubon was Raining's first. Eventually she graduated to the vastly superior watercolor technique of the great bird painter J. Fenwick Lansdowne, but Audubon still had her heart.

She loved Audubon's willingness to use any medium to accomplish the task at hand. It was from him she learned to use pencils and watercolor together, letting the graphite give a sheen and iridescence to wingtips and eyes that watercolor alone could not achieve. Often he would use coats of resin, particularly on the eyes, to add gleam and luster. From his paintings of smaller birds she learned some basics of composition. These paintings, filled with wrens or finches in flight around tangles of bramble or willow leaves, allowed her an opportunity to use her love of detail without creating mere jumble.

For a while she believed these small studies had allowed her to master the difficult art of perspective. She was quite pleased with her development—until the Southside humbled her.

When Raining first came to Nick's country, she tried to make the sky too small. The scale of the prairies nearly defeated her. The action in her paintings took place in spaces little larger than the living room in Cedar House. She never saw the narrowness of that vision until she stood before her easel in Nick's farmhouse, looking out at the immense emptiness of the plains.

It destroyed her perspective. All her techniques for conveying depth and volume relied on the massing of detail; objects in front of other objects, gestures from foreshortened arms, the neat tactical gradations in size that separated her teacup on the windowsill from her mother's cup on the coffee table. Her tricks of hand were no use to her here. The prairie obliterated them.

Watercolors were her best medium, but she knew they

did not have the strength to grasp that naked land. Perhaps a genius, a Turner, might have been able to bend them to the subject; but even Turner's great sea-and city-scapes depended on the gauze and lambency of rising steam or rolling fog or falling rain. It did not rain in Nick's country, not in winter, and the only fog came with your breath. In winter even the snow fell dry as ash.

She settled on oils. Acrylic would probably have been a more reasonable choice. She could have grasped the flatness of the prairie with it. But to paint the snow fields in flat matte white would have been a terrible lie.

It took her weeks to learn to render snow. Nick had mixed a gallon of wonderful zinc oxide white paint for her, using a recipe from her Companion to Art. In Vancouver she had long been forced to make do with lead-white. This meant scavenging lead from old car batteries and exposing it to urine. The mixture had to be left buried for weeks under a midden heap. This made for a lovely warm white, very opaque and easily mixed with various media, but it was highly reactive when exposed to air or other pigments. (The reactive properties of lead-white and lead-yellow were responsible for any number of medieval Miracle Paintings: black Madonnas, weeping Christs, bleeding saints and so forth.) Using the stuff required absolutely painstaking glair work, using an egg white medium to seal the lead paint so it didn't touch any others. And of course the lead was poisonous. But here on the Southside, Nick had dared the Stelco plant and salvaged a veritable trove of zinc oxide, bringing Raining's whites into the modern era.

Only she found she couldn't paint the Southside winter in plain white. She had to learn to break her colors completely anew. She tried the ecstatic white fire of Monet's cathedrals first, only to abandon it and walk snow-blind into a different kind of whiteness: the whiteness of Munch, broken into heavy blues and strange, cold greens.

She had to learn to lose the liquid shimmer of coastal air. Always before, unthinking, she had been painting filtered light. Light coming through clouds, through leaves, through windows, through the heavy sea-level air; light sinking into the ground like water. On the prairies, the sun burned untouched through emptiness. She went nearly crazy trying to capture the fierce light until the day she understood that here it shone not only down from above, but sprayed up like white fire from the snow.

In Nick's country she learned to paint with new clarity and harshness. Gone were the encircling trees of her childhood, whose knotted limbs were the truest geometry to her eyes; to be replaced at first by the long, receding angles of snowdrifts, highways, fence lines. Finally, she gave up all her old tricks of perspective, stopped adding those fake positional markings where they didn't exist, and went back to Turner to learn atmospheric perspective, situating objects spatially by changing their color values: realistic colors close, trees and hills dark and darkly shadowed in the middle distance; then, at the edge of sight, dim shapes in blue and lavender.

There was a certain picture she painted using the driver-side window of Nick's truck as a frame. The cab of the truck was a welcome brown touched with warm highlights: perhaps light reflected from a flannel shirt. On the far left, through the crack of the opening door, the plain swept into eternity. Small copses of scrubby trees dotted the prairie around Nick's farm, mostly bare-branched cottonwoods huddled around a creek or pond, or more occasionally, stands of birch and pine. She painted herself standing beside the nearest cottonwood. She was too far from the truck for her features to be visible, but still she was careful in the modelling of her own figure: her body hunched inside her heavy coat, her shoulders tight, a touch of red at her mouth. One arm raised to touch the cold trunk of the nearest tree, uncertain. Even the trees were different here, their muscular forms wasted to cylinders and sticks.

The warm truck door—opening? Closing? The silent fury of the snowy field. Herself, standing by the shelterless trees. Waiting.

This was her marriage.

CHAPTER 7

The bells of St. Paul's on the Southside had just chimed midnight. The last guests in the Visitors Pavilion sat talking over chicory and nibbling leftovers. Eight hundred kilometers west, in the Southsider barracks at the edge of Chinatown, there was still an hour of Friday night left. Emily's banished governess, Claire, had gone to bed early and lay among scores of sleeping soldiers. She was dreaming, and in her dream she knew she had to die. That much was expected of her.

She stood alone in Parkallen Cemetery. No one had bothered to attend her funeral. She was forced to prepare her own funerary pyre. With no one else there to pass the sacrifices through, however, if she cut her throat or chose to shoot herself, she would arrive on the North Side cold and naked. It was a problem.

So they had abandoned her, even in this.

She was surprised at how bitterly alone she felt. Emily had always said how cold she was, how unfeeling, and secretly Claire had agreed. It had never occurred to her to think, *But there is one thing you feel, and that is alone.* Alone like the white prairie in winter. Alone like the endless empty sky.

But there it was, no one would burn a sacrifice for her. She studied the funerary pyre. Then she leaned forward, gripped the edges of the brazier, and like a woman thrusting

her head into cold water at daybreak, she plunged into the
coals.

Claire woke from the nightmare gasping and unbearably hot.
Her heart hammered painfully in her chest. She was lying
on an army-issue cot. Her cot. It was dark in the barracks,
and hot. Agonizingly hot and close. The darkness like hot
cloth, stifling her, smothering her. She shoved a thin foil
blanket off her body and gripped the edges of her cot. Her
forearms were rigid and her chest heaved as she tried to
catch her breath in the oven heat.

Soldiers slept in tiered bunks all around her. The aisles
between the bunks, and the paths to toilets and exits, were
traced by glow-in-the-dark orange arrows that burned like
embers in the coal-black floor. Thirty meters away, at the
far end of the barracks shell, a few soldiers were still awake,
playing cards.

Claire was burning up, but she wasn't sweating. Her skin
was dry as wood baking in a kiln. She remembered feeling
like this once before, running a 40° C temperature with a
bad case of pneumonia. With shaking fingers she flicked on
her bunk light and pulled on a shirt and pants. Picking up
her familiar, she buckled it around her waist. It felt like a
band of fire. She queried her temperature.

—One hundred seventeen degrees, her familiar responded.

—Celsius, please.

—One hundred seventeen Celsius.

—That's impossible. That's over the boiling point of water.

—One hundred seventeen Celsius.

She burned her fingertips taking the familiar off. The plastic buckles were going soft with heat. Nobody else was waking up. At the other end of the barracks, the card players
dealt another hand.

She stood up. A black char-mark outline showed where
she had been sitting on the bed. She followed the floor lights
toward the end of the barracks. The synthetic flooring stank
with heat. She felt it stick to the bottoms of her boots. She

couldn't breathe. Her chest was heaving but there was no oxygen in the furnace air.

The card players had all taken off their familiars to make the game more sporting. "I call. Three queens," one of them said. His hair was on fire. "What have you got?"

His opponent put down a fan of cards. They blackened and began to bubble. "Read 'em and weep." He reached to gather in the pot.

Lieutenant Jackson, the man with three queens, swore and threw down his hand. Black patches spread across his uniform and flowered into flame as he glanced up at Claire. "Hey, Grandma. Got any money worth losing?"

"Split lip keeping you up, Claire?" The victor stacked his winnings. "That slant really stung you. Dirty bastard." Fire burst from his eyes.

"I-I need some air. I need to step outside."

"You on perimeter tonight?" Jackson said. Claire shook her head. "Go ahead, then. But stay within easy radio range, and stay on the Chinatown side." He waved her away. His hands had burned down to the bone.

She stammered her thanks and fled.

Outside, the night was cool and damp. It must have rained earlier in the evening. Reflections from their perimeter floodlights gleamed wetly on the asphalt. Steam rose hissing around her boots.

A dim figure in white walked slowly out of the parking lot and onto Carrall Street. Claire knew at once it was the white goddess Southsiders called The Harrier. The Harrier was Claire's mother, and all Claire's visions came from her. Claire ran after her, footsteps loud in the night, breath ragged. Without her familiar she was blind. No ghostly UV vision. No blocks of color scanned in infrared to show her the position of the perimeter pickets. Just shadows and cloudy sky, hazed into brightness around the lonely street lamps.

The sound of her footsteps changed as she hit Carrall Street, echoes slapping back off the storefronts. She was closing quickly now. "Mother!"

The white goddess did not stop.

Aged in casks of fear you came
Whiskey-eyed, ten thousand dragon

And cut the strings of my derelict limbs,
And careless, spilled red wine from my brothers.

But this is only poetry. I hide
Behind words as well as wine.

What is real? My weeping son. Honor.
This broken cup. Overhead,

Two gulls wing strongly into twilight,
And vanish into the borderless dark.

Water Spider's father had written that.

The whiskey-eyed dragon kept pace with him as he
walked the empty streets back from his prostitute's apartment in the New Moon Manor. It was late Friday night in
the hour of the Rat: a weak, cunning time of night, in which
the streets were always full of headless ghosts. Water Spider
felt them as a stiffness in his back and shoulders. A fair
price for what he had put Jen through the previous afternoon, he supposed.

There was a reason Water Spider was out so late alone
and unguarded; his prostitute, Pearl, was Jen's mother. Water Spider was careful that the boy not be with him when
he visited the mother. Both had their pride.

The fourth streetlight he passed had burned out. An unlucky sign. Water Spider's sword in its leather sheath
slapped gently against his left calf, and his boots went tip-
tap, tip-tap, on the weathered cement. Timbers creaked and
groaned in the building beside him as a ghost scampered
through its walls; he glimpsed it in the glass window-front.
With the sword he wore, Water Spider was not afraid of
ghosts. He smiled a little, remembering how Jen had tried
to get him to trade in his antique for a fine new weapon
with a ceramic body and a flaked diamond edge. Jen's sword
would cut through a lamppost as if it were cobweb—but

would pass through a ghost as if it were empty air. The Old Man at Water Spider's side knew the color of spirits' blood.

Pearl was only seven or eight years younger than the Honorable Minister for Borders. Water Spider was too old to listen to what a mere girl had to say, and too wise to care about impressing one. Life had given Pearl a more complex flavor, like a better quality of tea. A disappointed woman, in his judgment, but she bore it with good humor. She no longer had expectations.

She never smelled of flowers. She used a scent like tea leaves instead, fresh from the canister. Sometimes, after they made love, he would sniff at her sweat-slick body, and arch his eyebrows, and ask her, Was she steeped yet? Still brewing, she would answer, and roll back on top of him to give him her taste, touching his lips with the fine, silky hairs under her arms if she was finished, or between her legs if she was not.

And each time he came to her, before they fell onto her rumpled bed, she would serve him tea, and take with hers a little pill. Once he had asked what the pill was for. She laughed and said, "This is the love potion my herbalist makes for me." Only tonight, after he had spent his seed, had he realized the pill must be a contraceptive. Odd, that this understanding had come to him so late. The knowledge had a strange effect on him. Her great aphrodisiac: not to bear his children.

He had never liked the hour of the Rat. Too late for people of good intention to be abroad. Too early for scoundrels to be in bed.

"To be without posterity . . ."—something something—"is an offense against the whole line of ancestors, and terminates the sacrifices to them." Meng-tzu, wasn't it? Meng-tzu and K'ung Fu-tzu were full of dictums and analects about how men of Water Spider's class could best fulfill their duty to the Emperor. But the throne in Government House had been empty for seventy years, after the Emperor had carelessly allowed himself to be slain before ensuring his posterity.

Perhaps Meng-tzu was right. Too many edicts. Too few children.

The streets seemed lonelier than usual. Where the street lamps shone, cherry and apple blossoms lay scattered on the road. He thought of Pearl in her small apartment, drowsing or asleep perhaps; or playing solitaire. Or entertaining another visitor.

What is real? My weeping son. Honor.
  This broken cup.

It occurred to Water Spider for the first time that perhaps they were both disappointed people.

The moon came around the corner, and the goddess of the moon, and met Water Spider on Pender Street. Her flesh was the color of bones. Beautiful and terrible she was as a hawk in flight; beautiful beyond all singing. She reached out with one hand to trace the line of his forehead with her finger. Her touch was the distance to remote mountains.

She beheld him utterly: his silk coat and his discipline and the fumes of his weakness. Her beholding dissolved him. His blood and flesh became knots of wind. The moonlight stirred in him. Seeing him thus, she bade him name his deepest desire, and he knew that she in the fullness of her power would grant it to him. Wisdom. Riches. Sovereignty. Anything.

He heard himself reply, "a cup of tea."

She stroked his brow a second time, her touch like deep snow falling. She laughed, and then she was gone.

Water Spider fell to his knees, empty with the absence of the goddess. And yet a last scent of her remained; the fragrance of that tea called Silver Needles diffused through his lungs and blood.

Footsteps pounded up the street, followed by a lean Southside woman, flushed and gasping. It was the one who had beaten Jen so severely. "Damn it!" she yelled.

"You look like her," Water Spider whispered. "The goddess."

This broken cup.

Claire ignored him. "Damn it, Mother. Come back! Why send me such a horrible vision?"

Water Spider was still staring at her when sudden fire burst into the night from the barracks behind her. Where Claire's fellow soldiers had moments before been sleeping or pissing or playing cards, there now came a series of deep, concussive blasts.

Then munitions detonating, like strings of deadly firecrackers.

Glass shattering.

Screams.

Volleys of startled gulls and pigeons rose into the sky from the rooftops of Chinatown, breaking and re-forming. A tremor ran through the sidewalk. Firelight and shadow wrestled madly across the streets and buildings. "Sweet gods," Water Spider breathed. "Your people were in there!"

Claire turned, crying out, and watched them burn.

Some parts of the nonflammable barracks shell were black, others milky. Large patches were completely translucent, accidental windows onto the inferno raging inside. Something had punched a hole in the shell and fired incendiaries inside. Fat arcs of current jumped and spat among the flames.

A yelling mob of nightmares roared from Downtown, the monsters the Southsiders were supposed to repel. In the throbbing firelight Water Spider could make out a dark carnival of the grotesque and deformed. A stick-limbed man as tall as a house, armed with a plastic spear; a four-armed woman, clutching a glass-tipped rubber whip in each hand; another man, long as a car, bounding on all fours, each foot shod with steel cleats; a man with faceted eyes that winked like gems in the firelight; a woman with a hole in her stomach; a huge man in a formal suit and tie who wore sunglasses and carried a semi-automatic rifle.

"Run!" Water Spider yelled, grabbing Claire's arm.

"Your friends are dead. There is nothing you can do for them."

Claire swore and turned and ran like hell and Water Spider followed, sprinting wildly, his sword banging at his side. If he died now, his bones would be devoured. If he died now, he would have no heirs to make sacrifices for his spirit. He would be a wandering ghost, a thin hunger without end. After all the duties of his life, after all his service, what a bitter finish: to be a restless nothing, an empty shadow.

A bullet hummed past and glass fountained from a nearby window. "Shit!" Claire cried.

The monsters roared, and started after them.

Water Spider refused to die. Not here. Not yet. "Follow me," he yelled. He ducked into an alley he knew, and raced for the heart of Chinatown.

CHAPTER 8

Back on the Southside it was almost one in the morning. Twenty-one hundred years ago, Emily thought, an angel had come to the Theotokos with tidings that would change the world. Had Mary been glad at that moment? Or had she bowed and trembled and wished some other woman had been chosen? For the first time Emily thought how terrible it could be to feel your own life lost, swept away into a great river of destiny you never chose.

A handful of talkers lingered in the Visitors Pavilion, ignoring the enlisted men who were cleaning up after the banquet. Emily was outside with Li Mei (and two unobtrusive guards) contemplating the frozen surface of Mayfair Lake when the angel's voice came suddenly inside her, like a hammer falling on a piano wire.

alas!

Emily gasped.

—What is it? her familiar demanded.

—Nothing. I don't know. Something bad.

—Your heart just practically stopped. Now it's racing.

—Shut up and let me think!

soon

Li Mei didn't seem to have noticed anything. Bundled in a borrowed foil parka, she stood at the edge of the lake.

Filled with her angel's premonition of disaster, Emily jumped up from the bench where she had been sitting and began to pace. Her guards stiffened. She glared at them. "It's too cold to sit still. I'm not going anywhere."

The cold was creeping across the front of Emily's thighs at the bottom edge of her coat, where her frozen pant legs touched her skin. Her familiar screened her self-profile on her contacts. Classic high-arousal pattern: elevated heart rate and respiration, pupils dilated, galvanic skin response up.

listen

Emily stopped. An instant later a message came spitting across her eyes, top priority, direct to her and Winter. When it was over she sat blindly on the bench and crossed herself. "Oh. Christ have mercy. Claire."

One of her guards stepped forward. "Something wrong, Miss Thompson?"

now!

Emily looked up at Li Mei. "A priority interrupt radio message has just come for your mother from Government House. Our AI has instructions to descramble and translate any incoming messages. The monsters from Downtown have attacked."

"What! How bad is it? Have the barbarians penetrated beyond Carrall Street, or have they been contained? Does the message come from Water Spider?"

Emily's angel and her familiar spoke in concert.

now!

—Now! This is your chance to work Li Mei for a quick passage out of town.

Emily knew they were right. It would be the most natural thing in the world for Chinatown's delegates to return to their airplane and race back over the mountains. The right words, the right glances and actions, and Emily could be on that flight, safe from Winter, with the angel in her breast untouched.

Now. Now was the moment. Now.

She stared stupidly out at the frozen lake. "Those things you call barbarians must have better tech than we thought. They took out our barracks. Found a seam somehow. Shot in incendiaries." One hundred of her people burned alive.

"Survivors?"

"Four. Maybe five. Exact numbers currently unknown."

The guards looked at one another, white-faced. Emily's familiar informed her that one of them had a brother in the destroyed cohort. Had once had a brother.

Emily sat on the concrete bench and stared at the lake. Claire had taught her to skate here when she was five years old. She remembered stepping out onto the ice, tiny old lady steps, ankles flopping over, mittened hands out. And two years later, learning to skate backwards, Claire weaving from side to side, her strong hands around Emily's skinny hips, Emily screaming with terror and delight, the two of them wiping out in a fluffy snowbank not far from this very spot, a tangle of limbs and skates and hair, and they had laughed themselves sick. Powdery snow exploding around them like cold white fire.

"Christ was made flesh to suffer," Emily said. "Oh God. God, I'm cold."

Li Mei turned to their guards. "You! Run at once to the Visitors Pavilion! Find Li Bing and tell her that your garrison has been destroyed in a barbarian attack."

The first guard nodded to his fellow. "I'll stay here. You run like hell." The second guard bolted.

Emily started to say, "But—"

quiet

listen

She tried to think.

—It's a trap. Li Bing won't be at the Visitors Pavilion. She is always in bed by midnight. Who could know her routine better than her daughter? Li Mei is up to something.

—But she just got rid of one of the guards for me.

—What if she has some hidden motive? the familiar argued. She may want to get you to Chinatown for her own purposes. Had you thought of that?

—Then we shall use one another, Emily answered, thinking furiously.

now

She had to get rid of the other guard.

Emily inhaled sharply. The cold air stung her nostrils.

"There are things you will need from your chalet," she said, holding Li Mei's eyes.

Li Mei nodded. "Of course." She began walking quickly back to her cabin. Emily and the guard came after her. Ice-crusted snow crunched beneath their hurrying feet.

—Temperature?

—Minus fifteen Celsius and dropping. You should have worn warmer boots.

"Where are your bags?" Emily asked Li Mei.

"In the back bedroom." They crested a low hill. The path led down to three guest cabins. Li Mei was quartered in the middle one.

"Chalet, open," Emily said clearly as they came to the door. It obliged. "You—Raymond, isn't it?—run and grab the envoy's bags. We'll collect whatever is needed from the front room." The soldier nodded and loped through the living room to the sleeping quarters.

Emily held up a hand to stop Li Mei from entering. "Chalet," she said. "Seal. Emily Thompson: my authority." Locks hissed and clicked.

—Confirmed, her familiar said. Boy, are you in trouble.

"All right," Emily said. "That should keep him for a while. Do you need to speak with Li Bing before we go?"

"You can seal these buildings from the outside?" Li Mei stared accusingly at her. "These aren't guest accommodations. They are prisons."

Emily shrugged. "Two for the price of one."

The sound of hammering and cursing came very faintly from inside Li Mei's chalet. The soundproofing was excellent. "And you can do this? On your own authority?"

My soul shall magnify the Lord. "Lady," Emily said, "I own this town. Well, Grandfather owns it, but I have a big piece of the action."

By two in the morning Li Mei and Emily were flying for Vancouver in Li Bing's plane. Li Mei said the trip would take about an hour and a half. It was dark in the cockpit of the *Phoenix*. The old manual controls were still in place, although it had been years since anyone except the plane's own AI had piloted it. Readouts glowed a ghostly blue on the wide dash: airspeed, altitude, tachometer, fuel levels. Li Mei had asked the plane to take them home at top speed. Now more than ever they would need the Southside reinforcements. And if she was required to sacrifice her career to ensure Emily would not oppose reinforcements—well, as her mother would say, life asks unfair things of us sometimes.

Inside the cabin, the passenger seats faced each other over a long low table of polished blackwood, ornately carved and heavy with lacquer. An old-fashioned tachometer, warped and broken, hung swaying from the ceiling. It was a lucky charm taken from a much older *Phoenix* destroyed in a crash eighty years earlier, from which the great-grandfather of the present owner had been able to walk away with only a sprained ankle.

"How brave they must have been, the people who flew in planes that did not fly themselves." Li Mei bent over to study the instruments in the cockpit. "I always wanted to try it."

"You? I wouldn't have guessed," Emily said.

"I am my mother's daughter," Li Mei said. "I am required to be brave, but forbidden to be foolhardy."

Outside, stars glimmered in the cold prairie sky. A few high clouds streamed below them, wind-tangled like the hair of a Sung beauty in an ancient poem. The *Phoenix* vibrated, her powerful engines sounding muffled and distant, as if they hovered motionless in the dark sky, while the spinning world thundered far below, clouds and fields and soon the onrushing mountains.

"By now your mother and Winter will be meeting," Emily said. "By now he must know I've gone."

"He will be angry?"

"Oh yes. This is the end for Grandfather and me."

"Families don't end," Li Mei said.

"Love can."

Li Mei shrugged. "But not family. You are the shadow cast by your ancestors. No matter how hard you run, you cannot escape them."

Emily smiled thinly. "If you're trying to cheer me up, it's not working."

"Do you regret running away?"

"Yes," Emily said. "But it had to be done."

"Good," Li Mei said. She ran her fingers through her short black hair. "Smuggling you out and risking the wrath of your grandfather will certainly mean the end of my career. I would be unhappy to think it had been for nothing."

"Surely they will understand that you had no choice. I wasn't bluffing. I would have pulled our troops out of Chinatown if you hadn't helped me escape. It makes no sense to punish you—"

"My mother's ambitions for me have died tonight," Li Mei said. She rose and walked to the galley. "Shall I get some tea?"

She returned with a teapot and two cups on a lacquered tray. A wingless whiskered dragon in blue enamel curled around the pot; his mouth was the spout. Li Mei poured ceremoniously, first for Emily and then for herself. The cups were eggshell thin, and hot from the tea inside. Emily had to hold hers with great delicacy, near the top.

Li Mei savored the aroma. "For three centuries you whites drank this rotten, you know."

"What?"

"It is true. The first Europeans, coming to China, saw how greatly the populace depended on tea. Determined to introduce the drug back home and make their fortunes, they shipped a great cargo of leaves. Unfortunately, sea water got to them in the hold on the long voyage back to Europe, and not far from Bristol the captain discovered that the leaves had all gone rotten. 'Spread them out on the deck to dry' said that quick-thinking man. 'No-one here has ever tasted tea. How will they know the difference?' As a result, Europeans became addicted to a tea you called black—and we called rotten."

Emily sipped her tea. It was hot and green-smelling, with a lighter, more herbal taste than the charred-stick flavor of hot chicory. "Is that a true story?"

Li Mei shrugged. Her shawl-cut burgundy jacket made

her shoulders look large compared to her slight chest. "Water Spider told it to me. He knows a great deal about tea."

Great shadows climbed over the horizon as the Rockies thrust up to meet them. The plane flew low into the first pass. Dark stone rose around them.

Li Mei contemplated her embroidered cuffs. "Now that my life of public service has come to this surprising end, I think I shall make dresses. Or design them, rather. I find needlework very dull."

Emily shook her head. "To waste your talents is a sin. Design dresses, Li Mei? I could never do that."

"True," Li Mei observed. "But I have taste." Emily looked up, offended. "I am no longer a diplomat," Li Mei said. "I need not worry about your sensitivities. I could even note that there are places in the world where the needs of every formal occasion are not met by a freshly pressed set of fatigues."

Emily Thompson colored. "This is your version of being hysterical, isn't it?"

"In fact," Li Mei went on, "I could remark that Southside architecture is without a doubt the ugliest I have ever seen." She stretched out one leg, admiring her black calf-high boot, its gold buckles gleaming. "I might mention that women in combat boots do not add to the grace of a social gathering, and that the beet, the odious beet, is a vile, repugnant vegetable that no compassionate peasant would inflict upon his pigs! That—"

"Shut up!"

For the first time, Li Mei allowed herself a small smile. "No." She smoothed her skirt and took another sip of tea. "You have liberated me, Emily Thompson. I am in your debt."

Emily scowled. "Don't mention it."

The night roared softly around them, heavy with mountains.

"More tea for the Empress of the Southside?"

"Is there chicory?"

"No."

"Then I'll have tea. And I will never be Southside's 'Empress.' Not after tonight."

"Don't be coy," Li Mei said, pouring. "It is beneath you. You most certainly will rule Southside, or die trying. Once you were to inherit it; now you will have to fight for it. That is the only difference."

"I will not kill my own people to get Winter's chair," Emily said steadily.

"Of course you will," Li Mei said. She raised her cup. "To the gods," she said.

"My governess was a devil's child."

"I beg your pardon?"

"Claire. My governess. Do you remember her?"

"The one with the skin defect?"

"It's not a defect. Her mother was a devil we call The Harrier. Claire calls her a goddess. I don't argue the distinction with her anymore. The Harrier, as is her wont from time to time, mated with a mortal man. Taking his seed, she rubbed it into a ball of snow between her palms. From this she fashioned a snowchild, with abandoned wiper blades for limbs and ball bearings for eyes. Then she left it on Winter's step to thaw."

"Go on."

"My grandfather knows better than to thwart the Powers of this world," Emily said bitterly, thinking of the twelve children sacrificed to the North Side. "He took the snowchild in and cared for it. When it had completely thawed, he found he had a baby girl. That was Claire. Most people shunned her. She grew up tough, and everything she had came from his hands alone. That was something Winter thought he could use. So he made her my governess."

"Ah. She was in the barracks tonight, wasn't she?"

"Stationed there. I don't know. Maybe she was one of the survivors."

"The gods look after their own," Li Mei said.

"Devils," Emily corrected automatically. "I hope so."

A smile flickered on Li Mei's face at this surprising theological position. She changed the subject. "You said the monsters Downtown had been beaten back?"

"For a little while. I've been out of radio reach since we took off, but the last reports seemed to indicate that the monsters were held in check. One message singles out some men for special commendation, men from a . . . club? Does that make sense?"

"The Hong Hsing Athletic Club?"

"That's it."

Li Mei's thin eyes thinned some more. "Curious."

Emily looked at her. "What?"

Li Mei raised her hands, palms out. "Probably it is nothing. But we have not seen anything like these firebombs from the Downtown barbarians before. Suddenly, here one is. Only one, mind you, unless you have reports that more have rained down on Government House or elsewhere in Chinatown."

"No reports to that effect." Emily was watching Li Mei intently. "Go on."

"The members of the Hong Hsing Athletic Club are soldiers too, in the service of the Dragon, the most warlike of Chinatown's Powers. How lucky enough of them were awake and armed and close enough to Chinatown's borders to throw back this unexpected attack!"

"You think there was a setup," Emily breathed. "You think someone in Chinatown knew this was going to happen."

"I would not say so much, so simply." Li Mei reached for the makeup case in the pocket of her jacket and slipped out a lipstick. She ran it quickly over her thin lips. "I would say that Chinatown has been . . . very lucky tonight."

Emily grunted. The *Phoenix* banked and began to climb, swinging wide and high around a massive peak. Emily touched the crucifix that hung around her neck. "It's not the worst way for one of us to die. Burning." She looked at Li Mei. "It's very cold, on the North Side."

They passed through the rushing darkness, heading west, while mountains like empires fell and rose beneath them.

CHAPTER 9

Back on the Southside, Wire woke with bad luck crawling on her skin. She rubbed her face and the back of her neck, then raised her head to look at the clock-face glowing faintly on the wall of her room. Almost two in the morning.

There it was, the sound that had awakened her. A muffled pounding. Someone trying to get into the chalet.

Wire rolled out of bed. She grabbed her banquet dress off the floor and dragged it up over her hips, tug, yank, the usual struggle to get her arms through the straps, and then the behind-the-back scrabble with the zipper. The pounding and yelling was clearer now. The sound of Lark's sleepy voice in the next room filled Wire with dread. She stumbled barefoot into the living room just as the chalet was speaking. *Shh!* it hissed. *I have guests in here trying to sleep!*

More swearing and pounding.

I am terribly sorry about this, the chalet said.

Raining peered groggily from her room. "Not at all. Open, please."

"Goddamn door!" Nick burst in, bringing the freezing Southside air with him. "Rain, thank God. You have to get out of here. Don't waste time packing. Get Lark in her coat and get to my truck. Wire too." They stared at him stupidly. "It's Winter," Nick said. "He's killed Li Bing. Within minutes our cities will be at war."

"Oh sweet gods," Wire whispered.

"My familiar got it straight from the Tory Building,"
Nick told them. "It happened in one of the family apartments. He hit her. I don't know if he meant to kill her but
she fell and cracked her head. I don't know why. My guess
is that soldiers will be here to take you hostage within ten
minutes. Maybe five."

"Oh, shit!" Wire said.

"Why would he have killed Li Bing?"

"Get your things, dammit Rain!"

Everybody try to remain calm, the chalet said desperately.
Extremely soothing music began to well softly through the
room.

They ran for the parking lot, Wire mismatched in her party
dress and chunky boots. Hadn't had time to tie them up, red
laces flying around her ankles, snow crunching underfoot.
Nick loped ahead with Lark in his arms, and Wire loved
him for it. He had given his daughter to the city once. Never
again. Even Raining must see that.

Nick slipped on a patch of ice, lurched crazily and almost
fell. Lark screamed with delight.

The parking lot was almost empty. The only lights came
from the hooded pathway lamps and from the Visitors Pavilion, where weary enlisted men were cleaning up the rem-
nants of the banquet. Wire scrambled into the cab of Nick's
truck and took Lark in her lap. Raining jumped in after her.

"Where are we going?" Lark asked.

Nick jumped in and slammed the door. "Got your seat
belt on? We're going for a ride, sweetie. Truck: take me to
the McKernan helicopter pads." The truck powered up and
rolled out of the parking lot, heading up the long hill to the
top of the river valley.

Lights started snapping on all around the Visitors Pavilion. The truck startled and strained to put on speed. "Good
boy," Nick whispered. "Come on, come on." The truck
crawled up Groat Road. "Go, go, go, go," Nick murmured,
eyes glued to the rearview mirror. "Go a little faster, *dammit*!"

Lark jumped.

Raining grinned crookedly at Nick. "I thought you were going to get a gas-powered truck instead of this little ethanol four-stroke."

"Never got around to it."

"I see that."

They were near the top of the hill now. The night bent around them, watching. Wire shrank down in her seat, arms tight around Lark's waist. Shit, shit, shit, shit.

"Just out of curiosity," Raining said, "where are we going to fly in your helicopter?"

"I don't know." Nick twisted in his seat to stare back at the Mayfair plateau. Someone had used a remote override to turn the Visitors Pavilion and all the surrounding chalets transparent, with their lights on full. There would be no place to hide down there now.

"Does this chopper have the range to get us to Vancouver?"

"No."

"Then how are we going to get back to Chinatown?"

"I don't know."

"Won't they see the helicopter on their radar and bring it down?" Wire asked.

"Can't you shut her up?"

"Certainly," Raining said. "Wire, shut up. Nick, where are we going to fly in your helicopter?"

They turned onto Saskatchewan Drive, picking up speed. Nick stared at his speedometer. Wire saw letters sparkle and dim on Nick's eyes. He shook his head.

Another coruscation. "No. I can't. Not with Lark."

"Can't what?" Wire said. "What is Magpie saying?" They were now going forty kilometers an hour. She wished Nick had gotten that gas-powered truck.

Nick said, "There is one place we could go where they couldn't find us, Magpie says. And they wouldn't follow us." He looked over at his wife.

Raining's eyes widened. "The North Side," she whispered.

• • •

Fifty minutes later they had swapped the tired old truck for Nick's helicopter and were crossing the North Saskatchewan River to the one place no one from the Southside would follow.

Nick was in the cockpit. Wire and Lark and Raining were in the back, perched on Nick's big tool chest. A foam pad had been strapped to the lid with duct tape to make a crude bench. The wrinkled tape left little sticky silver smears on Wire's gown. It was a beautiful dress, forest-green rayon with rust-colored trim and a fitted scoop-cut bodice that showed her breasts to advantage without looking trashy. Now she would never get that tape off it.

"Dammit!" Nick said.

"What?"

"Shit. It's Magpie. My familiar. She's gone."

"Gone?" Wire said. "What do you mean?"

"I mean the instant we crossed the river she was gone. No answer. I don't seem to have a familiar anymore."

Lark squirmed in her mother's lap and prepared to whine.

Well, Wire thought, Raining's forest didn't much care for technology either. Although they were fading, the Powers were still Powers, and mighty on their home ground. Wire gave Lark her best conspirator's smile. "Isn't this an adventure?" Poor little Lark, big eyes blinking like an owlet, halfway between sleep and scared. The only charm Wire had was Raining's locket, hanging on a chain just at the top of her breasts. She touched it, wishing she had brought something luckier. "Can you make it any warmer, Nick?"

He shook his head. "This is all the heat we've got. That's the old municipal airport down there," Nick said. "It's always winter on the North Side, but there have been patches of thaw the last few years. This is one of the biggest ones. I was going to risk a quick trip in two or three years, if the thaw held, to see if we could salvage some jet fuel."

"Why should it be thawing here more than anywhere else?" Wire asked.

Nick shrugged.

"Magic runs differently everywhere," Raining said. "There was barely any of it in the Western world from the

Enlightenment to the Second World War, after all. And it clots thickest where you have a lot of people jammed together. An airfield is mostly machines and empty land. Somebody's day job.''

The helicopter drifted down, gentle as a snowflake, feeling its way. A few cold blue strip lights still gleamed in the darkness on the runways to the west. "No, over to the buildings," Nick said. "The runways still get some traffic." The helicopter obliged, sidling toward the big sheet-metal hangars. "Lots of nights you can hear the phantom planes taking off," Nick said. "Every now and then one actually comes up over the skyline."

"Where do they go?" Wire asked.

"We don't want to find out," Raining said.

Nick shrugged. "Ask John Walker and his legion of ghosts. Still, it's our only hope of cover. Right now all the Infants know is that you weren't where they expected you to be."

"Infants?"

"Infantry. Regular soldiers. For all they know, you found some way to sneak back to the coast. Or you all might be"—he glanced at Wire—"out, um, drinking, say, with some new friends."

Raining shook her head. "The chalet will tell them you came and got us."

"Oh. Yeah."

The helicopter settled with a bump. A line of hangars marched off behind them, big hollow buildings with open mouths. Just to the side stood the airport terminal, with the control tower at one end. All its lights were on. In the reflected glow, stretches of tarmac gleamed with black ice.

"I'm hungry," Lark said sleepily.

"Sorry, sweetie," Raining said. "We don't have anything to eat right now. Try to get back to sleep."

"But I'm hu-uh-ungry!" Lark whined.

Large blue letters glittered on the helicopter's windshield. *If you want me to hump three adults and a kid over the mountains, I'm going to need some real fuel.*

"I've been thinking about that," Nick said.

Jet fuel. Gas at least.

"Yeah, yeah, I hear you. Now shut up," Nick said mildly. He got out of the pilot's chair and came back to where the others were, stooping under the helicopter's low ceiling. "Okay, here's the plan," he told the chopper. "I'll go scavenge some airplane fuel to start us off. But even with full tanks, that's not going to get us all the way, right?"

No.

"So what we'll do is take off from here heading north-west, as if we were just another mystery flight from the North Side going God knows where. We'll stay under radar until we're thirty or forty miles away. Then we swing south and head for Banff. If we can pick up the old Trans-Canada Highway we should be able to follow it all the way to the coast and tap gas out of the service station tanks along the way."

Okay.

"Just like when we went over to Osoyoos. But if anything starts to go wrong, if you feel any threat at all to Lark, I want you to get the hell out of here, understood? If that means leaving me on the ground, so be it. If it means turning yourself in, you can even do that." He glanced over at Raining. "It won't be fun, but it will be better than some things the North Side can throw at you.—As for you," he told the helicopter, "if I'm not around, you take directions from Raining as if she were me. Do you remember her?"

<Grunt>

Raining sighed and glanced at Wire. "I wonder if it was easier when you only had to impress your in-laws."

Nick decided to take Wire with him to do the fuel tap. He gave her his foil parka and dug an old dirty down-filled coat out of the back of the chopper for himself. He rummaged in his toolbox until he found a tight wool toque and pulled it down over his ears. Wire struggled into the parka. "Put your hood up," Raining said. "You lose thirty percent of your body heat through your head. So my husband told me once."

Wire nodded. Nick reached over and pulled the tabs on

the foil parka twice, letting it puff up for better insulation. Then he pulled the foil gloves off Wire and put them on himself. "Jam your hands in your pockets. They'll be warmer there than they would be in gloves, as long as you don't need to use them."

"I won't need them?"

"Tapping is a one man job. Just watch carefully. That way if something happens to me and you have to fuel up, the chopper can talk you through it. Ready to go?" She nodded. The cold rushed in as Nick opened the helicopter door. He asked Wire to pull the tap out from the tool chest in the back. She grunted and muscled it out. It looked like an ice-auger, or an oversized pogo stick. Nick took it from her and leaned it against the side of the chopper. "There should be a few rods of raw ceramic there."

"How many do you need?"

"One should be enough. We're only going three or four meters down."

"Shit." Wire slid the big bar of ceramic across the floor to him. "Heavier than it looks." She grabbed a box of bits and scrambled out of the helicopter. Nick slid the door shut behind her.

Outside, the night was hard and clear and black. Small blue lights burned low along the runways. It was very cold. Their feet on the icy tarmac made tiny creaking sounds, quiet but clear.

"It's so *quiet*," Wire said.

"I thought you'd notice the cold more."

Wire shook her head. "No. I mean, yeah, it's cold enough to freeze the tits off a polar bear, but that's not . . ." She looked around. The dark bulk of the hangars. Cold white light from the windows of the terminal building. Small trucks parked around the tarmac. Everything still. "I thought the North Side was supposed to be spooky," Wire said. "Where your ghosts went. And I thought it would be like, I don't know . . . like being lost in the Forest. Eyes watching you from behind every branch. Things you couldn't see. But here . . ." She shook her head. "Look at the helicopter. Just sitting there like a dead thing. Like it didn't have a voice at all."

Nick was looking at her curiously.

"There's a path you take to Raining's house," Wire said. "You can hear him talk. Here he would just be dirt. Frost. Sidewalk."

Nick nodded. "Raining said something like that once. I had just taken her out to the farmhouse for the first time. It was winter, and she stood there on the middle of the lone prairie. She hated it. Said she wasn't used to being ignored."

Wire laughed. "That, I believe." She shivered and stamped her feet. "Shit though, it is cold. Your piss would freeze before it hit the ground. If you were a guy."

Nick looked at her.

"Not squatting. You know."

Nick grinned. "Ahem. It's only minus twenty. Okay, not tropical, but you can see that it's thawed here not too long ago." Runnels of ice lay on the tarmac where water had crept within the last few days. "Five years ago you could fly over the whole North Side in the middle of summer and never see the ground beneath the snow."

"Lot of Powers fading, these days." Wire's breath smoked in the cold air. "Still, this place makes little ghosts run around inside my bones."

Nick nodded at the nearest fuel pump, which was about fifteen meters away. "We're going over there." He hefted the heavy tap. "You bring the rod of ceramic and the drill bits."

Hangars loomed on their left. Ahead of them was nothing but empty fields, runway, and half a mile away, the back of Edmonton's abandoned downtown: windowless brick and concrete walls that were just as ugly and featureless now as they had been when they were first built in the 1940's.

Nick bent to study the ancient fuel pump that reared like a tombstone from the flat tarmac. Rust and frost were breaking up the red body. It still sported a gas company logo, long faded, and a hose, its rubber rotted by the gasoline, attached to a rust-clotted handle. Inside the airport some kind of announcement came over the PA system, unintelligible. Nick pretended not to notice. Wire figured she ought to do the same.

From where they stood now, they could see into the nearest hangar. A sixteen-seat commuter plane took up the whole far wall. "Could we just take that?" Wire asked.

"Those are dumb machines, no familiars or AIs. We'd have to actually fly it ourselves. Which we can't." Going back to the chopper, Nick flipped the cap off its fuel tank and clipped on one end of a length of hose. Unrolling the hose, he clipped the other end onto a short length of tubing that dangled from the top of the tap. "You can't work these old pumps directly. Too much decay. We're going to punch down into the tank."

"How do you know where to drill?"

Nick ambled onto the tarmac, glanced around, spotted what he was looking for, and began setting up the tap. "Well, this thing has a subsonic sensor on it. So I could fit casters onto the legs and drag it back and forth across the ground until I got a crude picture of what was down there." Nick picked up the tap and flipped out its three support legs. These rocked and settled, adjusting their lengths for maximum stability. With one booted foot he gestured at a small steel disc set flush with the tarmac. "Or I could look for the intake pipe."

"Oh. Of course."

When the tap was stable, Nick fed the rod of raw ceramic into its barrel. He squinted. "Two and three quarters," he decided. "Go."

The tap spun and hummed, warming up. Then with a whirring, grinding noise, it extruded a stiff tube of hardened ceramic about a handspan long and just over an inch in diameter. Wire crouched down in fascination. "It's already grooved."

"Mm." Nick looked through his bits. They looked like lampreys: gaping circular mouths ringed with vicious little teeth. He chose one and crouched down to screw it into place. "And now, since I don't have to make myself look smart anymore, I will turn on the subsonics, so the tap knows how far down it's supposed to go."

The tap began to drill, extruding an ever-lengthening tube of spinning ceramic.

"Why did Winter hit Li Bing?" Wire said. "I can't believe it."

Nick rested his full weight on the tap's t-bar as the snarling drill tore into the asphalt. In fifteen seconds it was through into the ground below. The drill bit held the tap in place now, pulling it down. "I have no goddamn idea. Metal fatigue, maybe. Happens to people too, sometimes. They look strong, they look good, you can't see the flaw, but the same tiny pressure builds up year after year and then one day they shear and fly into pieces and you never saw it coming. This hasn't been a good time for Winter. I heard a rumor that Emily has been under arrest for the last three days."

The tap chimed politely.

"Congratulations," Nick said. "We hit gas."

Disaster struck just after they filled the helicopter's tanks. Wire had disconnected the rubber hose from the chopper and then climbed in to get warm. Nick was still out by the pump, fixing a cap to the new line he had run down into the fuel tank.

Suddenly the helicopter's rotors screamed into motion, throwing Wire out of her chair. "What are you doing!"

Visitor. Walking toward Nick.

They saw Nick face the approaching figure, then turn, waving frantically upward. "Go! GO!"

The chopper bucked like a nervous horse and jumped into the air.

"Wait!" Raining screamed. "You can't leave him there!"

Blades screaming, the chopper banked up and away from the airfield, gathering speed. *The first sign of trouble.*

"I order you to go back and get him! You can't decide to leave him to die! You're just a machine!"

The chopper ignored her and raced away, heading northwest. Lark was crying. Numbly Raining put her arms around her daughter, and looked through the helicopter's glass body at the rushing darkness.

In the abandoned municipal airport on the North Side, Nick stood waiting for the stranger to approach. He was wearing an ancient Southside regimental coat with general's insignia, old winter fatigue pants, and army-issue boots. Under one arm he held a bundle of black clothing.

Raining and Lark were safe, Nick thought. The rest didn't matter. "Nicholas Terleski," he said, and he held out his hand.

The stranger took it. "John Walker," he said.

CHAPTER 10

It was cold on the North Side, and still. The lights were all out, the windows broken. Edmonton's downtown was dressed in ancient Christmas finery. Brown wreaths hung from the streetlights lining Jasper Avenue, and pairs of candy canes, each the size of a man, still crossed above the traffic lights. Every building stood profoundly untenanted. The North Side was landscape, nothing more. The skyscrapers were outcrops of steel and glass. The roads were paths for the wind.

There was no trace of the people of the North Side, those that had perished there in the Dream, or the Southside's dead since collected by John Walker. No ghosts in the houses, no spirits in her streets. No sign of any animate thing, dead or alive . . .

. . . Except for the birds. In all that empty landscape, only the birds remained. Winter wrens huddling like cold children in bare hedges. Cedar waxwings searching for shrivelled berries like women combing thrift store sale racks. A portly, good-natured owl hunkering in the chairman's office at the *Edmonton Journal* building. A white hawk, of the kind men called a harrier, wheeling high over the Bridge.

A single magpie fluttering through the darkness of an empty hangar at the airport.

·   ·   ·

When they were done talking and John Walker had left, Nick considered what to do. It was 2:45 A.M. according to his watch and very cold.

The dress boots he had been wearing for last night's banquet were better than nothing, but their fleece lining was still a far cry from the self-heating thermal work boots back at his apartment. His toes had begun to stiffen while he was tapping fuel for the helicopter, and during the whole conversation with John Walker he had been subtly rocking back and forth, trying to press blood into every part of his feet. He kicked his booted toes at the tarmac a couple of times each.

He wished he knew the temperature. Close to $-30°$ C, he guessed, and still falling. Overhead the sky was clear and hard. Stars driven into it like nails.

He wished Magpie were here. But Lark was safe. So.

He could try to walk through the haunted city, heading south until he hit the river valley. Then walk along the bluff to the Bridge, then over and home. But his hands and feet were already stiff. Between the collar of his coat and the bottom of the cap jammed over his ears, his face was tight and hurting. It would be very difficult to find his way through the North Side in the dark. He would have to expect frostbite if he tried the trip. And there were the ghosts. He would be better off to build a fire for the night, and make the trip the next day, when it would be warmer and he would be able to see.

All this presuming he wasn't dead already.

He didn't feel dead. True, he had spoken with John Walker, who brought the souls of the city's dead back to the North Side to rest. But Walking John had not told him he had died. Had not seemed to kill him, either. Nick didn't know what to make of it. They had talked about duty, some. John Walker asked him why he had taken Lark, his only precious child, down to the Bridge. Nick hadn't answered that.

Then there was the bundle of clothes John Walker had given him: a shiny black waistcoat, pants, a top hat, and a pair of gleaming black boots. John Walker's famous black suit. "Take these from me," the king of North Side's dead had said. "I will not wear them anymore. The North Side's long night is nearly done. Dawn is coming. I do not mean to bring back any more of the Southside's dead but one."

"What one?" Nick asked.

"My father," John Walker had said, with a curious, cold smile. And that had been the end of their speaking. Strange.

Well, if Nick was dead he was dead. He didn't think he would feel the cold so badly if he was, though. He tucked the bundle under one arm and headed for the nearest hangar. The fronts of his thighs burned with cold. He walked stiffly, trying not to let them touch his pant legs. His steps were beginning to jar as his feet stiffened and stopped flexing and rolling smoothly. Strides like the thump, thump, thumping impact of crutches, or wooden legs.

He would definitely need to build a fire.

He had two main problems as he saw it, the cold and the dark. In the hangar he would be out of any wind, thankfully. As for the darkness, he was already working with no more than starlight and the blue runway-indicators. Inside the hangar it would be very dark indeed. He had an excellent service-issue igniter and compact flashlight, along with eight unused Hot Spots, in the pockets of the military grade heavy-duty foil parka he had given to Wire. No doubt currently lying over the toolbox in the helicopter. Or possibly serving as a pillow for Lark.

The second hangar turned out to have a major advantage over its neighbors. Weighed under by a century's accumulation of snow and ice, a large part of its roof had collapsed, letting in the starshine. The drifting snow that covered every surface inside also helped reflect the light. It was terribly dim, but it was a long way better than pitch black. Nick went looking for a prop plane near some kind of light. The old Piper he settled for was farther from the hangar doors than he would have liked, but standing only a few meters from the debris of the collapsed roof, it got a lot of starshine. He couldn't read the lettering on its fuselage, but at least he could see where it was.

He started to put down the bundle John Walker had given

him. Changing his mind, he tried the pilot-side door on the Piper. He found his fingers had stiffened badly with the cold. He could not make them curl around the handle. Instead he pushed his hand down inside it, then lowered his wrist. The fingers bent readily enough, and stuck. He pulled. Nothing happened. The door was jammed shut or iced up.

He placed John Walker's shiny black clothes on the snowy floor as reverently as he could. Then he took off his gloves, stuffed them in the pocket of his coat, and thrust his hands inside his pants and down to his groin to get warm. He was going to need to use his screwjack, and he couldn't afford to be handling its flaked diamond cutting blade with hands made slick and clumsy with cold. His scrotum recoiled, the skin on his balls puckering. He pressed his hands out flat, then rubbed them vigorously against the insides of his thighs. He shovelled a clear space in the snow with the side of his foot. Once again he kicked his toes against the concrete floor.

When his fingers were warm enough to grip, he took his hands out of his pants and pulled his cold gloves back on. He thumbed the screwjack's control. Cultured ceramic pressed slowly out into a knife-blade shape, wrapping the flaked diamond band around one side to make the cutting edge.

Crouching down to peer at the Piper's door as he worked, he cut the lock out first. When the door continued to jam, he cut a good-sized hole straight through it. He picked up John Walker's fancy clothes and put them in the pilot's chair. Then he retracted the screwjack.

Next he felt his way to the back of the hangar where there were bound to be chairs, rags, solvent; maybe even matches and paper, though he would have to get lucky to find them under the snow that had drifted everywhere. He hurt himself twice fumbling through the dark, once stubbing his toe painfully on a wooden chock block, once cracking his head against a plane's wing, which promptly dumped a little pile of snow on his head. That seemed almost comical, until he thought of it melting against the exposed flesh on his face and neck, sucking off precious heat and maybe freezing again. Then he batted fiercely at the dry snow with his gloved hands.

He wondered why he hadn't run for the chopper when he heard it starting to take off. Why had he sent it away without him? Thinking it over now, he was sure he would have had time to get in before it took off.

It was very cold. He poked his cheeks with his glove a few times. The skin on his face was definitely going numb. His feet shuffled and slid across the snowy concrete.

A step behind the tail of what he guessed was the hindmost plane, he almost ran into an oil barrel. He stopped and thought. Placing himself exactly behind the barrel, he took a measured step toward the back wall. Another. Another, and he was there; a faint white shelf, just at waist level: a counter, running along the back of the hangar, lightly dusted with snow. His eyes were tearing from the cold and the strain of staring into the darkness. He kept wiping off the tears, not wanting them to freeze on his skin. He brushed lightly along the countertop. He quite irrationally disliked the idea of the snow touching his gloves. He listened very carefully for the rustle of paper, the clink of glass or rap of wood. Nothing on the first pass.

He took one measured step to the right. He wanted to be sure he could find his way back to that oil barrel. This time he felt his hand encounter something light and stiff. It fell off the counter. He sank down very cautiously. The numbness in his feet was throwing off his balance. He very much wanted not to trip and get his legs snowy. If his body heat thawed the snow enough to get his pants wet, he would have to take them off and dry them on his fire, and he wasn't sure he could survive that. Probably, if his fire was brisk enough, but he didn't want to risk it.

He patted the floor until he found the thing he had brushed off. He raised it to his face; peered; sniffed. If his face could have moved, he would have grinned. A rag! Not just a scrap, either, but a piece of cloth the size of a tea towel. He stood, hoping there would be another nearby. His luck held and he found a second. Now, with the luxury of having two rags, he stuffed the smaller one into his coat pocket. The larger

one he wrapped around his face, leaving only his eyes uncovered. It was too short to wrap all the way around and
have the ends return to the front. His fingers were too stiff
to knot it behind his head. Damn.

He forced himself to remain patient. He put the bigger
cloth—stiff as papier-mâché—on the counter before him,
and set about taking off his gloves. He couldn't close the
fingers of one hand tightly enough to pull the glove off the
other, so he pinned the fingers of his right hand against
the front of his coat with the palm of his left and then pulled
the right hand free of its glove. He repeated the process and
jammed the gloves back in the coat pocket that wasn't full
of frozen rag. Then he put his hands inside his pants again.
They warmed up more slowly this time, stinging fiercely. It
certainly was very cold.

When he had movement back he reached out, grabbed the
rag off the counter heedless of snow, and knotted it quickly
around his face. As his breath warmed the rag it began to
soften, smelling of gasoline and methyl hydrate. It was good
to smell something again. He put his hands back inside his
pants.

It wasn't everyone who met John Walker and lived to tell
the tale.

He realized he had been standing still a bit too long. It
was lovely, warming his hands, but he was doing it at the
expense of his feet. In the long run, he needed the feet more.
He would have to walk out on them tomorrow morning. He
took a second step to the right, a third, then a fourth. On
the fifth, he found what he was looking for: a chair. He
wasn't sure it was wood. He thought so. It might be a metal
chair, but he thought it was wood. He dragged it five steps
back. If he faced away from the counter, he should be able
to find his oil barrel.

He had a rag to use as a wick. He could get a spark with
the plane's magneto. If the chair was wood, it would give
him something to burn. Now all he needed was fuel.

He carried the chair back to the Piper, considering. He
wasn't sure whether or not he should put his gloves back
on. He was certain they kept him no warmer than having

his hands in his pockets. Still, he couldn't very well carry the chair with his hands in his pockets. So. Now that he had something to cover his face he felt much better. More alert. Cold was only cold. It was only dangerous, not malevolent. There was nothing covert about it. Nothing evil. Just cold. And he had won the first battle.

Warming, his cheeks began to burn.

His first thought was to cut the plane open and siphon some fuel out of the tank, but he quickly thought better of it. What fuel there was would be frozen stiff by now. Sludgy, at the very least. The freezing point of decane was . . . what? $-29°C$? Something like that. He was very sure it was that cold. Of course, if this was a functioning airfield, he would try it anyway. Warm the sludge with his hands. But these planes had been here for seventy years or more. Every volatile gas would have evaporated long since in the eternal arid winter.

Besides, there was bound to be methyl hydrate. Not only had they used it as a common solvent before '04, it was also their gas line antifreeze of choice, with a freezing point below $-90°C$, if he remembered right. It was cold tonight, but it wasn't that cold. He'd been in colder weather. He had seen the wrong side of minus 50 a few times; -58 once, up in the mountains. It wasn't that cold now. That time, when you spat, you could hear it crackling in midair, freezing before it hit the ground. It wasn't that cold now. Of course he had been a lot better dressed for it then.

He was pretty sure he had glimpsed a line of plastic bottles above the counter at the back of the hangar. For a moment he wondered how he would find the right bottle, with it too dark to read. It would be disaster if he soaked his rag in soda pop or water, and then died waiting for it to ignite. A moment later he laughed out loud, shaking his head at his own foolishness. The smile jerked on the drum-tight skin of his face. He made his way back to the counter. When he found the bottles, he started squeezing. He had lost his grip strength again, so he squeezed them between his palms. The first bottle was hard. Hard. Hard. Soft. The fourth one gave between his palms. Because methyl hydrate had a freezing point of −90°C. Which was the whole point.

He stopped back at the oil barrel, warmed his hands again, and then used his screwjack to cut all the way around it, at about two hands height. The top four-fifths of the barrel boomed and crashed when he kicked it off its base. What was left would make a good dry fire pit.

He sheathed the screwjack and pulled on his gloves. Next he put the bottle of methyl hydrate in the barrel bottom and carried them both over to the Piper. He placed the barrel bottom in the shadow of the Piper's wing, where a little less snow had made it to the ground.

Then he cut the chair into shavings. Sharp as the screwjack was, it felt different cutting through metal than it did through wood. Though his hands were numb, he thought the chair was wood. The legs were too thick to be plastic. It was bound to be wood. It was surprising how much you depended on vision and texture to tell you these things. He took a chair leg and banged it against the snowy concrete floor, listening. Chonk, chonk. Definitely wood.

Making kindling required a great deal of hand-warming at the expense of his toes. His feet hurt terribly. It was also very delicate work, very still. Just at the end he started to shake. "No," he said. He stood up quickly, sheathed the screwjack, and jumped in place until he landed so badly on his numb feet that he almost fell over. After that he did deep knee bends until he was breathing hard, sucking big gulps of frigid air through his facecloth.

He suddenly thought he might be breathing through his mouth too hard. He had been a cadet with a guy who had overexerted himself in extremely cold conditions and froze a lung. You were supposed to breathe through your nose as much as possible, to give the air extra time to heat before it reached your lungs. This fellow had lived. Discharged on a medical.

Anyway, the knee bends seemed to have worked. He had stopped shaking. His body must be using a lot of calories to keep warm. Well, he would eat when he got back to the Southside. And every dish would be hot.

Normally he would have taken great care getting to the

Piper's engine, but his hands were stiffening up much faster now. He formally apologized to the plane, and then used the screwjack to hack through to the engine block as fast as he could. He cut away great swaths of metal just so he could see. It had definitely been a good idea to pick the plane in the best light. Even so, he had to find the spark plugs partly by feel. He tried to unscrew one using the palms of his gloved hands, but the work was too fine. So he warmed his hands once more in his pants. They lay between his thighs like two pieces of cold wood for a long time. Too long. The cold closed over them like hard wax as soon as he took them out and put his gloves on again. He had to force himself not to hurry.

He unscrewed the spark plug, still attached by its wire to the magneto. He brushed a clear spot on the nose of the plane and laid the plug down gently, as if his life depended on it. Which it did.

He could no longer feel his feet. In one way this was a blessing, as the pain had made it hard to concentrate. Still, it wasn't a good sign. Even if he got the fire going, it was possible he was going to lose a toe or two to frostbite.

He never had cared much for the boots on these dress uniforms. Ha ha.

It was cheering to find he still had a sense of humor. He went about his business with some energy. He piled the kindling carefully in his makeshift fire pit. All that remained was to soak the rag in methyl hydrate, that wonderfully flammable substance, wrap it around the spark plug, give a good pull on the propeller, which he could do even without much mobility in his hands, and he would have lovely, fat, hot sparks jumping into his rag, one after another.

He retrieved the plastic bottle. It still sloshed: good. He felt as if there was something else he wanted to remember. Perhaps his brain, too, was having trouble starting in the cold.

It was really too bad of Magpie to desert him.

He crouched down with the bottle between his knees. Too late to worry about snowy knees now. If he got the fire going, they would dry easily enough. If not, he would have bigger problems. He tried to twist the cap off the methyl hydrate. He had no play left in his fingers, so he had to clench the cap between his palms and twist. Nothing happened.

Patience.

Standing up, he shovelled up the Velcro tab over the screw-jack, grabbed the handle between his palms, raised it to his face, and punched the "knife" button with his front teeth. The screwjack slipped out between his stiff hands and clattered to the floor. "Shit."

Taking off his glove, he laid his right hand on the snowy floor, palm up, next to the screwjack. With his left hand he pushed the tool's hilt into his right hand, and then pulled his fingers around it. He leaned on his fist, to make it tight. Then, kneeling with the methyl hydrate bottle between his knees he cut the top off. There. Simple.

Classic cold-weather slapstick comedy. Once when he was nine he had been out working with his dad, trying to get a combine to start for over an hour in freezing weather. When they finally gave it up for lunch and came inside, he desperately needed to pee, but even in the warm house he couldn't regain enough strength in his fingers to unzip his coat in time. To his horror he had peed his pants standing in the kitchen. For once his dad had laughed instead of getting angry. Said it was his fault for keeping them outside so long, and that anyway it was a good lesson.

He put his right hand back in his pants to warm. With his left he pulled the second rag out of his pocket and prepared to soak it. His hand froze over the bottle.

Carbon tetrachloride.

That's what he had been trying to remember. He had found a lot of carbon tetrachloride out at the International Airport when he'd been scavenging there. Another excellent solvent with a freezing point at least as low as that of methyl hydrate. Smelled like it too. The difference was, carbon tetrachloride wasn't flammable. Not just something that burned badly, either. It had actually been used in fire extinguishers. If he was soaking his rag in carbon tetrachloride, he would die waiting for it to catch.

His first thought was to take the bottle and walk out to one of the blue runway lights to read the label. But he was already very tired and cold, and he had no feeling at all in his feet anymore. He was definitely going to lose a toe or two. And he had just cut the top off the bottle. He couldn't screw it back on. What were the odds he could stagger out over the icy tarmac all the way to the lights with an open bottle, read the label, and stagger back, without slipping or dropping it from his wooden hands?

(At eighteen months Lark feared nothing on earth but dogs and people singing—who knew why? She could run like a rabbit. So when Nick stood at the head of the Bridge and put her down, her fear had come like a miracle, a blessing unlooked for. Because he had known, at some terrible level, that she was too precious to him not to be taken. He had known her sacrifice would be demanded.)

Whoa. No time for that. Focus.

To soak the rag now, or carry the bottle out and read the label? There were risks either way, and one took more time. He soaked the rag, tipping the bottle over so the fluid ran onto it. Then he picked the bottle up between gloved hands and shovelled it into the fire pit. The rest could pool there, in the bottom. If it turned out to be carbon tetrachloride, he'd tear some upholstery from the Piper's seats to use as rags and go looking for another bottle.

Barehanded—it couldn't be helped—he wrapped the rag around the spark plug, leaving the dry end hanging loose so he would have some place to hold it. He pulled on his gloves, now stiff with cold and his frozen sweat. He stumbled up to the front of the plane.

(It was one thing to take your child down to the Bridge, not knowing. It was a terrible risk, but a needful one, and so few were chosen. But to know your child would be called away and still to go through with it . . . Oh, of course, he had been wrong; Lark didn't go to the North Side. But he *had known*, so he thought. And he had taken her down anyway. What sort of father did that make him? Even his own dad wouldn't have done that. His father knocked him around on occasion, true—but he would beat the living shit out of any other man who laid a hand on his boy, no doubt.)

Focus. Focus.

It certainly was very cold.

Nick reached up high, hooked his numb hands on the propeller, and pulled down hard. The rag burst into flames.

He carried the burning rag over to his fire pit and dropped it in. The remaining methyl hydrate—or ethanol, it could even be ethanol, he thought—blazed up immediately.

It was frightening how long it took the larger pieces of the chair to catch. If he had gotten too rushed, if he had failed to take the time to cut kindling in various thicknesses, he might have had a brisk ethanol fire for thirty seconds, followed by a cold and lingering death. Now that the fire was going, he could admit that he was in a very bad way. He was probably in some stage of frostbite in a lot of places, especially his fingers and toes. The way his thoughts were beginning to wander, he might well be in the early stages of hypothermia as well.

The fire was a feast. Not only in its warmth, though of course that was the most important thing. But to see! To have light enough to actually read the words ''Methyl Hydrate'' on the twisting plastic bottle as its label bubbled and blackened. Death is cold, Nick thought, and the cold is still. To see the red fire bend and flicker, to hear it hiss and pop; to feel the shadows jumping at the edge of vision was to feel life rejoicing in that terrible, cold, lifeless place.

He swore then that he would follow Raining back to the coast. It was too cold here. She was·right, it was too damn cold on the prairies. They went whole years without snow at her house, she said. Heaven.

She had told him stories about that house, and Wire had too: the hidden home, now near, now far, a lost and secret place in the tangled Forest's heart. It came to Nick then, alone in the terrible cold and hunched before his little fire, that Raining was like her house, forever hidden; and it would always be like this. Even if they were to get together again, even if he won his way back across the Bridge and became Lark's daddy and Raining finally admitted that he

loved her and he always would, there would never come a
time when he could hold her hand and know that they were
together and it was forever. For all the long years of their
lives there would be days, many of them, when she left him
for the secret places of her heart, sad or angry or hopeless
or alone, and he would not be able to find her. In the end
the truest part of her life would be lived in a place he could
not reach, lost beneath her tangled branches. Alone in her
empty house.

Well.

First things first. He still had to get back to the Southside.
But he would leave that until the morning. Nick's explosives
instructor in the Sappers always used to say, "The proximity
of death always adds great singleness of purpose." Certainly
all the time Nick had been working to build his fire he had
given barely a thought to the ghosts and revenants supposed
to haunt the North Side. Nor could he find it in himself to
worry about them now. Instead he hunched by his little fire,
swearing softly as the blood inched back into his hands. By
firelight they looked waxy white, very bad. Still, a little
movement came back, and after a great deal of awkward
struggling he was able to pull off his boots and socks. He
put them on the ground and rested his bare heels on top,
presenting his nerveless feet to the warm fire with a sigh of
pleasure.

A shelf of snow slid off the Piper's tilted wing and into
his fire, dousing it utterly.

The darkness was absolute. His eyes had adjusted to the
sweet red and yellow firelight. It would take a minute or
two for them to make do with starshine again.

The heat. The heat coming up from the fire had worked
its way into the snow on the Piper's wing. He should have
thought of that. He should have thought to clear the snow
off the wing.

He scrabbled in the fire pit, grabbing sticks out of the
snow. He found two bigger pieces still embering. The
smaller ones had been doused, but these two still showed
orange lines. He blew on the orange parts, first one stick,
then the other, like a child licking two ice cream cones.

After the first ember died, he concentrated entirely on the second. There was a fissured orange coal, perhaps half as long as his thumb. It was a fiery orange when he blew on it, with wire-thin seams of hotter yellow. When he stopped breathing on it, the seams dulled immediately, and the rest of the coal turned blood red, with black spider-leg cracks.

The smell of burned flesh came to him, and he realized he must have grabbed some blackened sticks that were still very hot. It was impossible to tell how bad the burns on his hands might be.

He had nothing to make a fire out of now. That was the crux of the problem. However long he kept this coal alive, the rest of his kindling was buried in snow. It might be useless already. The first thing he needed to do was to dig it out and shake all the snow off and hope there were still some dry parts left. Or he could find another chair.

He was shaking very hard.

The seats in the plane would be made of fire retardant foam. He just remembered that.

He was certainly in very bad trouble now.

He would have to go back to the counter. With luck, he could do it in one trip. Get another bottle of methyl hydrate and find either a chair or some more rags or something. The fire pit was fine, he could just empty it out and use it again. He would have to make sure he got all the snow out. And he would have to brush off the wing.

He had never had the shakes quite so badly. He'd run a fever over 40°C once when he was eleven, and then he'd had the shakes pretty badly, but he thought this was worse.

The stick fell from his hand. It was very hard to hold, between the shaking and the lack of feeling in his hands, and he had dropped it. Not that it mattered, really: the thing to do now was to get the methyl hydrate. He wished he wasn't shaking so much, though.

Where was Magpie?

It occurred to him that he could remember taking off his boots and socks, but he couldn't remember putting them on again. He was probably crouching in the snow in his bare feet.

He would pretty much have to lose some toes now. Still, he didn't have to paint with them. Men could walk on crutches. All he had to do was get back to the counter. One quick trip to get another bottle of methyl hydrate and he would be set. He stood up to get the methyl hydrate. It was very difficult, because his balance was thrown off by not being able to feel his feet, and because he was shaking so much. Still, he was standing now. The rest would be easier.

Gravely, carefully, with great patience, he reached into the cockpit of the Piper and took out the bundle of cloth John Walker had entrusted to him. That was an honor, wasn't it? How many men had met John Walker and lived to tell the tale? Let alone been given something to keep for him.

He spread the coat out on the floor beside the fire pit, then sat down slowly, careful not to lose his balance. He didn't want to hit his head on the wing and have the snow slide down on him. He could see again, a little. The coat was a strange, shiny black. Bright black, if there was such a thing. He sat cross-legged. The shiny black material slid and whispered under his cold skin.

The boots he set next to the waistcoat, for when his feet were warmer.

Because really, thinking it over, he'd had more than enough time to make it back to the helicopter. But he hadn't tried. Instead he had turned to them and said, "Go!" It was a very curious thing.

He had stopped shaking, which was a great relief, and he thought he might be feeling a little warmer.

CHAPTER 11

Far away, across the mountains in Chinatown, it was loud in the night. Above the hissing rain, women shouted news from balcony to balcony, cymbals clashed to ward off spirits, hens squawked and cats quarrelled and men yelled. From time to time rifle shots popped and cracked from behind the barricades the men of the Hong Hsing Athletic Club had put up on every street that faced Downtown. The rain had begun again. Thin and relentless the raindrops came, making cherry blossoms bob and shake. Puddles spread and joined, stretching across streets empty of all save soldiers. The Southsider barracks, now mostly black, still smoked and steamed.

Water Spider strode down the tiled halls of Government House giving orders to the two aides who trotted after him. "One rifle at every barricade. If you can't find rifles, use bows. If you can't find bows, make slingshots. Under no circumstances should we engage in direct combat unless the barbarians come over the barricades. We can't afford any casualties now while our own people are still waking up. I need every soldier alert and uninjured."

He turned to the second aide. "Have any barbarians made it past the barricades?"

"Twice, Excellency. Two large monsters sprang over the Keefer Street barrier and ran through the streets until scared off by firecrackers. A stronger attack came down Carrall

Street. Hong Wu believes they had a railgun scavenged from one of the Southsider perimeter pickets. They cut through the barricade and the five men defending it in seconds. We had just placed a rifleman in an apartment overhead, according to your earlier instructions. He shot the monster with the railgun. The other monsters broke then, with two retreating, and three charging the rifleman. Reinforcements found him dead, along with two monsters. There was no sign of the third monster. We must assume it is still within our boundaries.''

''And the barricade?''

''A team is rebuilding it as we speak. Hong Wu took the liberty of assigning three rifles to this point until the barrier has been rebuilt.''

''Good man.''

Water Spider had made it back to Government House at 11:35 Friday night. In the two hours since then, runners had been coming and going in a steady stream, each bowing quickly and then pouring out his burden of information, until Water Spider felt like a water wheel, ceaselessly turning, scooping up casualty reports, readiness assessments, and countless enemy sightings. All inaccurate, no doubt.

At least he didn't have to worry about troop placements. He had so few soldiers, assigning them was easy.

Water Spider stopped before the great black doors of the conference chamber. ''Send Hong Wu my commendations. In the East Wing you will find the Ministry for Wellness charm-makers hard at work. Take the amulets they give you and deliver them. Some will need to be posted on roadways and over doors. Government House has already been protected. Others will be for personal use by the Hong Hsing Athletic Club. Still others are to be swallowed by the sick, the possessed, or the very unlucky. Use them with discretion. Make sure to take one each yourselves: you are my eyes and ears.''

''Yes, Your Ex—''

''Go!'' he said, brushing off their bows. ''Run! There will be time for courtesy later.'' Their footsteps raced away as he turned and swept through the conference chamber doors.

Heads snapped up around the table. "What's going on?" Huang Ti complained. The puffy-eyed Honorable Minister for Interior Affairs sat blinking in a gold robe belted hastily over silk pajamas.

"Water Spider! So glad you could come," said Johnny Ma. The Honorable Minister for the South took a joint from between his lips and grinned. "It wouldn't be the same war without you." Unlike Huang Ti, Johnny was fully dressed and wide awake. He looked as if he had just strolled out of a casino, which he probably had. "You do love a good crisis, don't you? It puts such a lordly purpose in your stride."

There were eight chairs around the conference table, one for each minister in the Government. Each was made of intricately carved blackwood, leopard-footed, with low arms and high backs, edged with beasts and birds and flowers, and gleaming darkly with sable coats of lacquer. Inlaid in the back of each chair was a different mother-of-pearl totem: a lizard, a monkey, a chrysanthemum, a wall, a purse, a ship, a pair of scales, and a lidded eye; but the Emperor's great red dragon chair at the head of the table was empty.

Water Spider, the Honorable Minister for Borders, dropped into the seat with the stylized wall. He looked at Johnny Ma. "I could use a smoke, if you have one to spare."

Johnny grinned and took out a gold-plated cigarette case. His portfolio as Minister for the South was to monitor the doings of the Double Monkey, the merchants' patron of the south side of Chinatown, a Power incarnating equal parts wealth and duplicity. Johnny shook out a joint and held it to a mother-of-pearl lighter. "Have you not told me many times that these are but the affectations of a foppish youth?"

Water Spider took the joint from him. "That was then. Now they are a vice of middle age."

On Water Spider's right, Grace Shih, the Honorable Minister for Wellness, chuckled. Her tiny hunched back was too short to obscure the pair of scales inlaid on her chair. Her old fingers rested briefly on his wrist, dry and light as twists of grass. "It is the great wisdom of age to know what you want, is it not?"

A cup of tea.

No time for that, Water Spider told himself. No time for mysteries. He took a drag on the joint. It was vile.

The Lidded Eye, also known as the Honorable Minister in Charge of Ministers, coughed meaningfully and began to call the roll. Present were Water Spider, the Minister for Borders; Johnny Ma, Minister for the South; Grace Shih, Minister for Wellness; Huang Ti, the Purse, or Minister for the Interior, and of course the Lidded Eye herself, the Honorable Minister in Charge of Ministers.

Absent were the Minister for Foreign Affairs, the Minister for the East, whose job was to monitor the doings of the Dragon, and the Minister for the West, who studied the Lady in the Garden. Water Spider thought it a bad omen that the ministers responsible for watching two of Chinatown's three Powers were missing.

The Lidded Eye rolled up her scroll and looked down the table to where Water Spider sat. "Begin."

Water Spider rose, bowing first to the empty chair and then to his colleagues. "The barbarians have destroyed the mercenary garrison at B.C. Place Stadium." Swiftly he outlined the tactical situation for his fellow ministers. Like Chinatown, Vancouver's downtown office district was one area that had not been overrun by the Forest in 2004. A Power of glass and steel had taken the people trapped there, twisting their bodies and minds. But now that Power had faded, or so said Chinatown's diviners. Leaderless, these altered men had begun to spill out from Downtown. Water Spider detailed what was known about the destruction of the Southsider barracks and what steps he had taken to defend Chinatown since. As he came to the end of his report, a heavy silence fell.

"But the monsters have not invaded our territory?" Huang Ti said.

"Not yet. Not in force. At last report, the barricades were still holding."

"But how did the Snows come to be defeated?" Huang

Ti pressed. "You told us we were paying for the best troops on the continent."

"I must accept some responsibility for this defeat," Water Spider said slowly. "Because the monsters from Downtown had attacked in so graceless a fashion, using homemade clubs and other crude weapons, the Southside commander and I foolishly assumed they had no truly superior technology. Now I must believe that we were wrong. They found a way to deliver incendiaries into the Southsiders' fortified barracks. Perhaps a rocket was used, or some device with a remote control."

Huang Ti glanced furtively at the glass-paned doors that divided the conference chamber from the Scholars Garden outside. "Could they do the same here?"

"We have placed many sentries around Government House, and very powerful charms—but yes, it is possible. But why haven't they used such devices before? I must still believe, looking at their troops, that their technological resources are limited. It is possible that they have more explosives, and that we are under surveillance. If so, the five of us currently gathered in this room would make a very appealing target."

"Perhaps in the future we should flock less thickly together," Johnny Ma suggested.

Water Spider nodded. "It would probably be wise to use runners to communicate, at least until we can get reinforcements from the Southside. And this time, may I suggest we pay for the Southsiders to attack barbarians in force. 'Crude yet quick strategies have been known/ But skill has yet to be observed in long operations.' "

"More Southsiders!" the Purse protested. "We have already paid dearly for the pleasure of cremating their first cohort."

"We have gone over this before," Water Spider said sharply. It was Huang Ti who had pushed to have the Southsiders come in the first place. He appreciated their usefulness for defending against the barbarians, but more particularly he had liked the idea of the Mandarinate having some muscle of its own for once. When the Southsiders arrived, he

had been quick to strike a deal with them to accompany his
men on inspections and tax collection rounds. The merchants hated paying any taxes, and bribed Johnny Ma scan-
dalously to look the other way. He claimed he passed all
the money he received to Huang Ti's treasuries . . . but there
were other kinds of bribes, and Water Spider was pretty sure
Johnny had accepted them all.

He still liked him better than pompous, greedy Huang Ti,
though.

"What of the dead Snows?" Grace Shih asked. "The
Southsiders will want to know about their sons and daugh-
ters."

"We do not believe there will be any survivors among
the troops who were in their barracks when the attack com-
menced," Water Spider said. "At least one guard on perimeter duty escaped and fell back to the barricades. Another
accompanied me from the scene. There may be three or four
more survivors, but I doubt any more than that. The monsters were extremely efficient."

"The white woman who came back with you," Grace
Shih said quietly. "Where is she now?"

"I have asked her to wait in my offices. I will want to
question her further."

"She must be in very great distress. Did you leave anyone
to attend upon her?"

Water Spider looked out the glass-paned doors, into the
darkness and the streaming rain. "But of course."

"You!" Claire growled. Water Spider had put her in the
care of the thuggy little streetfighter who had spat in her
face. Charming.

Jen shrugged. "Hey, fuck you. First my charm is broken,
now I get stuck with your cold luck. Brr. Look what happened to the rest of your friends."

Claire went still. "What a lovely thing to say."

"You broke my luck."

"You spat in my face!"

"I've wiped my nose on my sleeve too, and once I picked
up my hand before all cards were dealt!" Jen said hotly.

"You don't break a man's luck for such a small-small thing! A finger perhaps. Even an arm, if your pride demanded it. This I can understand. But to break my luck!"

"But—!" Claire collected herself. "You're right. I should have broken your arm."

Jen nodded stiffly. "I accept your apology." He studied her. "You could use some hot wine."

"No thank you."

"The Minister told me to see to your needs. Would you like your wine plain or spiced?"

"No thank you."

Jen threw up his hands. "Fine with me."

"Fine."

"Good."

Claire looked at the floor. "Spiced, please."

Jen nodded. "Wait here." He ducked around a folding wall and pattered off.

While Jen was gone Claire examined Water Spider's office. The furnishings were elegant but austere: a single low table, its top faced with black marble, rested in the center of the red tiled floor. A great blackwood desk dominated the western wall, its vast area divided into hundreds of drawers, cubbies, trays and cabinets, a honeycomb of tiny doors and slats, minutely carved and ornamented. Like the Mandarinate itself, Claire thought.

She tried not to think of the burning barracks, the screaming men inside.

Looking through the north-facing window, Claire could see the rooftops of the Lady's Garden across the street. Lady in the Garden, the Dragon, and . . . oh, the trickster god. Double Monkey, that was it. Yuck. Much nicer to live as they did back home, with all their gods and spirits locked away on the North Side, instead of having them everywhere underfoot as they were here. Claire looked at the Garden and shivered. She had heard that the seasons ran differently there, and now she could see it was true. Although in the world's time it was the middle of a damp spring night, summer sunshine shone through the Garden's piecework windows, and glowed above its red-tiled roofs. Unnerving, that.

It was Jackson who had told her the rumor about the Garden. He was dead now. They were all dead now, pretty much. Everyone but her. "Why couldn't you save the rest of them?" she whispered. But if The Harrier heard her somehow, she made no answer. She had saved her daughter's life and then disappeared, leaving the rest of them to die.

How many times had Claire tried to tell Emily this: the gods are cruel, and do not care as we care.

No sign of heating vents or air conditioning in Water Spider's room. Claire remembered Emily telling her that it was a point of honor among the Mandarinate's scholar officials not to seem soft. Their life was to be given in service to the Emperor, not to their own creature comforts. Sounded like a good deal for the Emperor. For that matter, Winter and Emily themselves were very good at substituting status for cash when it came to paying their prized retainers. A nifty sleight of hand. Hell, it had worked on her.

No, that wasn't fair. Emily hadn't swindled Claire's duty out of her. She had paid for it as her grandfather had taught her to, with the coin of her own fierce loyalty. There could be no truer currency.

Emily must have heard about the explosion. No doubt the girl would be praying for her. A rush of gratitude surprised Claire.

The only homely detail in Water Spider's room was the sideboard that stood against the southern wall. Here was a kettle and a tiny kerosene burner, a ceramic teapot no bigger than a man's fist, a set of terra-cotta cups and saucers, and a row of canisters filled with teas, their names written in Chinese characters, and below in English in a fine copperplate hand—oolong in two varieties, pearl tea, ginseng tea, lichee fruit tea, blackberry and raspberry teas, First and Third Quality jasmine tea, and three First Quality teas in special brass canisters: Emperor Tea, Dragon's Well Tea, and Ti Kuan Yi, under which was written *Iron Goddess of Mercy*.

There was no reason she should feel guilty for wanting

to take a closer look at the tea. Claire glanced around. No sign of Jen yet.

The brass lid of the third canister was cool to her touch as she lifted it off. The tea inside was a mottled green-black; whole leaves, not flaky or powdery as she had expected, but tightly withered, like the mummified hulls and wings of some insect. The hilt of a steel scoop showed through, and she caught the faint dry subtle scent of the Ti Kuan Yi, its breath of burning autumn leaves. Of sorrow accepted.

A runner bowed in the doorway of the conference chamber. "Radio message from the Southside, Your Excellencies."

"Li Bing at last," the Lidded Eye said. "Water Spider, would you act in place of the Honorable Minister for Foreign Affairs?"

The runner wheeled an enormous blackwood cabinet into the conference chamber and opened its ornately carved doors to reveal the radio within. He adjusted the controls, and then surrendered them to the Honorable Minister for Borders. "Li Bing!" Water Spider said, in the old Cantonese.

"I'm sorry," a pleasant voice answered in English. "This is Major David Oliver speaking."

"May I speak to Li Bing?"

"I'm afraid she is not available at this time."

"Not available!" Water Spider dragged on the vile marijuana cigarette. "Then may I ask you when your reinforcements will arrive?"

"I am afraid there is a small problem we must discuss first."

"What?" A dull premonition of disaster began to settle in the pit of Water Spider's stomach.

"The airplane which originally carried your delegation is on its way back to you. It may well be nearing your local airspace as we speak. Your Li Mei is on this airplane. So is Emily Thompson."

Water Spider's eyes narrowed. "We are honored that Southside's heir wishes to survey the situation in person."

"Winter requests that you send this flight back to us as

soon as possible. Once Miss Thompson returns we will be more than happy to send your reinforcements.''

Water Spider rolled his eyes but kept his voice polite. ''How do you suggest we accomplish this?''

''What?'' Puzzled. ''Order the airplane to turn around.''

''Ah. I am afraid this is not possible. Your military aircraft, I now recall, are all set to respond to a central authority. Ours, however, owe their allegiances directly and only to their owners.''

There was a pause. ''You are joking.''

''Not at all.''

''You sent a diplomatic delegation in an aircraft you could not control from the ground?''

''We have no other kind.''

Another pause. ''To whom does this particular airplane belong?''

''One of the leading citizens of Richmond, a sister community of ours. He lent its use to Li Bing. Unfortunately, this gentleman is presently beyond my ability to contact. You may recall there is an invasion in our streets. If you must persuade the *Phoenix* to return, your best strategy would be to ask Li Bing to speak to it, as its owner has temporarily transferred its allegiance to her.''

''I am sorry, but I do have to ask again—are you joking?''

''Major Oliver, I am in no mood for levity.''

''The airplane owes a personal allegiance to a friend of Li Bing's.''

''Correct. The machine has been in the family for years. I believe its personality was originally that of a much-loved summer cottage. When flooding made the cottage area undesirable, they had the program retrained and fitted into the aircraft.''

There was a long pause.

At length the Snow began again, more slowly. ''The situation is rather delicate. While we are not suggesting that Li Bing's daughter actually abducted Ms. Thompson, I am afraid that is the way some people will take Emily's absence. As I am sure you are aware, Ms. Thompson is a woman with considerable responsibilities on the Southside. Her disappearance cannot be disguised or overlooked.''

"I appreciate the delicacy of your—of our situation," Water Spider said. In fact he appreciated mostly that this idiocy was costing precious minutes without reinforcements.

"There is also the possibility that Ms. Thompson was a willing party to this escapade," the Southsider continued. "She may invent stories about her life at home, or plead for sanctuary by trading on your feelings. I want to emphasize that this cannot be allowed."

Water Spider coughed out a cloud of acrid smoke. "May I remind you that you have, in essence, made the safety of Chinatown contingent on her return? How well Miss Thompson attends to her responsibilities you know better than I. But as Li Mei's superior, let me assure you that no circumstance exists in which she would put Miss Thompson ahead of the welfare of her people."

"Perhaps then you could contact her on board the aircraft and convince her to return to the Southside immediately. We would be far more comfortable if they did not land at your end. Once on the ground, it becomes so much easier for something unexpected to go wrong."

"What do you expect us to do?" Water Spider said, exasperated. "Shoot the plane down?"

There was another long pause. "That would seem unwarranted to you."

Oh. "Yes, it would." What under heaven could Emily Thompson be doing that would make her grandfather willing to shoot down the plane she was on? Water Spider took another drag on his cigarette. "Please. Accept my word on this. As soon as I can reach Li Mei, I will explain the situation. You will have Miss Thompson back as quickly as humanly possible. Your reasons for wanting her back, whatever they are, can hardly be as pressing as my reasons for wanting your soldiers."

"Excellent," the Snow said. "We have already dispatched two aircraft in pursuit. They will be arriving there shortly, in case it seems more appropriate for Ms. Thompson to return in one of our planes. Let me assure you, we have three squadrons of heavily armed troops standing ready to be delivered to your doorstep in thirty minutes."

Water Spider hung up. "How reassuring."

Johnny Ma grinned. "Have you ever heard a promise that was at the same time so neatly a threat?"

"Two planes are on the way. It is perhaps eight hundred kilometers from Southside to here, over the mountains," Water Spider said, calculating. "An hour and a half if their planes have pontoons and they can land on English Bay. Longer if they have to land at the old Richmond airport. I am fairly sure they have pontoons, though. In which case, we can have another regiment of Snows to help us within two hours, as long as we can give them Emily Thompson when they arrive."

"What will we do?" Huang Ti said, wrapping his robe more tightly around his waist and glancing anxiously at the windows as if a barbarian incendiary bomb might come hurtling through them at any instant.

"What can we do? For the next two hours we wait. We try to hail Li Mei. We defend the barri—" The barricades. A sudden map of Chinatown jumped into Water Spider's mind. "Pearl," he whispered. His prostitute's little apartment was two blocks beyond the barricades. Two blocks west, toward Downtown. It was a Sunken District, home only to whores and beggars and other misfits, and he—the colossal complacency of it! The thoughtless arrogance!—he had never thought to extend his defenses out that far.

And Pearl, his Pearl, Jen's mother, was out there tonight, alone as he had left her—or perhaps with some unlucky other man—while monsters prowled through the streets and gunfire echoed all around. There would be no marksman to stop the barbarians from swarming into her apartment, if they chose.

The other Ministers were staring at him.

He found he was standing. "My apologies. I must go."

"Minister!" said the Lidded Eye. "While this crisis continues, your duty is at your post!"

"Not so long as that chair is empty!" Water Spider shouted, pointing to the red throne at the head of the table.

He found he was furious and he did not know why, which frightened and angered him more. "People, not positions, must hold our deepest loyalty. As long as the throne sits empty, I will not betray people for empty air."

He strode from the chamber, and slammed the door behind him.

"Well, well," Johnny Ma said thoughtfully. "Must remember not to give him any more dope."

The Minister in Charge of Ministers made a long notation on her scroll.

"There is a touch of heaven on him," Grace Shih, the Minister for Wellness, said. "I smelled it when he entered the room. A ghost, a god, a demon perhaps, has been with him." Johnny Ma looked sharply at her. Her old black eyes were thoughtful.

Huang Ti grunted. "Blood will tell," he said. "I knew there had to be a taint of the father in the son. Blood will tell."

Water Spider was sitting at his desk some minutes later when Johnny Ma found him. "You don't have to pretend you were working," Johnny said.

Water Spider smiled faintly. "How did you know?"

"Hard to write with no ink on your brush."

Water Spider put the dry brush down. "True. So, how did you get stuck with the task of bearding me in my den? Lose a cast of dice?"

"I never lose at dice," Johnny said. "It's part of the portfolio."

"Ah. True."

Water Spider waited politely for Johnny to speak. He had no intention of admitting that he had rushed back to his offices so he could send Jen to rescue his prostitute. Jen and the Snow too, Heavens forgive him. At the time it had seemed like mercy, to give her something to do other than sit and brood over her slaughtered comrades.

What had come over him?

It wasn't that the decision to rescue Pearl was so right or so wrong, but that he had lost all ability to tell which. He had never been one to crack under pressure, but now his judgment eluded him. It was all Water Spider could do to sit still and try not to show how badly he was adrift.

Johnny wandered to the sword shrine under the north-facing window and admired Water Spider's ancient blade. "Actually, no one sent me. I came on my own." His hand hovered over the hilt of the sword. "May I?"

"No."

Johnny smiled and lifted his hands. "Not promiscuous, is she?"

"He. And, no."

"Let me suggest that you keep the Old Man close." Johnny dropped into an exquisite cherrywood chair. "You do realize you're being worked, don't you?"

"What do you mean?"

"Huang Ti is in the service of the Dragon."

Water Spider drew in a long breath. "You know this?"

Johnny shrugged. "It is my instinct. And it was Chou Shou's as well."

"Ah." It was the responsibility of Chou Shou, Minister for the East, to watch the Dragon, and deal with those humans who owed him their allegiance, or fell under his influence.

"And here we are, in a time of crisis that could have been avoided if Huang Ti had been willing to pay for destroying the barbarians entirely and razing Downtown. Instead, Huang Ti used the Snows to harry the Double Monkey's people, my merchant friends. Let me tell you, they have not been at all pleased to have this plague of big, white, incorruptible tax-collectors visited upon them." Johnny held Water Spider's eye. "I can think of many traders, who deal in many strange devices, who will not be sorry to hear that the Southsiders have, ah, gone away."

"Are you saying the Snows were betrayed by someone within Chinatown?"

"Somehow Chou Shou, that most reliable of men, is nowhere to be found," Johnny Ma went on. "And our respected strategist, Water Spider, has misplaced his strategy, and the Lidded Eye is making ominous markings about him in her scrolls. Who then is great among the Ministers? No one ever trusts any Minister for the South—with good reason!'' Johnny added, laughing. ''Grace is very old. But Huang Ti: he is in his prime. He is not tainted by any of the Compass portfolios.''

Water Spider frowned. ''But what could the Dragon gain from such chaos? Or Huang Ti, either?''

''There is that empty throne,'' Johnny said.

''You can't believe Huang Ti imagines he could be Emperor. Even his arrogance would not support such a dream,'' Water Spider said flatly.

Johnny Ma shrugged. ''Perhaps you are right. But I would look to your back these next few days, Excellency. As for myself,'' he added reflectively, ''when all this settles down, I believe I shall ruin the smug prick.''

''Pray, not on my account,'' Water Spider said, smiling.

''Not at all, not at all. I shall do it for myself. Not even for the sport of the thing, you understand, but because it is Right.''

''It has been observed,'' Water Spider said drily, ''that to fitly serve the State is the only true joy.''

Johnny Ma nodded, eyes narrowed to slits amid a haze of sweet smoke. ''The ancient precepts must be heeded. And if I am a rogue sometimes—and I admit I am—I endeavor always to be a pious one.''

Water Spider smiled, but his mind was back on the disturbing conversation with the Snows. ''Johnny?''

''Yes?''

''I begin to think there could be a war waiting at the end of this. A real war, with a real enemy.''

''The Snows, you mean?''

''If someone did betray them, that person is a fool. You have not seen them fight as I have. You have not seen the reports from their other wars. This is an enemy we dare not make, a war we could not win.'' Water Spider looked at Johnny Ma, face drawn. ''I think we need to find Emily Thompson. I think we need to do it very soon.''

CHAPTER 12

Jen was trapped in his mother's apartment building. He had
come with Claire, the white bitch who broke his luck, to
rescue his ma, who was also Water Spider's woman. The
stupid pompous prick had finally learned, a little late in the
fucking day, that loyalty is owed blood to blood.

Claire and Ma had gotten away. Jen hadn't.

Well, he'd been meaning to come visit, hadn't he? Ha ha.
Only now gargoyles squatted on every gable, and he was
trapped in a dingy flat across the hallway from his childhood.

He rehearsed his Long Fist form. He crouched in the cat
stance, front toe touching the hardwood floor, just touching:
no weight on it, not so much as a feather. He had been doing
forms for a long time now. His hams were shaking with
exhaustion and the sweat ran in streams down his face.

*By Buddha's black balls, I don't want to die here. Please
don't let me die like this.*

Don't think. Don't think. "It is your own fear that draws
the demons to you," Water Spider had told him once. "It
is your own hate that gives them life." Trapped in a haunted
apartment building like this, demons crawling everywhere,
if he wasn't careful, if he let himself think, if he let himself
despair, it would come back to him, oh yes. Like a pearl
growing around a grain of sand his demons would grow
flesh and hunt him down. That's what minotaurs were, Wa-

ter Spider said. Fear made flesh. Nightmares in the waking
world.

Quick block left arm/ step front, punch right/ punch left/
recoil.

Snap back, humming. Body like a spring, like a wire.

The thing about practicing is that you have to do it con-
sciously. It isn't enough to go through the motions. You
have to think deeply into every move, you have to imagine
your enemy at your fingertips, you have to feel the flex of
his limbs, drawing away from you. When you block, you
have to feel the wind of his fist across your face.

Sweat. Sweat everything out. Sweat fear, sweat rage,
sweat like cool rain, drumming down, drumming down.

Sad thin little rains. Creaking on the window like a bed
creaking in the next room.

Hands and arms a cage, left toe touching—just touching—
next to right foot, *explode*: left back knuckle/ recoil/ right
punch!

So Jen had stayed behind to buy time for Claire to get his
ma out of the building. Stayed behind with his sword raised
against the demon. Showed no fear. Only the joke was on
him, the demon had no face, couldn't see how brave he was.
Ha ha. And his lovely sword, his lovely north wind sword,
his kick-ass, split-balls, high-tech, lowlife piece of *shit*—

Well, it was gone now.

And the sound of the rain had come drumming down, not
loud but everywhere, creeping over him like sad clouds.

But he did the brave thing. He didn't run back the way
his ma had gone. He ran for the stairs instead. Pounded up
the threadbare red carpet, bits of wood showing through
just as he remembered it, raced the length of the building
on the second floor. By now they were sure to be out, he
didn't even look behind him, just heard the rain falling sad
in his head and yelled to shut it out, down the back stairs
four at a time, huge flying leaps with his life in his throat,
stairs-landing-turn, stairs-landing-turn, stairs-landing-turn,
stairs. . . .

Stopped on a landing, chest heaving. He should have been

out by now. Should have made it to the ground floor. In fact, counting landings, he should be on floor -3, pretty funny except there wasn't any basement in the New Moon Manor.

It was very quiet.

He looked down over the banister. The stairs went twisting down forever; he couldn't even see the bottom. "Wonder who has to clean the carpets," he said. He used to once, for pocket money.

From Uncle Lui he had learned to joke at the worst things.

When he spat down the stairwell, he couldn't hear it hit.

Here's a memory for you: lying face down on that worn carpet, three guys beating the shit out of him which happened a lot when he was oh eleven or twelve, and he never fought back, didn't believe in fighting, he was a pacifist, very noble, and knew in his heart how much braver he was because of it. They beat the shit out of him pretty good pretty regularly and looking down through puffy eyes where his split lip was drooling blood on the carpet and thinking: shit the stain, never clean that one oh well maybe it won't show, red on red anyhow.

Story of his life, hey? Red on red.

Half horse stance, forward posture. Left back knuckle/ recoil/ right punch.

Hammer fist, dropping to crouched-toe stance.

Wait.

Still as dew trembling on the edge of a leaf.

At least he was smart enough not to go to his mother's apartment. Didn't know much about demons, but knew that much. Felt his childhood stalking him like a shadow. Didn't matter how many stairs he went up or down, he always came out on his mother's floor, see. But he was too smart to go into her apartment. Too much past there, no shit.

Fucking Snow broke his luck, would you believe it?

Listened at the doors. No one home in Number 32 so he went in there. It was next to Ma's, but at least he wasn't back home, not all the way. Some sounds from her apart-

ment, though, sometimes. Didn't like that much. A few
sounds. Creaking floorboards maybe. Creaking bed. Like
that.

Don't listen don't listen don't listen don't listen.

Don't think don't think don't think don't think.

Creak, creak. Creak, creak.

There was a baby crying in the next apartment. It cried a
lot, even for a baby. Long, whimpering cries. Not loud but
steady like the rain. Sometimes someone shouted, across the
way, or there was a thud, or a crash like pans smacking
together, and the baby would stop for a long moment and
then start in again, louder. Jen figured it must have been
about the saddest baby in the world.

Shouter and Shrieker lived next to the baby. Fought like
bad-tempered parrots. They might have moved in before Jen
left home, he wasn't sure. There was always a couple like
them, though, in all the New Moon Manors he and Ma had
lived in over the years. Most times they went quiet when he
passed their door. Except for once, when he thought he
heard her crying, very softly. He almost knocked that time.

Maybe Shouter knocked her around, maybe he didn't.
Maybe she deserved it if he did; if Jen had learned one thing
from Water Spider, it was that there were two sides to a
story, plus a top and bottom and a few other angles. Hell,
he'd done things that—that would have been hard to explain.

But still he thought maybe he ought to knock. Do the
right thing. Like staying behind while Claire and his mother
got away. That had been the right thing to do. That helped.
There weren't so many times in your life you could be sure
you were doing the right thing. There were a lot of people
you wanted to beat the shit out of, but you could almost
never be absolutely sure it was OK.

That was the best thing about working for Water Spider.
The Honorable Minister for Borders did not have these
doubts. He was very certain he knew which things were
right.

Oh, the lovely freedom from doubt. Jen could hold back

his fist in certainty; and let it fall, likewise. Not that Water Spider was always right. The pompous hand-jobber. Only a fool, blind with his own rank and smarts and obvious personal worth, could be so sure of himself. So smug. But that wasn't Jen's problem. He had dished off those particular responsibilities. He had gone to some trouble to get right and wrong defined as narrowly as possible.

Not because he was stupid. Because he was smart.

So here he was trapped by a demon in New Moon Manor, practicing forms until his muscles burned and the sweat soaked his shirt because the moment he let himself think, maybe a minotaur would form around his fear, his ugly thoughts. Maybe a demon would come and he would be dogmeat.

Must be a fucking genius, hey?

And up, Drawing the Bow, left toe out, and: *coil down*!/ back knuckle/ left hand block, next to shoulder: grip: pitchfork to forward stance.

Step into Number 8 Long Fist. Then up to reverse punch in low horse forward stance. Crescent kick/back kick.

Grab/ head butt/ *throw*!

And stop, terrified, at the sound of something hitting the floor. A quiet thump, like a cat jumping to the ground. The memory of weight spinning over his hip. Cool fingers wrapped for an instant around his wrist, opening when she hit the floor.

There had been a ghost in his arms. Something taking flesh from the thick enchanted air around him.

Don't think don't think don't think don't think.

She?

Here's a memory for you: thirteen years old and he finally fought back, swung like a maniac no fucking science at all broke three knuckles and *crushed* the fucker. That's when he found he had no fear left. No fear left—fucking amazing, hey? No courage in him exactly, just so much anger, so much rage there wasn't room for anything else. He held the fucker up so the fight wouldn't be over, kept him from folding with horrible stomach shots Pow Pow Pow and then Boom across the side of the head again and drove him into the concrete piling of the underground parking lot. Boom. Pow Pow Pow and again. Boom Boom Boom Boom.

Buddha's balls, broke three knuckles. No science at all.

Pretty clear pretty soon the guy wasn't going to be okay. Shouldn't have kicked him in the head. Should not have done that. Classic early mistake. No reason. Fight over, point made. But so much anger. Managed to stop himself after a couple of kicks but even then he stood over the other boy with blood running down his hands and screamed at the unconscious body. Screamed and screamed. The sound huge in the parking lot, like metal tearing.

In a way it worked out for the best. The kid didn't die, quite. But every time he went by, it sort of told everyone else not to fuck with Jen, hey: this sorry flat-faced fucker smiling or drooling or whatever, his eyes like shop windows after closing time. Good advertising. Discouraged anyone else from taking a run at Jen, which was lucky because there was absolutely no fucking science to him back then.

But oh, it had been sweet and dreadful, to find his boy's body thickening with muscle, to discover he was good at this. Lots of other stuff on top: pacifism too simple a response, times you have to fight for what is right, how about defending the weak? But at the heart of it, that moment, standing with his hands running red and screaming at Chinatown's next village idiot, screaming fucking berserk Don't *fuck* with me, you cock-sucking butt-cunt I'll fucking kill you, you fucker, *do you hear me?*

Story of his life, hey? Don't fuck with me.

The idiot gave him the creeps. That was way worse than death, that blank smile. Sorry, wrong number. Nobody home. Call again. Any fight after that, Jen stopped the moment the other guy went still. Totally involuntary. They noticed it in the gang he ran with for a while. Other guys would get him steamed and then play dead and he would stand there like a guilty john who couldn't get it up, no come in his fists at all.

Always meant to marry a passive woman for this reason.

Always imagined maybe a slap from a feisty girl, just enough to draw the lightning from him, the big red spark of his violence jumping between them and then her on the ground bleeding or god knows what, it scared the unholy shit out of him and he touched girls like eggshells, like fine china. Couldn't risk one who would hit him.

Not because he was stupid. Because he was smart.

So after being a little runty kid all his life his chest got deep and his short little legs and arms got stubby with muscle. Black curls of hair on his chest, would you believe it?

One day he realized he must have been a rape baby. Made sense. The hair, the muscles. The violence in him all the time. The rage. His mom so young and the way she never talked about his father. Not ever.

Maybe it wasn't true. But it felt true. He carried that rape inside himself, like a disease. He didn't ask his mother.

Unbearable, to have violated her like that.

There wasn't much furniture in the empty apartment. What there was he shoved into the kitchen or carried into the hallway. Then the empty main room was just big enough to practice in, bare feet slapping and squeaking on the worn wood floors.

He lost his feel for the passage of time. The past seemed a long way away, though. At the bottom of those stairs, maybe. A long way. As for the future . . .

Don't think.

He wasn't very sure about day and night, either. Maybe days and nights were going by, but whenever he thought about it, it seemed to be maybe pretty late at night. Couldn't be sure, though. There was nothing but a bamboo blind over the window, he could always check.

Choking horror came over him whenever he moved to pull the blind. It was a funny sort of war going on within his body: his eyes showed him only little red tasselled blind pulls, but his hands shook and his heart hammered as if every other part of him besides his brain and eyes knew they weren't just cords, they were snakes/ death/ poison, dangling there.

He remembered Water Spider's story about the little girl's house with the gargoyles outside and he left the blinds alone. His body had always been a lot smarter than his brain.

Here's a memory for you: sitting cross-legged on the floor with his ma and Uncle Lui. Dinner time. Bowls of steaming rice with little bits of apple cut in, one of his mother's staples. Fish soup. Ginger pickles. Ordinary stuff.

Uncle Lui has had a bad day. You can tell because he smiles a lot. He does this when he is angry. He sells shoes. He has many reasons to get angry, but salesmen only sell things when they are smiling. He can be very charming.

Jen's mother knows him well enough. She does not ask about his day. But it is part of Uncle Lui's nature not to brood in silence. It is important to show that these things do not bother him. He makes a joke about his surly customers.

The rice is a little dry. Some on the bottom of the pan is burned. Jen's mother apologizes.

Uncle Lui waves his hand. "No, no, not at all. It is very complicated. Hm. Rice. Water. Fire. Hm. Very complex." He grins.

Jen's mother does not say anything. She is hurt but she does not say anything. She desperately wants them all to get along. She will do almost anything to avoid fighting, especially in front of her son.

And because Jen knows this, he too cannot say anything. He knows his mother's loneliness far better than he knows any other feeling. He knows he must not do anything to upset Uncle Lui. Jen is ten years old and quite smart enough to realize that Uncle Lui could leave at any time, like Uncle Chan. Uncle Lui has been living with them for a year but they are not a family. He has no reason to put up with Jen. Jen must be very sure not to make him angry.

His mother has never said this to him. She would die rather than say this. But exactly because she would never ask him to sacrifice himself, he is very careful with Uncle

Lui. He has no interest in Uncle Lui, (the feeling is mutual), but Jen would never do anything that might risk the relationship between Uncle Lui and his mother.

She wants them to be a real family. Jen has even tried that. Once he called Uncle Lui "Dad." It was awkward for both of them. He didn't try again.

So they can't be a family. But at least he can keep her from her terrible loneliness. She never speaks of it, but he knows it like the smell of her hair.

His mother ladles fish soup into a bowl and passes it to Uncle Lui. "I am not a stupid woman," she says.

"Of course not! Of course not. . . . A stupid woman would have burned the pickles!"

Uncle Lui laughs toward her. He has this little laugh, this little teeth-baring good humor. Many years later, Jen will be sparring in a gym with an older man whose whole style is to hide behind a little left jab, poke poke poke, and he will remember Uncle Lui's little laughs. The quick little challenge in his eyes. His bare teeth. Ha ha ha. Ha ha ha. Jen broke his arm. Cost him dearly in apologies and errand-running and even a little cash. He laughs at himself when he remembers it.

Uncle Lui left Jen's mother two years later. He said he had found love with a girl in a fish-seller's shop.

Uncle Chan used to knock his mother around, but surprisingly, in later years, it is Uncle Lui Jen will fantasize about beating. A frightening number of times he has twirled his nunchuks and imagined whipping them across Uncle Lui's smiling face. Blood squirting. Shattering the little white teeth.

But now he is ten. He is a pacifist. He understands his mother's loneliness better than Uncle Lui does. Better than she does herself. So for four years he sits very still and says nothing to defend her from Uncle Lui's sarcasm. Not because he is a coward. Because he is brave.

There are three of them he can remember well, Uncle Chan, Uncle Lui, and Uncle Huang.

They are not really his uncles.

Uncle Chan has a round head and a big laugh and often smells of wine. He lives with them for two years when Jen is six and seven. He has hair all over his body. He shaves his face twice every day with a straight razor, leaving coarse black bristles in the sink. Jen does not like the sour man-smell Uncle Chan leaves on the towels.

Uncle Chan is quite a sentimental drunk. The times that he beats Jen's mother he is completely sober. At first he does not touch Jen. But after they have been living together for more than a year, he begins to spank him for his misdeeds. When Jen breaks a jade amulet he has been told several times not to play with, Uncle Chan beats him with the leather razor strop.

This turns out to be the end of their time with Uncle Chan. Jen's mother had tolerated being hit herself, but when Uncle tells her he has been forced to whip Jen with the leather strop, she throws him out of the house. The parting is very angry. Uncle Chan warns Jen's mother that he was her only chance for respectability. Without him, she will become a whore and Jen will grow into a whore's son and a thug. She spits at him.

When it is over she kneels before her son and takes his face in her hands and promises she will never let anyone hit him again. And Jen's mother, who will pay for the broken jade amulet with years of bitter loneliness, kisses him gently on the forehead, as if she were the one who had failed. As if she does not realize that Jen is to blame for everything.

Three years later she meets Uncle Lui. From him Jen learns to joke. He brags to other boys about the sharp deals Uncle Lui has made and retells his jokes and ignores him mostly and despises him sometimes.

Jen is quite a loner during this time. Other kids his age seem to work on very simple principles: they like or dislike, love or hate. Their friends are wonderful, their enemies dirt. It all seems very simple.

Not having any friends, Jen finds his reactions more complex. He finds it easy to admire his enemies' strength or daring, even if he thinks them stupid and vindictive. He is grateful to those kids who are friendly to him but he never forgets their limitations. He is physically small but he is funny and that is enough to get by. The only common thread in his feelings about other people is that aside from his mother he knows no one he respects.

Uncle Huang is different. He is an important man in the Mandarinate. He does not move in with them. For a while Jen thinks they will go to his house, which is certain to be very grand. This does not happen. Instead, Uncle Huang visits once or twice a week. He almost never stays the night, but Jen, who is now seventeen and old enough to be tactful, makes sure to be out on the evenings Uncle Huang is due to visit.

He catches them at it once, accidentally, coming back from a night of smoking marijuana and drinking cheap plum wine. His mother's bed is behind a screen in the living room. He stumbles in, worried in a drunken way about the noises coming from behind the screen. For some reason he becomes convinced there is a raccoon in his mother's bed.

A comical interlude ensues.

The one time they talk about it, afterwards, even his mother thinks it funny, though she does ask him, exasperated, how he thought a raccoon had made it to the third floor. After that he always stops at the apartment door and listens for the squeaking bed.

Uncle Huang leaves presents. These make Jen's mother very sad. Jen asks her why. His mother does not answer him directly. "What do you think of Uncle Huang?" she says.

He shrugs. "He's okay, I guess."

"Yes." She looks at her son with a sad smile. Sad. Not weak, never that. "Exactly." She fingers the little jade ring the Minister left for her the night before. "Jen, are you ashamed of me?"

"Never think that."

"I do sometimes." She puts the ring down on the table. "I want you to be married, you know. I am not one of those mothers who tries to eat her son. Any girl you like well enough to marry will be good enough for me."

"Ma, I'm seventeen."

"Are you having sex?"

"Ma!"

"If you are old enough to be a father, you are old enough to be married," she says drily. "Remember that. You just rent your heart to a lover, boy of mine. Your child owns it."

He is too old for the two of them to hug, so he makes her tea instead.

It is through Huang that Jen's mother met Water Spider. By this time something has changed in his mother's heart. He knows she will not be living with another man. Not while he is still at home. This is one of the reasons he moves out. Besides, his night life is getting pretty wild; it is time for him to move on. Six months later, his best friends are dead. Went to rob a wine store for the hell of it and got shot through the head by an owner with no sense of humor and an ancient .32 automatic. Two weeks later Jen is working for Water Spider.

It is from Water Spider he learns that Uncle Huang is the Minister for Interior, and a married man. He had started coming to Jen's mother after his first child had been born deaf and blind. The visits stopped two years later, after his wife gave birth to a healthy baby boy.

To put it in the worst light, his mother had been taking money to sleep with a married man. When Water Spider tells him, Jen stands silent for a long moment, afraid that he will break his promise and feel ashamed of her. To his intense relief, this does not happen. He feels sad for her, yes, and that hurts. But ashamed? No. Never that. He knows her too well.

Water Spider was not inconsiderate. "Truth is hard, but it lasts," he had said.

The prick.

Creak, creak. Creak, creak.

Don't listen don't listen don't listen don't listen.

Right cross/ stomp to knee/ left kick at hip. Now he is a grown man and his sweat smells sour, like Uncle Chan's.

Grab/ spin/ hold elbow: *snap!*

—But the imaginary arm between his hands bends before he can bring his elbow down to break it. A hip curls into his belly, his arms jerk, he shoots around an invisible pivot and slams into the hardwood floor.

There's a knee on his throat, his legs whip up and wrap around her neck and he arches. Dragging her off his chest, he rolls sideways and comes up in the cat stance, breathing hard.

He can't see her but he can smell her hair.

The floorboard squeaks a warning, he hops back as a foot flashes in a sweep kick below him. He snaps out with a quick kick of his own, feels his foot connect, a glancing blow.

Red silk flowers in the air and vanishes.

Then it's a side kick to the stomach and he doubles over, whooping. He knows better than to hold her foot but he coils down, one arm under her ankle, his other elbow pressing down at the knee, it can't help but bend. She doesn't even try to stop the fall, just lets it happen, lets his turn torque her body so her other heel comes hard for his head but he knows that one, he broke seven teeth for a fucker under the Main Street Skytrain station with that one. He pulls his head back until her foot is by and then drives forward so now she's flat on her stomach on the floor with him on top, pinning her arms beneath her, his hips against her hard ass, his head in the crook of her neck, it's covered with sweat, her straight black hair in his mouth, the smell of it like flowers and cordite.

"Who the fuck are you?"

She squirms underneath him until she is lying on her back and says, "Your luck, fool."

She looks at him as if she owns him. Lazy pleasure at the corners of her mouth. Her look opens his heart like a door and walks in. She is evil. Her arms like creepers wind around his neck. She drags him down to her mouth. It tastes of blood. He has never feared anything as he fears her. He has never desired anyone as he desires her.

She lets him go. He gasps.

She laughs and says, "Every woman hides herself in a different part of her body."

Then he sees Uncle Chan's razor in her hand. She snaps it open like a flick-knife, faster than he can follow, and slashes down his cheek. Blood flies over them both. It drips onto the skin of her neck and the top of her breasts, mixing with her sweat.

He rapes her, crying. The floorboards crack and squeak beneath them like a rickety bed.

Afterwards, she takes the razor and shaves the hair roughly from his head, leaving his scalp a lace of blood. Then she cuts away his mustache. Then his eyebrows. Then the hair on his breast and belly. When he is as smooth as a boy, she licks the blood from his face and offers him the razor.

He refuses.

Across the hall, Shouter and Shrieker are quarrelling again. A baby sobs in the next apartment. Rain gusts and sighs outside, running down the windows of New Moon Manor like tears from a sky that will never stop crying.

CHAPTER 13

Water Spider was alone in the Scholars Quarters, a chamber
empty save for two stone benches. He had pulled open its
sliding doors and sat gazing into the cobbled courtyard. It
was deep in the night, and pouring rain. Wind shook the
curtain of water dripping from the porch. He listened to the
rain falling, falling.

A message had come from Raining Chiu that the Southsiders had killed Li Bing. In the *Phoenix*, Li Mei and Emily
Thompson were not responding to radio hails. In the midst
of this chaos the Lidded Eye had requested his resignation.
He had given it. He was no longer the Honorable Minister
for Borders. He could do nothing now but wait for Jen and
Claire and Pearl to return.

He often came here to meditate. He liked the chamber's
emptiness and its strong bones, the pillars of nan wood polished and painted with cinnabar lacquer. Glassless apertures
in the walls framed the Three Friends: pine, bamboo, and
winter-flowering plum, whose blossoms now lay scattered
and drowning on the cobbles outside like the intentions of
youth.

Men were afraid of the outside. How much it hurt their
pride to think they were part of the world only as the otter
was, or the pine bough, or the drop of rain! So they retreated
Inside. Inside cities, homes, palaces; drawing back into a
world small enough that they could matter. But through all

the long years of history, sages had lived apart from this peopled world. The wise man in his mountain cave felt the hard stone beneath his feet; felt the cold wind on his face. He did not delude himself. He did not make himself large by shrinking the world around him.

Water Spider found he was shivering in the damp chill. He remained still, letting the shivers pass through him like gusts of wind. This bare stone room, into which the darkness rushed through open doors, was his cave in the mountains. His task was to hold his spirit upright in it, clear as a candle's flame. Clear as a lantern in the night.

A knock came at the side door, and his prostitute ran in. "Jen is trapped at my apartment. You have to get him back."

"Pearl!" Water Spider leapt up. The Southsider, Claire, followed Pearl into the room.

"I wanted to go back, but this Snow wouldn't let me," Pearl said. She spoke Cantonese, ignoring Claire. "Maybe I would be no use there, okay. But you must get Jen."

"What happened?"

"The gargoyles came first," Pearl said. "Squatting on the rooftop as if to take a shit."

In English, Claire said, "We went upstairs and got your— Jen's mother. On our way back there was a demon waiting for us. I shot him five times, but all that did was blow the glass out of the front door. Jen yelled at us to run out the back way. He said he would give us cover. A gust of air came through the smashed doorway and his sword faded in a little puff, like a cloud."

"You should not have sent him for me," Pearl said.

Rain fell in the Scholars Courtyard. Water Spider stood and kissed Pearl lightly on the forehead. "That may have been the only honorable decision I have made this cursed night. It was the right thing to do. But it means that now I face another task." In English he said, "Claire, leave us please. I wish to speak to Pearl alone. I will see you in my office shortly."

Claire nodded and withdrew.

"This is not the time for talk, Minister. My son is trapped in a gargoyle house. You must rescue him."

"Marry me."

"What!"

"Marry me." Water Spider took Pearl's hand. "Have no fears about Jen. I will get him back, I promise you."

"He's a good boy."

"He is," Water Spider said gently. "Tonight, when I found you were in danger, it was as lightning to me. In that fierce white instant I saw how arrogant I had been. Marry me, Pearl. I was a fool to snatch a cup of tea with you once a week. You are worth so much more than that." Her hand in his was strong, no girl's soft damp clasp. Her hair was pulled tightly back and fixed with a tortoiseshell comb, leaving plain her wide forehead, her thick brows and the strong bones under her eyes. No Sung beauty; and yet how much more real than those poetical ladies. "I am a connoisseur. I want to savor you. Marry me."

She said, "My name is not Pearl."

"What?"

"It's not Pearl. This is your pet name for me. It is not my name. My name is Po Yin."

"That is a lovely name too," he said. He held her hand more tightly. In the weak yellow lamplight he saw she was weeping. He brushed a tear from her cheek.

"Don't do this, Minister. It is cruel. Your dignity could never allow you to marry a woman like me. You have a position, appearances. An honorable family."

"My father was the most famous coward of 2004," Water Spider said softly. "I have been a coward too, I know. No longer. I want you for my wife. I have no wish to wed the gossips of the court or the Honorable Minister in Charge of Ministers. Yours is the only censure I will fear. Pearl, do not cry."

She wiped away her tears and said, "These are not for you."

He flinched and drew back his hand.

"Look at you." Pearl drew in a long, shaking breath. "Look at you! Even now you cannot imagine I will refuse.

Well then, Minister, let me speak more plainly. I will never marry the man who took me for his whore. Do you understand, you pompous prick?'' Her voice rang in the Scholars Courtyard. ''Who else could use a woman like a whore and then expect to be loved for it! Not even the Very Honorable Minister for Borders may do that. And yet you have the arrogance to stand here, expecting me to throw myself into your arms, while *my son may be dying*. He is your man. Throw me over, throw me out, now that you have forced me to say these things—but remember what you owe him.''

Water Spider felt his face go numb. His chest was a wooden box. He bowed and said, ''I never forget my debts.''

Pearl covered her mouth with her hands. ''I am sorry. Forgive me. I should not have spoken so.'' *Not because you have hurt me*, Water Spider thought. *Only because you might have injured your son. Isn't that right, Pearl? Not Pearl. Po Yin.*

At that moment it struck him with terrible force that each man is born alone and dies alone; in between we are candles in the storm, that burn singly and singly gutter and go out. ''I never knew you,'' he said.

He turned to leave. ''Minister?'' she said from behind him. He looked back. Pearl's wide face was weary. ''You are not a bad man.''

''Merely arrogant and obtuse.''

''Only a little.''

His heart twisted at her tired smile.

Claire was waiting in his office. So was his missing subaltern, Li Mei. ''At last!'' He strode quickly across the room and gripped her by the shoulders. ''Where is Emily Thompson?'' he demanded in Cantonese. ''Quickly!''

''I do not know,'' Li Mei said.

''What!''

''I do not know. I set Emily Thompson down some distance from here, and left immediately. She did not wish to be found.''

"I heard Emily's name," Claire said in English. "Is she here? Where is she? I want to see her."

"Please accept my resignation," Li Mei said, ignoring Claire and continuing to speak to Water Spider. "I acted entirely on my own, with neither the knowledge nor the consent of yourself or my mother. I am prepared to swear this at any inquiry, or to the Southsiders." Her mouth quirked in a brief smile. "I believe I was destined to design dresses after all."

Water Spider looked steadily at her. Li Mei faltered, and began to flush.

"What's going on?" Claire said. "Where is Emily?"

Water Spider switched to English. "I am afraid I am unable to accept your resignation, Li Mei."

"I—I did not imagine there was a chance my career could be saved. Surely the Southsiders will demand my resignation?"

"I am no longer the Minister for Borders. The Honorable Minister in Charge of Ministers retired me at two-thirty this morning. You are an hour late. Your resignation, though utterly appropriate, will have to be offered to someone else. Wei Lin, probably. Or possibly Wan Chu. A good man."

Li Mei sat down heavily. "Oh no. Not you," she whispered. "I . . . How could the Lidded Eye ask that of you! How could she throw away her most able Minister at such a time? It is outrageous! I took every precaution to ensure you could not be connected with my decision. I answered no radio hails, left no messages . . ." Li Mei looked up, eyes widening. "The Lidded Eye cannot think my mother was involved. Above all things, no one must think she was to blame."

"Li Mei—"

"I will take all dishonor upon myself. I understand this. But my mother is guiltless. If she has shame to bear, it is only for conceiving me. The Heavens know that will be enough."

Like distant thunder, a low roar rumbled from the sky, swelling gradually. "Those will be the first planes from the Southside," Water Spider said. "Li Mei, shortly after I sent

Claire and Jen to rescue his mother, we received a radio message from Raining Chiu. She is making her way home by helicopter. She says that Winter killed your mother earlier this morning. The Southsiders will neither confirm nor deny this report, but we have yet to hear from Li Bing. Surely if your mother was alive and unharmed, they would have had her speak to us.''

"No. Oh no.''

"The Southsiders consider Chinatown to have provoked a confrontation by the abduction of Winter's heir, Emily Thompson.'' The roar of jet engines throbbed through the darkness. Water Spider glanced at Claire. "While I am no longer privy to the doings of the Council of Ministers, I believe that at this moment our two cities are at war.''

"You can't hope to win,'' Claire said.

Water Spider nodded. "No, I don't believe we can. Winter means to have his heir. Having gone this far, I do not think he will stop now. He will send his troops to occupy Chinatown. Perhaps they will merely search for her. Perhaps they will execute hostages until she is produced. So you see,'' he said to Li Mei, "I really must know where she is.''

"In the Forest,'' Li Mei said, her face ashen. "I could tell a strange destiny was working her. She said she dared not come into Chinatown, in case her people were waiting for her. The plane landed on English Bay. I asked it to taxi up False Creek. I let Emily off at the south edge of Chinatown, where it gives way to the Forest. She meant to hide there. I—'' Li Mei bit her lip. "Oh, Mother. And now I have betrayed Emily too. Everything I touch turns to ash.''

"Emily Thompson must be found and made to speak to her grandfather,'' Water Spider said. "I expect you to do this.''

"I thought you weren't giving orders anymore,'' Claire said.

"Li Mei placed this destiny in her mouth,'' Water Spider said curtly. "Now she must swallow it.'' He took a moment to send a runner to the radio room, to tell the Southsiders that Emily Thompson had been dropped off at the Forest's edge. When he was done he turned back to Claire. "You could help search for her, I think. You know Miss Thompson as well as anyone. Will you not find her, and ask her to end this war?"

"I will help find her," Claire said slowly. "She will make up her own mind. But what about you? If finding Emily is so important, won't you come with us?"

Water Spider walked over to the sword rack and took down the ancient blade that rested there. "I have my own destiny to eat." He buckled the old sword belt firmly around his waist. "Thank you for bringing back my Pearl. I will not forget it. Now there is another who must be returned. Jen gave his life to me. I must try to give it back."

CHAPTER 14

"You were with Emily," Claire said to Li Mei, as soon as Water Spider had gone. "Why has the fool of a girl run away?"

"I don't know. She said it was important. She promised me."

"Emily doesn't break her promises," Claire said. "One of her many little failings, that."

Li Mei's thin eyes were bloodshot, her angular face drawn tight with exhaustion. "Will she help me feed my hungry ghosts? Hey?"

"Emily did not kill your mother," Claire said. "You can't blame her for that."

"You think it is an accident Winter killed my mother after Emily ran away? I do not. I think we were the cause of her death. Who shall I blame besides Emily? Myself? Believe me, I am already doing that. I find there is too much guilt. It fills me up and overflows me. Emily Thompson is a strong woman. She can carry her share."

Gunfire rattled outside. It faded, and rain filled the silence left behind. "You two are very much alike," Claire said.

"Has she also killed her mother, then? Oh, I suppose she has. The mother died in childbirth, I recall." Li Mei walked behind Water Spider's desk and bent to study her reflection in the window. She bit her lips to bring the color back into them and brushed at her hair with her long red fingernails.

"Or were you referring only to our beauty?"

"You are both very young, and you take yourselves extremely seriously," Claire said. "Come on. You need to eat and sleep."

"We are not the same." Li Mei straightened and turned back from the window. "And you are not my governess. Please do not presume. More people will die because of what I did unless we can find Emily."

"You saw Water Spider send a runner to the radio room," Claire said. "Soon Winter will know that you left Emily on the south side of Chinatown at the edge of the Forest. If Winter can't find her there with a squad of trackers, we certainly won't be able to. It's out of your hands now. May Emily's God help her when Winter catches her."

"What if Winter does not catch her?" Li Mei said. "The Forest is a Power. It will decide where Emily goes, and who finds her."

"I always forget how superstitious you wetlanders are."

Li Mei arched one thin eyebrow. "Superstitious, yes, but very pragmatic. You Southsiders, on the other hand, are very rational and terribly idealistic; a dreadful combination. You are not eight hundred kilometers away on the bald prairie now. There is no North Side here, we have not fenced all our gods onto a single reservation. They lie thick as leaves on the ground, not just in Chinatown but in all the Islands, the little pockets of humanity left where once Vancouver was. I wonder how long it will take your people to learn that lesson?"

Claire regarded Li Mei. "A sort of condescending mysticism is another unlovely trait you and Emily share."

Li Mei went back to the window. From the inside hip pocket of her jacket—low enough not to spoil its shape— she slipped a thin wood case, inlaid with mother-of-pearl. She opened it and took out an eye-stick, touching subtle hints of brown around her eyes, repairing the damage that rain and tears had done. It required great patience, as her hands were shaking badly. From time to time another tear would interrupt her work, and she would have to draw a makeup cloth from her pocket. "You are right that we cannot compete with Winter's men. If we are to find Emily, we must guess where she will go.''

Claire watched her work. "It is not Emily's way to run and hide. Not forever. Oh, right now I'm sure she is confused, and angry, and scared half out of her mind. But in the end she will want to face Winter again. There is not much subtlety in my little babushka. She will want things settled face to face. That's how her grandfather raised her, and she loves him more than anyone in this world, or the next.''

"Forgive me if I find no love for him in my heart.''

Claire nodded. "Hm. Well, he is not easy to love. Even for us. But he is a great man.''

"Never," Li Mei said. Her voice was light and dry with anger and despair. " 'Never has a man who has bent himself been able to make others straight.' There is no greatness without virtue. And there is no virtue in murder." Li Mei turned away. Tears crawled from her thin eyes.

"Sleep," Claire said. "Then we will find Emily.''

Li Mei blotted the tears with her makeup cloth. "And virtue will be restored, and all will be right under Heaven.''

"More or less," Claire said.

Li Mei refused to go home immediately, saying that she needed to go to the Garden to get special funerary offerings for her mother. Claire trailed behind her as she crossed the street to walk beside the wall of the Lady's Garden. To Claire's ears most parts of Chinatown were hideously noisy, even now at nearly four o'clock on Saturday morning—full of shouting people, screeching gates, wind chimes that clanged or clacked or boomed or rattled, chickens that clucked and pigs that squealed, plus an assortment of whistles, gongs, fireworks, mysterious chants, and drunken singing. But all that was muted around the Garden. Gentle sunshine from some other season spilled over the Lady's walls into the night, making fugitive rainbows dance and flicker there.

A red-crested woodpecker watched them from the Lady's wall. As Claire passed he cocked his head. When their eyes met, his beak gaped as if he were laughing. Claire shivered and hurried on. "I thought it was impossible to enter the Garden and return."

"This is true," Li Mei said, turning the corner at Columbia and walking along the Garden's back wall. She headed for a small door Claire had not noticed before. "But we aren't going into the Garden. We are going to its gift shop. I should warn you, nothing there is cheap."

"Gift shop?"

Li Mei opened the door and motioned Claire inside. "We are an entrepreneurial people."

Claire slowed, then stopped before the doorway. The child of a goddess, she had never been able to ignore the invisible world the way most Southsiders did. She felt the pulse and rhythm of a great Power beyond the threshold.

"What is it?" Li Mei asked.

"I'm . . . It sounds odd, but I am wondering whether I can pass through this door without being destroyed," Claire said. She was The Harrier's child and a thing of the prairie, after all: created from snow and steel and great solitude.

Li Mei's eyebrows rose. "It's a gift shop, governess."

Claire exhaled, and nodded. "Mm. I suppose you're right. Still, can you blame me? Imagine what they would stock in the North Side's retail outlet."

"You have a point." When Claire made no move to enter, Li Mei waved her in again. "Please—age before beauty, and reason before superstition."

Claire looked at her. "You are not entirely alike, mind you. Emily was at least a little more earnest."

Li Mei followed her. "When you must maintain your nation on a diet of beets, there is much to be earnest about."

A wizened little Chinese woman in black pajamas peered at them over a pair of wire spectacles as they entered the shop. She said something in Cantonese, which Li Mei answered. As usual it sounded to Claire as if every phrase ended with an exclamation point. She imagined most conversations in Chinese went something like,

"Hello! How are you, you pig!"

"Fine, dying dog!"

"The sky weeps little shits, eh! Tomorrow I shall execute my wife!"

The clerk waved at Claire impatiently. "Go look, please. You see what you like. Many good things. Beautiful things. You need this good luck, hey?" She pursed her lips disapprovingly at Claire. "Too thin, and funny color." She said something to Li Mei in Chinese. Li Mei looked at Claire and smirked before replying. The old woman closed her eyes and wrinkled her nose as if smelling dead fish, then waved her tiny hands and turned away. They laughed together, Li Mei's white teeth just showing, the old woman sniggering with a hand over her mouth.

Li Mei caught Claire's scowl. "Please. Pay no attention."

Claire looked for something to hit her with.

The Double Happiness Gift Shop had a very unusual selection of things for sale: joss sticks; I Ching coins; charms brushed in red ink on gold paper, or carved into jade, or burned into shards of bone or horn or tortoiseshell; amulets made from bird tongues, old transistors, spark plugs, spent bullets, ancient American Mercury dimes, and lacquered ginseng root, suspended from cords of red silk or gold thread or braided dog's hair or salvaged TV cable or stripped electrical wires. There were rows and rows of small glass bottles with powders inside, labelled in Chinese characters with pictures of butterflies, chrysanthemums, hummingbirds, turtles (lots of these), pearls, bones, and, confusingly, clocks. Vials and vials of liquids: oozy black ones, watery gold ones, red ones that looked like blood; liquids clear and clotted, dense and mottled, liquids gently bubbling, and opaque mixtures that seethed unnervingly from within.

Also available in glass, gold, brass, crystal, bone and wood, were chimes, bells, gongs, whistles, combs and dice. There were books, too: books written on rags of silk, books etched on thin bamboo scrims that rolled up like little blinds, cheap holographic books whose texts changed when you looked at them from different angles, books brushed on paper and plastic. Claire saw at least one whose every page was made from mother-of-pearl, with Chinese characters inlaid in gold.

And of course there were seeds—in glass jars, in silk bags, seeds in paper packets with gaudy pictures on the outside, seeds in jade boxes and clay pots and oyster shells, seeds that grew into flowers and trees and appliances, if the pictures on the outside were to be believed.

Every item's price and description was meticulously labelled in Chinese characters that Claire, without her familiar, had no hope of deciphering.

"Ah." From a tall urn Li Mei drew out three long sticks of incense.

"You too, yes?" the old woman said, looking at Claire.

"Me?"

"You have many dead. They sit on your shoulders." Claire peered down at her shoulders, square beneath her scratchy fatigue shirt. "Hungry ghosts!" the old woman said, with a jab of her finger. "Give them some smoke to eat, yes?"

"All ghosts are hungry," Claire said.

Li Mei drew out three more sticks of incense. Claire followed her up to the counter. The old woman laid the incense in a balance she kept next to her register. She eyed it professionally. "One day, each."

Li Mei looked at Claire. "I told you they were expensive."

The old woman rang up their purchases—

—And Claire woke up ten years old in her bed in the Tory Building. It was dark and she tried to go back to sleep but her body knew it was morning. Finally she gave up and opened her eyes. "Seven-sixteen," the room said.

She climbed out of bed and dragged on her long johns and pants and undershirt and a sweater, brushed her white hair away from her hateful ice-cube-colored eyes and headed down to breakfast.

She no longer woke up every morning wondering if she would see her mother. It had been three years since the last time. The memory of that meeting had blurred and faded like a snowy track worn away by the wind, its edges crumbling, dry and indistinct. Blowing away through the years.

Claire wasn't exactly anybody's charge, but a couple of the women in the Tory Building cafeteria were pleasant enough. Winter was understandably cautious in his dealings with The Harrier's daughter, and though he never treated her like family, he did at least get rid of the overtly cruel or superstitious members of his personal staff. Claire did not mistake this caginess for love.

It was boiled wheat and honey for breakfast, with a cup of hot chicory to finish. Then off to McKernan Elementary and Junior High. School, while still hellish, was marginally less purgatorial this year than last; over the summer three girls in Claire's grade had developed perceptible breasts, thus drawing a certain amount of the fire formerly reserved for her. Some of the other girls, God help them, were jealous. Claire supposed it made sense, if you were desperately worried about your long-term popularity with boys.

The Harrier didn't much go in for sexual subtlety. Her mother's habit was to snatch an unsuspecting man under cover of a blizzard or other natural crisis, use him up like a box of matches, and then throw him in the snow. Watching the boys of her class snapping bras and peering under changing-room doors, Claire was coming to appreciate the virtues of this approach.

Curiously, she was the only offspring to result from The Harrier's indiscretions, as far as she knew. A dubious honor.

Things were vastly better inside the classroom, where pulverizing tedium replaced the more ingenious cruelties of her peers. They were well into their second week on the internal combustion engine. Claire barely managed to reassemble her little motor in the hour and a half allotted, and she had three pieces left over, which couldn't be a good sign. The motor started anyway. A pleasant surprise.

At the end of the day it was skiing. When she got to her cubby she found someone had stolen her wax, but she had long since given up complaining. Even if her teachers were honestly willing to help, the wax wasn't going to reappear, and it was beneath her dignity to whine. That's what They wanted anyway. She went out on unwaxed skis, with predictable results. Trying to go up each hill of the route was like trying to scale a glass mountain in greased boots. At the halfway point she was almost a kilometer behind; it would be dark by the time she got back, and the school would be deserted.

She had become quite expert at making a virtue out of solitude.

She turned back from the river valley, heading south. She made the long hill up to the University Hospital and paused at the top, breathing hard. A cold white magic gathered in the December air. To one side, a brace of cedar waxwings hopped through the bare branches of a mountain ash, looking for any shrivelled red berries others might have missed. The parking lot behind the abandoned Cross Cancer Institute stretched out before her, a sheet of white too dazzling to look at, as if a glass sun had been smashed to splinters and strewn across the plain, every crystal still burning with cold fire. For the second time in her life Claire saw sun dogs. Two pairs, flanking the sun in the ice-blue sky.

Then her mother was there. The sun dogs snapped and quarrelled around The Harrier's heels, balls of white fire, flashing and winking. Clouds of fine white snow fountained at their feet, hung fretted and sparkling in the freezing air, and then frayed into tatters of white smoke. They stood by, panting, as The Harrier crouched down and touched her daughter's cheek. Their breaths smoked up together in the cold winter air and Claire felt a sudden rush of joy, as if her mother was *giving* this to her. The snow. The sun with its hounds at heel. The burning sky. The enormous silence.

Her fingers were halfway to frostbite by the time she got back to the school, and she was forced to endure the inevitable lecture on Proper Waxing Technique. That night, while her classmates were home eating dinner with their families, she was in the Tory Building cafeteria eating tasteless breaded perch fillets, which she despised.

But when she had labelled her Four-Stroke Engine Diagram, read over the day's math homework, and then screened herself to drowsiness, she lay in bed in her night-gown, closed her eyes, and held the vision of the sun dogs and the snowy field like the memory of a mother's kiss, until sleep took her.

—The cash register clanged in the Double Happiness Gift Shop.

Claire felt as if sixteen hours had passed, as if she had just lived out that day of her tenth year, second by second. She felt the memory slipping away like a dream on waking. She tried fiercely to hold on to it, the snow and the blue sky, the smell of her room, and her mother was in it some-how, but the harder she tried to remember, the faster it dis-appeared, like a snowflake melting in her hand.

Then it was gone, and she knew it was gone forever, and she would never get it back. Her mother had given her something very precious and she had lost it, lost it. She turned and found Li Mei crying in silence. No sobs or gasps: just a steady flow of tears down her narrow cheeks.

On the counter before them, a white diamond and a tiny seed were lying in the old woman's balance. The diamond glittered like frost in the sun. The old woman scooped each one up and popped them into small plastic containers.

Li Mei touched Claire's hand. "They will go into the Garden."

Claire's heart was broken, but she didn't cry. Her mother had given her that, too. Frozen her up inside. "I didn't want to lose that day."

Li Mei took the incense after the old woman wrapped it. "Our dead didn't want to give up their lives."

The incense wasn't all Li Mei bought. There was paper jew-elry too, and spirit money, a hundred million dollars of it. "For my mother to buy her way into Heaven," Li Mei explained. They watched it burn in a little brazier back at Li Mei's home. Then they ate. Claire coaxed Li Mei into drinking two cups of plum wine, and carried her into her room when the young woman finally fell asleep, still silently weeping.

Then Claire sank into a soft couch in the front room. The air was still heavy with sad smoke. "Emily, you idiot," she whispered. "What have you done?" Probably she would get herself killed and what would Claire have done to stop it? What had she ever given the girl but wariness? Even her own cursed white cold bitch goddess mother had given her something, something terribly precious, if only she could remember it.

She was crying, damn it. She hated that, but she couldn't seem to stop.

She finished the bottle of plum wine herself, hoping to let sleep sneak up on her, but she was still too wary for that. She wondered what had happened to Jen, and whether Water Spider would get him back from the haunted apartment building. She remembered cards bubbling and turning black. Players' hands burning down to the bone.

She tried to remember the day that had been taken from her in the Lady's gift shop.

Tap, tap.

She remembered The Harrier turning the corner onto Keefer Street last night, white and cold and distant as a star. Claire supposed she should feel grateful, she should feel blessed that her mother had cared enough to save her. But instead she felt angry at her for letting the others die. And absurdly jealous of Water Spider, whom the goddess had touched instead of her.

Tap. Tap. Something was knocking on the window of Li Mei's house. Groggy with incense and exhaustion, Claire pulled herself back from sleep and struggled up from the couch. **Tap tap tap.** She fumbled in the dark, smacked her shin on a coffee table, cursed, and limped across the room to the window on the north wall. The sky outside was finally paling. The long night of horrors was almost over. **Tap tap tap!** "I'm coming, for Christ's sake."

The tapping stopped, and a horribly burned and disfigured face pressed up against the glass. It was Lieutenant Jackson. Claire screamed.

Jackson grimaced. "Glad to see you too, sweetie." His voice was faint. It was hard to hear him through the glass.

"Oh God, you're alive, oh shit we have to get you to a doctor—"

Jackson shook his head. "Uh, negatory, Claire. I'm dead. We're all dead, actually, except for you and Lamont and Nagy. I don't think Nagy's going to make it, though."

"You're dead?"

"No shit, sweetheart." Half his face was burned down to the bone.

"Then why . . . I mean, what . . . ?"

He grimaced again. "I don't know. The captain doesn't know. We're not in great shape, I'll tell you that. Most of the guys don't have enough left to drag themselves out of the barracks. I was taking a piss when it hit, don't know why that would make me a good ghost, but who knows anything about this shit? I followed your incense here. It's killing me to hold on so far from my body, though, so I gotta make it quick. John Walker hasn't showed up, Claire." Lieutenant Jackson grunted and closed his one good eye. "Christ. Lord have mercy. Yeah, anyway: no John Walker to take us to the North Side, so, uh, there we sit in a parking lot on the edge of this godforsaken slant village. And we can scare the shit out of a few Chinamen, I suppose, or haunt a monster, but Christ's sake, we just want to go home. We just want to go home."

"I, I don't know—"

"Shit. Ow, shit. Daybreak coming," Jackson said. He started talking faster. "Yeah, anyway, we figured the White Bitch bailed you out, and maybe you got connections or something. Ask her to tell John Walker to get his ass over here, okay? Christ, Claire, we're a long way from home—"

A cock crowed, and he was gone.

May Emily's God have mercy on my soul, Claire thought, staring through the window at the dawn. Rain hurried down the gutters outside. *John Walker has not come and the ghosts of Southside's dead are trapped in Chinatown and begging me for help. What am I going to do now?*

Sleep crept up on her as she tried to decide. Whether it

was fate, or weariness, or just plum wine, Claire remained asleep even when Li Mei rose and left the house, and only woke when a squad of Southside's trackers burst into the room and put her under arrest.

CHAPTER 15

After Water Spider took his leave of Claire and Li Mei, he arranged a billet for Pearl. As he finished this business he turned to find the Honorable Minister for the South leaning in the doorway. "Where to now?" Johnny Ma asked. Even at four in the morning, he looked fresh and immaculate, as if his evening were just beginning.

"I have a certain task to perform."

"May I walk with you?"

"My path leads me to Hastings Street."

The Monkey's eyebrows rose. "Then I shall definitely come with you. It isn't safe to go down there by yourself. But I suppose you know that."

"Forgive me, Minister; while of course you are always a delight, I am afraid I would be poor company tonight. My thoughts and I need some solitude. I am sure you understand."

"Perfectly." Johnny belted a stylish trench coat around his waist. "Are we ready, then?" He dug a gold-plated cigarette case from his coat pocket and flipped it open. "Want another?"

"Under no circumstances."

"Probably wise." Johnny clicked the case shut. He lit his joint and then pointed at the sword belted on Water Spider's hip. "Taking the Old Man out, I see." Water Spider retrieved an umbrella from the stand.

They went out through the front doors of Government House and stood for a moment under the Dragon and Phoenix carved on the North Gate. It was still dark. Still raining. "Not so much gunfire," Johnny said.

"Wait a few hours."

"The Southsiders, you mean?"

"My people tell me their planes are taxiing on the waters of English Bay now."

"Do your people know they aren't your people anymore?"

"We value loyalty in this government," Water Spider said.

Johnny pulled thoughtfully on his joint. "Huang Ti has been given the Borders portfolio for the duration of the emergency."

"I hope he can find some clothes. The men and women of Borders are not accustomed to taking orders from a Minister wearing a bathrobe."

Johnny laughed. "You always were a pompous prick."

"Hm. Well." Water Spider reflected. "Winter and Emily Thompson have dealt with us, with the Mandarins," he said. "How will Huang Ti explain that Chinatown's real power lies elsewhere, with the Lady and the Dragon and the Double Monkey, and the chosen puppets of these Powers? I rather pity the new Minister for Borders."

"Pity Huang Ti, eh? Well, you are a man of more generous sensibilities than I," Johnny said. "Are you still seeing that concubine of his, by the way?"

Water Spider put up his umbrella. "No."

"Pity. She suited you better. I always thought she was a bit too clever for him. Better he stick to his wife. A good soul, and slow enough to make even him feel clever."

"Shut up, Johnny. Respect the woman. She is raising two children, one of them very difficult."

"No harm meant, my friend. No disrespect intended."

"You think that charm and wit forgive your moments of viciousness. Your improprieties. They do not."

Johnny looked at his colleague and took another drag on his joint. "You shame me."

Water Spider grunted and walked out into the rain. "Flippancy is a habit, Johnny." He thought of Huang Ti, taking his pleasure with Pearl while at home his wife struggled with their deaf and blind child. "So is betrayal."

They walked the block along Keefer to the barricade at Columbia. "I lost one man around two this morning," the captain reported, shaking his head. "Zhang jumped over the barricade. One of the monsters had a gun. Popped Zhang and ran. Not much action since then."

"I am grieved by your loss."

"Minister? We've been hearing aircraft. Are the Southsiders coming?"

"Yes." Grins broke out on the faces of Water Spider's men. They cheered as he walked away. He did not tell them not to.

It was a block down to Hastings Street. Neon hummed and crackled in the air: dragons and stars and falling coins. A huge purple Buddha let gold coins fall through his fat electric fingers over the Number One Son Casino. "You didn't tell those brave soldiers back there who the Southsiders might be coming for," Johnny said.

"Six men on that detail." Rain drummed monotonously against Water Spider's silk umbrella. "Do you know how long it would take one of the Snows to kill them all?"

"All of them? All six?"

"Less than a second," Water Spider said. "Less than the time from one heartbeat to the next."

Johnny had no clever remarks.

Water Spider picked a gap between two rickshaws and plunged into Hastings Street. The instant he left the sidewalk, he left Chinatown proper and stepped into no man's land. Crowds of sharps and pickpockets swirled around him, cripples and charm-sellers with crepe-paper necklaces, prostitutes wearing rented smiles, the old, the poor, the foolish and the reckless: all flowed around him, a river of disrepute, and at their touch he felt everything he had been diffusing from him, all his duty and scholarship, all his hard work and propriety, as if he himself were a kind of tea, his virtue seeping away into their dirty water. It was a different world on the far curb, and a different man who stepped into it.

"I am greatly honored by your company to this point," he said to Johnny Ma. "I will go on from here alone."

Johnny nodded. "What have you come here for, Spider?"

"My father," he said.

Water Spider's father lived two blocks north of Hastings in a small apartment at the corner of Columbia and Cordova. Nobody lived north of Cordova, no matter how desperate or deranged; from Cordova to the docks was a three-block strip of hell, stretching from Centennial Pier in the west to the abandoned fairgrounds of the P.N.E. park three kilometers down the shore. Throughout the twentieth century Vancouver had been Canada's California. Dreamers and rogues and folk too poor to survive the brutal Canadian winters had fled there. Those whose luck or hope ran out ended up on the Lower East side, strewn like sea wrack at the edge of the Pacific. The Dream of 2004 had come there like the end of the world.

In Vancouver, the greatest battles of '04 had been fought along Hastings Street. In cities all around the world, nearly every community that bordered on a place like the Lower East Side had run mad with minotaurs, or been consumed. But Chinatown, deep in a magic of its own, and blessed with the leadership of Wu Lei, the angel they called the Emperor, had fought the darkness to a standstill. The final engagement had come at the Carnegie Library at the corner of Main and Hastings. There the Spider Darkness and the Emperor met, and there they both fell.

Wu Lei's followers had revered him as a hero, as a god. When he died, those of his knights who survived put on their mourning and became the Shrouded Ones. All but one. Alone among that honored company, Water Spider's father, Floating Ant, had chosen to turn his back on the Emperor, and Chinatown, and honor.

Water Spider knocked on Floating Ant's door. "It is me, Father."

"You? Who are you?" An iron bar slid back in the center of the door and two eyes peered out. "Spider! Only much older and wetter. Why are you here?"

"Will you let me in?"

"Of course, of course! Only, tell me why you've come."

"Father? Why do you sound afraid?" The iron bar shot back. Bolts slid, chains rattled. The door swung slowly open. "You're already up," Water Spider said, surprised. Instead of a bathrobe or a dressing gown, his father was dressed formally, in a long tunic and pants of white silk, with pearl buttons in gold mounts. Looking past his father's shoulder, Water Spider saw three old men sitting cross-legged on the floor around a small, low table. One was dressed all in gold silk, with a pair of white boots. The second wore only red, save for a pair of white gloves. The third wore a long black robe, belted with a white silk sash.

A pot of tea sat on the table—almond from the smell of it—but there was only one cup, before his father's empty place.

"You are all wearing white," Water Spider said. "Who has died?"

His father gave him a curious look. "Well, Spider. Come in, come in. You look cold and empty and careworn."

"I am all those things tonight. If you could spare a cup of that tea, I would be very grateful, " Water Spider said, heading for the low table.

"No, not this," his father said, snatching the pot away. "I will make you something better. Something better, for a connoisseur." He opened the window above the sink and poured the tea outside into the rainy night. Floating Ant still moved spryly and his back was straight, as if he carried on it only sixty of his ninety-six years. Water Spider felt older than that, this night.

But this had been his father's gift, and curse: to live, and live, and live, while everyone around him perished, in body or soul. No doubt he would outlive his son, as he had outlasted his wife and the comrades he had deserted at the Carnegie Slaughter. For years he had seemed to live on nothing but plum wine and marijuana. His body had not

decayed, but become small and leathery and tough, as if the
wine had pickled his insides, and the smoke from the joints
had cured his hide. But this morning Floating Ant was uneasy. Old ghosts haunted his eyes and hands.

While his father rummaged in a cabinet for tea, Water
Spider placed his umbrella in the stand by the door, and
turned politely to the silent gentlemen waiting around the
table. They regarded him, unspeaking. There was something
in their looks that disturbed him. Their eyes were still water;
he could see his own reflection there, trembling and shallow
on the surface. Any thoughts that might move in the depths
of their silence were hidden utterly from him.

"Aren't you going to introduce me, Father?"

Floating Ant turned. "Introduce . . . ? Ah—no. No, I
don't think so. This isn't actually the best time to visit, Spider. In fact, of all the days in the six years since you last
came—"

"Five, Father."

"Five, then. In all those years, I don't think there·has
been a worse day for you to drop by. So I think perhaps a
cup of tea, and then I must send you back to composing
edicts and scheming for power. Very sorry, ah?"

Water Spider went to the little coal stove and squatted
before it. Something had been burning in it recently; great
curls and flakes of black ash rustled in the wind of his coming. "I need your help," he said.

His father laughed.

"It is not a time for laughter. A young man I sent out
tonight has been trapped in a gargoyle house. A demon
guards the door. I need you to take me to a Shrouded One."

A silver tea ball swung, forgotten, from Floating Ant's
ancient fingers. "Oh," he said.

Water Spider warmed his hands before the fire. "This is
not a good day for me either. Over this night I have lost my
servant, my woman, and my position in the Government.
Daylight may well find Chinatown occupied by a foreign
power. Forgive me if I sound intemperate, but I doubt your
night has been worse than mine. I need—I am begging for
your help. If all my work must be ashes, at least let me

rescue this one poor boy, whose only fault was that he followed my orders."

Floating Ant filled a copper kettle and brought it to the
little stove. "That's a busy night," he said. "So your career
is ruined, ah? Well." The old man ran his long fingernails
through Water Spider's hair. "Now you see why you should
have had children. The only true comfort in one's age." He
gave a dry little laugh.

"What right have you to mock me?" Water Spider said.
Pearl's great aphrodisiac: not to have his children. "If you
had been more of a comfort to me in my youth, perhaps I
would be a greater solace to your age. I will drink plum
wine in your room until I pass out, though, if that would
ease you. Or smoke hashish, or eat poppy bread. Any of
these little attentions that draw a family together."

"Enough," said the stranger in black. His eyes like cold
stone wells were deep with years.

Water Spider turned, furious. "Sir, I do not believe we
have been introduced."

The old man in gold smiled and said, " 'A youth, when
at home, should be filial, and, abroad, respectful to his el-
ders.' "

"Very well, you can quote K'ung Fu-tzu. But does not
the Old Man also say, 'If a man lose his uprightness, and
yet live, his escape from death is the effect of mere good
fortune'? If you do not remember what it was like in our
house when I was young, perhaps you are of an age, venerable sirs, to remember what my father did in the service
of the Emperor. Or rather, did not do."

The old man in red looked at him contemptuously. "Boy,
you can't even remember the things your father has tried to
forget."

The man in gold looked past Water Spider to his father.
" 'Things that are done, it is needless to speak about,' " he
said gently. " ' . . . Things that are past, it is needless to
blame.' "

But Floating Ant said, "The boy is right."

Twists of paper curled and twisted between the coals in
the little stove. Surviving scraps still huddled in the corners,

spotted with ink. There was a great deal of ash. "These were poems," Water Spider said suddenly. He looked at his father in shock. "You have been burning your poems."

His father laughed. An old sound, like twigs rubbing together. "I did not think you of all people would be concerned."

"This was your life!" Water Spider tried to reach into the stove and pluck out one of the pieces of paper, but the heat was too fierce. He looked around for a pair of tongs. "This is ridiculous. Take them out. How many did you burn?"

"Only the bad ones."

"How many, Father?"

"All of them."

Water Spider looked at him in horror. For some reason this seemed worse than what was happening in Chinatown, worse than Pearl's furious refusal. He felt like a little boy. He wanted to cry.

His father patted him awkwardly on the hand, and shuffled back into the kitchen. "I will make that tea." Water Spider sat before the fire, devastated. With every breath, every movement, tiny ripples of air shuddered inside the little stove. His father's life smoked and trembled.

The old man dressed all in red silks said, "Floating Ant has been a warrior, a poet, a husband, a father—What have you done, hey? Boy?"

Water Spider's father washed out the teapot and returned it to the table with a spoonful of dry tea inside. When the kettle began to sing, he poured the water into the pot. The scent of tea stole through the room, pungent as crushed herbs, light as a summer breeze. When it had steeped, he poured a cup for his son.

"Thank you, Father."

"Easy now, Spider. My old heart cannot withstand too much filial piety all at once." Floating Ant watched his son drink. After a while he looked around the room. "Ah, what a group of terrible old men we are now, ah?" In his beautiful recitation voice he bagan to chant.

> "I heard the old, old men say,
> 'Everything alters,
>   And one by one we drop away.'
>   They had hands like claws, and their knees
>   Were twisted like the old thorn-trees
>   By the waters.
>   I heard the old, old men say,
>   'All that's beautiful drifts away
>   Like the waters.' "

Water Spider felt his father's old fingers against his cheek. "Are you crying then, Spider? Well, that's one good thing. If you can cry at a poem, there is hope for you yet . . . But as for the Shrouded Ones, they—"

"They are dead," said the man in gold. Water Spider's father blinked. "Tragic," the man in gold continued, sadly shaking his head. "Wan Lu was slain by a demon seven years ago now. Or was it eight?"

"Eight," the old man in red said seriously. "And Jimmy Kwong died of drink a year after that, wasn't it? Under a cherry tree. They found him covered in blossoms."

"Oh, did they?" Floating Ant said.

"And of course, poor Wei Ping!" The man in gold sighed and shook his head. "Gored by oxen, you know. Tragic, tragic."

One eyebrow rose on the face of the laconic man in black. "Gored by oxen?"

"Trampled too," the man in gold said solemnly. "They didn't have the heart to show the body at the lying-in. Just propped a picture of him in front of his urn."

"I . . . hadn't heard," the man in black said. "How melancholy."

"Now cut this out," Floating Ant said.

"So it seems you are left with only one choice," the man in red said to Water Spider.

"Oh no," Floating Ant said.

Water Spider looked around, bewildered. The man in gold smiled. "After all, you do know a man who served the Emperor."

"Oh no you don't!"

"Who has fought—and vanquished—many demons in his time."

Water Spider blinked, and looked at his father. "Him?"

"No!" Floating Ant said indignantly. "Not me! The Emperor is dead, and I am no soldier. I am a poet."

The man in black looked to the little coal stove, where the ashes danced. "Not anymore."

"You?" Water Spider said, looking at his father. "You have bested demons? But I thought you were the one who ran . . ."

"I did."

The man in gold said, "Remember, Carnegie was but the last battle in a long war."

Water Spider reached out to his father. "If the Shrouded Ones are gone, then you are my only hope. Jen's only hope. Please. He is very young and terribly profane. You would like him. Please."

His father stood with his eyes downcast.

"You can take life by the haft or by the blade, old friend," the man in red said to Floating Ant. "But take it you must."

Water Spider's father looked up with hunted eyes. "I cannot."

Water Spider sighed, and stood. "You must do what seems right to you," he said. "I will not question your decision. Thank you for the tea, Father. I will be going now."

"Going? Going where? You said yourself you have nothing to go back for."

"I told you, there is a man of mine I swore to rescue. If there is no help to be found, I must try the thing myself."

"You! Don't be ridiculous, Spider." His father snorted. "You have spent your life on the wrong side of Hastings Street for such a business, boy. Writing edicts will not help you now."

Water Spider smiled. " 'If a man in the morning hear the right way, he may die in the evening without regret.' "

"If you must quote, pick someone who could write," his father snapped. He rocked back and forth on his heels. Then with a snarl he crossed the room and pulled a coat from a hook on the wall. "If you had sired a child, I would have let you go, you fool."

"Yes, Father."

"But here you stand, threatening to end my line by throwing away your own ridiculous life. Idiot." He belted the coat around his waist, old fingers shaking.

"Yes, Father."

"And children are better than poems, ah? Ever read *Municipal Gallery Revisited*?"

"No, Father."

"Well, you should." He jammed a small black hat over his bald head. "What's wrong with you, then? You like boys better in your bed?"

Water Spider colored. "No, Father." The man in gold was smirking at him.

His father held out his hands expectantly.

"What? That is, how may I serve you, Father?"

"The sword, child," said the man in red. "Give it to a man who can put it to some use, will you?"

"I don't have to take insolence from you," Water Spider snapped. He schooled his features and unbuckled his ancient blade. "Only from him."

He belted the sword around his father's narrow hips, and then, gently, placed his hand around the pommel. Floating Ant's fingers curled blindly around the grips, sure and instinctive as a baby's fingers closing around its mother's offered thumb. Water Spider examined his father, a funny old man in a tattered raincoat, with an ancient sword slung by his side. "Any stirring last words, honored progenitor?"

His father opened the door. "Oh, be quiet," he said.

CHAPTER 16

The flight back from the Southside was a long one for Raining and Lark and Wire. The helicopter's top speed wasn't much above a hundred and fifty kilometers an hour, and they had to stop twice at ancient gas stations to tap extra fuel. Wire managed all that, talking with the helicopter. Raining stayed inside, stroking Lark's hair.

She decided to make Nick's pyre on a certain hilltop clearing in the heart of the wood. She meant to do the thing immediately, even before sleep. The Southsiders believed that John Walker took their dead naked into the North Side, and there they stayed in the bitter cold with nothing but what was burned in offering for them. She would hurry back to her house to collect pictures of herself and Lark, and a lighter, and a knife, and thick socks and underwear and a woolly hat of her father's, who would not grudge it. She didn't know if only things that burned would cross through the fire, so to hell with it, she would put everything on and let the fire take what it could. And she would bring Lark with her, because she owed him that, too.

It was almost seven o'clock in the morning by the time they made it back to Vancouver. Dreary day had broken; the clouded grey sky over the Forest was weeping. The helicopter received instructions from someone in Chinatown about a good landing place, a grassy open area less than a block from Wire's apartment. The chopper had no difficulty landing, and wearily they climbed out.

Seconds later Southside infantrymen charged from cover, jumping out of doorways and rolling from beneath abandoned cars. There was a burst of railgun fire, over so fast that all Raining could see was a line of steam smoking in the air. The chopper's rotors clanged to the ground like four steel petals blown from a flower.

"Holy shit!" Wire said.

"Mom!" Lark yelled. "The copper breaked!" Raining grabbed her hand.

A soldier walked out to meet them. "Captain Ranford. Sorry if we caused you undue alarm," he said unapologetically. "We're in a hurry this morning. We are looking for Emily Thompson and we're hoping you can help us find her." Another soldier came up behind him, a tired-looking man in a rumpled dress uniform. Intelligence, no doubt.

"You blew up the helicopter," Raining said. "That's my husband's helicopter. He went all over the place in it, salvaging things." She found she was crying. "You broke it."

"It can be replaced, Ms. Chiu," said the Intelligence officer. *Ms. Chiu*, she thought, not Mrs. Terleski. This fellow knew something about her. "I'm afraid we very much wanted you not to run away again. The Mandarinate is cooperating with us on this, Ms. Chiu. That's why their people had you set down here. If we can just stay calm, I think we'll see that working together is in everyone's best interests."

Lark pouted, dragging on the hand that Raining held. "Mom, I'm hungry. Is it break-tast yet?"

Raining kept her eyes on the Southside officers. "Later, sweetheart."

"When is it going to be later?"

"Look, we'd love to stay and chat, but we have a job to do," the Southside captain told Raining. "According to your people, Emily landed about three hours ago. We found the place where she left the water and tracked her to a path at the edge of the Forest. She went down it. We want you to help us find her."

"Emily Thompson is nothing to me," Raining said. "You know where the path is. By all means, go and get her."

The captain grunted. "Very kind, I'm sure. But Major Oliver here has suggested that we had better have you with us. You will help us search."

"Mo-om, is it later yet?"

"Not yet," Raining said.

Wire was looking very worried.

"All right, Captain." Raining tried to keep her voice level. Remember those computer familiars, she told herself. The Intelligence man would have one that was very good at telling truth from half-truths and lies. "Take however many men you feel you need, and follow me."

The captain gave his orders.

"Eight men?" Wire said incredulously. "You need eight men to go down a path and find one girl who's supposed to be on your side?"

"We may need to split up and search. And, unofficially, shut the fuck up. Ma'am."

Raining cut in before Wire, furious, could get herself in any worse trouble. "Let's go, shall we? My daughter needs to eat and go to bed."

"Ms. Chiu, where is your husband?" Major Oliver said gently.

The grey sky wept and wept. "On the North Side," Raining said. The Southside soldiers flinched and glanced at one another.

Major Oliver nodded. "Yes. That makes . . . I am very sorry." He turned to Captain Ranford. "It's my guess that going into the wood could prove dangerous, even with Ms. Chiu. I suggest—" He hesitated. "I suggest we take her daughter into custody while she is in the Forest."

"You sister-fucking son of a bitch!" Wire yelled.

"Shut up, Wire."

"How can you—"

"Please," Raining said. She looked at Ranford. "You can't take my daughter." She spoke as calmly and steadily as she could. "That isn't right. I told you, listen to me,

Emily Thompson means nothing to me. You can have her. You can have her with my full cooperation. But don't take my daughter.'' Major Oliver started to shake his head. ''Listen to me! Ask your familiar! Am I lying? I'll do what you ask, goddammit!''

''Major?'' Ranford said.

The Intelligence man looked away from Raining. ''It's not just her. It's a matter of motivating the Forest itself. We believe the Forest is a Power, like the North Side. We think it has the interests of this family at heart.'' He looked at the captain. ''I really think it would be safest this way. For the men. That is my considered opinion.''

''Your opinion!'' Raining tried to make her voice sound less hysterical. ''Listen to me. The Forest doesn't think like that.'' She looked back and forth between the two men. ''You want the truth? Here's the truth. Anyone who comes into the wood with me under threat is not coming back. That's the truth, all right? Spare your men. Spare yourself.''

''This solicitude is late in coming,'' Captain Ranford said. ''Arnott, you've got kids, right? I'm putting you on the little girl. You'll stay out here under the command of Major Oliver until relieved.''

''Mommy, you're hurting my hand,'' Lark said.

''How am I supposed to explain it later?'' Raining said, her voice rising. ''I'll come out of the wood tomorrow, alone, to get my daughter back. What will I say? How will I convince your people that I tried my best?''

''I guess you'd better not come out alone,'' the captain said. ''Wilson, Conrod, your teams are with me.''

''No! You don't understand—''

''Ms. Chiu,'' Ranford said, ''shut the fuck up. And that's for the record.''

Corporal Arnott stepped forward apologetically. ''I'm awfully sorry about this, Mrs. Terleski. I knew Nick a little, back in Compulsory. I promise you I'll take good care of the little one.''

''You had better, mister.'' Raining did not release Lark's hand. She looked at Major Oliver. ''She's the daughter of my House. Whether I am dead or alive, there's no bolthole in hell that will save you if anything happens to her.''

The Intelligence man nodded gravely. ''I understand.''

Lark's little face began to crumple. ''Mo-om,'' she wailed.

''Do you hear me?''

''Pay no attention to her, Major. Let's get moving.''

Major Oliver said, ''I hear you.''

Wire stepped forward. ''At least let me stay with Lark. She knows me. I volunteer to come with her.''

''That's an excellent idea,'' Major Oliver said gratefully. ''I think that would help both Ms. Chiu and her daughter. Not to mention me.''

Wire looked at him with loathing. ''Go lick a cat's ass, you toad.''

Raining knelt in the wet grass and cupped her hands around Lark's little face. The streaming rain had soaked them both. Lark looked back at her unhappily, her bangs slick with rain, her black eyes wide and solemn. ''Sweetheart, I have to go with these men for a little while. I need you to go with Wire and Corporal Arnott and Major Oliver here until I get back. Can you do that for me?''

Lark sniffed. ''No.''

''We have to.''

''No!''

Raining hugged her very tight. She wanted to hold her forever, but she could not bear the thought of soldiers pulling them apart, so she ended the hug before Ranford could get angry.

''Mom?''

''Yes, sweetheart?''

''Even you'll come back next day, won't you?'' Raining nodded, unable to speak. Lark looked gravely at the soldiers preparing to go into the Forest. ''But not them, right?''

''No,'' Raining said. ''Not them.''

Lark and Wire stayed behind with Arnott and Major Oliver. Raining set off into the wood with Captain Ranford and his men.

The day was dark with rain. The trees towering around

them were many times as thick and tall as the scrawny little things the Southsiders were used to. Any coastal wood would have been a revelation to them—and this Forest was awake as other woods were not. The air was heavy with its green power. The Southsiders were very professional, but Raining could tell they were edgy. Telling them they wouldn't come out alive probably hadn't relaxed them, either. Southsiders tended to think of themselves as rational people, but in Raining's experience they were as superstitious as anyone, and more scared of the unseen for denying it.

They went quickly, following Emily Thompson's trail. Raining felt badly for the girl. She had not failed to notice the lack of her usual stumpy good humor, or the traces of bruising around her eyes. But nothing that could happen to Emily—nothing—was worth Lark's life. Or even the lives of these toy soldiers and their despicable captain. She could not imagine what earthly reason the girl could have had for coming to the Forest.

Raining reminded herself that Emily was in her twenties now. She was a woman, not a girl anymore. Raining was finding it increasingly difficult to take any woman seriously if she didn't have children.

"You're smiling," Captain Ranford said suspiciously. "What are you thinking?"

"That it is hard to take men seriously under any circumstances at all."

"You're very humorous, for a woman whose husband has just died."

"Oh, well," Raining said. "Any skull can grin."

They picked up speed, running now, the tracker Johnson first, then Raining with Captain Ranford, then six enlisted men in loose single file. The path was very muddy, and dotted with pools of standing water. Raining's dress was soaking wet and filthy. It stuck to her legs as she ran. It made her furious that her best silk dress should be ruined like this. Heavy boots pounded through the puddles at her back.

They came to a fork in the path, but Johnson barely hesitated before taking the right-hand way. Rather than having the usual HUD contacts, his familiar had been augmented with a special visual array. The lenses were the size of glasses, with IR and UV emitter penlights attached. The whole assemblage was bolted to his face with screw-plates attached directly to his bones. Raining had never seen a tracker in action before, but she'd met a couple off duty. They tended to be a little flamboyant; good fun compared to the average stuffy Southsider. The one she remembered best used to wear little pieces of steel jewelry screwed into his faceplate when he wasn't on duty.

"Let's go," Ranford said. "Emily's prints will get harder to follow if the rain picks up any."

One of the enlisted men said, "Where are Bishop and Ozolinsh?"

"What was that, Mister Lubov?"

"Bishop and Ozolinsh, sir. And Smythe. And Grant." Private Lubov kept his voice steady. He seemed poised and professional, like the rest of them. But young, so young. He couldn't be more than a year or two past his Compulsory, Raining thought. Twenty-three years old, maybe. Body like a god, no doubt, beneath his mud-splattered uniform whites. But such a young man. "Maybe they took the other fork in the path back there."

Ranford stared down the path behind them. "What in hell . . . Johnson?"

The tracker turned and loped twenty paces back along the way they had come. "No sign, sir." His voice was a little shaky, but he steadied it. "No tracks, no traces. No IR signatures within visual range."

"That's impossible. We've only been on the trail three or four minutes."

"I know that, sir. They're just . . . gone."

Ranford stared at Raining. "Where the fuck are my men?"

"I don't know." She kept her voice very low and steady. "You would be making a mistake if you thought I controlled this wood, Captain. I do not. I don't know where your men are. If I did, I would tell you. Please remember that seeing you out of here is my only hope of getting my daughter back.''

"Fuck." Ranford turned away. "Shit. Shit."

"Sir?"

Ranford waved Johnson back. "Yes, come on. They'll have to make their own way out. We can't let Emily make up too much time on us."

They went fast. Raining had expected the Southsiders to be slowed by the twists and turns in the path, the sudden dips and puddles, the roots and deadfall that cluttered the trail. She should have known better than to underestimate the Southside soldiers. Nick's familiar had been so full of crusty humor, salvage lore, chemical specs, and site information that she had forgotten what five years with a familiar devoted to physical optimization could do to a man. The Southsiders' reflexes were unbelievable, their movement through the wood fluid and incredibly fast. No doubt they could keep at it for hours too. Raining was quickly gasping for breath. She wondered how long it would be before she was picked up and carried.

If the Forest was going to let them find Emily, they would be on top of Ms. Thompson very, very fast.

"Help!"

The line of running figures froze.

"Who the hell was that?"

"Samuels, sir!"

The voice seemed to be coming from a few dozen meters away.

"How the fuck did you get off the path?" Ranford demanded.

"I don't know, sir!"

"Calm down, son. Yelping won't help. Are you standing still?"

"Yes, sir. Didn't want to risk getting lost, sir."

"Good man. Now listen, Samuels: can you fire a burst straight up to give us your exact position? I think I can spot you, but I'm not quite sure."

A railgun hissed somewhere to the right. Raining thought

she caught a glimpse of the beam between some branches.

"Johnson?" Ranford said quietly.

"Got him, sir. Twenty-seven meters along this line." The tracker pointed. His lenses were cloudy with green shadows.

"But he was right behind me," Lubov said quietly. "I mean right on my tail. His splash was on the back of my leg."

"Cut the chat—Samuels, we're going to fire a burst. Tell me when you see it." He nodded to Lubov.

"Got it," Samuels called.

"All right. I want you to take five steps through the forest towards us. Go around a tree if you have to. Cut through any underbrush, though; try to keep a straight line. When you've taken five steps, I want you to stop and fire again to give your position. Is that clear?"

"Yes, sir."

"All right, go ahead. I'm going to keep talking now, so you can use the sound of my voice to orient by. Nice and easy. Don't panic and you'll be fine. A little wet in the pissing rain, but—"

A line of tracers flared in the undergrowth. A moment later they heard a branch come crashing down. "*Shit!*"

"You okay, Samuels?"

"Yes, sir. Barely." Samuels laughed shakily. "Nothing spooky, sir. I cut the fucking branch off with the gun and it just about brained me falling down."

Ranford grinned. "Watch your fire there, Mister."

"Sir? He isn't any closer," Johnson said quietly. He scratched at the side of his face as if brushing away a cobweb.

"What?"

"Samuels is now at twenty-eight point five meters, this line." He pointed.

"Goddammit."

Ranford turned on Raining. "You go get him."

"Sir?" the ensign said.

"What the fuck is it, Lubov?"

"If she goes off the path for Samuels, that leaves us on the path without her. Sir."

Ranford swore. "Right. Shit."

"Samuels, are you holding your position?" Johnson called.

"I can hear you better," Samuels called. "Hang on." Shambling noises came muddily from the undergrowth.

"Don't move!" Johnson yelled, and Ranford added, "That's an order, Mister!"

"What?" It was harder to hear Samuels' voice.

The soldiers with Raining shouted. "Don't move—stay still you stupid fuck—stand and fire, dammit!"

The movement in the undergrowth stopped. Another burst from the railgun. "Thirty-eight meters from this position," Johnson whispered. His lenses were green discs now, set flush into his face. In this light, Raining thought, he looked as much like a creature of the Forest as her mother. Rain crept in tracks down his flat green eyes.

"Lord have mercy. Christ have mercy. Lord have mercy," Lubov said.

They kept trying until Samuels panicked.

When the last sounds of the lost soldier had faded into the Forest, Ranford turned and spat. "We're going back."

"Thank you," Raining said.

Ranford nodded tightly. "I am not an idiot. Or such an asshole as you think. If Emily is in here, she's either coming out when the Forest wants her to, or not at all." He looked at Raining. "This place is like the North Side, isn't it?"

"I tried to tell you."

He nodded. "That you did, Ms. Chiu. But I had my orders. You'll have to accept that."

"Tell it to your men, Captain. They're the ones who are paying for it."

Johnson moaned. Lubov looked sick but determined. "There's the matter of your daughter too," Ranford said. "Or had you forgotten?"

"I hadn't forgotten."

Ranford took a deep breath. "Well my lads, here's for it. Everyone hold hands now; no more getting separated. We're going to head back the way we came and hope Ms. Chiu can get us out of here alive. If not, I'll see you on the North Side in a few day's time, eh?'' He shook his soldiers' hands, Lubov first, then Johnson. ''Are you all right there, Mister Johnson? You feel a little shaky.''

''I don't—I think I'm getting sick,'' Johnson said, breathing raggedly. ''Get me out of this hellhole and I'll be fine, sir.''

''Good man.'' Ranford clapped him on the back. His eyes were anguished.

They had just made it back to the original fork in the path when Johnson dropped to his knees, whimpering. ''Oh God, Oh God, leave me alone!''

''Christ, Johnson. Johnson! What's wrong?''

Johnson's body convulsed. He shrieked and started tearing at his face. Ranford grabbed his hands but Johnson bucked, throwing him aside. He had dug bloody welts into his face. Blood and mud were smeared on his lenses. His fingers clenched as if trying to pluck the lenses out, but slid down their smooth surface. He shrieked again and again.

Lubov and Raining watched in horror.

''Stop it! Stop it!'' Ranford shouted. His railgun was trained on Raining's face. ''Make it stop.''

''I can't!''

''If he goes, I swear to God I'll kill you too. Do you hear me?'' Ranford yelled at the Forest. ''Leave Johnson alone or your pet human buys it. Are you *listening?*''

''It doesn't work like that.'' Raining was crying. ''It's not a person, Captain. You can't bargain with it. It doesn't understand anything you say. All it knows is that you might hurt me, and you made Lark sad.''

Johnson stopped clawing at his eyes. Gurgling, he smashed his head into the ground, once, twice, again, again. Finally his body slumped and stilled. Ranford looked from it to Raining. Tears mixed with the tracks of rain on his face. ''All this? All this because a little girl might be sad?''

''Mercy is a human thing,'' Raining whispered.

''Oh my God,'' Lubov said.

Green shoots and little white runners had pushed out from under Johnson's lenses. A faint green blush of something like moss showed in the bloody runnels around his eyes.

Ranford looked at Raining. "You're dead."

She screamed. Shadows burst from the forest as a line of white fire tore steaming through the wet air.

Ranford blew apart.

Raining gasped.

Beside her, Lubov put his steaming railgun gently on the ground. Then he popped out his contacts. Holding them in one hand, he unzipped his uniform jacket and unwound the computer-gel pack from around his waist. He put the components of his familiar on top of the gun. He rolled up the leg of his uniform pants and unbuckled a knife sheath from around his calf. He dropped that on the pile too.

Then he looked at Raining. "Please, miss. Can you get me home?"

"I'll try," she said.

She prayed for him and she held his hand, she did everything she could, but finally she stumbled over a hidden root. She let go of his arm as she fell and the Forest swept between them like a river and carried Lubov away.

Two minutes later the path turned a corner and she was home.

CHAPTER 17

David Oliver waited at the edge of the wood for Captain Ranford to return. They were very close to Wire's apartment, so he sent Corporal Arnott there with Lark and Wire and a couple of extra guards. He stayed at the edge of the Forest, pacing back and forth under the blossoming cherry trees, wondering if he should have let anyone go in there. A light, steady rain was falling.

After a time he heard what sounded like railgun fire. Dread crept into him. His worst fear was that Raining had been killed, that Lark had been orphaned because of him.

More waiting. Then more shots. Then there was only the rain.

An hour passed. There was no sign of Ranford and his men. David posted two pickets to watch the path, in case anyone should come out. Then he walked to Wire's apartment to collect her and the girl. He called for a helicopter and in a few moments they had been flown to Government House, where the Southside forces had set up their temporary base of operations with the support of Huang Ti.

He felt terribly weary.

After seeing that Wire and Lark were safely under guard in a small shrine room on the first floor, David turned his attention to Emily's governess, Claire.

Claire had turned up rather by accident. Huang Ti had told the Southsiders the location of Li Bing's house. David had immediately detailed some men to see if Li Mei was there. In fact, she had come and gone again, but when the trackers arrived, they had found Claire asleep on a couch in the front room.

David spent more than an hour going over Claire's story, trying to sift through what she remembered of Li Mei's comments for any extra clues to Emily's movements or motivations.

"Christ have mercy, how many times have we covered this?" Claire said wearily.

"I sympathize with your frustration," Major Oliver said. "I'm tired too. Let's try leaving the question of Emily and going back to the massacre at the barracks."

"Sweet Jesus."

"Try to sympathize with the families of the men and women who died."

"That's a cheap shot, Major."

"Is it? They died. You didn't. Naturally we are curious. Now, you said you had a dream."

"Not a dream. A vision."

"Could you explain the difference?"

"A dream comes from inside. A vision is sent."

"Thank you. And you believe The Harrier sent you this vision?"

"To get me out of the barracks. Yes."

"In your mind, then, your survival was not a matter of chance."

"No."

"And then you followed your mother—The Harrier is your mother, correct?"

"Can't you tell by looking? I have the family nose."

"Mm. You ran after her, turned the corner, and found yourself face to face with our Chinatown liaison. Water Spider."

"That is correct."

The man from Intelligence looked up at Claire. "You are convinced that your mother acted deliberately to save you. Presumably she also meant to bring you together with the

Minister for Borders. Can you tell me why she would have done that?''

Claire remembered Water Spider, standing on the side-walk in his elegant silk robes, all his arrogance gone. Eyes defenseless; his life unfolded by The Harrier's touch.

For the first time, Claire wondered what it had been like for her nameless father to be borne up by The Harrier and joined to that clear infinitude. Like falling toward the white stars, maybe. Like falling between them.

"Ma'am?"

"I don't know," Claire said. "Why Water Spider? I never thought of that. I truly don't know."

The Intelligence officer looked at her. "Now we're getting somewhere."

In two hours of questioning, Claire hid nothing . . . but she was disturbed to find how much she wanted to hide. She did not want to tell Major Oliver about the little dead boy haunting Emily's dreams, or her mother's visitation, or what she knew about Water Spider and Li Mei. The urge to con-ceal these things made her feel guilty and uneasy. So she washed out her memories of the last few days with truth as if with iodine, hoping that after the sting would come heal-ing.

"All right," Major Oliver said at last. "That will do for now. You will be reassigned to light duty, but I will request that you be stationed here, where we can talk to you im-mediately should the need arise. Accommodations have been arranged for you."

"Thank you, Major." Claire rubbed her face with her hands. "Was I hallucinating, or did I really see Jackson's ghost this morning?"

"In my professional opinion?"

"Yes."

"At the time you saw Lieutenant Jackson's ghost, you had barely slept for twenty-six hours. Under extreme stress for the last seven. Could it have been a hallucination? Of course. But I wouldn't rule out other possibilities. Vancou-ver is a funny place. Eight of our men were swallowed whole by a forest this morning. You have a very odd history yourself, Claire." He shrugged.

"In other words, you have no idea whether I'm crazy or not."

Major Oliver gave her a tired smile. "You are welcome to seek out a second opinion."

The Southsiders had taken Wire and Lark to Government House—in a helicopter yet, though it couldn't be more than a mile and a half from where the Snows had ambushed them on the edge of the Forest—and put them in what must have been a little altar room cluttered with Buddhas, and left them there so long that Lark finally fell asleep on the couch. With infinite caution Wire eased her lap out from under Lark's head, terrified the girl would wake up, but badly needing to stretch her legs. She had just managed to shift Lark's head onto the couch and stand when the wooden door of their little holding cell slid open and David Oliver walked in.

Wire held a finger to her lips. Major Oliver nodded. Silence hung heavily in the air. The long night without sleep had finally caught up with Wire, leaving her limbs feeling heavy and slow, her skin sensitive, almost feverish. Gold and blue peacocks peered up from the gorgeous carpet underfoot. "What time is it?" She murmured, the words thick and muzzy in her mouth.

"Almost noon."

Wire wondered if there was still a guard outside the door with Major Oliver here. Probably. "Funny place to keep your prisoners," she said.

"The dungeon's full up."

She couldn't tell if he was joking or not.

The first time Wire had called them prisoners, back at the edge of the Forest, Major Oliver had argued with her. That was before the railgun fire had started inside the wood. It seemed like a long time ago. But Captain Ranford's men had not come back, and neither had Raining. There was no question that she and Lark were anything but prisoners now.

"We have an arrangement with the Mandarinate," Major Oliver said. "Is there something I can get you?"

"Out of here." No response. "Water, then."

Oliver slid back the door and said a few words to the guard. (Aha! There *had* been one out there.) Footsteps hurried in the corridor, voices called in Cantonese. Wire couldn't hear anything clearly enough to make sense of it. Someone beat a small gong. Then the door slid shut and the noise fell away as if cut with scissors, leaving the same heavy Buddha silence behind.

Major Oliver was in his early forties. No bulky muscles: rather ropy for a Southsider. Lean-faced. The young men from the Southside had always struck Wire as loud and silly, but somewhere around the age of thirty they all seemed to grow into a curious kind of silence, different for each one. In Nick's case the silence shut you out, empty as the prairies while he worked on a truck engine or studied circuit diagrams. Major Oliver had a different kind of silence, a listening kind. His listening was like a well so deep you found yourself talking into it; your words falling into that deep quiet. You leaned forward, straining to hear the echo.

"Anything else?" he asked her.

"More food. Apple juice for Lark, when she wakes up."

"We'll get some."

"She can't drink that disgusting soy milk stuff, and I don't blame her."

"We'll get the apple juice."

"Yeah, well. Okay. Thanks."

Major Oliver smiled briefly. Tired crow's-feet gathered around his eyes. "Do you still want me to lick a cat's ass?"

"Until it bleeds," Wire said. They both laughed at that, and then immediately Wire hated herself for laughing with him. Traitor. The deep silence started to close over them again. "Sorry about your men," Wire said.

"Are you? I'm surprised. We just chased you across the mountains. Took your friend's daughter by force. Brought you both here against your will. Why shouldn't you be glad Ranford's men haven't come back?"

"That's sick." Wire grimaced. "They were just doing their job. Good grief, they're only boys with muscles."

The major regarded her. "I wonder if I would be so understanding."

"I know what it's like to be lost in the Forest," Wire said. Remembering the way the cedars creaked and swayed overhead. The way the rain dripped down. She touched the locket at her throat, the cameo Raining had made for her.

"Ms. Chiu painted that charm, didn't she?"

"How did you know?"

"Part of my job. As the Intelligence man with the Chinatown file I studied a lot of tape of Ms. Chiu. Looked at a lot of her work. She's very good, isn't she?"

"Did you have Nick's apartment bugged?" The Southsider had the manners to look uncomfortable. Wire laughed. "Boy, I'll bet you got an earful." She stopped. "Did he ever hit her?"

"Nick Terleski was a good man."

"Did he hit her?—Look, *I've* hit her, okay? So you don't have to cover for Nick."

Oliver looked away. "I don't know for sure. Maybe shook her once or twice, early on.—Did you know he played hockey?"

"Nick? I had no idea."

"Not in the Infant's league, of course. But there's a six-team league from the other Service units. No familiars. He played left D. Not a great skater. A lot of grit. You try to get the D rattled. Forecheck hard. We had a guy on our team, Dan Sheehy. Always a yap or an elbow. Nick drove him crazy. Could not get a reaction out of him. Eventually Dan just left him alone. He knew Nick would always take one for the team." Oliver glanced at Wire with the ghost of a smile. "I tell you, our boy Dan could have learned a few things from Ms. Chiu."

Wire laughed. "You want to see my Fat Picture?" she said, taking the locket off. The major crouched down next to her. He needed a shower. But then, so did she. There hadn't been much time for anyone to bathe or sleep in the last twenty-four hours. Oliver turned the locket over. Wire liked his hands.

Suddenly he cocked his head as a priority transmission

came through. He listened attentively. Moments later a supplementary landscape of data began to slide across his contacts like reflections of a countryside streaming across a truck window. "I have to go," he said, rising and returning the locket. Halfway out the door he turned and gave her the strangest, most attentive look, the brother perhaps to his curious silence. First at her; then, even longer, at Lark. Data slid before his eyes, unread. "I wonder how this will all turn out," he said.

"No you don't," Wire said, surprising them both. "You think you already know, don't you?"

Silence. "I have to go."

"Don't you?"

He turned away.

When he was gone the silence settled back like a fat man sinking into an armchair. "Well, damn," Wire said. Lark was still asleep. Wire fingered the locket. Her own face, running to fat. Hair done up. Raining's little threat that she would turn into her own mother.

No, that wasn't fair. The woman carved on the locket could be in her future. That was one of Raining's great gifts, really: to look into the future and face the hard things there. And Wire had always said, what use is that? You have to look for the sunshine if you want to find it. . . . But maybe Rain was right, maybe she would grow old and plump. Not, oh, of course, someday—but for real.

Maybe Ranford's men would never come out of the Forest. Maybe David Oliver would be killed by sniper fire. Maybe Lark—Stop. Stop that.

One of the Buddha statues began to hum.

No, several of them were humming. And they hadn't just begun, they had been doing it all the time since she and Lark were brought to this room. Before that, probably. Wire hadn't noticed it before, that was all. The chanting was very soft, quieter than silence even, but very powerful. The planets might make such a sound, spinning and swinging through space. "Well, what do you think about all this?" she whispered to the nearest smiling Buddha. He was made of carven jade; tiny rubies glittered on the side of his nose, and one above his left breast, and one gleaming richly from his naval. Two more hung in his pendulous ears. "Is everything going to be all right?"

The jade Buddha regarded her with a benevolence that could shatter stone. A serenity that could unmake worlds. It beheld her utterly, and she dropped her eyes. Then, with glacial slowness, the stone Buddha winked.

Wire scowled. "Oh, sure, fine," she growled. "What do gods know, anyway."

CHAPTER 18

While Wire and Lark were confined in the little shrine room in Government House, Water Spider was waking up on the wrong side of Hastings Street to the sounds of his father making tea. His mind was hazy with sleep. They had rescued Jen, though: he remembered that. His father's old fingers had gripped the hilt of his ancient sword and a power had woken in him that Water Spider had not seen before. For the first time he beheld the man who had been one of the Emperor's knights in the dark days of '04.

Then they had come back, stopping at Li Bing's house to get Li Mei. Water Spider made them do that. He knew Huang Ti would sell her to the Snows. That fat man had loved the idea of importing some muscle for the Mandarinate. Now the muscle was sitting with its boots on Huang Ti's desk. Water Spider wondered how much the pompous fool was enjoying the sensation.

He opened his eyes and winced against the daylight. How long had he slept? Three hours? Four? He was getting too old for this. His father was ninety-six and perfectly spry, but that was magic, no doubt. Magic or the pickling effects of decades of plum wine.

The good-tempered kettle chuckled and wheezed. Small cups and saucers rattled from a cabinet. Then *clink*, the lid of the little teapot coming off. Then his father prying up the tin lid of the tea canister, *squeak*, and the spoon, *shtump!*

digging into tea dry and brittle as beetle shells.

The wonderful musty secret dark green smell.

Dry tea scooped into the pot, rattling like rice falling on a tile floor. Floating Ant's stove got to its punchline and the little kettle shrieked with merriment. Floating Ant picked it up. Hot water, still laughing helplessly, tumbled into the teapot. Water Spider imagined the tea leaves unfurling, opening their arms to the hot water as to a lover's embrace.

Water Spider wanted only to curl up and go back to sleep while his father took care of everything . . . but he was not a boy anymore. The cherry blossoms were beginning to fall for the forty-fourth time since his birth. An unlucky year, Pearl had teased him. Her fortunetelling appeared to be reliable.

He remembered his parting with Pearl.

His father's wrinkled face appeared, bending over him. "Come," the old man said quietly. "Take some tea with me."

Li Mei slept on a pallet, her mascara smeared. Jen lay on the floor, snoring lightly, with a pile of clothes for a pillow. Water Spider and his father took their cups out onto the balcony, stepping quietly so as not to wake the sleepers. The balcony faced north. Water Spider's heart leapt to see the white-capped mountains there, cold and pure. As always their distance, their cold serenity, infused his spirit with feelings of honor and mystery. "I have missed this view of the mountains," he said. "I had not realized how much."

Chickens clucked on the next balcony over. Floating Ant poured the first cup of tea from his small pot and held it up to the mountains. "Greatest health," he said, and then dumped the tea out into the street below. He had done this for as long as Water Spider could remember; a fit and pious way to dispose of the first cup, which connoisseurs usually declined to drink, anyway.

Floating Ant had made some of the precious Ti Kuan Yi for them, the Iron Goddess of Mercy. The color was perfect, the pale green-gold of new leaves; the taste was delicate yet dark, an elusive, acrid yin flavor, like the smell of hemp burning out of sight on a damp day. "I was amazed to see you drinking almond tea when I came here yesterday, Father. What happened to the man who said, 'You may drink low wine, for wine leads down to the Nine Hells; but to drink poor tea is blasphemy, for tea leads up to Heaven'? Next I will find you drinking lowest quality jasmine.''

"Never! I was not drinking almond tea. Impudent child."

Water Spider grinned. "What was it, then? A white lichee? With *milk* in it?"

His father did not answer. Curious, that he should deny it, but Water Spider remembered the almond smell clearly, sweet and bitter at once. Then he remembered the smell of burning paper. And his father, all in white. "Oh." Water Spider's hand froze in the act of bringing his cup to his lips. "It was White Blossom in that pot." A traditional suicide in some of the older parts of Chinatown. "That was why you would not let me drink it," Water Spider said. "That was why you wore robes of white. The death you had dressed for was your own."

"We do not need to talk about these things," his father said.

"Those old men were there to see you to the spirit world."

"I will not talk of this with you."

The wind had come up like Heaven's broom and swept the sky clean while Water Spider slept. In the clear afternoon sunlight he could plainly see the forests on the lower slopes of the North Shore mountains. Higher up, their snowy peaks blazed with white fire. Together they drank, father and son, and beheld the day.

"Your man is hurt in spirit," Floating Ant said, glancing back at Jen. "His body sleeps, but his soul is wounded."

"He is lucky to live at all. Lucky that you came to draw him out of hell. I am ten thousand times grateful. You saved my honor with his life."

"Hell is not so easy to leave as that." Floating Ant closed his eyes. "Our darkest hells we carry within." He glanced at his son. "Do you know that saying, 'Cowards die many times before their deaths; the valiant never taste of death

but once'? No? Well, you always were shockingly ignorant.''

"How can I express my grief at having failed you?"

"Wah! Now, no need to get all stiff and offended." Floating Ant laughed. "You always were a little crab: mince,
mince; pince, pince! No, heavens, Spider: I am ninety-six
years old. Of course I know more than you. Shakespeare,
that was. From *King Lear*. No, *Julius Caesar*. *Lear* is 'Thou
shouldst not have grown old, before thou wert wise.'
Well . . ." He sipped his tea. "Remember, I grew up in a
Peach Blossom time, an ordered, peaceful world. I did not
need to learn how to fire a gun or purify water. As a young
man I visited Shanghai and Paris and New York, and it was
easy. It truly was a global village back then . . . and we the
village idiots. We felt we had tamed the world. We forgot
we lived only at its whim, like pilot fish swimming at the
shark's flank. Then the world woke up, and reminded us."

He took a little more tea.

"I suppose you have wondered why I chose to die a thousand deaths, ah? Why your father, one chosen by the Emperor, should have been the only one to betray him, to run
from the great battle at the Carnegie and live forever with
that shame. You need not answer. I know this must be true.
. . . Do I know the answer to this question? How can I? It
was very long ago. But I can tell you what I think I remember, looking back through the long wine-colored years.

"You see, I had a little boy at home. I had a little boy,
and the times were very dark. Many parts of Chinatown
were *taonan* then: the crazy fear, the mob fear that makes
a man kill for a cup of rice, or a bicycle, or a gun. Everyone
was desperate to run, but there was nowhere to go. To the
east, the Hill had woken, born in the dungeons of Simon
Fraser University. An evil set of buildings if there ever was
one. Dark monsters spilled from it. Downtown was swallowed overnight in a Dream of glass and steel. The bridges
were clogged with panic; monsters rose up to feast on the
people trapped there. For a time, Main Street remained clear,
but then the Sikhs walled off Little India to outsiders, and

that route was closed. A warlike people. I don't know what became of them.

"Up the Fraser Valley, the rivers threw off their dams. They did no other evil to people that I heard, but thousands drowned in the floods. Everything ran on hydroelectric power then; within three days it was gone. By then, the water was going bad.

"How could I leave my wife to this? My little son?" He looked at Water Spider. "I could not find the way. Some did. Not many of the Emperor's men had families, but some did. Those men managed to find a way to die. I could not."

Water Spider held up his empty cup. "So, in a way, I am responsible for what you did that day."

Floating Ant blinked. "Of course not. This was more than seventy years ago. You were not that boy, Spider. That was my first son. We named him Chang An, but called him Peanut, because of how he looked on the ultrasound at fifteen weeks. By the time he was born, we were in the habit of using this name."

"I have a brother? Where is he?"

"Oh, he is dead. He died only a few days after the Carnegie battle. Maybe ten. The water was very bad. He took a fever and all the water left him, shitting and vomiting. He burned down like a birthday candle, not even one year old. Poor little Peanut. . . . No brother. Very sorry. No need to cry, Spider. This was all a very long time ago. I made many tears for this boy already, and for his mother. Their spirits rest easy. Here—wait only a minute. I shall put the kettle on again, and refresh the pot."

Floating Ant paused at the balcony door with the teapot in his hands. "So, Spider?" he said softly to his son. "Did you think sorrow was new?"

To the north, the mountains were just as they had been before Floating Ant began his tale. Just so cold and pure and distant. *What is real? My weeping son.* Floating Ant said, "Sorrow is a hidden continent. Only when a man discovers his own grief does he see the broad landscape of sorrow, stretching away, away."

"More tea," Water Spider said. "Please."

He only slept, I said. The herbalist agreed.
"Here," he said, his nails the color of the moon
    Tapping my boy's cheek,
Light as moths bumping on a bamboo screen.

"The shadow passed him over, like a cloud,
  Nothing more." Our manly paper drum confidence.
    I smiled and held my wife's hand
Feeling the thin sand trickle of my luck running out.

They had clams and noodles for breakfast, fried together
with duck's egg. Floating Ant was a very loud cook, rattling
and banging his skillet on the iron stove, cursing the food
when it had the impudence to burn and fussing over his
teapot like a hen with a prize egg. Water Spider was used
to his father's cooking, but the red chili paste Floating Ant
had worked liberally into the noodles was a shock to Jen
and Li Mei. Sleep fled their bleary eyes as if pursued by
demons.

"The sauce I got from a friend in the building, who
knows someone in the Marina, who got it from a sailor in
Seattle, who got it from a man in Portland, who makes it
with peppers from Baja." Floating Ant peered at Jen, who
was slowly turning the color of a lobster. "Is it too strong?"

"Pain is the way of the warrior," Water Spider said cal-
lously. "Your story is impossible. We don't have that kind
of trade."

"You mean the official government of Chinatown has not
sanctioned it. But there are plenty of merchants in Double
Monkey's part of town who are doing a nice underground
business. Every day cargo comes through the port that you
never see, because you don't look on the north side of Hastings Street." Floating Ant refilled Li Mei's cup. "Have
something to drink. Sometimes that helps."

Li Mei looked down at the fresh tea, which was still boiling hot and smoking fiercely. "Ten thousand thanks," she
gasped.

"Wah! I have made your breakfast too spicy! My hum-
blest apologies."

"Nonsense. 'Sdelicious," Water Spider said, scooping another mouthful from his bowl. "You can't be serious about people shipping goods up from Downtown East Side docks. Too dangerous."

His father shrugged. "Not so dangerous as it was once. And for the right price, you know . . . We have a great spirit for business, in this community."

Water Spider laughed and shook his head. "I wonder if the Minister for the South knows of this."

"Open-palm Johnny? Of course he does. That is his job."

"You know him?"

"He is often in this neighborhood, Spider."

"I did not know that."

His father grunted. "Then I suppose you were not meant to." He swirled a noodle around in a blob of chili paste. "The world is getting smaller again, I think. More dry land between the Islands, less ghost-water. Easier to get from city to city. More radios. Maybe soon mail service, weather reports, newspapers. TV! There is money to be made. Mind you, we will not make it if the Snows take over our little town."

Li Mei coughed. "Has it come to that?"

"Well, not officially, but you see how it goes. The Snows are in Government House, at the invitation of the Purse, your Huang Ti."

"Dog-fucker," Jen growled.

"What is he to do?" Water Spider said. "You know what the Snows are like. If they occupied the building first and asked my permission after, I would smile and serve tea too."

Jen grunted. His hairless head and face were hatched with thin scabs and stubble. "What happened? Why should the Snows fight with us?"

"We are not fighting," Water Spider said. "We would be mad to fight. The heir to Southside has run away from home and Winter is here looking for her."

"He also killed my mother," Li Mei said. "Or had you forgotten?"

Floating Ant stood noisily. "More noodles for anyone?"

"If this is not a time to fight, what is?" Li Mei said.

"Provocation is irrelevant," Water Spider said evenly. "As servants of the Government, we may not allow our personal feelings to color our judgment. We must do what is best for Chinatown. And no matter what outrage the Southsiders commit, we dare not fight with them. We simply have no hope of winning."

"Not with surprise? A concentrated attack, when they are not expecting—"

Jen grunted. "The Snows are always looking." Warily he picked up a clam with his fingers and scraped the chili paste off on the side of his bowl. "We could attack them with guns while they lay asleep in their beds with five to one odds and be lucky to get out alive. Compared to them, we have no fucking science at all."

"The barbarians found a way," Li Mei said. "Perhaps if—"

"No chance," Jen said flatly. He rubbed his chest. "The Honorable Minister was careful to prove this to me. White devil broke my fucking luck," Jen said between mouthfuls. "Ballsy, though."

Water Spider remembered walking down Pender Street, the moon in his breath, the goddess asking him to name his heart's desire. A second later she was gone, leaving Claire behind like her shadow. "The Iron Goddess of Mercy," he murmured.

The others looked at him. "Mm. Nothing." He wondered about the white goddess and her daughter. He wondered about the half brother he had never known, dead of cholera or dysentery before his first birthday in the dread days of the Dream. He sipped his tea. The flavor spiralled down into him, a secret road. Where would it lead, if he chose to follow it? He could not say. The continent of sorrow, perhaps.

"Our best policy would be to find Emily Thompson," Water Spider said. "When Winter has his missing heir, he will become more tractable."

"Do not be ridiculous!" Floating Ant snorted. "Of course we must repel the Southsiders. What kind of Minister could hand over his government so easily?"

"An unemployed one?" Li Mei suggested.

"Father, you do not understand what kind of soldiers these Snows are."

Floating Ant waved the Snows away. "Big guns, big muscles, yah yah yah. Irrelevant." He began to declaim:

> " 'Those who win one hundred triumphs
> In one hundred conflicts
> Do not have supreme skill.
> Those who have supreme skill
> Use strategy to bend others without coming into
> conflict.' "

Li Mei winced. "Quoting Sun Tzu. Emily Thompson does this too."

"You say, quite rightly, we cannot fight with the Snows," Floating Ant said. "Therefore, we must make the Snows leave of their own will." He put another helping of noodles into his own bowl. "There are ways of doing that besides acceding to their every demand."

Li Mei's thin eyes thinned some more. "I begin to think you may be a very cunning old man."

"A lovely idea, Father. But how do you propose to execute it?"

"They are very superstitious," Li Mei said thoughtfully. "They are not at all comfortable with the depth of ghosts and demons out here."

Jen said, "They are right to be scared."

"Then perhaps we should ask the Shrouded Ones to stand aside," Floating Ant suggested.

Li Mei blanched.

"You said the Shrouded Ones were no more, Father!"

"I did no such thing. Don't glare at me, Spider. Jimmy Kwong told you that. He was the one wearing gold."

"Then there are Shrouded Ones still?"

"Of course there are, you ignorant boy. You wake up alive in your bed every morning, don't you? Who do you think has been keeping the demons from your streets?"

"But I thought you said—"

"True, yes, very true: things are less dangerous than they

were. But some demons still prowl—as poor Jen here has learned to his cost. In fact, as the Powers unravel, there may be more minotaurs now than years ago, albeit smaller and less powerful ones. Perhaps we should ask the Shrouded Ones who remain to come back to Chinatown at last; to cross Hastings, and let the demons come too, under their watchful eyes. It is a risky plan: but the things that creep forth from the wrong side of Hastings Street will not be so easy for a Snow to dismiss with a burst from a gun, ha?''

Li Mei sipped her tea. ''Yes. You are very definitely a cunning old man.''

''I am a poet—or I was once,'' Floating Ant remarked. ''Do you know that wonderful line by Emily Dickinson? 'Tell the truth/ But tell it slant.' ''

''There is a Mandate for you,'' Water Spider said sourly.

Floating Ant was unperturbed. ''Your problem, Spider, is that you keep thinking about your enemy, about these Southsiders. In fact, they are irrelevant. This is Chinatown. It is the Tao of Chinatown you must heed. The Dragon, Double Monkey, and The Lady in the Garden are the Powers here. Align yourself with them, and you cannot go astray.''

CHAPTER 19

After eating, Floating Ant sent Water Spider and Jen out to purchase groceries and spy on the lay of the land. Once they were gone he shuffled around his apartment, performing a sort of feeble tidying. "I am afraid it has been a very long time since I entertained a young lady of consequence," he said to Li Mei.

One corner of her mouth quirked up. "Pray, do not trouble yourself. Yesterday, it is true, I would have been appalled by the company I am keeping. Today I am merely another unmarried woman without family, unemployed and in disgrace. Ask yourself, rather, if you care to be associating with me."

"My dear girl! Your presence illuminates the day. In future years I will devour the memory. Remembrance is the food of the old, you know."

" 'What does a memory weigh?' " Li Mei said.

"Wah! You know this little poem of mine?"

"My mother was a great admirer of your verse. She gave me a book of it once, for a New Year's gift." Closing her eyes, Li Mei chanted:

> " 'What does a memory weigh?
>   The bed we shared is light, now;
>   Heavy the sighs of our parting.

My soul in my breath, my breath
In my oath. My life pawned,
Flesh and sinew for air and angels.

Now you are dust; my words only air.
What can I do, kneeling in the garden,
But eat these stones?' ''

Li Mei opened her eyes. ''The words don't die. And their beauty does not grow old.''

Floating Ant grunted. ''Hm, yes: to escape time through art. Can't blame the ones who try. Nobody wants to die, ha? Nobody wants to grieve. Hm, hm, yes: 'gather me into the artifice of eternity . . .' and so on. Art to cheat death! . . . 'Once out of nature I shall never take/ My bodily form from any natural thing . . .' '' Floating Ant glanced sharply at Li Mei. ''Famous poem, that one. Taught it in schools, when I was young. But the same man, older, wiser, wrote, 'I must lie down where all ladders start/ In the foul rag and bone shop of the heart.' ''

Li Mei said, ''When Grandmother was lying on her death-bed, my mother cut the flesh from her own arm to make a magic soup to make her well. Tears ran down her face and blood fell on the floor. I can remember her holding Grandmother's mouth open, trying to make her drink this soup, but she would not. Her spirit ran away that night and hid. I was a little girl then. All my life I have wondered if I would be brave enough to cut out my flesh for my mother. Now I know I would have done that too. Only I was not given a chance to be brave. I made one mistake and then there was no time to fix it.''

Floating Ant touched her hand with his old fingers. ''There is this about life: it will always give you another chance to be brave. Sorrow for your mother, yes, do! It is right and proper. But do not believe this will be your last chance to grieve.'' He shook a finger at Li Mei, pretending to scold. ''Regret is a luxury you have no time for. Think! What will you do about these cold white strangers in your kingdom?''

"I told you. I no longer work for the Government. I am the disgraced attendant of a dismissed Minister."

"You are waiting perhaps for Huang Ti to solve the dilemma?"

Li Mei laughed raggedly. "Hm. You have a point."

"One does become wise with age. Otherwise, why bother growing old? Merely to feel your joints swell and your bladder shrink?" Floating Ant sniffed. "So. You know this man very well, Winter, the leader of the Snows. Think like him. Become him. You have brought your people to this alien land. You are looking for a jewel of great price." Li Mei closed her eyes, nodding. "You have been here one day. Now, relax all the way down to *dan tien*, and ask yourself—

—"Well, gentlemen: what do we do next?"

Silence around the table as Winter met the eyes of his staff. David Oliver noted his own discomfort, put it aside, and met his commander's gaze. He had become quite good at detaching his feelings from his actions. Still, he was surprised to hear himself say, "I suppose that requires a clear answer to another question: why are we here? Sir."

Winter regarded him. "Repeat that question, Major."

"Why are we here, sir? What precisely is our objective? The men feel some confusion on this score."

"And you, Major? Do you share their confusion?" All eyes turned away from him, except for Winter's. Narrow blue eyes in a seamed face.

"Sir, I do."

Winter leaned back in the red lacquered chair at the head of the conference room they had borrowed from the Mandarins. Most of the men looked absurd, sitting in these ornate thrones inlaid with emblems in mother-of-pearl. Winter alone was at ease seated in the Dragon chair at the head of the table, one booted foot crossing his other knee, his old frame still lean and tough as a hank of wire. "Why do you think we are here, Major? Give me your honest analysis."

"First, to respond to the massacre of our men and fulfill the contract between ourselves and the Mandarinate." David

listened to his calm voice tick on, mindless as clockwork.
"Second, to recover Emily."

"Those are our two principal objectives, Major. You may
tell the men as much, when they come to you to profess
their confusion."

David wondered if it was simple weariness and lack of
sleep that had created this frightening sense of disconnection
between himself and what he was doing. He could even feel
the pressure of the situation, the fear of drawing down Winter's enmity; but he felt it distantly, like an argument coming
from a neighboring apartment.

Ah. He was speaking again. "The problem, sir . . ."

"You have balls, Major. I like that." Winter smiled.
"The problem is that the men think I've gone crazy, to send
them out here in these numbers to claim back one young
woman. If they have to put the good of their community
ahead of their wives and family, why shouldn't I? How can
I risk widowing their wives over a family quarrel between
Emily and myself? Is that an accurate summation, Major?"

"I think that covers it, sir."

Winter looked slowly around the table. "If I go to Hell,
gentlemen, it will be because I chose the good of my community over the good of those close to me. If I go to Hell,
it will be because I decided a long time ago I would rather
be damned on behalf of my fellows than saved at the cost
of their lives. Yes, of course, it makes sense from a purely
military perspective to commit ourselves fully to the conflict
with the Downtown barbarians. History is full of half-assed
campaigns that turned into fiascos because the man with
overwhelming force on his side was too timid to deploy it.
Economically, Chinatown has been unwilling to pay for an
operation of this scale. I chose to go ahead anyway. It sets
a bad precedent, everywhere our troops are hired, if we are
willing to let them be destroyed piecemeal.

"A student of Chinese history could put a darker inter-
pretation on the Silks' unwillingness to recruit us in force.
Isn't it reasonable to assume that the Mandarins would prefer that there be very few heavily armed foreigners occupying their territory at the conclusion of hostilities with

these barbarians? History teems with people conquered by the very armies they asked in to help them fight some third foe. I direct your attention to the conquest of Spain by the Berbers, for instance.

"Still, the question remains: how can we pay for this operation? Partly, we must use this exercise as advertising. Communication technologies are re-establishing themselves at a tremendous rate across the continent. I now talk regularly with representatives of dozens of major population centers. Such a thing would have been unheard of even twenty years ago. So, we have an ever-increasing number of potential clients, and an ever-increasing opportunity to advertise."

He stopped and looked around the table. "Advertise. You don't know this word, do you?" He shook his head. "To make other people aware that we have a military product of proven efficiency." He ran his hand back through his white hair. "We may also find that if we present a complete bill for this operation to the Mandarinate, the presence of large numbers of heavily armed troops will make them think twice about refusing to pay it."

Is it true that you beat Chinatown's ambassador to death last night? David said. Oh, no, no words came out this time. And how does this figure into the long range diplomatic relations between our communities?

No. No words came out.

Winter opened his hands. "And yet, clearly there is a personal side to this. I want Emily back. This is not a secret. Why? Why was I willing to risk, and to lose, a platoon of men just to bring back one twenty-year-old girl? I am right on this one, Major. We are classing Captain Ranford's men as missing and presumed dead, are we not?"

"I believe so. Sir."

Winter closed his eyes. Opened them. "If Emily were only a member of my family, I would let her go. Hell, plenty of kids need room to grow up when they get to be her age. She's had a lot of responsibility put upon her. And it isn't just that she is going to be my successor, either. It would be a pain in the ass but I could train someone new, if that was all there was to it. It is not. There is a compact between myself and the North Side. A contract. As far as I know, the Southside is the second largest single community on the North American continent. There are cities with a higher total population, if you look at the Dream metropolitan areas. Here in Vancouver is one. Minneapolis-St. Paul, Little Boston, and San Diego are others. But those populations exist in islands separated from one another by no man's land. On this entire continent, I believe only Madison, Wisconsin came through the Dream with a larger unified core of survivors.

"Believe me when I tell you, we owe our very existence to the contract between myself and the North Side. Blood is required. But I can't live forever, and Emily is the last of my line. She in turn must pay the price for our collective survival. That is why we are here, gentlemen. We are here to recover my granddaughter. As soon as Major Oliver and his fellows in Intelligence produce her, we can go."

It was almost a relief to feel the axe come down, David thought. "Do you have any suggestions, then, sir? Emily appears to have entered the Forest. As I feared, we have been unable to penetrate it."

"Burn it down," someone grumbled.

David sat bolt upright. "I strongly recommend no such action be taken against a Power, gentlemen. Need I remind you of what happened with the napalming of Harlem, or the Tampa Bay nuke?"

"No, you needn't," Winter said drily. "Obviously, we don't want to deal with any Powers, let alone provoke them. And napalming a forest to get Emily out of it would leave me with a barbecued heir, eh, Mike?"

General Beranek sighed. "I just hated losing the men. I don't like fighting here, sir. The terrain is so ridden with minotaurs . . . It gives the men the creeps. Frankly, it gives me the creeps. And the food!" He glanced at Martha Antoski, the quartermaster. "The stuff your men have been buying . . . Some of it gives me the shudders, Martha. Little crispy green things that used to live in the sea. With too many legs. I mean, I don't know what half this stuff is. And when I ask, I wish I hadn't."

Winter laughed out loud. "Oh, the soldier's life is a hard one, eh?"

"Sir, I know it sounds foolish, but these can be serious concerns. Morale is not good to start with. First the massacre. Now stories about Ranford's men are getting around. The food is one more thing to make the men uneasy."

"Then let's get this thing done, shall we? I want a three-block-wide firebreak cleared on the Downtown side of Granville Street, gentlemen. I want to make it clear Downtown that their party is over. Major Oliver, I very much wish to speak to Li Bing's daughter. It is now almost three o'clock Saturday afternoon. If we still haven't found Li Mei by tomorrow morning, I want you to start going door to door."

"With respect, sir, that will ruffle a lot of feathers."

Winter shrugged. "If it reduces the length of our stay in Chinatown, it will be worth it to the slants as well as us." Winter rubbed his eyes. It occurred to David that the old man had probably had even less sleep than he had since Friday morning.

"I just worry that out of ignorance we may—"

Winter held up his hand. "Don't out-subtle yourself, David. Of course this culture is complex. We can never understand it as these people do. Don't try. I realize that the role of Intelligence is to understand the opponent. But you can't allow the opponent to dictate the nature of the engagement. We must play to our strengths. We have enormous tactical and technological superiority on our side. Let that be our Alexander's sword, shall we?"

Perhaps like a weary chess player Winter wanted simply to clear the board as fast as possible and get to the endgame, rather than thinking through the ornate complexities of the earlier positions. But ornate thinking was David's job, and he was very tired of it. He had not slept in thirty-two hours, and although he was still thinking lucidly, the widening split between his feelings and actions was disturbing.

What if Raining had been killed by Ranford's soldiers? This was the nightmare that haunted him. What if Lark's mother was dead, and he was the cause of it? How could he face that little girl? How would he take care of her?

It was a great relief to see Winter, almost three times his age, with his city at war and his family falling apart, still strong enough to take the responsibility from David's shoulders, and put it back on his own, where it had lain so heavily for more than seventy years. Which was why, however many times he disagreed with Winter on this policy or that decision, David Oliver would have followed him anywhere. Winter never shirked. He took responsibility, he led from the front, and if they had to send an army into Hell, he would be the first man to step through the hot black gate.

—But of course Li Mei cannot understand that about you, Floating Ant thought. You hard old man of the prairies.

It was almost six Saturday evening and Floating Ant was watching the sunset from his balcony.

She is angry and guilty and bitter, and shocked by the touch of grief. Oh, but you and I . . . Grief no longer sneaks through the window when she visits us. She comes to the front door now, and we have won the bitter wisdom to open it when she knocks.

A beautiful sunset. "It ended as it began—" No. Ah. How about:

> The day was dying as it had lived;
> In splendor.

Nice. So I fiddle, while the city burns.

Chickens clucked on the neighbor's balcony. Floating Ant held a little cup of wine. Winter, he thought, your men would look at me, an old Chinese man, half-drunk poet and notorious coward, and think we could not be more different. That young lady in the other room, or my son with her, washing up the dishes, must see you monstered in hideous white, a hero to your half-machine men, the cold north like a raven on your shoulders. Who could be more different?

The young are aliens to you and me.

Can you remember the great Edmonton Oilers teams of the 1980's? Gretzky, Coffey, Messier, Anderson, Grant Fuhr the best goalie in the world: a black man playing hockey, can you imagine? I never saw the old Canadians, of course, with Jean Beliveau and Maurice Richard and all the rest of them, but I still think the '87 Oilers were probably the greatest single hockey club to ever play the game. If not the greatest, surely the most beautiful.

You will want Li Mei. You have to, I can feel it. She thinks she is the cause of your invasion, because she brought your granddaughter here. Maybe she is. She is part of the fate which has pulled your child's child from you, the last of your line. That's the thing that hurts, isn't it, old man? We all try to cheat death. And you, you were smarter than I. All those years that I pursued my Muse, you already knew that way was hollow. You were nurturing your people and your family.

Now that I consider it, you will find Li Mei, won't you? Unless we hide her well. These young ones don't remember DNA fingerprints, protein analysis, police dogs, spy satellites. But you do. Too much of that technology has military uses for you to have lost it entirely. Maybe you have nothing more advanced than dogs, but you'll use anything you've got. The end of your whole line is at stake. The great death.

I was a fool to dawdle here. I should have had the Shrouded Ones meet us somewhere else. I too have become accustomed to this latter age; I think myself invisible because I live on the north side of Hastings Street. But you don't care, do you? This neighborhood holds no awe for you.

Where could we hide her? Where could she go that you could not follow?

Floating Ant took another sip of wine. Ideas came to him. Weak ones at first, then steadily stronger, like tea steeping. And finally the beginnings of a very deep idea indeed.

Sun Tzu wrote:

"Skillfulness in moving an opponent about comes through
        Positioning the opponent is compelled to follow
        And gifts the opponent is compelled to take."

"No," Floating Ant whispered, shocked at the thought which had come to him. "You cannot ask such a thing of me." But an idea had come to him, a dark idea that would not leave. It remained, insistent, like a poem that had to be written. Like a baby whose birth could not be refused.

There was a knock at the door. Floating Ant did not rise. If it was a friend at his threshold, he could finish his wine. If it was an enemy, there was no point in resistance.

Jimmy Kwong's jovial voice filled the small apartment. Floating Ant smiled and sipped his wine. Moments later Jimmy found him on the balcony. "So then, old man! How did it feel to wrap your fist around a hilt again? Is that what put that smile upon your wrinkled face?"

"Actually, I was musing on time. What a lie it is, that time makes one suffer less. In truth it merely teaches one to suffer with more poise."

Jimmy's smile faded. "You speak truly there." His hand on Floating Ant's shoulder was cold. "After the Emperor died, when the rest of us put on the white, I set aside all fear and care. For many years I thought the Shrouded Ones would be forever—like candles with their flames pinched out, never burning down. But the world is changing, the magic is wearing away, and we are wearing with it."

"Do not say such things."

Jimmy shook his head, smiling a little. "The Shrouded are not in the world of good luck or bad. We speak the truth we see. Our time is coming to a close. But enough of this! I bring gifts from the Lady in the Garden." Floating Ant saw that all three of his friends had come: Jimmy in gold, Wan Lu in red, Wei Ping all in silks of black and trimmed with the white the Shrouded always wore.

"These are the men who were with you yesterday morning," Water Spider said. "*They* are the Shrouded Ones?"

Jen and Li Mei were frankly staring.

Jimmy Kwong held up a flat cherrywood box, lacquered red as blood. He bowed before Jen, whose eyes lit up. "The Lady returns to you something you had lost." He raised the box lid and took out the Lady's gift. It was an ordinary straight razor, the folding kind that opened with a flick of the wrist.

Jen recoiled, horror working his young face. "No! Take it away!"

"Did you not realize that the gifts of the gods can be cruel?" Jimmy said. "Do you not understand they may not be refused?"

"Please," Jen whispered. "Please. I can't. That thing is evil."

Jimmy held out the razor. "But is it yours?"

Tears spilled down Jen's scarred cheeks. Finally he nodded.

"Then you must take it," the Shrouded One said.

Jen grabbed the razor. He held it so tightly in his bunched fist that the skin above his knuckles turned white and the tendons in his wrists stood out like cables. "Never trust the fucking gods."

Jimmy Kwong came to stand before Water Spider. "I have learned to fear these gifts," Water Spider remarked. "Would you oblige me, and give me mine in private?" He stepped over to the balcony.

Jimmy nodded and followed. When they were away from the others he opened his white-gloved hand. In it lay a small ring with a green-gold band, the color of sunlight streaming through new leaves. The setting was of a lotus flower, made of white gold so delicately shaped it seemed it must tremble if a breeze slid by. At the flower's heart, a single diamond glittered like a star caught in a chip of ice; like frost burning in the winter sun.

Water Spider reached and took the precious thing. "There must be some mistake," he said. "This is too small for me." It was evident at once that the ring would fit on none of his fingers. "Perhaps the Lady meant this for Li Mei."

"The Lady does not make mistakes."

Water Spider closed his hand around the ring, and then put it in his pocket. "I shall treasure it," he said. But inside, he was disappointed. However terrible Jen's gift had been, it was clear he understood it. But the ring was a mystery to Water Spider. He felt curiously left out. Ever since the moment he had realized that Pearl's great aphrodisiac was not to bear his children, he seemed to have been losing direction, losing focus. Twenty hours later he no longer had his lover, position, direction, or security. He, who had worked all his life to avenge his father's disgrace—avenging it on his father, as well as the rest of the world—now found himself adrift.

And all the while, that same disgraced father condescended to him, and charmed his subordinates, and was held in esteem by the Shrouded Ones he had betrayed. It was unfair, terribly unfair. Water Spider felt he must choke on the gall of it, but the long practice of politics kept expression from his face. And what a strange, empty triumph that was, too.

He returned to the others with a careful smile.

"Well," said Floating Ant, with forced jollity. "Don't these gifts always come in threes? What about me, ha? What do I get?"

Jimmy Kwong looked at him in surprise and gestured at Water Spider, Jen, and Li Mei. "Why, *them*, of course."

Li Mei's thin eyebrows rose. "Us?"

"Don't be coy, Ant," said the Shrouded One in red, testily. "We fought our battles. You must fight yours."

"But I am a poet, not a soldier!"

"You were a soldier for the Emperor," said the Shrouded One in black. Each word terse and final as stones dropping into a well. "You can never leave that service."

"You have only been on leave," Jimmy said. His smile was tired. "But now it is our turn to rest, my friend. Your long holiday must come to an end. You earned it: we know that. You alone among us had to go on living, and living, and living; perhaps all those years awaiting this day, though you did not know it. Do you not see? You are the Lady's chosen champion. This struggle is your gift."

The Shrouded Ones departed, leaving their gifts behind. They had agreed to withdraw the protection from spirits and demons that had kept the borders of Chinatown safe. (Water Spider's Borders, whose security he had arrogantly assumed to be his own doing.) They would try to follow any demons or minotaurs who chanced into Chinatown, limiting the damage where possible.

"We should not leave Li Mei here," Floating Ant said nervously after the Shrouded Ones had gone. "So. I have, have some friends. Both at the Hong Hsing Athletic Club, in the heart of the Dragon's domain, and in the Lady's Garden. I will take Li Mei to one of these places, where she will be safe from the Southsiders."

"No one can enter the Garden and return," Li Mei said.

"Well, now, that is a popular, but, ah, misguided belief. There are ways. I lived here before the Powers woke, you know. Few people understand Chinatown better than I."

Li Mei looked impressed and dubious at the same time.

For his part, Water Spider felt little. "As you wish," he said. He had a cup of his father's wine in his hand. He was no very good drinker of wine, but he was thinking he would try to get the knack of it.

"May I ask Jen along?" Floating Ant said. "It is dark and the streets are rough this side of Hastings."

Water Spider waved with the hand that held his wine cup. "As you wish, Father. Honored Father." He laughed. His other hand was in his pocket, fingering the ring the Lady had bestowed on him. It yielded no secrets.

There was a brief bustle as the others prepared to leave the apartment. Then Floating Ant was beside his son. "Have you ever made a study of Tu Fu?" Even through the blur of wine, Water Spider thought his father seemed agitated.

"As you wish, Honored Father. Ha, ha."

"You should." Floating Ant pressed a small book into his son's hands. It was in the old Chinese style, a long panel of bamboo rolled into a cylinder and held closed with a ribbon, with characters painted inside in Floating Ant's matchless calligraphy. "Tu Fu was a scholar too, you know. Trained for the highest office, a brilliant student. And then, unaccountably, he failed his exams. This was to be the pattern of his life: always torn between the service he so desperately wished to give his Emperor, and his other life of family, and wine. It was a terrible time; the very end of the

T'ang dynasty. Barbarians pressed always on their border as they press on ours. We have no Emperor; theirs was weak and fickle.'' Floating Ant pressed Water Spider's hands around the bamboo book. "These are some of his poems. They have meant much to me. I always wanted you to have them. I suppose I thought they might help you understand . . . oh, everything. My life. All lives.''

"Father," Water Spider said, moved by Floating Ant's strange intensity. "I will read them. The book is short.'' The bamboo scroll was little more than a handspan wide. Unrolled it would be as tall as a tall man. "Perhaps we can discuss them tomorrow.''

Floating Ant searched his son's face. "Perhaps," he said.

The sun was setting as Floating Ant left with Li Mei and Jen in tow. Water Spider refilled his cup of wine and lit a lamp and kept his promise. He read *For Li Po* ("Given to the wind, yet resolute—so brave, and for whom?'') and *An Empty Purse*:

> . . . In fear
> Of shame an empty purse brings, I hold
> In mine this one coin I keep, peering in.

He lingered over *Reflections in Autumn*, which his father had said was the greatest poem ever written in Chinese, with its devastating last lines:

My florid brush once defied the shape of things. I watch
Now, nothing more—hair white, a grief-sung gaze sinking.

He cried when he came to the end of *Meandering River:*

> Drift wide, O wind and light—sail together
> Where we kindred in this moment will never part.

He lingered longest, though, over an early poem, *New Year's Eve At Tu Wei's Home*. Objectively he knew it was not the strongest piece, not so complex or profound or beau-

tiful as many others. Yet he found himself reading it over
and over.

> The songs over pepper wine have ended.
> Friends jubilant among friends, we start
> A stabled racket of horses. Lanterns
> Blaze, scattering crows. As dawn breaks,
>
> The fortieth year passes in my flight toward
> Evening light. Who can change it, who
> Stop it for even a single embrace—this dead
> Dazzling drunk in the wings of life we live?

He was murmuring these words aloud when the Southside
soldiers burst through Floating Ant's apartment door like
summer lightning and caught him there, with his naked eyes
still leaking tears onto the little bamboo book.

CHAPTER 20

The Southsiders did not torture Water Spider, not right away. Instead they carried him back to Government House and put him in a deserted office under guard. It was the private office of the Chrysanthemum, the Honorable Minister for the West. Apparently Betty Hsiang, whose job it was to study the Lady in the Garden, had still not been found. Dead or in hiding, who could say?

Betty's brush was famous. On the wall facing her desk hung a mountain scene, grey and cloudy; distant horsemen struggled through a treacherous pass. The characters of a poem hung in the high air like valley mist:

> Songs say the roads of Sanso are steep,
> Sheer as mountains.
> The walls rise before your face,
> Clouds grow out of the hill
>   At your horse's bridle.
> Fragrant trees line the stone roads of the Shin,
> Their trunks bursting through the paving,
> And freshets burst their ice
>   at the heart of Shoku, a proud city.
>
> Men's fates are already set,
> There is no need of asking diviners.

Upon the desk, an arrangement of dried flowers, exquisite. Surely, Water Spider thought, a man could not be tortured in such a place as this. He found his hand closing around the ring the Shrouded One had given him. For the first time he could remember, he wanted to pray to the Lady, that she protect him.

The anticipation of pain, Water Spider discovered, was bad for his character.

He had always told himself that he had the kind of courage most men lacked: the steady, selfless application that saw him accepting ever more responsibility, rising ever higher in the Government, always reliable, always efficient. Physical courage was common; even fellows like Jen possessed it in abundance. After all, that was why he employed Jen, wasn't it? To supply a certain complement of animal force and brute bravery.

But Jen wasn't with him now. He was alone. The only stocks of courage he had to draw on were his own.

What could he know of interest to the Snows? What could they hope to force out of him that they would not have already received full willingly from Huang Ti? (Johnny must be wrong. It was impossible that the Dragon should work to put that bungler on the throne. Ridiculous!) There was no information of value the Southsiders could get from him. Except he knew that the Shrouded Ones had been withdrawn. And he knew his father planned to drive the Snows out of Chinatown with ghosts and spirits. And he knew where Li Mei was to be hidden.

"The determined scholar and the man of virtue will not seek to live at the expense of injuring their virtue. They will even sacrifice their lives to preserve their virtue complete." Not so difficult for K'ung fu-tzu. He knew he would live on in his disciples. He knew he had descendants to burn the offerings to his spirit.

Not so easy for Floating Ant's childless child.

Meng-tzu said, "There are three things which are unfilial, and to have no posterity is the greatest of them." Water Spider had betrayed more than himself in failing to find a wife and start a family. He, who was so correct and so upright, had failed his father. He had performed the most vicious sort of blasphemy, using the very precepts of K'ung fu-tzu and the other scholars as a weapon against his father. What had the Shrouded One in scarlet said? *You cannot even remember what your father is trying to forget. He has been a poet, and a warrior. But you?*

In his pocket the Lady's ring warmed to his touch. He felt no salvation from it.

He wondered if the Snows would break his fingers.

Oh, the shame that would be his should he betray Li Mei and his father! The humiliation he would have to live with if, through his revelations, the plans to defeat the Snows were to collapse! What would he do when—

—No. No use. However hard he tried to focus on the shame of giving up his secrets, his imagination eluded him, returning to his body. Imagining the Snows brutalizing him. Imagining the pain they could bring to his fragile fingers. His lips. His eyes.

Water Spider's face was clammy with cold sweat. Careful, careful. Deep breaths. Deep breaths . . . Very nearly fainted there.

Perhaps the thing to do would be to confess immediately. Tell the Southsiders enough truth to seem credible, but withhold certain key things. Distort them. He would need to have something to give them, a little piece of truth. They were going to learn a certain amount anyway. What honor would there be in accepting pointless pain or disfigurement?

Water Spider half-smiled. No, the anticipation of pain was definitely not good for his character.

Do not think about what is to come. There is only this moment, this time. Do not anticipate.

> Men's fates are already set.
> There is no need asking of diviners.

It was impossible to torture a man in so refined a setting, he thought. But when the interrogator arrived, Water Spider was moved to another room.

It was quite different from Betty Hsiang's elegant office.

Small and cold. Bare shelves. Concrete floor with a drain in the middle. Even though this room was in Government House, Water Spider had never seen it. A converted pantry, probably.

Brawny Southside militiamen strapped him to a table. The interrogator, a major, stood behind them watching. "I am very sorry about this," he said.

Water Spider yelled as one of the Snows put a blindfold around his eyes. This was worse than anything he had imagined. He had imagined threats, yes. Beating. Broken fingers. But not this. Not strapped blind to a table in a cold little room. He stilled himself. "You cannot do this to me. I am a Minister of the Government."

"Not anymore. We have spoken to Huang Ti on this matter. He understands our need for immediate, accurate information."

"He said to torture me?"

"I have no intention of torturing you. I would rather not use force. If I have absolutely no other way to get the information I need, then I will consider it. But that will be your decision."

"You do not think I will believe this, Major? These are the oldest words of the torturer: this is your choice. Your fault."

"My name is David." Two clicks then, like the clasps of a briefcase opening. Tiny sounds of glass and metal as the interrogator picked something up. "I'm going to give you a needle now. This will hurt a bit, but only a little. It will help us talk more freely. There will be no permanent effects."

"If you rape my mind, this is permanent. If I tell you things against my will, the words will not jump back into my mouth when we are done." One of the guards rolled up Water Spider's left sleeve and tightened a pressure cuff around his arm. "You have no answer for this, David? Why are you not speaking?"

"Because you're right," Major Oliver said.

The needle hurt. Water Spider hissed at the pressure of strange fluid pushing into his blood. A thin cold current whipped down the length of his arm and then went whirling through the rest of his body, limbs and belly and brain and lungs.

"Now we wait for that to start relaxing you." David Oliver paused. "Here is the truth. I am going to ask you some questions. About your subordinate Li Mei, for instance— Ah: you were waiting for that one, weren't you? Let me tell you how I feel about my job. I hate this part of it. It disgusts me to do this. But I do it because someone must. There are lives at stake—many more than just yours or mine. We will not leave your city until we have recovered Emily. Right or wrong, this is the truth. Li Mei is part of that puzzle. The longer it takes us to find her, the longer we will be here, and the greater the chances are that men will die. There have already been fights between your people and mine. Two fatalities. Are your feelings of personal honor really more important than the well-being of your people? Mine are not. That is why I am here. I do not wish to cause you any pain but I will if I have to. Too many lives are at stake. Can you see that?"

It was cold. Water Spider found he was shivering.

"Minister?"

"Your words seem wise to me." Water Spider wished he could see. He wished he could touch the Lady's ring inside his pocket. "But it is easy to find good reasons to betray. Simple to find reasons to run from pain. The mind is easily confused by fear. In times like this, I think, a man must listen to his heart, not his head."

"Do you not feel for your people?"

"Major, you have closed my eyes. How can I see such a ghost idea? I can see my father, though. I can see Li Mei." The drug was beginning to work on him, whatever it was. A laugh slipped out of him. There was a long silence. Pressure grew on Water Spider to fill it. "My father was a very great poet. Did you know that?" The words spilled out of Water Spider's mouth. How surprising. "Would you like to hear one of his poems? It is called *In Time of War*.

"I would like that very much."

"It is more subtle in Chinese but I will tell it in English. But the Chinese is better. You will see it is very appropriate.

Through crossing streets the spilled men pool and
    stream, shouting
Under the mountain. There, mouths closed, the fallen
    snows
    lie, unspeaking.

"Snows, you see? Snows. Yet this was written long ago, during the Dream. A prophecy. I do not wish to speak to you!" Water Spider bit his lip until it bled, to stop any more words from coming out. *I am a spilled man. I am a spilled man.*

"What else can you tell me about your father?"

Water Spider smiled and shook his head. Very carefully he said, "I think you must torture me. If my honor must be broken, Major, at least I will take yours with me."

"You are a brave man," David Oliver said. His fingers closed around Water Spider's wrist, checking his pulse. His fingers were warm, so warm against Water Spider's cold, cold skin. He wept at the touch. Surely his life was lies and illusion and the touch of human skin was the only truth to be found in the lonely middle world. *It's a trick. It's a trick.*

"You will get a fight you did not expect, Major!"

"I don't doubt it," David Oliver said softly.

It took him less than an hour to learn everything Water Spider had to tell.

Li Mei had never been on a houseboat before. She was not enjoying it. She did not like the way the floor rocked queasily beneath her feet. She did not like the tiny dark room with its slanting walls. She did not like the stink of brine and tar and old shellfish, made worse by the smell of opium and the incense that hung around her and Jen in ropes. Instead of heading back across Hastings Street toward the Garden or the Athletic Club, Floating Ant had led them north, through the wastelands and down to the harbor, where this dilapidated boat lay moaning quietly against the pier. "A little dark hole to hide in while I make certain inquiries,'' he had said.

And so they waited in the cramped, old sea-smelling darkness.

Li Mei's mind felt dull and confused. She wished they hadn't gone through the opium den. That had been another one of Floating Ant's ideas. He wasn't sure how good the Southsiders' chemical trackers were, but at the very least they could bring in dogs. The owner of the houseboat they were hiding in had cast off and let the wheezing diesel motor drag them a mile up the inlet, close to Coronation Park. Here Floating Ant disembarked to collect more information, leaving Li Mei to the tender care of Jen, who was not much fun. Although the tiny cabin was not nearly large enough to prowl in, Jen prowled in it.

Hours passed.

The stars were still out but the black sky was beginning to pale when Floating Ant finally returned. ''Disaster! Terrible luck! I have not been able to find my friends who could hide you in the Garden or the Athletic Club. Worse than this, the Snows have taken my son!''

Jen cursed.

''I am so sorry,'' Li Mei said. ''But do not despair. They have no reason to harm him. They will question him, of course. But I would be very surprised if anything worse were to happen.'' Of course, what reason had there been for Winter to kill her mother? Li Mei forced a lightness into her voice. ''And there is at least a small pearl of luck hidden within this oyster. Water Spider will tell what he knows to the interrogators. If we had managed to get to the Garden tonight, we might have found the soldiers at our doorstep in the morning.''

''Well, we must stay here for now,'' Floating Ant said. ''We should be safe for a day or two at least.''

Suddenly Li Mei wished very much there was enough light in the little cabin to see the old man's face. ''Jen has been finding this hole unbearably cramped,'' she said. ''Do you think it would be safe for him to go out, now that you are here? Perhaps he could keep watch.''

"Mm. I don't see why not. If you like, Jen. Patrol the dock."

"Anything for an hour or two outside this hellhole," Jen grunted, slipping out.

Li Mei waited until he had disappeared through the hatchway. "You knew," she said to Floating Ant.

"Ha?"

"You knew the Snows would find your apartment. It was only a matter of time." Her mind was working clearly now. "I was right, there is no way to leave the Garden, is there? But the Snows can't know that. Sooner or later, Water Spider will tell them I am there, or in the Dragon's temple."

"And there they will go," Floating Ant said quietly. "With their guns and orders."

"Oh, you cunning, cunning old man. You will make the Snows fight Chinatown itself. You will let them throw their guns against the Lady and the Dragon."

"That war was already underway," Floating Ant said. "It was we who betrayed the Snows. One of the Double Monkey's puppets, a certain merchant I will not name, made a deal with the Downtown barbarians and sold them the rocket that killed Winter's men."

"I wondered, when I heard," Li Mei whispered. "But why?"

"Huang Ti was using the Snows as incorruptible tax collectors. It upset the balance of power for the Mandarins to have soldiers of their own. They were supposed to be a bureaucracy, nothing more. They inconvenienced people," Floating Ant said. "And of course the presence of a foreign army on Chinatown's soil was nothing but a goad to the Dragon."

"This merchant must have tipped the Dragon's men to watch for the Snows' destruction."

"I do not know this," Floating Ant said. "But if I had sold the barbarians the means to wipe out the Southsiders, I would make sure that Chinatown's borders were not defenseless, lest the barbarians become overenthusiastic about pursuing their advantage."

"Johnny Ma should be fired for this," Li Mei said

fiercely. "He should have known what was going to happen."

Floating Ant looked at her. "What makes you think he didn't?"

"But—But why . . . ? He voted in favor of bringing in the Southsiders, didn't he? He did. I remember Mother talking about it. But if the Snows had not been killed, Winter never would have called my mother to his offices last night. She would still, would still—"

Gently Floating Ant laid a hand upon Li Mei's shoulder. She shook it off and drew something the size and shape of a pocket watch from inside her jacket. She pressed a spring and the lid popped open, revealing a tiny mirror. Li Mei went to the spluttering kerosene lamp and studied her thin face by its light.

"Johnny is a subtle man," Floating Ant said. "Perhaps he is one of those who feels that Chinatown needed an immediate threat to unite. Perhaps the Snows were cutting into his bribes. Perhaps he laid a bet on the outcome of the invasion. Open Palm Johnny is not a man whose motives are easy to fathom."

"It's part of the portfolio," Li Mei said.

"That sounds like a quote."

"One of his favorite sayings." Li Mei snapped the little mirror shut and tucked it back in her jacket pocket. "You are not easy to fathom either. I understand your plan, I suppose. You want the Snows to provoke the Powers of Chinatown as openly as possible. You want to let the Powers break them, instead of us poor mortals. But why did you let them take your son? Was there no other way?"

The houseboat beams creaked and shifted, the small constant complaints of its unquiet sleep. Floating Ant's voice was no more than a whisper.

"Skillfulness in moving an opponent about comes through
      Positioning the opponent is compelled to follow,
         And gifts the opponent is compelled to take.

"Sometimes I hate these wise old men," Floating Ant said. "Sun Tzu, K'ung fu-tzu, Chuang Tzu and the rest of them. They see too clearly for compassion. Perhaps there was a better gift to give our enemies. I could not see it. And this strategy is so clear. So elegant. . . . Once before I had the choice to sacrifice a son. I did not." Floating Ant's old voice was calm. "Now I can tell you that both cups are bitter at the bottom."

CHAPTER 21

It was still early Saturday morning when Raining lost her grip on Ensign Lubov and felt the Forest like a river bear him away. A few minutes later she was home. She had slept one hour of the last twenty-six. Her voice was clipped and flat as she told her parents why Lark wasn't with her, but her body betrayed her, pacing through the house, her hands jumping like small birds, jerky and nervous. Her mother offered a box of joints to help her sleep, but Raining did not want sleep. She did not want tears or food or drink or comfort. She wanted to paint.

She painted while she told her parents what had happened to Nick. Painting, she told them that Lark had been taken from her and that the Southsiders would not give her back. She told them about leading the Southsiders into the Forest, and how the Forest had taken them, one by one. Her mother made her tea and her father brought her salty fried potatoes and a plate of fish. She painted while she ate, wiping her fingers on her dress. When her parents finally left her and went to bed on Saturday night, she was painting still.

"Hello! Hello, little girl," Nick had said to the baby in his arms as he paced gently around Raining's maternity bed the day Lark was born. Lark was just a scowl in a blanket, peering up at him. Not even as long as his forearm. How tiny she was! Her whole head fit inside his cupped fingers.

"Sit down," Raining said. "You're making me dizzy."

"Mm. Okay, okay, here we go," he said, nodding to Lark as he folded himself ever so slowly into the big armchair. "Whatever Mommy wants, Mommy gets after this night's work, hey?"

Lark continued to stare at him. Raining would never have imagined two-hour-old eyes could measure you so deeply.

"Tch tch tch—there we are, there we are. All sitting down. Now what?"

She could remember thinking, He doesn't even know he's smiling. "Okay," she said. "Now you put her on *your* tummy." He grinned, settling deeper into the chair, and did as he was told. "Ha! Bliss," Raining said. "I've waited nine months for that." The sight of her baby, lying swaddled on his big man's chest, rose through her like wine and made her eyes fill. Never had she felt so keenly how sweet life was. How sweet and how fragile. "Oh, Nick. Is it going to be okay?"

Nick lifted Lark up between his big hands. "What do you think?" he said to the baby. "Do you think it's going to be okay?—Yes, Mom!" he answered in a high squeaky voice.

"Quit that! Nick!"

"Yes, Mom. It's going to be fine, Mom." Gently he laid the baby on Raining's chest, the poor kid still as solemn as a priest in her blankets, slate-blue eyes regarding her, regarding her. The scent of her, the secret boiled milk smell of the lost world inside Raining's womb. "Yes, Mom. Everything will be okay." She felt the faintest, faintest warm touch of the baby's breath on her cheek.

In his own voice Nick said, "I promise it."

Now Lark had been taken from her and Nick had been left to die in the North Side's terrible cold. So much for his promises.

She painted and hated her painting and felt only fury and despair and painted that. Technique is not enough, she told herself angrily. It is not enough to draw and plan, compose and construct, to arrange your subject and know your theory and choose your paints and bend your wrist just so in the

execution of your comma strokes, because your feeble useless little-girl art can't resurrect the dead. And if it can't do
that, what the hell is it good for?

Only fury can bring back the dead.

Paint with your hand, your hand! Not your eye, stupid.
Feel the weight of every muscle. Feel the pull of blood. You
paint too thin. What are you saving it for, hey little girl?
Art is not about mercy. Compassion, yes. Mercy, never.
Never anything but the truth. Use more paint, goddamn it!
Layer it thick and smelling of oil and powdered bone, thick
enough to touch, heavy against the brush, feel the way the
bristles pull through the heavy paint, slow and painful as
divorce.

She painted Nick who had been her husband, who had
lived once, who loved her still. You wanted landscape?
Well, here it is. Here is a man with the man gone from it.
Here is a portrait with only landscape left. Landscape is not
pretty. Paint cold dead forehead white and still as his hateful
country. Paint the cold that cares not one damn for you or
anything you love. Hold it, hold it, hold it, *hold it*; crush it
in your fingers until welts show on your hands, until your
finger bones snap, until your blood is rubies.

No crying! No crying. Save it for the painting, every bitter
tear.

Sometime in the middle of the night, Raining stood staring
at the canvas she had been working on all day. She had
slept one hour in the last forty-three. Her hands were shaking and her skin felt thin and dry like paper and easy to rip.
She knew she must be tired, but she could not feel it. She
took a step back and examined her work. It was Nick and
Lark and they were standing in a snowy country, standing
together at the top of the Bridge on the Southside, and it
was Raining who was not in the picture, Raining who was
not there. Raining who had abandoned them.

Her mother, Bell, came downstairs, belting her dressing
gown. "Rain? Go to bed, sweetheart. You won't be able to
think until you sleep."

Raining laughed without looking away from her canvas. "I guess they aren't going anywhere."

"You can't help Nick or Lark by making yourself sick."

"I can't help them any way at all, Mom. I made very sure of that."

"You did what you could do."

"Yes, it always feels that way." Raining picked up a morsel of white paint and cut it roughly into some dark blue with her palette knife, careful not to blend the colors too much, then picked up the paint on her little 00 brush and touched a few more highlights into Lark's black-shining hair. "Everything I do feels right at the time . . . and somehow, I always end up here in the Forest. Alone."

Bell sighed and touched her daughter's cheek with her birch-white hand. She looked at the painting. "That's very good."

"Wu Tao Tzu once astonished the T'ang court by creating a marvelous celestial landscape for the Imperial Palace, and then walking into the painting. That would be good magic, wouldn't it? I could paint Lark, maybe, and pull her out. Drag Nick back from the North Side."

"Can I make you some tea?"

"I was always afraid to paint like this," Raining said. "Yes please. Blackberry."

The cookstove was down to a dull orange ember. Bell widened the flue and dug another piece of dried poplar out of the woodbox. Opening the stove door she blew gently on the coals until the fire turned yellow. She stuffed in the new faggot. The fire clasped it with thin yellow arms and licked black lines onto its pale flesh. Bell went to get the kettle.

Raining stood back from the painting. She had taken extraordinary trouble over Nick's hands, his thick oil-stained fingers. In all his enormous silence it was always his touch she understood, his hands speaking even when his voice was silent. Silent, silent, silent under the snow.

Bell came to stand beside her. "This is the best thing you've ever done."

Raining touched up a shadow under one of Nick's eyes.

"Yeah. And you know what I have now?" she said. "Paint . . . Nothing but goddamn *paint*."

She took her palette knife and stabbed into the canvas. It wouldn't go all the way through. She swore and slashed up and down the painting, smearing the paint around, picking up big gobs of blue and green from her palette and splattering them like mud across the surface. Then she fell into the big armchair and doubled up with her face in her hands and wept, huge shocking sobs, her eyes blind with tears, her heart dissolved in utter desolation.

When the tears finally stopped, her mother and the fire still remained. Raining watched the fire for a long time.

Finally she rose. Into a basket she put a suit of her father's good warm clothes, a box of wooden matches, and a pair of wool gloves. From the kitchen her mother brought her some bread and dried fish and mushrooms. From her studio Raining gathered a set of paintings, miniatures she had made while still on the Southside: one of Lark on her first birthday, and one of them all together as a family. Then, reluctantly, one of herself, a little self-portrait she had made, back when she and Nick were very much in love. It hurt to look at it. Then she took a matte knife from her studio and cut a long tress of her hair and put that in the basket too. Then she took a handful of kindling from the woodbox beside the stove. Last she took the painting she had made that day, with the spatters of blue and green paint she had flung on it like tears, and the rips where she had punctured it unmended.

She crept to the hallway closet, eased out a wool coat and pulled on a pair of canvas shoes. Her mother brought her a flashlight from the oddments drawer in the kitchen and kissed her on the cheek and held her for a long moment. When she let go, Raining eased the porch door open and stood on the threshold. Then she stepped out, and the door closed behind her with a click. She thumbed on the flashlight and made for the nearest path with her basket of sacrifices. She was half hoping Wire would be waiting for her at the edge of the wood, but she wasn't.

It was deep in the night. Far above the treetops the sky

had cleared, and a cold wind had sprung up from the north. The towering Douglas firs swayed and rocked, shaking the day's rain down in gusts. The cold drops fell on Raining. She did not put up her hood but let them fall.

A long time she walked and always climbing, heading for a high and secret place she knew. At last, breathing hard with her basket at her side, she came into a clearing on the top of a great hill. The wind blew hard and cold. Stars shone above her between rags of flying cloud.

There was a circle of stones in the center of the clearing and there she built her fire, with paper on the bottom held by rocks against the wind, and twigs on top, and kindling, and above that a few dry sticks. The wind played tricks on her ears. Downslope, an animal seemed always to be scrambling up through the brush. Branches squeaked and moaned. Far away she could hear the distant buzz of Southsider helicopters patrolling the edge of the Forest, reluctant to venture inside. Raining smiled mirthlessly. As well they should be.

She set a match to the paper and nursed her fire, sitting with her back to the north wind so it would not rush among her little flames and blow them away. The fire flared, flickered, struggled, caught. She tended and fed it. When it was strong enough, she sat back, feeling the damp earth cold and wet beneath her haunches.

The wind was strong. It pulled the flames into giddy tornadoes that swirled and vanished over the pale wood. The fire's movements were jerky, sudden, desperate. It curled steadily around some logs, blue flames bending like stalks of grain before a smooth wind. Elsewhere it burst into incendiary blooms. She wished she could paint in those hungry colors.

She put in the things she had brought for Nick, the clothes and the food and the pictures of their family, and the fire consumed them all, and she put in the tress of her own black hair and the fire bore it away. Last she put on the painting she had made that day and it blazed up, smoking and stinking of oil. The canvas went black and rotten with fire and then the flames devoured it.

When the fire had taken everything she had to give, it shrank, falling in on itself, sinking down. The wind seemed colder now, stealing the flames' warmth away, but when she tried to sit downwind the smoke choked her and burned her eyes. She settled for stretching one leg downwind so the heat could pour over it.

The fire gave off many sparks. These the wind pulled into thin, glowing streamers. One by one or in groups of four or five they threw themselves out of the embers and rushed into the night. Most were instantly extinguished. Some lasted six or seven meters before dying. A very few curled over the slope of the hill and hurtled out of sight, still burning. She watched them go. The stars above her burned and burned, and the wind rushed under them.

Slowly Raining stretched her hands out above the fire. Heat welled up in her palms and the firelight filled them with trembling shadows, so they were strange to her. She was grateful for the warmth that filled her hands. Sparks whirled and jumped around her fingers. At first she was cautious, bracing herself for quick needles of pain when they touched her, but they never did. Whether the wind flowing around her fingers carried the sparks away, or for some other reason, she was not burned. Slowly her shoulders relaxed. She no longer heard the sound of animals in the brush. The fire was everything, its flames and embers.

Long, long into the night she hunched over it, dipping her hands into its light as if into holy water. Watching as the sparks whirled and flew, light breaking around her hands like water streaming around a rock. Ten thousand fragile threads of flame, slipping between her fingers and rushing into the enormous dark.

From out of the night a voice said, "I have come."

Raining jerked her head up and stared, her eyes blind from staring at the fire. Flames still seemed to dart and flicker before her. "Who are you? What do you want?"

"I saw your fire," the voice said. It was a man's voice, a god's voice, not harsh but weary. To hear it was to feel the silence of long journeys. Raining thought she had never heard a voice that sounded so alone.

Her eyes were adjusting to the darkness a little, and she could make out the dim shape of a man across the fire from her. He was seated downwind; the smoke from the fire blew around him like clouds, revealing and obscuring his pale face. He did not seem bothered by it, but leaned forward as if to warm himself. His two hands broke into the field of firelight. They were pale hands, thick-fingered and worn with hard work. Somehow they reminded her of Nick's. "Who are you?" she whispered.

"The Southsiders call me John Walker."

"John Walker!" Raining said, but she did not disbelieve. "But—Why have you come here?"

"I saw your fire," he said again. A corner of canvas writhed and twisted on the edge of the fire, sending up a line of oily smoke. "You called for Nick. He could not come, so I came in his place."

"You know Nick?"

John Walker held up his hand. "Wait! Someone is coming." Branches squeaked and twigs snapped, heading up-slope out of harmony with the wind.

A moment later a last branch shook and two more people stumbled into the clearing. Raining could make out nothing in the darkness, but John Walker seemed to know them. He stood. "I have been waiting for you," he said.

CHAPTER 22

Emily had been lost in the Forest for what seemed like a very long time. It was late, it was dark, and though mercifully the rain had stopped, she was fairly certain that if someone had offered her a stiff shot of rye she would have taken it and to hell with religion. "'So dear, what have you given up for Lent?'" she muttered. "Sleeping and eating, to start. I'm drinking nothing but muddy rainwater. I have also decided to magnify the Lord by going without conventional toilet supplies. Or toilets."

She hadn't started talking to herself until nightfall. Until then, the Forest had been bearable. Cold and wet and gloomy, yes. Horribly cramped, God yes. Her eyes had literally ached with the desire to look across an expanse: snow, water, plains, anything. But in the Forest every view was choked off, smothered by brambles, tree trunks, limbs, dips in the path. It had stopped raining some time in the late afternoon, but if there were stars above the tangled branches, Emily could not see them. A wind had come up, making the pines wave and bend like stalks of prairie grain. It was much louder than she would have expected, gust after gust of wind crashing and foaming through the treetops. Branches cracking and splintering, dead limbs breaking off and smashing to the ground.

Even above the noise of the wind she could hear the helicopters. Back and forth, farther and nearer, sweeping overhead with methodical efficiency. She had been involved in a lot of search-and-rescue operations looking for stray troops or lost children. She knew the drill. Except this time, she guessed, they were looking for her.

She had been so focused on getting Li Mei to smuggle her out of the Southside before Winter could cut her angel free that she had eaten little at the banquet last night. All day long she had been regretting the cabbage rolls and perogies she had left uneaten. Served her right for not attending to basics. She spent a miserable hour in the late morning remembering the exact smells of steaming borscht and hot raspberry cobbler.

Here her Lenten training did her some good. Five times a year she observed total fasts, no food at all from sunset to sunset, so at least she was familiar with the pattern of her body's complaints and seductions. In a way, this fast was easier than most; usually she had to use tight discipline to keep her desires in check. But this time there was no food to eat, no temptation at all, and she could indulge herself in food fantasies that were positively explicit.

She was also extremely lucky to still be wearing her foil parka. Even though the temperature here in Vancouver was laughably mild compared to what she was used to at home, Emily kept her hood on and drawn tightly around her face, and she tried to keep moving. She was afraid that if she stopped and gave in to sleep, she might slip into hypothermic shock. Even lost in the Arctic she could at least have built an igloo and let the snow insulate her sleeping space, but here in this damned wet wood everything conspired to leach heat away from her. Never too much at a time, it was too mild for that, but a small, steady drain. Bleeding warmth as if from a small cut that would not close.

The infrared scopes her Grandfather's trackers would be using were the other reason the parka was a godsend. Besides being an excellent insulator, the foil was also highly reflective; standing on the prairie without it, she would have glowed like a bonfire in an IR scope. A tracker's familiar might well be trained to pick out the heat signature of a soldier wearing foil gear, so she kept her face turned down

and her hands jammed into her pockets to make her IR profile as scant as possible. She wondered what her signature
looked like. A fox? A badger? Hopefully this wood was
crawling with such small heat traces.

Saint Barbara and Saint Simeon, it was chilly. She
couldn't keep walking forever. Sooner or later exhaustion
and hunger would catch up with her.

At first, fear had kept her going. Early in the morning she
had actually heard sounds of pursuit behind her. Terrified,
she had labored to put on speed, running through an agonizing stitch in her side. Then she tripped over a root hidden
in a puddle of water and fell so hard her head rang. Covered
in mud, she clawed wildly for purchase and lurched back
into a run before the fog had fully cleared from her eyes.

She had dropped into a stumbling jog soon after, her lungs
beating like dying moths in her chest and her mouth feeling
as if it were stuffed with wet wool. Then down to a walk.
Then down to the ground. She lay there for some minutes,
heart pounding so hard it hurt her chest and made her body
shake, trying to listen through her own ragged, whooping
gasps for sounds behind her. She was determined to stagger
off the path and into the bush to hide if they were still
coming. They weren't.

Long minutes had passed. From time to time she heard
distant shouts. Twice she caught the sound of railgun fire,
very far away. Once, much later in the afternoon, a soldier
had cursed and stumbled through the bush shockingly close
to her. She had crept behind a tree and crouched there, frozen, until long after he was gone.

She wasn't sure why she hadn't been caught. Any good
tracker should have been able to follow her, even in the rain.
And any group of infantrymen should have been able to run
her down without breathing hard. Whether she would have
been able to suborn them and turn them to her own uses
was another question. That was the sort of thing her familiar,
and her angel, and her life, had made her good at. She was
Winter's heir, the second-most powerful person in Southside. She owned their loyalties, now and in the years to
come.

—Used to own them, her familiar said. You abdicated, remember?

Emily nearly cried then. Not quite, but nearly.

As the day wore on, exhaustion made it hard to sustain a good, useful fear. The midafternoon was particularly unpleasant; a long, aimless journey on shaking limbs weak from hunger and a fevered mind dizzy from lack of sleep. She had actually walked into a tree, which was painful and a little funny. The second time she did it, it just hurt.

By dusk her body had found its second wind. Burning up muscle tissue now. Hooray. When dark fell, her fear came back. A good dose of fear, Emily discovered, could clear her head wonderfully.

She wondered if it mattered which trail she picked to walk along. Would this one more than another lead her to Raining's house in the wood, and some hope of sanctuary, or at least to the edge of the trees, or the sea? Or was she destined to wander in this Forest until it chose to let her go? Or maybe she was going to wander under the light-strangling trees until she died. There was no divine plan, and Emily's only hopes for salvation lay in her own rapidly fading powers. That's what Claire would say.

She walked unsteadily into the darkness. It had stopped raining hours ago, but cold water still dripped from the cedars. There were a lot of noises in a dark forest at night, she discovered. She was surprised by how much she hated not knowing what made each one.

She wondered how long the flashlight Li Mei had given her would last.

"Ninety-nine bottles of beer on the wall,
   Ninety-nine bottles of beer!
   If one of those bottles should happen to fall . . .
   Ninety-eight bottles of beer on the wall!"

"Fifty-four soup bowls of borscht on the floor,
   Fifty-four soup bowls of borscht!
   If I were to eat just a little bit more,
   Fifty-three soup-bowls of borscht on the floor!"

"Eight roasting squirrels on a homemade spit,
    Eight roasting squirrels on a spit!
    I'd have no problems devouring it,
    Seven roasting squirrels on a homemade spit!"

There was a very depressing moment when she reached
zero. She was getting very hoarse, and she thought she
might as well lie down here as any other place. She had
done her best and tried her hardest, but she didn't know
what to do anymore; she was tired and cold and filthy and
shaking with hunger and if her best wasn't good enough,
then to hell with it. As her soldiers said. She looked for a
long time at the gaping mouth of a split-trunked cedar,
where she could probably just squeeze in. If she was lucky,
it wouldn't get much colder than the
    —six degrees Celsius, her familiar said,
it was already, and anyway she had tried. She really really
had, and damned if she was going to cry, she had nothing
to cry about. It would have to be someone else who rescued
those children; poor unlucky innocents, they froze too, out
there on the Bridge, because even God could not reasonably
ask her to do anything more in this hateful freezing eternal
hell of a forest. Not even God.

She climbed into the cedar's trunk. It was dark inside and
smelled of wet wood and mud and mold. The floor was a
litter of dead leaves and pockets of moss and pine cones,
obviously cached here by a chipmunk or a squirrel. Emily
forced her way into the hollow trunk and sat staring out into
the wet night's darkness for a long time. Then she com-
mended her soul to the Almighty, turned off her flashlight
to save the battery, curled up, and tried to doze.

Brightness exploded across Emily's closed eyes as her familiar tried to wake her by firing every pixel on her HUD
lenses.

Someone was shaking her by the shoulder. "Miss Thompson? Miss Thompson?" A male voice. Southside accent.
Had to be a soldier. She had been caught. A flashlight beam
played over one side of her face. "Miss Thompson?" His

fatigues rustled as he bent over her. "Miss Thomp—"

Emily jerked up, smashing his nose with the back of her head. Twisting, she drove an elbow into his stomach. "Goddammit!" The soldier's flashlight fell to the ground but didn't break. Emily dove out of the tree trunk and tried to scramble into the forest.

The soldier was faster. Incredibly fast. One arm grabbed her around the waist. She folded, then snapped back with her head. This time he was ready for it and she missed. He grabbed one of her wrists. She spun into him, free arm going for a back-knuckle strike. He crimped her wrist in a joint lock. Sparklers of pain went pinwheeling up her arm and suddenly she was on her belly trying not to scream.

"I'm not out to get you. I'm a friend."

"From the Southside?"

"Yes."

Emily went limp, as if sobbing with relief. The soldier crouched behind her. "How long have I been lost?" she said.

His fingers loosened around her wrist. "I'm not sure. More than a day."

"It seemed like forev—" Still talking, she jerked her arm back, hard, smashing his nose again with her elbow. He staggered back and she jumped down the path.

She got maybe three meters before he tackled her. This time he put an elbow lock on her. It felt like her cartilage was tearing, burning, bleeding. She couldn't think for the pain. She found herself trying to burrow through the ground to escape it, twisting, anything to take the pressure off, driving her face into the cold wet ground of moss and mud and cedar needles. "Ah, please! God! Please!"

"Shut up." Blood from his nose dripped onto her neck. He spoke very softly. "I am your only friend in this world, Miss Thompson." He slid his hand down her arm to her wrist. Much of the pain in her elbow faded immediately, leaving a hot, torn, buzzing sensation behind. His knowing fingers slid one thin pain into her wrist like a hot needle and held it there. "Are you done running?"

She didn't answer.

"Are you?"

She didn't answer.

"You better be."

She wished she could see him. When he touched her, her familiar could pick up GSR figures, but she needed a better look to get an I.D. No pupil dilations in the dark either. She remembered the weight of his body on top of her and the agony in her elbow. "Are you going to rape me, soldier?"

"No!" Genuine shock.

Thank God. "Kill me?"

"No."

"Then let go of my wrist."

Silence.

"Let go of my wrist."

"I think you broke my fucking nose." Silence. "I'm not a fucking saint, you know."

Hope began to bloom wildly in Emily's heart. He was just a kid. One of her kids, one of her soldiers. Sorry for himself. Thank God, thank God, thank God unto the ages and ages.

He let go of her wrist.

Emily fell forward and gave herself a moment to lie curled around her poor wrist. The pain began to fade, but the wrist still felt loose and weak, as if he had unscrewed it, stripped the threads, and then stuck it back on.

He picked up his flashlight, held it inside the cedar's trunk so its light wouldn't spill outside, and turned it on. The glare dazzled her. His voice was flat. "My name is Ensign Jacob Lubov. I want to take service under you."

Her familiar screened his file. Twenty-three years old. Good record. One commendation. Just past his compulsory service. "Are you a deserter, Lubov?"

"Is that what you think?"

"You tell me."

"No ma'am," he said. "I'm not a deserter. I'm a traitor. Like you."

Lubov told her he had been sent into the Forest to find her, only the Forest had consumed his patrol. He had shot his

CO to save Raining's life, and his own. But Raining had been unable to hold onto him. Instead he found himself on a trail that after many wanderings had led him to Emily. The Forest, Emily thought, was a strange, dark, green Power. But then, Christ too was terrible, and the Spirit blinding, and the face of God more fearsome than the face of Satan. Providence had brought her this soldier. For now, he was all the army she had.

Lubov shone the light on his face while Emily dabbed carefully around his nose with a bit of bandage from the first-aid pack in his vest pocket. "This is twice I've had it broken, and both times by girls."

"Wow. How humiliating."

"Are you making fun of me?"

"Yes."

". . . Oh."

Emily laughed.

"If I hadn't been trying not to hurt you, you would have been dead the next second," Lubov said.

This was obviously true. "That's got the rest of the blood," Emily told him. "It's going to hurt for a while, I'm afraid, and your profile is going to have a little more character. I shouldn't have been able to catch you like that. What happened to your familiar?"

"I took it off," Lubov said. Emily's familiar, long-practiced in the art of reading men, watched his GSR spike suddenly and his pupils widen. His heart rate climbed to ninety-two beats a minute, almost twice his resting rate. "The Forest doesn't like them," he said.

They tallied their equipment. Emily still had her cultured ceramic knife, plus a foil parka with four hot-paks in the pockets, and her familiar. Lubov carried standard field kit, including field glasses, a foil pup tent, and rations: packets of juice crystals, powdered milk, salt, and vitamin-fortified beet and beef pemmican strips. Hunger must have been naked on her face, because he handed over the pemmican before she could ask for it. Ravenous as she was, she couldn't eat more than two strips. "This stuff is awful."

Lubov raised an eyebrow. "Complain to the civilian authorities."

"Very funny."

When she had finished eating, Emily said, "Do you want to know why I left the Southside?"

"No."

"If you take service with me, you deserve to be told."

"I said I didn't want to know."

Emily touched his hand. "Lubov?"

"Yes."

"You did what you had to do."

"I guess," he said.

A while later he said, "We should start walking. We need to get out of here before hypothermia gets us both. We need to try to find Mrs. Terleski's house."

"I think you're right."

Neither of them moved.

"I purely hate this fucking Forest," he said.

"Me too."

"We were in there, and Wilson went, and Johnson died, and the captain, everybody dead. And I knew I wasn't going to get out alive. That even if . . ." The words stopped. He stared into the fire. "That even if I got out, the Forest was inside me. It's in me, you know. Like it got into Johnson. And no matter what happens, it will always be in me now."

"I know." Emily remembered walking through the woods until she was dizzy, banging into tree trunks, the sad rain dripping on her hood, the choked view, the trees dark and everywhere. Then she thought of her grandfather, his face cut by the cold prairie wind. "But you know, the Southside is like that too."

They had been walking some time when Emily's angel spoke.

up

Could you be a little less cryptic? Emily thought, annoyed. Why always these blind urges, these cloudy visions? Why can't you just, I don't know, write a letter. Be specific.

up

Emily grunted. "Does the path seem straighter to you?"

"Yeah." Lubov walked beside her, tireless. They did keep these boys in good shape, anyway. "All day long I felt as if I were just . . . waiting. As if it didn't really matter where I walked. But now . . . now I feel like we're going somewhere."

"Up," Emily said, puffing.

"The exercise will keep you warm."

"Not on next to no sleep and food it won't."

"There's always another ration bar," Lubov said sweetly. Emily did not dignify this with a response.

Still the path climbed and the wind blew.

"Hey! I see a light!" Lubov said.

"Where?"

"Up ahead! Come on!"

Emily grabbed his arm. "Wait. Slow down. We don't know what it means, or who's there. What if it's some of your buddies, or some monster or something?"

"As if the Forest isn't going to take us where it wants," Lubov said. "Do you really think you can run away from wherever we're going?"

up! said the monotonous angel. Emily grunted. "You have a point."

A few minutes later they stumbled into a clearing on the crown of a tall hill. Just up the slope from where they stood a small fire blazed and crackled, blown to brightness by the hard wind. A man and a woman sat by it.

Suddenly the man stood. "I have been waiting for you," he said.

Emily's angel pulled violently toward the man, as if drawn to a magnet, but something in his cold voice filled her with dread.

The woman at the fire scrambled to her feet. "Mrs. Terleski!" Private Lubov cried.

Raining stood for a moment with a look of terrible anguish, and then she ran down the hillside and grabbed the young Southside soldier and held onto him for dear life. "Oh, you made it, you made it. I was so sure you were all dead, that everyone was dead. I killed you all. Oh God," she said. "Oh God, you're alive."

Lubov glanced uncertainly at Emily and then put an awkward arm around the small woman from Chinatown. "It's okay," he said gently. "I'm all right. We're all going to be all right."

"No, not everything is right." It was the other man, who had stayed by the fire. "Not everything will be all right." Slowly he rose and walked toward them.

join
meet
touch

But for once Emily did not trust her angel. "Back off," she said. "Keep your distance. Who are you?"

"My name is John Walker, my name is Walking John, my name is Blackshanks and Halterman and just plain Death, and if you don't know me, you should, Emily Thompson, for you are the one who has called me home, and here I am at last."

At this point Ensign Lubov made a funny wheezing kind of noise and fainted dead away, slipping through Raining's arms. "Now isn't that just like a Southsider," she said, laughing and crying at once. "One little god and they go all to pieces."

"Not quite a god or a Power," John Walker was saying a few minutes later, when they had Lubov propped up and recovering beside their little fire. "In some ways I am even less than an ordinary man. I started out as only a fragment of Winter, after all. But a child too starts as nothing more than a muddled mix of its parents. It grows. I have grown, as have all the other children who came across the Bridge. You call them demons," he added, glancing at Emily. "Philandering Meadowlark and bright Finch and The Harrier, that fine white hawk of a woman."

"Those . . . that is what became of the twelve children who crossed the Bridge."

"Thirteen, if you count me," John Walker said. "And I do. We peopled the North Side, and we did our jobs, and for years we were content. In my own way, I was as great in my kingdom as Winter was in his, and for many years I thought little of him. But lately. . . . Everything is changing. The Powers are waning as once they waxed. If the world fell into a Dream in 2004, then it is almost morning, I think. The snow on the North Side has begun to melt. Powers are dwindling, dying, drying up.''

"Wire has been telling me that for years," Raining said. "She used to talk to my dad about it. He thought the barbarians from Downtown had attacked us because the Power that knit them together had unravelled." Coals popped and flared in the dying fire. The cold wind was bitter with the smell of Raining's burnt offerings, wool and canvas, oil paint and green wood.

"But what does this have to do with you, exactly?" Emily asked. "Or with me? Did you send the visions to my angel?"

"I do not know what visions you mean," John Walker said. "You burned the sacrifice for me. That fire was the first time I had felt warm since the moment Winter cut me from his belly." John Walker paused. "He had no right to cast me out. I have come to reclaim what is mine. All these years he has been warm, over on the Southside. While I have been so cold."

"I do not think Grandfather wants to see you," Emily said, and she touched the skin just below her right eye, where Winter had hit her when he found her crouched over the funerary pyre she had made for the little dead boy. So he was right, she thought, and I have made anew the link that he had severed between himself and that dead boy, between the Southside and the North.

"Nobody has ever wanted to see me," John Walker said. "I come for them just the same."

"Winter can see you all he wants," Lubov ventured. "Hell, I'm all in favor. But if he sees us, he's going to have us shot. It's not much of a threat to you, I guess, but Anna Lubov's little boy doesn't want to be blown into three hundred pieces."

"Would he really shoot his own granddaughter?" Raining asked.

Emily grunted. "Next question? Grandfather responds to
leverage. Unless I have an army at my back, the best I could
expect would be to be clapped in chains at once. As for
Ensign Lubov here, after what he did to save you, the best
he could expect would be summary court-martial and execution."

Rain pulled her coat more tightly around her shoulders.
"If—*if* you promise to get me back my daughter, I can
supply you with food and drink and a warm place to sleep
tonight. But an army I can't provide."

John Walker looked up and laughed grimly. "I can," he
said. "Ninety-seven of Southside's finest. There's only one
problem with them."

"What?" Lubov said, bewildered.

This time it was Emily who was quickest to catch on.
"They're dead," she said.

CHAPTER 23

Water Spider woke on Sunday morning to the smell of tea and the sound of running water, hidden deep and rushing like the blood beneath his skin. *I am a spilled man, a spilled man.*

But the silent mountain is waiting always.

He was lying on something softer than the table they had strapped him to for his interrogation. He tried to twitch his fingers. A rough hempen sheet rasped against his hand. He opened his eyes. He was lying on a cot in the interrogation room. The only light came through the latticework above the door lintel. It seemed to be quite bright beyond his cell. It was at least midmorning. The gurgling water sound came from the drain in the middle of the floor. Perhaps it was raining again outside. He did not know.

A wooden crate was his bedside table. The tea smell came from a small cup on top of it. He remembered asking for tea many times during his interrogation, but he did not remember anyone bringing it. It seemed very sad to him to have wanted something so badly, and then have no memory of getting it.

Wraiths of steam coiled and drifted from the cup, fragrant ghosts.

He pushed himself up on one elbow and reached for the tea. A twinge of pain tweaked him where David Oliver's needle had gone in. He was glad someone had brought tea.

The cup was empty. Not only empty, but cold. And dry on the bottom.

He set it down. It was still steaming. Inside the cup, autumn leaves burned in damp air. Smoke swayed and thinned. Water Spider blew out a little puff of breath—*fweh!* Steam roiled, bent, and gradually straightened. He picked up the cup and tipped it. Nothing came out. He tipped it more sharply, until he was holding it upside down. Not a drop. Warmthless steam crawled around his fingers.

Water Spider eyed the empty cup. Then he lifted the ghost tea to his lips, and drank.

A knock came at the door. It was Claire.

"Come in," Water Spider said.

"You're smiling."

"Curious: to kidnap a man, tie him down, shoot him with needles—then knock for permission to come in! Very polite! Late. But very polite."

"You know me, always the lady." Claire stepped in, closing the door behind her. She dropped a bundle of clothes on the crate beside the cot, a red silk tunic and rust-brown rayon pants. "Major Oliver told me you were here. I brought you something to wear."

Water Spider picked through the soft cloth. Tears crept over his face.

Claire stood by the bed. She seemed enormously tall, stooping over him. Hair the color of frost, eyes pale watery blue. Heavy black boots and camouflage pants, a khaki shirt with the sleeves cut off, exposing her lean shoulders. Her skin was white like snow on the mountain.

"Aren't you cold?" he asked.

"Not very often, even at home. Here, never. You look better. The first time I dropped by you were still strung out on the S and D."

"S and D?"

"Seconal and Dexedrine. Stimulant and Depressant. First they knock you out—almost. Then they jerk you back with the dex. Then they peel you like a hard-boiled egg."

There were tears on Water Spider's face again. He

couldn't seem to stop them anymore; they fell when they would, like the rain. "How much did I tell them?"

"Everything."

So.

"I don't know that," Claire said. "Major Oliver didn't tell me that. But you can't keep anything from Intelligence, if they really want it. Not someone like you."

"Someone like me?"

"Smart people always break. Thinking people. Only the fairly crazy or the really stupid slip by. So I'm told, anyway."

"So. Everything." Water Spider nodded. "Would you step outside, please? I would like to dress."

"Maybe I'll stop by again tonight. See how you're doing."

Water Spider touched the clothes—lovely, clean, soft clothes, without the stink of his fear. Without the memory of his cowardice and betrayal on them. "Why are you doing this for me?"

"Major Oliver thought it might be a good idea."

"Ah."

"And I liked what you did for Jen. Going back to rescue him."

"After sending him on a fool's errand to start with."

"Why shit on your good deeds? You don't screw up enough?"

Water Spider smiled. " 'The superior man will not manifest either narrow-mindedness or the want of self-respect.' "

"What you said. Now, would the superior man like to manifest some clean clothes?"

"Yes please, Lady North Wind."

Claire cocked an eyebrow at him. She turned to go.

He called to her. "Do you have another moment?"

"What do you need?"

"Nothing. Go."

She waited.

"Would you stay and talk to me?" he asked.

Claire looked at him. "Okay."

She waited outside while he changed. It took him longer
than he expected. He was weak and his balance was not
very good. He undressed lying on the cot, then slowly sat
up. The concrete floor was cold and damp under his bare
feet. He felt horribly weak and shaky inside. Vulnerable as
a little boy. His throat was raw and his eyes hurt. He dressed
deliberately, with slow, steady movements and a face empty
of expression.

Steam within a china cup.

He dressed himself and invited her back in. "You said
you saw me, earlier?"

Claire sat on the crate. "Yeah. You were asleep all right,
but your whole body was curling and uncurling like a piece
of bacon frying in a pan. That's the Dexedrine."

"Was I weeping?"

"Yes."

Water Spider sat on the edge of his cot, facing her. "You
do not look like your mother."

"What?"

"Your mother. The goddess. You do not look like her."
Water Spider studied Claire's features. "Her eyes were nar-
rower and further apart. Your nose is quite different, and
the set of your mouth. There you take after your father."

Claire seemed genuinely taken aback. "I . . . I don't
know. I don't know who my father is. It never occurred to
me to find out."

"That is unforgivable."

"He hasn't bothered to get in touch."

"Perhaps he is dead, ha? Who will burn the offerings for
him, if not you? You see, this much I know about your
people. Perhaps he died when your mother took him up;
gods are seldom easy on their consorts. Then he waits, as
you believe, on the North Side, dark and cold, for the fire
that you have never burned."

"The dead are not the business of the living."

Water Spider waved her off impatiently. "You do not
believe this. This is only something you say to make things
easy for you. Most times, you like to think a harder way
from your fellows—I know this from reports—but this time

you are lazy." Water Spider regarded her with a slight smile. "Come. Your one life is not so big a thing. Many bodies already walk the planet. We are only great when we serve greatness. When we work for our family, our people."

"My people have never seemed too interested in my contributions."

"Does this absolve you of your duty to serve them? Of course not. This is a problem for the Southside, as for any very young community: you have no sense of shared history, of collective effort."

"We seem a lot more tightly organized than you do, to my eyes."

Water Spider said, "A chain of command is not a community."

Claire regarded him. "I'll bet you made an insufferable boss."

Water Spider smiled and raised his hands. " 'There is no attribute of the superior man greater than his helping men to practice virtue.' "

"Is that Confucius?"

"Meng-tzu."

"I need to screen some of these guys just for self-defense. The devil might as well quote Scripture for her own purpose, as Emily says."

"Mm. 'There are three things which are unfilial, and to have no posterity is the greatest of them.' You might start with that. I have produced no sons to light the sacrificial fires for my father."

"How old are you?"

"Forty-four."

"I'm thirty-six," Claire said. She swung herself off the crate.

"You never wanted children?"

"That's none of your business."

Water Spider held up his hands. For a time they were silent. Then he said, " 'When Heaven is about to confer a great office on any man, it first exercises his mind with suffering, and his sinews and bones with toil.' " He looked around his little cell. "I expect this to lead to great things."

"Did she say anything to you?" Claire said. "My mother, I mean."

"She asked me to name my deepest desire."

"And?"

"I had never considered such a question. I did not know what to tell her." Water Spider looked down at his hands. "I said a cup of tea. Heaven knows why."

Then he told Claire about the ghost tea he had drunk just before she entered the room, the steam rising from his empty teacup. She picked up the cup, which was still sitting on the crate next to her thigh. She peered inside. "So what happened when you drank? Did you taste anything?" He shook his head. "So there was nothing in it after all?" Claire said.

"Oh, North Wind, I would not say so. I would never dare go that far."

Claire laughed. "What strange people you are. Have you any idea what this fragrant apparition is supposed to mean?"

"None at all." Water Spider looked about his austere accommodations. "I may have ample time to contemplate the matter."

Claire laughed again. She promised to have some real tea sent to him, and to return at the end of the day. As she left, he said, "In the spring, a north wind often rises after sunset," even though it wasn't true. And though he had called her the north wind, the cell seemed colder when she had gone.

An hour later he was taken to see Winter. The lord of the Southside had made his quarters in Betty Hsiang's offices. Major Oliver was also in the room. The calm-eyed composure Water Spider was famous for had fled from him. A flush of terror spread through him like warm water running over his skin. He knew the other men saw it. His long, graying hair hung loose and tangled and he was ashamed. He looked away from David Oliver and pretended to study the painting of the travellers picking their way through the fog-bound mountains. *Men's fates are already set. There is no need asking of diviners.*

"I have a problem," Winter said. "I'm hoping you can

help me with it.'' Water Spider did not answer. Winter continued. "I have asked Major Oliver to stay with us. If necessary he will put my questions to you, but I would prefer not to do that."

"This delicacy is late in coming."

"Yes, and I don't apologize for that. We needed to get your information as quickly and reliably as possible. You would have done the same. Or at least you would have if you worked for me." Winter smiled briefly. "But men are like machines: if you break them enough times, they can't be fixed. I prefer not to do that."

"How fortunate for me."

"You believe there were certain people whose job it was to protect Chinatown from minotaurs, deal with ghosts, and so on."

"The Shrouded Ones," David Oliver said quietly.

"Thank you, Major. Do you remember speaking of them, Minister?"

"Perhaps." Water Spider shrugged. "I can remember very little of the talk I had with Major Oliver. The Shrouded Ones have been asked to withdraw their protection."

"Who asked them to do this?"

Water Spider's face stilled. "I prefer not to say."

"Do you want to go back on the table, Minister?"

"No."

"Who asked the Shrouded Ones to withdraw?"

No answer.

Winter sighed. "Major?"

"His father, sir. A manservant was also present, along with Li Mei. I have tapes of the interrogation, if you want them."

"Maybe later. Christ, I'm tired." Winter closed his eyes and rubbed his forehead. "The older I get, the more dangers I see down every path. Things turn out so surprisingly in life. It paralyzed me, for a time. So many unforeseen consequences ... But grow a little older still, and you realize there is no escaping from the world. Even doing nothing is an action, with its own set of results. In the end, all you can ask for is a chance to make your own decisions, and the strength to accept what comes from them.'' He met Water Spider's eyes. ''I could have Major Oliver here take you back to your little room and hook you up to an S and D drip and let you babble. Instead I am offering you a chance to make your own decision.''

Silence.

''The Shrouded Ones have withdrawn,'' Winter said. ''I have no way of forcing them to return. I suppose I could threaten your life, hoping your father would persuade them to come back. I doubt your father could be squeezed that way. He lived through the Dream, didn't he?''

Water Spider glanced up, surprised. ''Yes.''

''Then he has known too much sacrifice to be intimidated.'' Water Spider must have looked dubious, because Winter laughed. ''Believe it. He and I are survivors, Minister. Our generation was forged in a hotter fire than any you have known. Those who came through it are made of harder steel, and we hold our edge.''

''I confess I had not seen him in this light.''

''Of course not. Children never do. But parents are always stronger, Minister. We have to be. We carry our children on our backs.''

A distant gong rang somewhere in Government House.

''So. Your father's strategy was to corrode my men's morale. Not difficult in a place like this. Swimming in spooks and specters, bad food, unclear military objective. It's what I would do. Unfortunately, I am on the other side. It seems clear that I must fight fire with fire. I need the protection of a Power, Minister. Would you agree?''

Water Spider shrugged. ''A reasonable analysis.''

''This presents more difficulties. A local Power would be best, I suppose—but your people are suspicious of us, despite the fact that we are here at the explicit invitation of your Chief Minister.''

''Huang Ti.''

Winter smiled at the measured disdain with which Water Spider pronounced his rival's name. ''So, I have decided to make an alliance with the barbarians. We will let the Power

Downtown decide what happens to the people of China-town.''

Water Spider jumped up. ''The barbarians! Are you in-sane! We hired you in good faith, paid you well, sent em-bassies back and forth, supplied you with medicines—and you would bring that on my people? Leave them like to be slaughtered or enslaved by the monsters from The Offices?''

''Major Oliver said you wouldn't care for that sugges-tion.''

''Major Oliver was right.'' Water Spider stood with his fingers on the edge of Winter's desk. ''You cannot make an alliance with the enemy that slaughtered your men.''

''Oh, but I have already, I think. Major Oliver believes our men here were betrayed by your people, don't you, Da-vid?''

''It's the most likely explanation,'' Major Oliver said. ''The Downtowners never showed any kind of rocket tech before. Analysis suggests a device of a type fairly common in the Portland campaign. Someone shipped it in. There's no evidence of anyone trading out of Downtown, but we have uncovered definite signs of a coastal merchant network among your own businessmen, Minister.''

Water Spider felt dazed and blind. ''What does Johnny—'' He bit off the question.

''Unfortunately, Mr. Ma seems to have vanished. I have trackers looking for him,'' David added, glancing at Winter.

Winter shrugged. ''So you see, from my perspective there is not much to choose between your people and the creatures you call barbarians.''

Water Spider started to speak, stopped short, and fell si-lent. ''Ah. I see,'' he said at length. ''I am to tell you how you can secure the aid of one of our Powers.'' He nodded. ''There is an elegant economy in this. I helped devise the strategy to make your troops withdraw; who better to betray the scheme? And how could I refuse, if I truly thought you would do the unthinkable, and invite the barbarians into Chi-natown.''

''Look at my eyes,'' Winter said, ''and tell me if I'm bluffing.''

Water Spider was silent for a long time. Finally he said, "Make an alliance with the Dragon."

"Why the Dragon? Why not one of the others?"

"You can't make a contract with the Double Monkey without being cheated," Water Spider said wearily. "It cannot be done. As for the Lady in the Garden, I am not sure that she could do what you ask, even if she were willing. It is hard to imagine what she would want. Impossible for you to provide it. You stupid Snows have parked ugly trucks before her windows; it may already be impossible to retrieve your position."

Major Oliver looked alarmed. "Just parking a truck outside the windows of the Garden would be enough to turn a Power against us?"

"Very possibly. Of course, if your driver parked in the right spirit . . ."

Winter laughed to see the consternation on Oliver's face. "But the hand grenade my soldiers tossed into the Garden this morning would pretty much have torn it, eh?"

Water Spider was shocked.

"Yes, yes, we too are barbarians. I know." Winter rubbed his forehead again. "That leaves the Dragon."

"He is your only real chance. The Dragon wants power, which is something you can actually give. His Big Man is Hsieh Wu." Water Spider stopped and bent his head. "I cannot do this. This is to betray my life."

Major Oliver looked away, embarrassed. Winter waited.

"Go to Hsieh Wu at the Hong Hsing Athletic Club," Water Spider whispered. "Offer him the city. No—not that. Offer him the Emperor's chair."

"He will accept?"

"He will accept."

Winter glanced from Water Spider's bowed head to Major Oliver, who nodded.

"David, get it done. And Minister, for what it's worth you did the right thing. This way, in a few months, everything here will be pretty much as it always has been. A new man in charge, but one of your own. Much different than what would have happened had the barbarians marched in."

"Would you really have done that?"

"Without a second thought. My duty is to my own, Minister."

"Even I despise you," Water Spider said. "Even I, the traitor."

A while later he said, "Why did you really bring me here? You could have slept while Major Oliver wrung this advice from me. And forgive me if I am not convinced by your pretty words about the nobility of being fully awake to savor one's betrayals. I do not wish to remember this moment."

"But it is important, Minister. It is terribly important to take responsibility for the damage one does. At least, it is to me," Winter said. "If I was going to make a Judas of you, Minister, I thought I owed it to you to do it face to face. Because that's my responsibility, you see? You are another load for my conscience to carry."

Water Spider regarded the leader of the Southside. "I do not think the load will break you," he said. "It is a strong thing, this conscience of yours. I am afraid of how much it can bear."

Winter turned back toward the window. "Take him away. David, let a corpsman do it. I have a question for you."

Water Spider left the room. David Oliver closed the door quietly behind him.

"It's always goddam raining here," Winter said. He looked out of Betty Hsiang's window at a drizzle falling along Carrall Street. It was raining everywhere in Chinatown, except for the Lady's Garden. There it appeared to be nighttime, and clear. Winter shuddered. He found himself leaning against the window, the glass cool against his forehead. "What I wouldn't give for a glass of rye and a good night's sleep. I haven't got the stamina for this anymore." Rain creaked and ticked against the glass. "Who would have thought there could be so much rain in the sky?"

"Yes, sir."

"But the summers are beautiful. Did you know that? I came out here the summer of—1984, was it? Vancouver was the only Western Canadian stop on Simon and Garfunkel's reunion tour. I drove out to catch the concert. Stayed a month with some friends. July in Vancouver. You can't beat it. Sunny every day, no mosquitoes. Nectarines the size of your fist. Every day for lunch I had one of those nectarines and a cappuccino yogurt. It was paradise."

"Yes, sir."

"You don't even know what a nectarine is, do you, Major? Or cappuccino, for that matter?"

David smiled briefly. "Just screened for them, sir. Got the fruit. Drew a blank on the other."

"Just as well." Winter looked at Oliver's haggard face. As the days dragged on, the lack of sleep was telling cruelly on his senior staff. "Major, you comfort me. I do believe you must be nearly as tired as I am."

"To be frank, sir, I am extremely tired."

"Do you like it here, Major?"

"What? Do I like Vancouver? I—I hadn't really given it any thought."

"The climate is superb, if you don't mind a little rain. Very temperate. The farmland in the Fraser Valley is some of the best on the continent. It would support a lot of people."

"I'm sorry, sir. Your point is eluding me."

"Do you think we could live here, Major? It's not a subtle question. Do you think our people could be happy?"

"Oh." Major Oliver looked at him for some time. "Ah."

Winter walked across the room and looked out another window, this one facing south. Battered brick tenements, faded banners, balconies covered in chimes and charms and flowering plants. Farther away, the concrete strings of the abandoned LRT line arcing by. Over in the west, the empty asphalt and the gutted barracks where ninety-six of his men had died. Or was it ninety-seven? "I just wonder about the rain."

"I don't pretend there aren't problems with the Southside," Major Oliver said carefully. "But I would be sad to see it vanish. If you're thinking of moving our people here, I would not like to see that. I am very sure that whatever makes us what we are, as individuals and as a community, could not survive such a transplantation.''

"I like you, David. You answer my questions even when you think I'm crazy." Winter turned away from the window. "I agree. You cannot escape your shadow, however fast you run. Major, in your professional opinion are we likely to recover Emily?"

"At all? Or alive?"

"Either. Both."

"Sir, I think the chances of getting her back are very poor. By this time she has either died in the Forest, found a safe haven there which we cannot penetrate, or slipped out beneath our guard. If she's in the Forest, we have no hope of getting her. If she's outside the wood, we can only hope she stays alive long enough to betray her location and allow us to capture her unharmed." Major Oliver shrugged. "The only thing we have going for us now is Emily's impatience."

Winter laughed. "Yes. She won't sit on her butt in a tree house forever. Not my Em. But my instincts run with yours, David. Christ, the mess you handed me when your men lost her back home."

"Yes, sir."

Winter rubbed his forehead. At least he had passed through the need for sleep. He could feel the fatigue consuming his body, like a long slow flame licking firewood, but it seemed to be attacking his limbs directly, eating his strength but leaving his mind clear. "If we don't have Emily, then I have a problem. My gut tells me I'm running out of time. We have fulfilled our contract with Chinatown. We'll wait another day or two and then pull out. If you can't produce Emily by then . . ."

"Sir?"

"I shall have to pursue another option to placate the North Side," Winter said. "Not one I like, but that's the hell of it in this life. I have asked too many sacrifices from the people of Southside to fail them from a lack of nerve."

"Would you care to explain your backup plan?" Major Oliver said.

"No," Winter said. "I would not."

"Sir, Intelligence ought to know. Not me as an individual, necessarily. But the service."

Winter shook his head. "It's easier to follow orders if you don't understand the reasoning behind them, Major. Once you know the reasons, you are obliged as a thinking being to judge their validity." He smiled briefly. "Frankly, David, on certain issues I am much too old and wise to be interested in your input. You're Orthodox, aren't you?"

"Yes sir."

"Good," Winter said. "I'm not a believer myself, but I like subordinates who are. I find Orthodoxy builds up a muscular capacity for faith, and a fine appreciation of sacrifice."

"Not to mention a great deal of reverence for the teachings of old men," David added drily.

Winter laughed. "That too," he said.

"Why did you kill the ambassador, Li Bing?" David asked. Winter did not answer. "Was it an accident? Were you angry about Emily's disappearance? Did she insult you? Or did you . . . had you guessed already that our men had been betrayed?"

Winter looked out the window. "You are dismissed, Major."

". . . Yes, sir."

And still it rained.

CHAPTER 24

A staff sergeant escorted Water Spider back to his cell. The Chief Minister, once Purse, was waiting there. "Huang Ti!" Tears sprang unexpectedly to Water Spider's eyes. "You came to see me?"

The Honorable Minister for the Interior looked up. His fleshy face was fearful, pale and sweaty. The cot was gone; the surgical table was back in its place. An IV loomed at its head.

"You are free to leave," the sergeant said in English.

Relief flooded Huang Ti's face. "Double fortune! You think different, ah?"

"We regret the inconvenience."

A long silence. Slowly Huang Ti turned to face Water Spider. "Oh, no," he breathed.

Headless ghosts gathered in Water Spider's stomach.

"I have been expecting you," Huang Ti said, switching to Cantonese. Deliberately he wiped the sweat from his wide forehead. "When the Snows roused me from my bed and took me to Winter, I thought of you. When I would not betray my people, they brought me here. They were going to torture me, I thought. I told myself it was no more than just punishment for my cowardice in letting them keep you here. At least, I thought, I will have company. For if I, poor fat Huang Ti, could choose to resist, then surely the great Water Spider would also. What was that line you used to quote to us, Minister? 'If a man in the morning hear the right way, he may die in the evening without regret'?''

Water Spider's mouth went dry. "They asked you about making an alliance with a Power."

"But you did not resist, did you, Spider?"

It was not possible that Water Spider could have done less than the odious Huang Ti. Huang Ti who cheated on his wife. Huang Ti who loved perfume too much. Huang Ti who hoarded his taxes.

The Purse's fleshy head shook in disbelief. "All these years you had us fooled. The virtuous one. The principled man. But you are no better than your father."

"Shut up!"

"I think you should go now," the sergeant broke in.

"Coward!" Huang Ti yelled. "You—"

"Shut up! Shut up! You don't understand, you fat fool! They were going to bring in the barbarians," Water Spider said.

Huang Ti with his two chins had resisted? Not possible.

"Of course they said that!" the Minister for the Interior shouted. His face was purpling with outrage. "Are you insane? Are you stupid enough to believe they would dare after what the barbarians did to their men? And even if the Snows did make an alliance with Downtown, this is Chinatown, you fool! No Power rules here save the Three."

Huang Ti had resisted. Huang Ti had refused to go along with Winter. This knowledge hit Water Spider like a kick in the stomach. He strained to breathe.

Huang Ti was yelling at him. "The barbarians could never hold what they tried to take. What do you think the Dragon would have done? Or the Lady? Or Double Monkey? You think they would be content to draw their pensions—Old Gods, just go now and read books, thank you?"

"They—they would have learned, anyway," Water Spider whispered. "On the table. You can't hide things from them." But was that true? You couldn't hide anything from the Snows, on their drugs, but you couldn't think, either. And it had taken thought for him to address their problem.

"You didn't even try," Huang Ti said contemptuously. "They did not have to lift a finger."

The sergeant took Huang Ti firmly by the arm and led him to the door. "Goodbye, Minister."

Huang Ti shook his arm free. At the door he turned, and gave Water Spider a deep, mocking bow. "Sleep well, Borders. Rest assured that our people will know to whom they owe the coming peace. I do not know what price you got for selling us to the Snows. Perhaps they will reward you with a post. I doubt it, though. Not even the rat-killer loves his poison."

He left. Petty, boastful Huang Ti. Who had resisted.

The sergeant followed Huang Ti out, closing the door behind him. Water Spider was alone. He stood on the cold concrete floor. From the drain under the surgical table came the gurgling of hidden water.

Huang Ti who had resisted.

But the Snows would have figured it out, surely? They had to ally themselves with one of the local Powers. They couldn't treat with Double Monkey, they had nothing to offer the Lady; it had to be the Dragon, that was obvious; any child could have told them that.

But it hadn't been any child. It had been him.

Trickle, trickle.

It had been raining while Water Spider sat in Winter's office. He wondered if it was raining still.

He was going to be found out. He was going to be found out. The Lidded Eye, Johnny Ma, old Grace Shih—Huang Ti would tell them all. And everyone would know that it was he who brought the Mandarinate to an end. A pretender would sit in the holy dragon chair and they would all know it was because of him.

Stop. Stop. Disgusting, to think of your own shame when the larger good of the people is at stake. Think of the people you failed, not of yourself and your little reputation.

Even Jen, even the drunks and the whores would look down on him. His whole life of service gone like smoke before a wind of shame. Even Pearl, halfway to a whore herself; she would be glad, glad she turned him down.

Stop! You disgust me.

He reached out and touched the IV stand. The steel was cool beneath his fingers. A half-full wrinkled bag of clear fluid hung at the top, dripping.

Drip.

Drip.

Drip.

Even the rat-killer does not love his poison.

You can't use a woman like a whore and then expect to be loved for it.

You didn't lift a finger.

You didn't lift a finger.

The straps and cinches hung loosely from the table, like his father's belts and robes, askew after days of drinking. Your father has been a warrior and a poet. What have you done? You cannot even remember what he is trying to forget. Our generation was forged in a hotter fire than any you have ever known. Parents must be stronger: we carry our children on our backs.

He had failed the test.

He had failed the test.

"The superior man is satisfied and composed; the mean man is always full of distress." "The determined scholar and the man of virtue will not seek to live at the expense of injuring their virtue. They will even sacrifice their lives to preserve their virtue complete."

Water Spider considered hanging himself. It might be possible, if he were ingenious. He would have to be quick and quiet, so as not to alert the guard outside the door. He deserved to die.

Coward. You are only running again.

No, that isn't it, it's justice I am thinking of—

Vile thing. You are thinking of your reputation. You merely flinch at the thought of your disgrace. Desist. This shame is of your own making. Claim it. Shame is the only son you will ever sire. *What can I do, kneeling in the garden, But eat these stones?*

• • •

Some hours had passed when Claire knocked softly on the door. "Hello?"

"Come in," Water Spider said. "Why do you bother to knock? Courtesy in a jailer is only arrogance." I have no walls; I am only doorways, only windows. I am an empty house and the wind blows through me. I will hide in my empty apartment like a spider on the baseboards.

The people will know to whom they owe the coming peace.

He will tell everyone.

"I'm happy to see you, too." Claire yawned. "Congratulations, you're a free man. I'm to escort you to your home. Major Oliver's orders."

Even if they did make an alliance, this is Chinatown, you fool. No Power rules here save the Three.

I cannot go into the streets, not in daylight. It must be dark, dark enough to creep through the rain like a spider at the baseboards, no one to see me, even the whores, even Jen and Pearl—she'll be glad she didn't marry me.

Use a woman like a whore and expect to be loved?

"Thank you." Water Spider found he was sitting on the edge of the table. He let himself down. The cold concrete pressed against his feet. He heard the distant murmur of water, deep down below.

You didn't lift a finger.

If only he had waited, if only he had refused, then they would have tied him to this table and maybe with the drugs in his blood he wouldn't have been able to think, he couldn't have told them any more, just babble, just the sound of wind through the branches, shutters swinging, bamboo chimes.

"Hey? Are you all right?"

"Fine, thank you. But I will not be going just yet. I find myself still somewhat tired."

"What?" Claire blinked. "What were you going to do? Crawl up on that metal table and take a nap?"

Water Spider edged back toward the corner of the room. "I will not leave at this time. Thank you. You may go."

"Do you have a fever? Let me feel your forehead."

"Get away! Get away from me! You can't make me go,

I can't, I can't,'' Water Spider cried. "They'll *see* me." Claire's hand touched him and he collapsed, hunched into a ball in the corner of the room. "I want to die."

"You don't mean that."

"I tell you my life is over!" he shouted. "I sold the man I was—he is gone. There is nothing to come back to. The house is empty. Huang Ti will tell everyone I didn't lift a finger. They will know who to thank for the coming peace. Even fat stupid petty Huang Ti, I betrayed him too." He felt her hands on his wrists. He struggled for an instant, then abruptly stopped. Of course he was no match for her strength. He would have laughed, if he hadn't been crying. "You do not know," he said. "You cannot know what it's like."

She knelt before him on the floor, her hands on his, their foreheads almost touching. "Hey," she said softly. "Can I tell you one thing?"

"You do not understand."

"Can I tell you just one thing?"

His chest was heaving with astonishing sobs. The tears flowed out of him, he who before the white goddess came had not cried since he was ten years old, and he was powerless to resist them; he did not lift a finger, he was a coward and he let them come, running from the dark emptiness inside.

"Can I tell you one thing?"

He wept. It was like dying, to cry like this. The surrender was appalling and the river went back forever.

"You're not that important," Claire said. She held his shoulders. "Nobody cares."

"T-they, th-they will." He had to fight to talk. To breathe, even. Anything.

"Well," she said, "I don't care, anyway." A little grave smile on her white face. Her pale blue eyes, like cold water in bone china.

"You don't?"

"About you? Not a tinker's damn. Couldn't care less."

A smile on his face, spun up on the river of tears—he had no control over his face anymore; it might say anything.

Who knew what the river would throw forth next? "You swear it?"

"I do," Claire said. "I solemnly swear not to give a good goddamn. Just some guy who needs a bath, as far as I'm concerned."

He laughed while weeping.

"Major Oliver got me thinking," she said, some time later. "Why did my mother take me to you, that night outside the barracks? It must have been part of her plan somehow." Water Spider did not answer. "We do the work the gods give us," Claire went on. "You don't know whose work you're doing. You don't even know what you've done. Not really. So, to hell with it. That's what I say."

" 'Where—' " He stopped to get his breath. " 'Where is this fleeting consequence you've tangled your life in?' "

Gently Claire let go of his shoulders and sank back on her knees. "Why on earth would The Harrier have brought me to that corner at just that moment? Was it to get Pearl back? Or to get Jen caught by the demon, for that matter?"

Water Spider blinked. His face still ran with tears. He wiped them off with the sleeve of his robe. What a fool he had made of himself.

Claire sat before him, waiting for an answer. "Do you have any ideas? What do you think The Harrier was showing you?"

Water Spider beheld her kneeling before him, ill-dressed in a white jumpsuit uniform, graceless and unrefined, sardonic and helpful. "A cup of tea," he said.

CHAPTER 25

"Wire? Wire?"

A little hand fell on Wire's shoulder. Jiggle jiggle jiggle jiggle. "Are you awake?"

"Unnh. 'Sleep."

"Oh."

Wire dropped back into sleep as if weighted with bricks. There had been tremendous activity in Government House all night long. She had spent most of it awake and worrying. Only in the last hour before dawn had sleep finally ambushed her, striking like a blow to the back of the head.

Jiggle jiggle jiggle jiggle.

"Hn!" Wire's brain felt stunned, smacked around between sleep and waking. Slow green ichor was oozing in her veins instead of blood.

Oh, sweet gods. Sunday morning.

"Wy-errrr!" Lark's straight black bangs tickled Wire's cheek.

"What! What do you want?"

"You're awake."

Wire glared through gummy eyes.

"Wy-errr, I want to tell something." Lark paused.

"What! What?"

"We-e-e-e-ll . . . Is it morning yet?"

Wire whimpered. "No, it is not morning yet! Go to sleep."

"Oh."

Blessed silence.

"Wire—"

"Shh!" Wire hissed. "You have to be quiet so people can sleep!"

"Oh."

Lark's little feet pattered away.

Another day with Lark. Sweet gods.

Wire turned to the wall. "Time?" The room didn't answer. Shit. What time was it, anyway? She could hear the murmur of people coming and going beyond the little shrine room, but they did that in the middle of the night, too.

She thought about getting up and asking the guard at the door.

A guard at the door! As if she would try to escape. Where would she go with a three-year-old? She had pointed this out to David Oliver at length, but he seemed to feel it was appropriate to have a watchman there. Wire had argued the point right up to the moment when she realized what he would never say: that the guard wasn't there to keep a little girl and an attractive woman prisoner in the room; he was there to keep Southside soldiers out.

It wasn't as dark as it had been. Not full light, definitely not. But lighter. It would be morning soon.

Wire felt like crying. Instead, she burrowed more deeply into the quilt David Oliver had provided. Like a rabbit in a burrow, snuggling down for the night. Like a dove nestled beneath its mother's breast. . . .

Jiggle jiggle jiggle jiggle.

"Ah!" Wire snapped into stunned alertness. "What? What?" Lark stepped back, startled. Wire blinked and waved one feeble hand. "'S'okay, honey. Must have fallen back asleep. What did you want?"

Lark tilted her head on one side. "We-ell," she said seriously. "When is it morning?"

"Not yet! It's not morning yet!" Wire crushed her voice down to a furious whisper. "I will tell you when it's morning. Now please, go back to your bed and *don't keep waking me up*. It will be morning in a while. I'll tell you. It will be morning when they bring our breakfast, okay?''

"At break-tast?''

"Yes. Breakfast. Until then, we will all try to sleep. Do
you understand?'' Lark nodded and pattered back to her
own bed.

Wire collapsed back onto her cot. Today she would talk
to David Oliver. She would demand that she and Lark be
taken back to her apartment. This was ridiculous. It had been
a full day since Raining disappeared into the Forest. Surely
it was clear by now that Lark could not be used as leverage.

Wire dwelt for some minutes on a pleasant fantasy in-
volving finding Emily Thompson and punching her in the
face before turning her over to Oliver and putting an end to
this whole horrible business. She closed her eyes. Sleep
came to her like a lover.

> "Mis-ter Sun, Sun, Mis-ter golden Sun
> Please shine down on, please shine down on,
> Please shine down on me-e-e.
>
> Mis-ter Sun, Sun, Mis-ter golden Sun
> Please shine down on me-e-e.''

Oh no. Lark was singing. Very quietly, under her breath,
lying on her cot like a good little girl. And singing.

> "Please shine down on, please shine down on,
> Please shine down on me-e-e!''

Wire's hands balled into fists inside her quilt.

By eight o'clock that morning she had decided she was
never having kids.

The first thing she did after getting up was to ask their
guard if they could have a clock. He brought back an ugly
brass one with a very loud tick, but Wire was grateful to
get it. She would have gone crazy if she couldn't see proof
that the day was passing.

It wasn't so bad for the first hour. Lark started by removing one of the silk table vestments and wrapped it around an especially jolly-looking bronze Buddha to make a skirt so she could play dolls. The Enlightened One regarded her with great good will. Lark picked the little statuette off the table and tumbled it artistically to the tile floor.

(High, squeaky voice) "Oh no! Buddy's fallen in the water! Help, help!"

(Gentle, motherly voice) "Don't worry, Buddy. I'll save you."

(High, squeaky voice) "Help! Help!"

This occupied her until breakfast. Wire gathered her resolve while they ate. It was a small room. There was nowhere to run from Lark, and no way to hide. Besides, if she felt miserable, how much worse must poor Lark be feeling? So. The thing to do was to give up on the notion of having private time to worry about herself. The thing to do was to throw all her energies into dealing with Lark.

The breakfast dishes were removed at seven-fifteen. When the guard had left and they were alone again, Wire told Lark a story, a somewhat garbled version of "Goldilocks and the Three Bears." She was amazed to find she didn't really know it. She got the porridge (hot, cold, just right) and the beds (hard, soft, just right), but what was the middle thing? She thought it might be chairs—she definitely remembered Goldilocks breaking Baby Bear's chair, but what was the problem with the other two chairs? Surely Mamma Bear's chair couldn't have been too low? Hard and soft didn't work either; she had to save that for the beds . . . She made something up about the chair backs and arms, but even Lark could tell she was fudging.

After the story, Lark taught her some songs. There was "Mister Golden Sun" and "The Alphabet Song" (this one Wire knew) and "Twinkle Twinkle" (which she also knew, but had never previously realized had the same tune as "The Alphabet Song"). There was one about a little white whale, but Lark couldn't remember many of the words. Most successful was "The (Somethings) on the Couch."

"The mommies on the couch go shh! shh! shh!

Shh! Shh! Shh!—Shh! Shh! Shh!
The mommies on the couch go shh! shh! shh!
A-a-ll da-a-y looooong.

"The grandpas on the couch go read, read, read, . . .
"The grandmas on the couch go sew! sew! sew! . . .
The chickens on the couch go cluck, cluck,
      cluck, . . .
"The sluggies on the couch go shlurp, shlurp,
      shlurp, ..."

And so on. And on. And on.

Then they tried drawing, respectfully removing a stick of
incense from one of the Buddhas and tracing out shapes on
the tile floor. Wire drew a cat, a person, a rainbow, a fish,
and Lark three times. Then she looked at the clock.

Seven forty-two. Twenty-seven minutes had passed.

Twelve and a half hours to bedtime.

It was four-thirty on Sunday afternoon. Wire had not stran-
gled Lark. She had tried to get someone to fetch David
Oliver six times. She had spent the entire day rehearsing
increasingly furious versions of what she would say when
he finally deigned to show up. But he was so haggard when
he came through the door, so worried and drawn, that she
threw out her prepared speech. "You look terrible."

"It's been a bad day." The first streaks of grey were
showing in David's black hair. There seemed to be more
lines around his eyes. He looked at Lark, lying listlessly in
Wire's lap. "The man said she was sick."

"I thought she was. Now I'm not sure. Maybe she's just
bored. She says she's thirsty."

"I'll tell the guards to keep an eye out. And I'll make
sure you have plenty of water."

"Boil it first."

"Okay." He didn't leave. There were sweat stains under
his arms. It had been several days since he had shaved. His
skin had a darker tone than most Southsiders. The stubble
on it was so black it was almost blue.

He caught her looking at his face. She colored and looked away.

"Mind if I sit down?"

Wire waved around the room. "Oh, please—enjoy the comforts of our little home."

He smiled and sat on the edge of a low table. "That's what you do, isn't it? Design houses."

"Break them in, anyway. Yeah. How did you know that? On second thought, I know, it's part—"

"Part of my job. Yes." He rubbed his hands wearily across his face. Wire didn't think he'd gotten any more sleep than she had last night. "By the way, I meant to ask what on earth you told that guard. He yanked me out of a top-level meeting and hustled me through the building like it was on fire."

"I swore him to secrecy and then told him Lark was your love-child. Gotten while Raining was married to Nick."

David's head snapped up. "What!"

"Not my daddy," Lark said. She turned her face away from him and burrowed closer into Wire's tummy.

Wire snickered. "I had been trying to get a message to you all day. It was the only thing I could think of to get your attention."

"Sweet Christ, Wire. Just the kind of gossip I need right now."

She looked at him. "Then I guess you shouldn't have kidnapped her. What if Raining—" Wire glanced down at Lark and bit her lip. "As long as we're prisoners, you are responsible for her. Right now, you and I are the closest thing she has to parents. You gave your word."

"I know." David closed his eyes. "The whole day has been an Intelligence nightmare. I've been putting out fires since three this morning, but I promise you, Lark has never been far from my thoughts." He was staring at the floor. "Neither of you has."

Feet hurried over tile floors beyond their door. Voices called. "We sent a squad into the Garden at first light," David said. "Over my protests. I told them to be careful, I told them only to negotiate. I was overruled. Three men went into the Inner Garden. When they didn't come back, do you know what their captain did? Threw in a grenade. Physically lobbed a grenade into the Lady's Garden. You can see right in, apparently; the wall between the public and the inner gardens is full of those leaky windows.''

''By all the little crawling gods! What happened?''

''The grenade exploded into red flowers. I am not making this up. I have a dozen witnesses. There was a flash, no explosion; and then a rain of red petals. A few of them drifted back onto the men watching. Also, according to six respondents, a pleasant smell, like crushed herbs. A few minutes later, a temple attendant came with a broom to sweep up.''

Wire laughed.

''Can you believe that? We walked into Chinatown and *attacked a Power*. The one *right across the street* from our base of operations. And do you know what Winter said?''

''Should you be telling me this?''

''He said, 'Patch it up. Find out what the Power wants and make a deal.' '' David's head was back in his hands.

''It doesn't work that way,'' Wire said. ''Can you make a deal with water to flow uphill?''

''I know. I know. He just doesn't understand. But surely what happened to Ranford should have made it clear. The Infants are rattled. They are really rattled. There's been a lot of talk about what happened to Ranford's men. Now our Chinese contacts are getting cold feet. Apparently the Shrouded Ones have abandoned Chinatown because the Mandarins are collaborating with us.''

''Oh gods. The Shrouded Ones have left?''

''If there really are such things as ghosts, there should be plenty to see now,'' David said grimly.

''If?'' Wire said, surprised. ''Haven't you ever seen a ghost?''

''Have you?''

''Dozens.''

He looked at her. ''Oh. Great.''

''You Southsiders are a strange bunch.''

Outside the door, the guard shifted.

"Am I a bad man?" David said.

The ugly brass clock tick, tick, ticked. "I don't know," Wire said. "Are you?"

"Ah." David stood up. "Wise woman. I'll send you that water and see if I can get something for Lark. I'll tell the guard—well, first that she's not my daughter—I'll tell him to come get me immediately if you ask for me, no matter what else I'm doing. For your part, try not to ask unless it's genuinely urgent. You may not believe it, but I'm one of the people trying to get us out of here as quickly as possible. I'm one of the good guys."

"I know," Wire said.

He looked away. "You are an exceptional woman."

Wire smiled. "Well, no—but flattery is always welcome. Goodbye, Major Oliver."

"David?"

"David. Goodbye."

She watched him go. Never saw a ghost. She shook her head. Poor ignorant bastards.

CHAPTER 26

Shortly before midnight on Sunday, Jen, Li Mei, and Floating Ant returned to Chinatown. It was raining. Crossing Hastings Street under the glowing sulphur sign of First Born Photo, they walked a block past Pender and stood for a moment under the back wall of the Garden, looking across the parking lot at the burned-out hulk of what had been the Southsider barracks. Although it was only midnight, the streets were unusually empty. Those still out hurried by with eyes downcast, flowing around the Southside perimeter pickets as water breaks around stone.

"You still feel you must do this?" Floating Ant said quietly.

Jen spat. "It is the meaning of the Dragon's gift. The Snows fear ghosts, you said. This will give the Southside's ghosts, and the living Snows who see them, something terrible to fear."

"Very well." Floating Ant was wearing a floppy black hat. Rain dripped from the brim onto his thin shoulder. "Go safe under the Heavens. We cannot be found here when the cry is raised."

Holding his hands at the height of *dan tien*, Jen placed his right fist against his left palm and bowed as he had to the Sifu who had taught him the way of fist and sword. Floating Ant bowed solemnly in return. "Goodbye, then. And good fortune."

Li Mei and the old man slipped away.

The straight razor the Lady had sent to Jen lay folded in his right pocket. So his broken luck had been replaced. The razor was bad luck, true—but it was his and his alone.

He plodded slowly up the road, head downcast. On a balcony across the street, four tipsy fellows stood bunched under a huge pink umbrella, singing an old plum wine song. The Snows had been given a place of honor among the vulgar lyrics. Across the way, Snows were stationed around the perimeter of Government House, tall and still and white as cranes. Jen decided to walk another block down Pender Street before turning up toward the barracks. He did not wish to draw the attention of the guards.

He had found only china flats to wear since escaping New Moon Manor and his feet were soaking wet. The red rubber soles went plash plash plash across the wet asphalt.

Here's a memory for you: bearing down as he raped his beautiful demon, red silk whispering between them, the slap slap slap of his hips against her thighs, his soul dripping from his mouth like spit. Her devouring it. And then, later, the blood trickling down his face as she shaved off his eyebrows. His blood on her lips, red on red.

Story of his life.

On the far side of BC Place, the old stadium in whose parking lot the Southsiders had built their barracks, a patrolling helicopter swept along the thin line of forest between the stadium and the seashore. As soon as it passed by, heading east on its patrol route, three figures slipped out of the wood and hurried forward. Clouds covered the moon and the night was very dark. "What if they see us crossing the parking lot?" Lubov whispered.

"I don't think they'll shoot strangers on sight," Emily murmured. "Besides, the barracks is between us and Chinatown's perimeter. If I know my soldiers, nobody will be anxious to get close to a ruin full of ghosts. Not when our friend here has left them to wander the night instead of carting them off to the North Side where they belong."

John Walker did not speak.

wait!

Lubov froze. "Someone's coming," he hissed.

"Where?"

"Over there, walking up from Pender street. Short guy dressed like a native."

Emily squinted, wishing she had her military kit, an IR scope, photomultiplier binoculars, *something* to make it easier to see in the dark. Lubov flattened himself to the asphalt and dragged her down. John Walker crouched beside them. Together they watched. It was hard to see the man; he moved quickly and quietly and stayed away from any lights.

"He's going to the barracks too," Lubov breathed. Good eyes on that boy, Emily thought. "What the hell is he thinking?"

Emily shrugged. "Lay low," she whispered. "Watch."

A few of the Southsider ghosts walked around the outside of the burned-out barracks. Most sat wearily within. They were hard to see, like faint stars that winked out when you looked straight at them. Jen found he could distinguish them well only when he was touching the razor the Lady had given him. When his fingers left it, the ghosts fled like minnows from his groping eyes.

"Visitor!" called one of the lazy sentry ghosts. Four or five of them gathered around Jen. Rain slid through them.

"Hey—isn't that the slant old Claire kicked the shit out of?" This ghost's shoulder insignia had burned off, along with the flesh of his back, chest, and lower jaw. "Hi-ya!" he said, lashing out with one phantom foot. Jen leapt back and slapped the kick away. He felt no charred bone or baked flesh; only the sensation, very slight, of the damp air gelling and splitting around his hand.

The ghosts stepped back, startled. "He can see us."

"I must speak to your captain," Jen said.

Two of the ghosts scrambled away. In a moment they returned with the CO who had refereed the match between Jen and Claire. Six days ago, was it? Jen looked with pity at the burned and crippled ghosts now thronging around. Six days and all their lifetimes ago.

"My fellows tell me you can see us," the captain said. "I figured there must be some kind of slant magic that would help. Can you talk to Winter for us? We want to go home."

Jen took a breath. Mind/no mind. "I come with a message."

Fist against open palm, he bowed very low, as he had to Floating Ant a few minutes earlier. Then he reached into the pocket of his shabby pants and brought out the razor. He opened it with a street fighter's flick. With the stroke called No Design, No Conception, he hit with his body, hit with his spirit, and hit from the Void with his hands, cutting the front tendons of the ghost's neck and severing his throat.

The Southside captain choked and fell jerking to the pavement. Instantly Jen was on top of him. The man was only a slippery half-there thing between his knees, but the razor slashed and bit as if cutting into real flesh. Jen's beautiful sword had vanished at a demon's breath—but the razor cut bloody into the invisible world.

Swearing and crying, the ghosts attacked him. Small winds tugged at Jen's hair and clothing as he hacked off the captain's head and then held it up by its hair. It swayed there, tugging on his hand no more than a balloon. "This is my message to the Southside. Remain here and you will never go home. Every Snow who stays in this city will die. Not only the body death, but the true death, the death of the Void. We will slay your very souls, and the sacrifices your sons burn for you will go unclaimed."

The ghosts of Southside's dead, who thought they had gone beyond all terror, looked at Jen with the head swaying in his hands and found fear again. Those strong enough to move scrambled away. Those too weak to leave the barracks wept and begged.

I want you to understand these Snows, Water Spider had said. *For one day, I think, I will need you to kill one for me.*

A distant voice called out. "Hey!"

"Shit," Jen whispered. Somehow one of the flesh and blood perimeter pickets had seen him—must have some equipment that let him see in the dark. The sentry started running toward him. "White bitch broke my fucking *luck*," Jen swore. He should have found a new one. Shit. Too late now. He turned and ran. Only trouble was, a real live Snow was going to be quicker and stronger than he was. Fuck.

He raced to Taylor Street and turned into it, feet slapping echoes off the pavement. His legs starved for oxygen and grew heavy but he forced himself not to let up, sprinting for the *Sing Tao* offices at the corner of Pender Street. He would feel better once he had buildings blocking the line of sight between himself and the Snow. Twenty steps, ten, five— home free!

With a hissing crackle of railgun fire, brick blew out of the corner of the *Sing Tao* building. A hot fragment slashed into his shoulder and knocked him down.

now

"What the hell was that all about?" Lubov said.

"I don't know, but he's gone and the guards are running after him," Emily said, scrambling to her feet. "We'll never have a better chance to get to the barracks and recruit our army."

She jogged toward the barracks with Lubov behind her and John Walker striding at her side.

"Sister-*fucker!*" Holding his shoulder, Jen staggered to his feet and hared off down the alley, running back toward Government House; surely they wouldn't guess he would go that way. A second later he remembered again that the fuckers could track people in the middle of the fucking night, by Buddha's three-pronged cock, but by then it was too late to change his mind. At least the alleys provided garbage cans for cover, and crates and junked cars. Precious good that would do against railguns that could cut through brick walls.

Out the alley, down half a block and along Pender—anything not to stay in a direct line of sight.

What the fuck was he going to do now? His legs were like burning logs. He was in good shape, but this was four blocks at a flat-out sprint. The spit in his mouth tasted like blood. Hell, maybe it was blood, maybe the brick shrapnel had cut him up. He couldn't feel anything from his wounded shoulder. Just as well.

He burst across Columbia and almost fainted. He was less than a block from Government House, which was crawling with *the other fucking Snow guards.*

Shit shit shit, better run like hell, better—

"Jen?"

He spun around at the sound of his name.

The demon who had come for him in the New Moon Manor was standing at the mouth of the alley. She was dressed all in red, with a red flower in her dark hair.

"I have to go," he said.

She walked slowly toward him. Soldiers pounded into sight behind her. She stopped. He had always loved her. "You are so beautiful," he said.

Red fire blossomed suddenly, everywhere, and he was lying on the pavement.

She knelt over him. He tried to speak, there was something he wanted to say, something terribly important, but she laid the red nail of one finger gently on his lips. She was even more beautiful than she had been in the New Moon Manor. His heart broke with desire. The dizzy scent of her filled the night, all flowers and cordite. He tried to speak again but blood bubbled from his mouth instead, red on red. Dimly he was aware there were men standing around him, their voices distant. Someone said, "The fucking slant's bought it."

The years of his mother's loneliness sprang to his eyes and he was sorry, so sorry he had failed her again. Failed her, failed her, failed everyone, and he had never made it right.

Then the woman in red bent down, her black hair sweet and smelling like darkness, and they kissed.

CHAPTER 27

When Water Spider's father found him just before midnight, he was sitting on his balcony and contemplating the wetness of his feet.

Water Spider's feet were wet because it was raining, again, interminably. While he had taken the precaution of bringing an umbrella out onto the balcony with him, the fact that he—sat? lounged? slumped?—on a wicker chaise lounge left his legs entirely uncovered below the knee. He had been drinking as steadily as the rain had been raining, and on balance it seemed rather less effort to leave his legs where they were than to move them. The lazy things would just have to fend for themselves.

The sun had gone down a long time ago. Just to the left of his balcony, clinging to the edge of the roof, a carved gargoyle of vengeful aspect vomited rainwater continuously between his stone lips. A knock came on the balcony door. Water Spider did not bother to turn around. "Enter. I mean, exit. Anyway, no doors here," he said. "Only archways and windows."

"Spider?"

"We are an empty building," Water Spider said. "*Un*-occupied," he added, by way of emphasis. "Hello, Father."

"You are drunk," Floating Ant observed.

"It is a pleasure to succeed at something."

"Do you mind if I sit down?"

"Hm."

His father settled into the other wicker chair.

They sat together in the rain. The umbrella did not quite cover Floating Ant. Rain dripped from the edges of his floppy black hat. A few apartments over and a few floors down, an altercation began. To judge by the sound, someone was beating a cat to death with a pair of cymbals.

"Not at all," Water Spider said.

"What?"

"Um." Water Spider felt some dim species of alarm nosing around inside him like a carp at the bottom of a muddy pool. "You can't be here. The Snows will have guards posted everywhere around me. Watchers."

"Not tonight," Floating Ant said. "They have other problems to concern them just now. I was hoping to show you."

"Wine is a very inferior drink," Water Spider said. "I have been studying it with some attention today and I must tell you that wine is a very poor habit compared to tea."

Floating Ant reached across his son's body and took the drinking bowl from his hand. He sniffed. "Ah. But you drink very excellent tea, whereas this is decidedly inferior wine. What do the words 'gas-line antifreeze' mean to you?"

"Not very much."

"I thought not."

"You betrayed me," Water Spider said. Floating Ant set the drinking bowl gently on the wooden deck. Rain splashed into the plum wine; ripples bloomed in it like roses. "I only figured it out this afternoon, after I started drinking. I was somewhere into my third cup when I remembered something Winter said, about how you and he had been forged in a different fire from the rest of us. I never would have guessed, but when I thought of you *as* him, you two terrible, hard old men, suddenly many things became clear to me."

"Indeed." There was a metallic crash followed by a protracted scream from the unseen cat, followed by silence and then muted cursing. "And what will you do with this new knowing, Spider?"

"Do?" Water Spider laughed. "I am not going to do anything. Knowledge can be entirely divorced from action, I have discovered. Knowing a thing changes the world not at all. I rather think that the more I know, the less I shall do. 'Cherish that which is within you, and shut off that which is without; for much knowledge is a curse!' as Chuang Tzu remarks."

Floating Ant laughed. " 'Begone! I too will wag my tail in the mud!' "

"And you did," Water Spider said. "All the years of my life."

"That is true," his father said.

People were gathering in the streets. This struck Water Spider as odd. He was not sure what time it was, but he knew it had been dark for a while. Someone in the crowd pointed up at his balcony and jeered. He turned away as if from a slap.

Well.

"I was to tell the Southsiders that Li Mei was hidden in the Garden," Water Spider said. "I was to bring them into open conflict with the Powers." He nodded. "An admirable strategy. Did it work? Are you not worried the Dragon will put Winter on the Emperor's throne? Johnny Ma has convinced me that the Dragon is working to fill the red chair, and Winter is the kind of man who might win the Dragon's blessing. Hard. Warlike."

"The Powers would never put a barbarian on the throne."

Water Spider glanced at his father with a flash of his old skepticism. "So Huang Ti said. No doubt the scholars of the court made such pronouncements daily as the Mongols swept down upon the Middle Kingdom."

"I came to tell you that the Snows are melting. Will you not come see?"

"Ah. All the people in the street," Water Spider said. "I will. It will be good for me to walk among them. I can explore the nuances of this surprising new infamy I have acquired."

"No one must accuse you," Floating Ant said. "I will see the truth is known."

"You don't know the truth, Father. Not all of it. Even at your advanced age I am afraid you will not be spared some disappointments—Hm." Water Spider frowned. "I find I cannot stand."

"Li Mei is brewing a pot of Tiger Health inside. It will steady you."

Water Spider made a face. "No doubt. Li Mei, did you say? When did Li Mei arrive?"

"With me. You talked to her just now, after I sat down."

"I did?"

"Yes."

"Oh." Water Spider kept his face expressionless. "I have no memory of this. How . . . unpleasant. I do not think I shall emulate your prowess with the drinking bowl, Honored Father."

"Good boy," Floating Ant said.

Claire was outside when the disturbance began. Unable to sleep, she had been prowling the two-block radius around Government House that was the limit of her "area of duty"—David Oliver's exquisitely polite phrase for the orbit of her house arrest.

She found she wasn't the only person waiting for something to happen. Although it was nearly midnight, the streets were crowded; umbrella spokes were a genuine menace, poking out everywhere like the spines of so many black sea-urchins. Claire felt even more conspicuous than usual, wading through throngs of small Chinese people like some strange white bird paddling on a sea of bobbing black and red umbrella tops. She wondered why hoods had never caught on here. She was very grateful for the one on her army jacket. Hell of a lot more convenient than an umbrella.

How alien the chatter and clang of Cantonese still sounded to her ears. Surprising how alone you could feel in a crowd.

She made her way over to the picket stationed on the southwest corner of Government House. "Quite a bustle out tonight, eh?"

"You said it. Do you know why the slants are so excited?"

Claire shrugged. "I gave up trying to understand what happens here."

"I tell you one thing, they aren't out to throw us a welcoming party." The guard was wearing night goggles and a radio clip. He carried the standard-issue railgun.

A chattering burst of explosions echoed from down the street. Claire jumped. The guard grinned. "Gets the old heart going the first few times, doesn't it? Just firecrackers."

"Are you sure? That sounded like railgun fire."

"Tell me about it. I nearly blew someone's head off my first night on duty. This kid—twelve maybe, thirteen at the most—this kid came up and threw a whole pack of firecrackers at me, right at my feet. Bam! Bam Bam Bam Bam Bammity Bam-bam-bam! I started to shoot his hand off when it went back for the throw, but he looked so young, you know. So I just stood there and then the crackers started going off and I thought, Well fuck it, Reniak, now you've gone and let yourself get dead."

"I don't envy your job."

Reniak shrugged. "The whole position stinks. I'm not some kid on his Compulsory. I'm career army, and this is the shits. Well, it's a living, I guess. You take the bad with the good."

"Can I ask you a question?"

"Shoot."

"Why are you talking with me? Most people are a little more . . . uncomfortable, when I'm around."

Reniak grinned. "You got out of the barracks alive, didn't you? Lady, you are the one person in this man's army we know is going to get out of Chinatown with her ass unscathed. As far as I'm concerned, you can stand at my station all night."

"Oh," Claire said. "Well, thank you, Private. I think. Is it just my imagination, or has the crowd gotten quieter all of a sudden?"

"Mm." Private Reniak's hands shifted on the butt of his gun.

A whisper ran through the crowd like a cat's-paw ruffling the surface of a lake. Then, through the sound of the falling rain and shifting bodies, the sound of a distant call, light and clear, followed immediately by a sentry's challenge.

"That's Nichols, over by the barracks," Private Reniak said. He stared intently into the darkness. Claire fumbled for the field glasses in her inside pocket.

"Oh my God," Reniak said.

"What? What?" Claire got her glasses out and raised them, forgot how to turn on the photomultipliers manually— damn not having a familiar—remembered at last and then was looking out through the ghostly night-vision world. At least she was getting some real value out of being tall, as she could easily see over the bobbing umbrellas.

A delegation was walking across the asphalt of the old parking lot from where the burned barracks had been. On the left walked a heavily muscled young man, army from his bearing, although he carried no weapons Claire could see. On the right, a tall figure dressed in an ancient army greatcoat like the one Winter used to wear when Claire had been a girl. And in between, straight-backed in a mud-splattered jumpsuit that had once been white, marched Emily, walking like she had the keys to the kingdom swinging on her belt. At her back, clearly visible, came a double file of Southside's dead, ghosts in nightshirts and pajamas; a smattering in full uniform. The men who had died in the barracks fire.

"Sweet Christ, girlchick, what the *hell* are you doing?" Claire murmured.

"Blessed Virgin," Reniak whispered.

"Well, no she isn't," Claire said, grinning like an idiot. "But don't say who told you."

She jostled and squeezed and elbowed her way through the crowd and arrived to find Emily and Private Nichols arguing. "I can't go get General Beranek, miss, as I think I explained. I am on duty at this position." He was shaking with fear and yet still he tried to hold his post. The poor dear brave little boys, Claire thought. No wonder Emily was so fond of them.

Nichols tightened his grip on his gun. His eyes kept flicking to the ghosts at Emily's back. "I'm afraid I will have to arrest you, miss."

"Are you going to arrest John Walker too?" Emily said. Nichols stared at the tall, silent man at her side and then moaned. Emily put a kindly hand on his shoulder. "Time is wasting, soldier. I'd like to see General Beranek, please. There are a lot of things we need to discuss."

"I don't want General Beranek," John Walker said. "I want Winter."

Emily flinched. "Please trust me," she said.

"Let me help you out," Claire said to poor Nichols, stepping forward. "I'll stay here with Emily. I'll even arrest her, if you want. In fact, I'd like that. You get General Beranek out here double quick."

Nichols' eyes flicked back to John Walker.

"Get on with it, Mickey," growled one of the ghosts behind Emily. Half his face was black, and when he made a shooing motion, bones showed through the skin of his hands.

Nichols looked at Claire. "Is that a direct order, Lieutenant?"

Claire's commission was so purely ornamental that she had forgotten all about it, but she took the hint. "Absolutely, Private. That's a direct order, and I will be responsible for the consequences."

"Thank God," he said. "Sir." And with that, he turned and ran for Government House like a jackrabbit ahead of a pack of wolves.

The moment he was gone, Emily lunged forward and hugged her governess. "Claire! You're alive! Thanks unto the ages and ages! God is merciful."

Claire laughed. "Yes, I'm alive. So are you," she said, stepping back. "More than just alive, it would appear. Do you know I was foolish enough to be worried about you?"

"You were right to be. Only Providence and the Forest saved me. And Lieutenant Lubov, of course. Ignore his stripes; Mister Lubov has received a battlefield promotion."

The young serviceman on Emily's left snapped off a salute. "Lieutenant."

"Lieutenant. Emily, you seem to have acquired some surprising troops."

"These men are not hers, they are mine," John Walker said.

"I have a claim," Emily said quietly, looking back at the burned and broken men who stood in ragged file behind them. "I sent them here. They died under my command. I have a claim." She turned back to Claire, and the governess could see the weariness and grief abiding in her.

"What if he kills you, Emily?"

"Then I will have one more soldier at my back," John Walker said.

"Have you met my father?" Claire asked him suddenly. "Where is he?"

John Walker gave her a curious look. "Your father lives in the attic rafters of a small house on the North Side," he said. "He is very cold."

The crowd of black umbrellas began to part. Claire could see it ripple all the way back to the doors of Government House. "It's General Beranek." He was flanked by four elite corpsmen, heavily armed.

When he reached them, General Beranek looked at Emily, and then at the ghosts behind her. "Christ. So," he said. "The prodigal daughter returns."

"Mike."

"This is a hell of a mess, Emily."

"I think we can clean it up."

"That will be your grandfather's call. I could cry to see you alive, Em, but you've put us through a hell of a time here. I don't think anyone is ready to forget and forgive. I'm not. And I don't think your grandfather will be either."

Emily looked at him steadily. "I am," she said.

"You don't have the right to be forgiving anybody, girl."

"General, I do. And I will." She held his eyes.

He shrugged. "Winter can decide that for himself. Come inside."

"No."

"What was that?"

"No. I'm not coming inside. Grandfather can come here."

"You're pushing your luck, Emily."

"It's not luck, Mike, and I'm not pushing it. I have no interest in going inside and maybe not coming out again. I like a nice public place, even if it is a bit damp." She raised her voice so that it carried clearly to the crowd and the soldiers stationed around Government House. "I am here to announce the end of the war!"

Soldiers cheered.

"Emily! You can't, you don't have the authority—"

"We can all go home!" More cheers.

Emily smiled. "Lighten up, Mike. I'm getting you out of this tactical nightmare."

His eyes narrowed. "What you're saying is that you have a little army of your own."

"General, my army is exactly as big as you care to make it." They locked eyes again, but it was the general whose gaze dropped first. "Oh, by the way, General, I should introduce Ensign Lubov, my second-in-command."

The general snorted. "Second-in-command! Christ, girl— *I'm* your second-in-command."

"Mike, that is my dearest wish. My current second would still be a private if I hadn't given him a field promotion. He's a little over his head."

"I'll bet." General Beranek looked at the ghosts. "And them? Are they sworn to you too?"

"They are mine," John Walker said. "And for a little while longer, until the North Side thaws, your dead will follow me. Enough talking. Bring Winter to me or I will come to him."

"John Walker. Nichols said, but I didn't . . ." General Beranek stood a long time silent. He laughed once. "Emily, you are without a doubt the sneakiest, ballsiest . . . Runs in the family, I suppose." He smiled and regretfully shook his head. "Emily, I know a little bit about honor. I won't be part of any palace coup, no matter how charming the plotter. I am Winter's man sworn, and I will not betray him."

"Nobody is asking you to betray him," Emily said impatiently. "I just want to talk to him. I give you my word no harm will come to him. I think he can still be brought around to see reason, but he won't listen to me if he doesn't have to, so . . ."

"So you thought you'd demand the surrender of his army to make your point?" General Beranek chuckled. "What a pair. You deserve one another. All right. This is what I will do. I'll send a runner to let him know you're here, and that you want to talk with him outside, and that in my professional opinion hauling you in by force would cause a hell of a riot and maybe more trouble besides. But if he sends back word that you are to be dragged in by your hair, then that is exactly what I will order done. Do you accept?"

"I do not," John Walker said. He stepped forward, and the line of dead men behind him stepped with him. General Beranek's bodyguards paled and raised their railguns. John Walker smiled at them, a little sadly. "Are you ready, then, to march with me?"

Private Nichols forced his way through the crowd, breathing hard. "He's gone, General! Winter is. Left half an hour ago in a chopper with Major Oliver and a little girl."

"Gone?" Claire said, mystified. "Where?"

"Lark! Christ have mercy," Emily whispered. "Oh no, Claire. Don't you see? If he can't have my angel for a sacrifice, he has to offer something else." *What do you suggest I do, Emily? Deliberately sacrifice a real human child?* "He's going to the Bridge." Claire looked at her in horror. Emily swung around. "Mike, could we catch him? Is there any way to get back to the Southside ahead of Winter?"

"No, not if he has thirty minutes on you. He can take his pick of planes. Besides which, I am in no hurry to let you go until I get some orders. Would you mind telling me what in hell is going on?"

"We'll never make it. Blessed Mary!" Emily's voice grew frantic. "Even if we had a jet parked here in the street we couldn't catch him now. Oh Mike, he's taking a little girl down to the High Level Bridge to be sacrificed. I'm sure of it. And God only knows if either one of them will come back.''

Claire looked around. "John Walker," she said. "He's taken his ghosts and gone.''

CHAPTER 28

Unknown to the picket soldiers, David Oliver had his own spotters positioned on several building tops watching the burned-out barracks. When Emily came there to reclaim her dead, he knew within minutes. "She came out of the Forest," he told Winter. "As close to the barracks as she could have. My guess is that Raining Terleski led her to the spot, but chose to stay inside the wood. There are two men with Emily."

"Identities?"

"Can't say yet."

"Do you think she's returning with a heart full of contrition, David?"

"No. She didn't just find a sentry and surrender."

"I agree. She thinks she's got an edge," Winter said. "If you knew what I did about her motives, you would be doubly sure."

"I wish I did, sir." Winter laughed at that. "Sir, the situation here is critical."

"David—"

"No, let me finish, damn it!" And despite everything, David waited for Winter to stop him, but the old man let him speak. "Sir. Two more pickets were mauled an hour ago by some kind of minotaur. The locals say this never used to happen. They say it's because the protection of the Shrouded Ones has been withdrawn. The men are talking, sir. They're talking about what happened in the Lady's Garden, the hand grenade that blew into flowers.''

"David—"

"*We are fighting Powers now*. Not people. Those things from Downtown, the ones the Silks called barbarians, they were just deformed men. This is different," David said. "Sir, I don't think we can win here. I don't even think we can stay. The men aren't in a military situation anymore. They're in a religious one, a supernatural one. We came in here too ignorant, and that's my fault, I know. We came in here and insulted the Powers of this place. It's not like occupying the Southside, sir. It's like marching across the Bridge to the North, and trying to hold that. There are some things flesh and guns can't do."

"You think it's time to retreat," Winter said.

David prepared to have his commission revoked. "Sir, I do."

"I agree."

"What?"

"I agree. It is time for us to decamp."

"Sir?"

Winter stood up from behind his desk and stretched. "Perhaps we could make a stand here. It's not impossible. If we worked hand in glove with the Dragon, maybe. As for Emily—I still think I could outfox her. For all her poise, she is very young. But maybe she has something unexpected up her sleeve. I would love to find out which of us is craftier, but Emily wants to make a mistake too grave for me to risk.

"We are awash in spirits here, David. I think that old man, Water Spider's father . . . perhaps he got the best of us. Looking back, I think he sacrificed his son to draw us into provoking the Dragon and the Lady. A cruel man, to do that." Winter nodded. "The more I consider it, the clearer the matter becomes. Let Emily have her way. Let her have the whole Southside. I trained her for it. She'll do a hell of a job. I don't want the power anymore. But there is one thing I must see done that Emily will not do."

"Happily, I have become used to suppressing my curiosity, sir."

"If I thought that were true I'd sack you, David. You need curiosity in Intelligence—But you need loyalty more. In a family or a city or an army. The world is a blind and separate machine; life is the only thing in it with meaning. Life is all that coheres." Winter stretched again. "I have a number of boring speeches. Perhaps I'll make them to you on the plane. We're going on a trip, Major. No need to pack your kit, we won't be long. But pick up the girl for me, would you?"

"The girl?"

"Raining Terleski's daughter."

"Why, sir?"

"She's the heir to a Power, isn't she? Important, to a Power's way of thinking. Surely, if we have learned anything in this spirits' playground, we have learned that." Winter picked his army jacket off the back of the chair where he had thrown it. "There's a helicopter waiting on the roof to take us to a plane moored on English Bay. I've had them there since morning. I'll meet you and the girl upstairs."

"Lark," David said.

"What?"

"Lark. It's her name. Lark Climbs Singing."

"Is it? Pretty name," Winter said.

They took the chopper to English Bay, where Winter's jet sat bobbing gently on long pontoons. David had a bit of a struggle getting Lark to step from the dock to the plane; eventually he had to pick her up and hand her over to Winter. There were sixteen seats on the plane, arranged in clusters of four. David and Lark sat side by side. Winter sat across from them, watching.

The computer gave them a smooth flight. There was a hail from Vancouver just as they reached the eastern edge of the Rocky Mountains, but Winter told the plane not to respond. Eventually the hailing ceased.

"Are we going to see Mommy?"

"Not right now," David said.

"Why?"

David didn't answer.

"Why? Why aren't we going to see Mommy?"

"We're going somewhere else right now."

"Where?"

"Southside. Where your daddy lives."

"Are we going to see Daddy?"

"No."

"Oh. Daddy died," Lark said.

"I'm very sorry."

"Why did he died?"

David didn't answer.

"Why did he died?" Lark wasn't crying. She didn't even seem upset. Of course, she hadn't seen her father in a long time. "Am I going to died?" Lark asked. David didn't answer. Lark waited. "Am I going to died?"

"Someday. Not for a very long time."

"Why? Why am I going to died?"

David looked helplessly at Winter. Winter was looking at Lark very carefully, like a man studying a scene he would need to remember. He said nothing. "It's what happens to living things," David explained. "All living things die some time. That's what makes them different from things that aren't alive."

"Are you going to died?"

"Yes. Someday. Not for a long time I hope."

"Is he going to died?" Lark said, pointing at Winter.

"Yes."

"Oh." She frowned. "Can a plane died?"

"No, it's not alive. Only living things can die. Plants and animals and people."

"I'm a people," Lark said.

David got up and walked to the galley. He found some crackers and brought them back for Lark. Crumbs got into her chair and scritched her and she whined until he let her take off her safety belt. She stood and he brushed the crumbs off her seat. Then she didn't want to put the belt back on. He insisted and they had a fight about it. He held her in the chair as gently as he could and buckled her in. She cried very loudly. The noise was amazingly loud in the small plane.

When she finished crying she undid the buckle. He pretended not to notice.

"Why is he looking at me?" Lark said, pointing at Winter.

"Why don't you ask him?"

"Don't look at me!"

It was a while before Winter spoke. "Would you like me to look somewhere else?"

"No! Don't look!" Lark said. She scowled and curled up in her seat. Then she held her hands in front of her face. "Don't!"

Winter looked away.

Later she asked if Winter was a stranger. "I guess so," David said.

"Mommy says I shouldn't talk to strangers."

"You're a stranger to me," Winter said unexpectedly. "Had you thought of that?"

Lark looked offended. "*I'm* not a stranger."

"You are to me."

She scowled and curled up in her chair again and covered her face.

"Are we going to see Mommy?"

"No, we're going to the Southside."

"Why?"

"I don't know."

David was surprised he had admitted that. Maybe there were things to be learned about interrogation from the little girl. Think of her as a fellow professional and maybe it would make the trip go faster. Maybe it would ease the dread.

He didn't feel the dread. Not really. He observed it. As if noting the progress of enemy troops on a war map.

The jet reached Southside eighty minutes after taking off. They were met on the ground by a curious sergeant who reported an urgent call from General Beranek. Winter said he would respond from the Tory Building and asked for a car. Lark wanted to ride in the front seat but wanted David to come with her, so all three of them sat in the front. Winter drove.

It was fifteen minutes from the landing strip to the outskirts of town. Hundred-year-old grain elevators stood like sentries along the empty highway. Then they were at the city, driving past Southgate and Lendrum, down 111th. Winter didn't go the usual way to the Tory Building. This made David very uneasy, he noticed. He had figured out something about what Winter was doing, that much was clear, but he wasn't letting himself know what it was. Odd.

They had left the clouds back in Vancouver, and the lit streets and the throngs of people. Here the night was black and still. They rolled through the silent city. White lines flickered into existence in their headlights and went pouring back behind them. They drove down 109th Street and did not turn to head for the Tory Building there either, but came instead to the top of the High Level Bridge. Of course the road had not been plowed. Winter shifted to first gear and began to creep slowly down the hill.

The terrible thing which was going to happen was now very clear and definite in David's mind, only he didn't know what it was. The sensation was like being in a dream where he had an urgent letter to read, but the words when he stared at them would not come, destroyed by a blindness that was not a blindness of the eye.

They reached the bottom of the hill. They were on the Bridge.

There was still a good deal of snow on the roadway, though clearly it had thawed several times while they had been in Vancouver. The top of the snow was icy, glinting and hard in their headlights. The whole road was slick with black ice. They crept along. When they were halfway across, David thought he saw a figure by the side of the road. A moment later Winter grunted and flicked on his high beams. A hundred meters ahead, a man stood on the roadway, watching. Winter slowed down further. The man began to walk toward them. Winter stopped the car and unbuckled his seat belt. "Time to get out."

David helped Lark with her seat belt and eased her out the passenger side door. It was cold outside. Not killing, but brisk. A few degrees below freezing. The icy snow crunched loudly underfoot and David found he had to be very careful stepping on the black ice. It was dark now that the car's headlights were off. Faint starshine the only light.

How hard it was to see the right course by that cold, distant light.

It was time to act. It was definitely time to act. He stood holding Lark's hand in his own and wondered what he was going to do. Winter came around to their side of the car and picked Lark up. "I'm going to carry you now," he said.

She looked scared. "Mister?"

"It's okay."

"He's a stranger."

"It's okay."

Winter walked to the right side of the road, ducked under a girder, and stepped up onto the cement sidewalk. He was now on the pedestrian walkway on the east side of the bridge. He started walking north. "Thank you, David. You should probably drive back now," he said.

The waiting man was now standing on the sidewalk about ten meters from them. He was wearing an ancient Southside greatcoat. He had a regiment of soldiers at his back. Many of them looked to be horribly burned, but they made no sound, and no steam curled from their mouths as they stood behind their commander.

With the ease of a practiced grandfather, Winter stepped a little to his right and shifted Lark onto his right hip. Now he was holding her just above the rail at the edge of the Bridge. It was a long way from the bottom of his right arm to the cold river far below.

David noticed his own hand was on the gun inside his jacket pocket.

The stranger in the greatcoat took another step forward. "Stop," Winter said. He looked more closely. "Oh. It's you."

John Walker said, "It always is."

• • •

John Walker. The king of North Side's dead faced them on the Bridge. An army of ghosts stood behind him, blackened and burned. The men who had died in the barracks, of course. David crossed himself. Holy God, Holy mighty, Holy eternal.

He said, "I don't know what your business with John Walker is, sir, but Lark isn't part of it. She made her trip to the Bridge like everyone else and she came back."

"Sorry, son. Desperate times call for desperate measures," Winter said. "I hope to hell nothing will be asked of her, but I don't know what the North Side will demand. She is the heir to a Power and she does matter. She can't help that, any more than Emily could, or I could." He shrugged and looked at the angel he had cut from his own flesh so many years before. "Hello, John. You have been shirking your responsibilities, I hear. I hope you don't blame that on me."

"I don't blame you. Not for anything," John Walker said. "Perhaps I did, once. When I was younger. But it is not for the child to judge his father. All I want now is to be with you. Let me come back across the Bridge."

"I made a deal, John."

"That was a long time ago," John Walker said. "That was a long dark time ago. And I lived by your deal, Winter. Father. You were over there with warmth and light and love—but it was John who kept the other kingdom. John who walked the dark landscape. John who lived in the empty house. All the grim years of your reign it was I, the boy you despised, gave up, threw away, I that did the coldest work. It was I who kept the night watch for you."

Winter's breath smoked in the cold air.

"But daylight will be breaking soon, Father. And I want to go home."

For a long moment Winter did not answer. David thought he would turn and put little Lark down and they would walk back up the hill to the Southside and make hot chicory and drink it together and wait for the sun to rise. But Winter shook his head. "I do not forget my responsibilities." He began to walk forward with Lark held over the edge of the Bridge railing. "I made a deal with the North Side once. I go to make another. Perhaps the magic will not demand her sacrifice. Don't try to stop me. That would only make her death a certainty."

"Mister?" Lark cried. Standing there on the cold dark Bridge, David found himself wondering, sadly, why he had never married. It seemed like a very important question. "Mister?"

Would he speak? No. No answer. But he had not forgotten the promise he made to Raining. He had not forgotten Wire, that extraordinary young woman who said, "We are the only parents she has left."

The question was, Where would the bullet drive Winter's body? Standing where David was, two paces behind Winter and a little to the right, could he shoot his commander in the left shoulder and hope the impact would spin the body around fast enough to keep Lark from falling over the bridge?

John Walker stepped forward.

What about a bullet to the leg? Would it buckle Winter's body and drop Lark below the level of the railing?

Winter shifted Lark again, holding her out in empty space. She whimpered.

John Walker stepped back.

David scrambled from the road onto the sidewalk and ran forward. He couldn't decide what to do, so he shot Winter through the brain and lunged for the girl. He missed her and she fell screaming as Winter's arm dropped beneath her.

She grabbed his dead body, little arms clutched around his bloody neck as he buckled, and David had another chance and this time he caught her. He tried to pull her back from the railing but she was screaming and wouldn't let go of Winter's body until David took her arms and held her and held her while she screamed.

John Walker knelt beside Winter's body, weeping. David looked up and met his eyes. "I promised," he said.

He went back to the car and used its radio to call for help. He explained that Winter was dead and that he had a little girl with him who might need assistance. Before he finished, an operator cut in to say that Emily was on her way and wanted everything left for an investigation. He was to wait and touch nothing.

He buckled Lark up in the front seat and turned on the heater. When she was safe and warm he got out of the car. Winter's body lay where it had fallen. Gouts of blood had already frozen into a crusty brown stain on the snow. John Walker was gone. The only trace of him that remained was a set of boot prints on the snowy sidewalk heading up the Bridge to the Southside.

David got back in the car. He cracked a window so he and Lark wouldn't die of carbon monoxide poisoning. The girl cried until she fell asleep. Together they sat in the warm car for hours. From time to time David spoke on the radio. Delays developed while people tried to decide whether to let Emily come down to the scene of Winter's murder. No one told David what was happening in Chinatown and he didn't care.

At last Emily arrived. David was taken into custody. The sky was just beginning to pale in the east. It was almost morning.

CHAPTER 29

Claire had never seen Emily so upset. The news of Winter's death unravelled her.

Emily had never been a worse politician than she was for the next couple of hours; silent and withdrawn with the enlisted men she needed to command, and, more damaging still, snappish and high-handed with the few Southsiders of her stature. She had even provoked Mike Beranek, who was, in Claire's jaundiced opinion, as level-headed a man as the army was capable of promoting. Claire had found herself in the highly unusual situation of having to shut Emily up and do her talking for her.

Things got so bad that at one point Claire feared there was a real chance of Emily's landing in prison. This was not the way she put it to Emily. Instead, she said it looked as if Emily would not be allowed to participate in the investigation into Winter's death. There was even talk, she said reluctantly, that Emily would not be allowed to pay her respects to his body before he was entombed.

A sneaky tactic and it worked. With a great effort of will Emily pulled herself together and began to coax, argue, wheedle, and bully the assorted dignitaries of Southside with something approaching her usual skill.

It went surprisingly well. The shock of Winter's death was very great on the Southside. Claire suspected that in their hearts, her fellow citizens were desperate for Emily to

take charge; their obstreperous behavior reflected their outrage that she hadn't stepped in and done so masterfully from
the start. As soon as Emily showed she had her touch back,
everyone was glad to accede to her wishes. She was, after
all, Winter's political heir and next of kin. Claire was able
to relax and observe the rest of the negotiations with what
she imagined must be the feelings of a proud mother with
no interest in hockey watching her son dominate his league's
All-Star game.

On the Bridge it was different. No politics there. No ma-
neuvering. Just the fact of Winter's body lying cold and stiff
on the icy sidewalk. Emily prayed over it, and wept. When
her tears were done she crossed herself and stood. "Claire?"

"Yes."

"I have to go across the Bridge. I have to . . . harrow the
North Side, you know. I have to make peace with those
children. I have to end Grandfather's deal."

"Do I hear something about Making a New Covenant?"

Emily laughed unsteadily. "That too. Claire? I'm frightened."

"Sensible."

"Will you come with me?"

Claire looked around. David Oliver had driven Lark up
to the top of the hill. He was probably being questioned
already; no doubt by one of his own men. "I didn't have
anything else planned," she said.

Pale morning light came as they began their crossing.

The river was almost free, now. The pack ice had broken
up; scattered floes drifted singly down the river's broad
brown back. Old snow still lingered in the dim river valley
and spread out across the wrinkled plains. The great red-
black bones of the High Level Bridge lay on that mute white
expanse like the skeleton of some huge iron beast. At the
north end of the Bridge, where it began its climb up the far
bank of the river, Emily crouched before a little mound in
the roadway. Brushing away the snow, she found a pile of
children's bones, tiny arms and feet and fingers, and twelve
small skulls. The bones were cold to the touch. To Claire's

surprise Emily did not close her eyes and pray, but only knelt before those dead children, unblinking. And she made there certain promises.

Then she stood and together they climbed up the hill to the abandoned city.

It was colder on the North Side, and still. The road forked after leaving the Bridge. Emily chose the right-hand way that skirted the edge of the old Legislature buildings. The pond before it was frozen, its fountain still. A few cars sat empty in the snow-covered parking lot. Then they went on, past the Legislature and up the hill, Emily puffing as they passed the YWCA and the *Edmonton Journal* building on the corner of Jasper Avenue. All the roads were empty and all the windows were dark. Everything human had been stripped from that place, every thought or purpose; every building and car and sign and street lamp was reduced to landscape only. Every work of man held only the same irreducible meaning as the barren trees, and the snowy fields, and the prairie sky.

"Look!" Emily said, pointing upwards.

"What? I don't see anything."

"It's a pigeon."

"What? Oh—there it is," Claire said. One pale grey bird peered down at them from a window ledge just under the eaves of the *Edmonton Journal* building. It cocked its head to one side, fluffed, and then rushed into the sky in a batter of grey wings.

"Ha!" Emily said. She was grinning.

Claire grinned back. "Nice to see *something*, anyway. Hey—look over there. On the streetlight. No, right on top."

"Magpie? No, a crow. Two crows. Let's go that way." Emily waved across the street to where the crows were. Claire went first, stumbling when she stepped off a curb whose edge was still hidden by the snow. "Look at our footprints!" Emily said. "Like being the first kid in the schoolyard after a blizzard."

"Big playground," Claire said. She felt herself smiling.

Three cedar waxwings watched them from the top of a

huge white marquee with the words FAMOUS PLAYERS
spelled out in letters a foot high. The marquee stuck out
above a pair of large glass doors rimed with frost. Emily
waved to their reflections in the glass; they very civilly
waved back.

There were more crows on the electric trolley lines now—
three, five, seven of them. Another waxwing perched in the
naked branches of a scrawny tree planted to beautify the
sidewalk untold decades earlier. A brace of singularly
greedy-looking magpies patrolled the park in Sir Winston
Churchill Square. And on the steps of the public library,
Emily and Claire surprised a whole flock of pigeons. The
birds scattered around them, booming and whirring.

The empty city was alive with birds, birds in every tree,
birds on statues and parking meters; birds perched on the
gables of old buildings or issuing suddenly from underground parking lots. Crows and magpies and sparrows,
finches and pigeons and little hedge wrens. Emily even spied
a first spring robin, red breast puffed out bravely against the
white of winter.

"Could they all be birds?" Emily asked.

"Could what be birds?"

"The dead. The ghosts. They live half in our world and
half in another. Grandfather said that."

"Oh," said Claire. "We should have asked John Walker."

The day grew warmer. Claire began to sweat in her parka.
The dry snow underfoot lost its squeak, then grew mushy
and clotting. Water stains spread down the sides of empty
office buildings. Still the birds came, scores of them, flocks
of them. Everywhere Emily went, the birds followed her.
The sparrows a-quiver, the pigeons disapproving and easily
offended, a source of endless amusement for the jeering
magpies, and the crows, who croaked out their own cynical
commentary on the whole business. By the time Emily
headed back for the Bridge, a storm cloud of birds wheeled
and hovered over her. From time to time she would raise
her hand and whirl it, and the whole vast twittering cloud
of birds would spin like autumn leaves stirred by the wind.

It was almost noon when they returned to the park at the head of the Bridge. Here the birds hung back, uncertain, settling on trees and park benches and bicycle racks. But Emily shook her head, and raised her arm again, and cried out, no stirring words but a schoolgirl's yell, and jogged to the sidewalk leading down the hill and began to run, quicker and quicker, and Claire loped alongside, and the birds began to follow, streaming out behind them like a banner. Faster and faster, slithering on the slippery sidewalk, Emily bounding down the slope, each stride huger than the last, and then they were running onto the very Bridge itself, and the sky was dark with wings.

Emily faltered, laughing, as her wind gave out. The cloud of birds swept by, crows beating steadily below the Bridge and magpies with them, little brown birds and dun-colored birds, spotted and stippled and speckled birds of hedge and limb, darting through the girders, and overhead the great rushing roaring of ten thousand beating wings. And then the birds were past them, driven like leaves on the wind. Over the valley they soared, and into the trees on the south side of the river. Some beat strongly up the hill, swirling among the university buildings or darting into the tangled hedge-rows of bare honeysuckle and rhododendron, or lifting up, higher and higher, to circle around the great dome of St. Paul's.

Then drifting, landing, perching, hopping, stopping, walking, watching, the birds came down, settling after so many long cold years among the streets and houses of the Southside, for once and forever.

Emily knelt again at the cairn of small bones and crossed herself and bowed her head.

A ring of birds gathered around her: a finch, a duck, a meadowlark; swallow, waxwing, snowy owl, chickadee, wren. A squawking crow. A white marsh-hawk, that men would call a harrier, fierce as the winter sun. Last to come was the woodpecker, winging not from the north, but from the west, coming up along the river. A faint sea-scent clung about his wings.

Emily touched the skeletons, their tiny skulls and finger
bones. "We should bury these." She stripped off her foil
parka and made a rough sling of it and put the bones inside.
Then she started walking back across the Bridge, for home.

One by one, the last birds lifted into the air and flew
ahead, arrowing for the Southside. Swallow, meadowlark,
finch, and the others, hopped, squawked, and flapped away
singing.

The Harrier landed on the bridge railing next to Claire.
With fierce pale eyes they beheld one another. Then the
white hawk leapt up, beating higher and higher, until she let
her wings open and soared toward the wooded southern
bank. She screamed, and split the day open with her fierce
exultation.

Some time later Claire realized Emily was looking at her.
She turned away from the girl abruptly.

"Well?" Emily said. "It's time to go home."

CHAPTER 30

That night was the worst of Wire's life.

She had given Lark up to be slaughtered.

David Oliver had come into the room and told her in his grave tired gentle lying way that he needed to take Lark with him for a moment, the *bastard* . . . Oh shit, oh gods. Had said he would only be a minute, and stupid worthless cunt she had trusted him, trusted a Southside spy. And let Raining's daughter go to die.

She cried loudly, hysterically, trying to lose herself in the violence of her own grief. But she never managed to forget why she was crying, so she stopped.

Oh Lark. Black hair bouncing, small limbs tireless in play. Small mouth open in sleep.

Oh Rain, what have I done to you?

Because he was a man, dammit. Because he was a man and he admired her and he had wanted to kiss her once, she felt it, and so she had liked him. And trusted him. She had sold her best friend's life for a few tired smiles from a stranger. Unbelievable.

If she could have traded places with Lark, she would have done it like a shot. She would have gone to her death weeping tears of joy. And it didn't matter a damn. Because the terrible mistake was made and it couldn't be taken back, not by a million good intentions, not by the most anguished remorse. Lark would die and Wire would live, because the universe is deaf and dumb and does not hear what we say and has no answers for us, but rolls on crushing and implacable, and our dreams and desires are less than ghosts to it. Less than smoke on the wind.

It never occurred to Wire to kill herself. She only imagined living in anguish, always.

The god came to her just before dawn, clothed in the body of a woodpecker—a red wingbeat and a faint smell of bark and stream water.

"You!" she whispered. He stood before her, smiling. Beautiful beyond hope. "I know you. You were watching me the day I went to get Raining."

He held out his hand and she knew she must stand and approach him.

Even smiling, his beauty was terrible. Unendurable. She fell to her knees and looked away, unable to bear his brightness. He took her hand. His touch was morning sun kindling the treetops; cold creek water over stone; deer in the forest. His smile was not serene but merry. He looked at her with rascal's eyes that promised everything, and kissed her hand, and like a miracle she was forgiven.

"I can't," she whispered. "I don't deserve it."

He laughed, annihilating all deserving. As if her guilt, too, was only smoke on the wind. And the touch of his lips on her hand was sweet, was sweet.

Early that morning a rumor of Winter's passing flew through the corridors of Government House, and was soon confirmed. Winter was dead and General Beranek was in charge until further notice. Someone back on the Southside, David Oliver perhaps, thought of Wire at last and sent word to her that Lark was safe. Wire was to be released and escorted to her apartment.

A few hours later she was home.

At the entrance to her building she said goodbye to the well-muscled escort the Southsiders had provided and climbed the stairs to her apartment, all seven flights. She came to her door still puffing and turned the knob. Her right hand was stiff and painful where the god had kissed it. She drew a breath and stepped inside. The hand bothered her again as she unlaced her chunky boots. Her apartment hummed and chortled, happy to have her back. A burner came on under the kettle. Pleasant music began to play.

Wire stripped off her socks and walked barefoot across the hardwood floors. She was grimy and weary from her days of captivity and she meant to take a bath, but first she walked over to her balcony door, slid it open and stepped outside. It had finally stopped raining; the grey cloud was beginning to break up. Here and there the midmorning sun slipped through, dancing on the water of English Bay.

No woodpecker regarded her from the branches of the cherry tree.

She never saw the god again, and her right hand, where he had kissed it, remained crippled with arthritis for the rest of her days. But on that morning, the feeling of joy and relief and grace, more profound for being undeserved, still abided deeply within her; and his rogue's kiss had been sweet, and the world was good.

Wire sat on her bed and pulled off her clothes, lifting Raining's locket off last of all. She held it up, and laughed at her fat future self there—thanks a lot, Rain. She kissed the locket and tossed it in the general direction of her charm box. Then she headed for the shower, wondering what she was going to eat for breakfast.

CHAPTER 31

When David Oliver woke he recognized his surroundings immediately. He was in the solitary confinement cell in the McKernan stockade.

He had done some work here. The room was very small and dark. The floor was made of concrete and very cold. He couldn't remember if he had been carried in or if he had walked. He was still wearing his fatigues, but his pockets had been emptied out and his rank insignia cut away. No familiar, of course. He blinked. Even the HUD lenses were gone. He felt naked without them. Nothing left but David now.

He had never married, and had no children. He had been very good at his job, but his job was gone. He had left it. So what was this thing, this David? What was left over when all the uniforms were stripped away? No answer.

By the book, he would be court-martialled and shot.

There would be a tremendous power vacuum with Winter gone. He could think of several people who might try to step into it. General Beranek, for one. Always ambitious, and convinced that he had the best interests of Southside at heart. Jason Paslawski another. Emily of course. Things might not be going by the book for a little while. Emily— so she had made it back after all—Emily wasn't the exe- cuting sort, he didn't think. Mind you, he had murdered her grandfather. Beranek would take no joy in it, but he would go by the book for sure. Paslawski would be genuinely pleased to see David executed. Prick.

David knew he should be thinking hard about these things, but his mind wouldn't stick to the task. It kept slipping back to what they had taken away from him. His uniform, his familiar. That's how rough interrogation worked. Strip the subject of the things that gave him his sense of self. Pressure him. Then give him something to rebuild on—yourself. Give him yourself. He wondered which of his subordinates would be working on him.

Even if they gave him his familiar back, what good would it do? It was trained to analyze politics and memorize maps, to perform unit conversions between greed and dollars and ambition and rifles and lust. Very useful for Major Oliver. Not much good for David.

His fatigues were taken away and replaced with clean ones. Food was left for him three times a day. After two days he had a visitor. "Come in," he said. "Hello, Lieutenant . . ." He waited for the name to jump into the corner of his contact lens, but it didn't. How odd.

"Lubov."

David nodded. "You look familiar."

"Yes, sir. Come with me, sir." Reflexively David noticed that Lubov's lieutenant's insignia were brand new. Field promotion in the Chinatown action, perhaps.

It was a watery spring day outside. The sun hurt David's eyes. Soldiers watched them pass. Lubov brought him to an army truck and asked him to get in. There was a spare foil parka on the front seat. Lubov told him to put it on. They drove in silence to the Parkallen Cemetery. Lubov parked the truck. "See the mausoleum at the top of the hill?" David nodded. "I'll wait here," Lubov said.

David got out of the truck and walked through the wrought-iron cemetery gates and up the south face of the hill. Single pine trees stood among the graves. Pockets of snow still remained in the deep gloom beneath their branches, but mostly it had melted away, leaving the graves bare. A few were marked with wreaths or recent ashes.

Three had braziers permanently installed within tiny ceno-
taphs.

Winter's mausoleum was bigger, of course; an open, pil-
lared enclosure about the same size as David's cell. Winter's
sarcophagus rested on a low stone table that took up most
of the chamber. Candleholders had been hung from each
pillar. Each held a beeswax candle. All the candles were lit.

Emily watched the man who had killed her grandfather walk
slowly up the hillside. She wondered if she could ever forgive him. But a real leader wouldn't worry about forgiving
him, would she? Winter wouldn't. Just use him. Use him to
the best effect.

Emily was no longer sure that a real leader was something
she could be. Ambition was another thing she seemed to
have given up for Lent this year. Truly a lean spring, then:
she had eaten ambition every day for a long time. She would
grow very thin without it.

"Hello, David. God bless," she said.

He reached the mausoleum, then stopped as if he had no
idea of what to do next.

—Very low arousal. Tremendously flattened affect, Emily's familiar said.

—Go away, Emily told it. I don't want you here.

—You can't afford to be emotional about th—

The blue letters scrolling down Emily's eyes faded
abruptly as she turned her familiar off.

"Why did you do that?" David said. Too much the Intelligence officer not to notice.

"I don't know," Emily said. She looked at the hand that
had fired the shot that killed her grandfather. "This is private."

She had set up a large brazier at the foot of the sarcophagus. Waves of heat rose from it, making the air shimmer.
She drew a knife from the sheath at her hip. Pushing back
her kerchief, she carefully cut a lock of her crinkly brown
hair and dropped it onto the coals. It smoked and writhed
and was ash. Then she took the knife and made very small
cuts in the fingertips of her right hand. She crossed herself

and then shook the hand over the brazier. A few droplets of blood hissed among the coals. Good night, Grandfather.

No answer.

She wished Claire were here.

Emily turned and looked up at the sky, as if contemplating some deep thoughts about eternity. Actually she was trying to keep the tears now pooled in her eyes from spilling down her cheeks. She'd had the idea she ought to handle David alone, but it was hard to feel like a tough-assed leader of men with her breath catching in funny little hiccups in her throat and her nose starting to run. Oh, hell. Here came the tears in earnest.

She cried.

When the worst of it was past, she whispered the Lord's Prayer; holy God, holy mighty, holy immortal. Praying for— what? Grace, perhaps—her prayers held out like the fingers of a blind woman for the chance to touch that serenity. To see a little better by that uncreated Light. Lord have mercy, Lord have mercy, Lord have mercy unto the ages and ages, amen.

There. Better. Silly girl. Be practical . . . Except now Emily knew how terribly practical grief was. How deeply the experience of grief ran into the world. How truly the Crucifixion taught.

She handed David the knife. He cut a lock of his own hair and then stopped, directionless. He stood with the hair in his hand for a while, then dropped it in the fire. More to get rid of it than anything else. "Oh David," she murmured. "You are lost, aren't you?"

He gave her back the knife.

All right, girlchick. Pull yourself together. "So, Major Oliver. What am I to do with you?"

"By the book? Court-martial and execute me."

"There's been enough killing already, don't you think?"

He shrugged, half-smiling, and said, "You at least I still understand."

"I don't think I can leave you in prison. Too destabilizing to have you there among us, like a bad memory."

"Then leave me in the stockade until someone kills me.

When I'm dead, mount a vigorous and ineffectual inquiry into the identity of my murderer.''

"I am never quite sure if you're joking when you say things like that, David.''

"Neither am I.''

"Ah. That explains it.'' Emily looked out over the hillside. Viewed objectively, it was a glorious spring day. The air felt warm and moist, the small white clouds were clean, the blue sky freshly washed. A few white crocuses rose blooming from their icy beds. "Do you think he'll go to hell, David?''

"Yes.''

"You seem very sure,'' she said sadly.

"He was willing to kill that little girl.''

"I know.'' Emily was crying again.

"Christ is merciful,'' David said awkwardly.

Emily bit her lip. "So they tell us. So we must believe.'' She wiped her face with the back of her hand and then wiped her hand on her fatigues, leaving a faint bloodstain. "I don't think he was evil. I still don't. He made a covenant and he strove to keep it. He saved us all, in the Dream. He just . . . couldn't change when the world changed underneath him.''

"He could not adapt to the New Covenant?'' David said. "Didn't recognize his granddaughter was the messiah, is that it? He could not hear the Good News.''

"Spare me your sarcasm, David.''

"I'm not sure I'm being sarcastic.''

Emily looked away. "The great pyre was yesterday. You weren't invited.''

"Thank you.''

"But I don't think he will wake up on the North Side. I think those days are gone. I think this age of the world is coming to an end. His body is in this stone box and his soul is in the hands of God eternal, amen, amen.''

"It isn't going to be easy for you to stay in power,'' David said.

"I'm not enjoying it much. I thought I would, you know. I didn't want him to die, of course. But I always looked forward to taking over the Southside. It was what I had been trained to do. But now . . .''

"Beranek thinks you're a mystic. Imagines you giving money to the Church. He doesn't think women should hold office. Worries what you'll do when you get premenstrual or pregnant or menopausal.''

Emily snorted. "He's getting a bit ahead of himself on the last two counts, isn't he?''

"Beranek is a good man," David said. "Paslawski is more problematic.''

"Meaning you don't have any dirt on him?''

"More or less. He's also very well off. He's actually worth more than you are.''

"That I did know. Winter and I talked about him. You think he has designs?''

"I would advise caution. But I'm not in Intelligence anymore, am I? Not in anything.''

"Only in yourself," Emily said slowly. "That, you always have.'' He shook his head abruptly. "You may not know what you are. But God does.''

David didn't answer.

Well, it probably wasn't the best time for Sunday School, Emily decided. If God wanted David, a path would be shown to him. Unless she had him shot, of course. That would rather cut short his chances of salvation. "I think I have to banish you," Emily said at last. "I don't want you killed but I can't have you around. You are going to have to leave the Southside.''

"Forever?" he asked. She nodded. "I understand." A little wind came up. The coals in the brazier breathed deeply of it, flushing as if at the taste of wine. "Is there anything else you wanted from me?''

Emily looked away. "Why didn't you shoot him in the knee, David? You were behind him, damn it. You could have taken a leg, a knee, a shoulder. Anything. Why didn't you?''

"I don't know.''

"That's it?''

He shrugged.

She turned to look up at the sky again, blinking. Damn tears. Go away.

weep

I don't want to cry anymore. Don't make me. I'm so tired.

weep

Emily looked into the fire. "I drew the hammer back," she said at last. "You just pulled the trigger."

CHAPTER 32

A week after Raining and Lark had been reunited, Emily sent a message to say that she had found Nick's frozen body in the Municipal Airport on the North Side. She offered to send him back to Chinatown. Raining accepted.

She made a travois, lashing together boughs of pine, and asked Wire to spend a day or two with her in the Forest. When word came early one morning that Nick's body had arrived, she asked her mother to look after Lark and told Wire to gather matches and kindling. Raining went to her room. From the bottom of her jewelry chest she took a small jade box, a gift from her grandmother long ago. Then she went into the kitchen and took one cloth bag.

The sky must have been paling in the world above the trees by the time she and Wire left Cedar House, for high overhead the first thrushes had begun to sing, but under the great limbs of cedar and pine and Douglas fir, the world was still dark. Grave and respectful, the path picked his way through the gloom, careful that Raining not stumble and fall, gathering speed only when daybreak finally began to filter down to the forest floor.

Three Southside soldiers waited by a simple wooden casket at the edge of the Forest. Raining asked them to lift Nick's body out and place it on the travois. This they did. When she told them they need not come into the Forest, they looked relieved but offered to help just the same. "The way will be short," Raining said.

Nick's body was still cold, and very heavy. It took all her strength and Wire's to drag the travois down the path. But Raining had been right about the length of her journey. Almost as soon as the Southsiders were out of view, the path entered a clearing high on a hilltop. The air was cool here, and the leaves on the birch and poplar trees were yet unborn, curled tight in their black buds. Raining undressed Nick's body. The skin on his face was white, his lips blue. Blue shadows in the hollows of his bony forehead. Curls of black hair on his white chest. Shrunken genitals. Nails blue on his toes and fingers. When she kissed his cheek it felt like cold leather.

"Build the fire," Raining told Wire. When it was ready they placed Nick on the pyre. Then they lit the kindling.

Raining cried.

Hours later, after the last flame had gone out, Raining crouched before the embers. From a fallen tree she cut a piece of bark as long as her arm and as wide as her hand. With it she stirred among the coals, clumsily sweeping up a pile of fine white ash. This she scooped into her jade box. Then she rooted through the fire-bed until she found Nick's blackened hand bones. These she wrapped in white cloth and put inside the cloth bag while Wire looked on, scared and unspeaking. Then they went home.

Back at Cedar House, Raining made up her paint. She separated three duck's eggs, letting the whites drip down into a clean glass bowl. These she whipped into a meringue. She placed the whipped egg whites on a shallow platter and collected the glair when it ran off. She divided it into two pots. To the larger she added the white ashes she had scooped from the hottest part of the fire, stirring until she had a fine, luminous white. Then she took Nick's blackened finger bones and made ivoryblack, scraping the carbon residue into a pestle where she ground it into finest powder. This she added to the smaller pot.

Then she painted the last portrait she would ever make, a study of Nick in black and white, a few simple lines, a man standing alone on the vast naked prairie.

Standing alone.

The rest of her art for the years of her life would be full of trees and rivers, branches and leaves, clouds and fish and her beloved birds, but never again would she paint a human form.

Five months after Nick had died, Wire stood peering up the stairs of Cedar House. "Rain? Are you ready yet?"

"Almost."

"You said that ten minutes ago."

No answer.

Lark tugged on Wire's leg. "I want to come too!"

"We've already been through—Aa! What have you done!"

Lark was splotched and splattered with red paint everywhere. It was on her hands, her clothes, her face, her hair. She looked as if she had been rolled through a slaughterhouse and then left to dry in the sun. To Wire's horror she could smell the musty woody smell of Western Hemlock bark. She and Raining had spent days, whole weary days, stripping flitches of bark from hemlocks in the Forest, and peeling out the soft inner bark to make the red dye now coating Lark. Tomorrow they were supposed to boil the bark with mordant and strips of thin hempen cloth which Raining could then use as watercolor cakes.

Lark beamed at her. "Even I been painting!"

With a little moan Wire jumped down the corridor to Raining's workshop. The big covered pail they had put the dyestuff in lay on its side like a pig with its throat cut. Rust-colored dye lay pooled on the stone floor. It was soaking nicely into the bottoms of a stack of canvases Raining had left against the wall. A wood chisel lay in a puddle of dye on the floor. Wire picked it up. You could see the ring of pressure marks on the dye pail where Lark had used the chisel to pry the lid open. Smart kid. Strong, too.

She heard Raining's voice coming downstairs. "Wire? Wire, what do you—Aaah!"

Shrieks, screams, tears, yelling.

More shrieks.

Wire squinched her eyes shut. Probably she ought to go back.

Raining had Lark by the shoulders and was stooped over her, yelling, wild as a hawk. "These are Mommy's paints! Mommy's! Not for you!" Shake. "Do you understand me!"

Lark flopped down on the couch—splat! "You get everything and I get nothing," she said, pouting hugely and trying to squirm away from her mother's grip. She used to cry when Raining yelled at her. Now, just shy of her fourth birthday, she was more likely to get mad. She was going to be some kind of teenager. Wire shuddered.

"Lark, why don't you get Grandma to give you a bath. Bell?" she called desperately. "Bell?"

"You're hurting," Lark whined. Raining hissed at her daughter; bit her lip; let go.

"That's good, that's good, all right," Wire said. "You really are too little to paint by yourself, Lark. Tell you what, maybe tomorrow Mommy could show you—" Raining made a low, snarling noise. "Maybe Aunt Wire and you could do a little painting together," Wire said quickly. "How about that? We could go back in the workroom— um, I mean, we could go out by the stream and take some pencils and draw together, how about that?"

"Want paint." Pout. Pout, pout, pout.

Raining's mother came down the stairs. "Wire? Did you—oh my." She blinked, looking at her granddaughter and then at her sofa. She grimaced, then smoothed her face over and smiled. "My, someone has been having a lovely time! Maybe we better go have a bath, sweetheart. Mommy and Wire are going to a very important dinner tonight and they need to get along."

"I want to co-o-o-me."

"Oh, not tonight, dear. They're going to be up well past your bedtime. But I promise you we will have every bit as much fun here. I was thinking I might make . . ." Bell pursed her lips and frowned at the ceiling. "I might make . . ."

"Cookies?"

"Cookies. That was the very thing."

"Don't want cookies," Lark said, scowling. Wire bit her lip to keep from smiling. Even Bell couldn't win them all.

"Want muffin."

"You know," Bell said, "I have some blackberries I've been meaning to use. Perhaps blackberry muffins would be just right."

Lark, much put upon, suffered herself to be led into the kitchen, making it clear with dragging feet and slumped shoulders that she had a very poor opinion of this transparent attempt to buy her off. Wire watched her go, exasperated when she was in the room, indulgent when she had turned the corner, and deeply affectionate when she had been out of sight for a minute or two. It was a very familiar sequence.

She looked at Raining.

"Shut up. I didn't kill her."

"Mm." Wire stood. "We better clean up."

Raining grunted.

In a few minutes she came to help, bringing a pail of warm water and a mop. Wire scrubbed the floor and took the cleaning supplies back to the kitchen. Then she settled into the armchair in the parlor.

Raining came in from the workroom, her lips quirked in a small smile. She spread her arms. "Well? How do I look?" Her hempen blouse was cedar green, with a black and red lacquered brooch at the neck. On her black shirred skirt she had slashed a simple design in the spilled red paint, half-drawing, half-calligraphy. It might have been poetry. It might have been leaves of bamboo.

"Gorgeous," Wire said.

"Nick always loved me in this kind of thing. I mixed some dye with glue and a powder thickener. It won't last through a wash, but for tonight . . ."

Wire smiled brightly against the heartbreaking unfairness of things which had put her in Cedar House tonight instead of Nick. How right Raining was. How his heart would have leapt to see her.

"I saw his ghost last night," Raining said.

"Nick?"

"I came into Lark's room to check on her on my way to bed. She was fast asleep. I bent down to give her a kiss, and when I stood up, he was standing beside me."

"But—I mean, what did he say?"

"Nothing, of course. He was never much of a talker," Raining joked. Tears stood in her eyes. "That's it. No more story. I guess that's why I made this dress. He would have liked it."

The silence stretched out. Raining went into the kitchen to have a quick word with her mother and then returned. Wire cast around for something to say. "Why do you even bother boiling bark and crushing shells and pissing on lead to make paint?" she asked. "Why not do all your painting on the Companion?"

"Yuck."

"Seriously."

"I don't know!" Raining threw up her hands. "It's—it matters, it's important to make colors from bark and shell and stone. To make glair from eggs and thinner from pine sap and mix your paints in gum arabic and linseed oil. That's what we are," she said. "Meat and fat and skin and muscle. That's the world. That's life."

Wire looked at her right hand that still ached where the god had kissed it.

"You better get changed," Raining said. "Your pants are all splotched. I probably have a skirt you could squeeze into. It will show a little more leg on you, but . . ."

Wire went upstairs to change.

It was the middle of August, high blackberry time. Emily Thompson had returned to Vancouver, putting the finishing touches on a series of diplomatic pacts. Southside soldiery was keeping the Downtown core from utter warlordism, if you looked at it one way, or enforcing martial law for its own purposes, if you looked at it another. It was not a comfortable situation, and Wire was glad she wasn't involved. She was, however, invited to the dinner; Raining had asked her along for moral support.

She finished changing out of her dye-stained clothes.

Chirps and exclamations came from the baking party in the kitchen as she came downstairs. No sign of Raining. Idly she picked up the Companion to Art. She wondered when it had been made, and by whom, and how much longer it would last. The magic was fading everywhere, it seemed. Raining's father agreed with her about that; he had been spending a lot of time talking to merchants and radio operators of late, listening to news from other cities, other countries. Wonders and miracles were seeping away as if a long night were passing at last. All the dreams of the world's troubled sleep were slipping away as daylight came, and one by one the dreamers all woke up.

Raining came out of the bathroom. "Are we ready?"

"Have you ever thought to look up yourself in the Companion?"

"No. And don't."

"Why not? I'll bet you're in here."

"It's too important," she said. She went into the kitchen to check on Lark.

When she left the room, Wire picked the Companion up again. "Chiu," she said.

The Companion's screen cleared and returned with a self-portrait of a woman Wire did not immediately recognize.

Chiu, Lark Climbs Singing
    The daughter of a laborer and a competent amateur, Chiu came to art after a troubled adolescence which saw—

"Clear," Wire said, and she closed her eyes.

CHAPTER 33

Mother should have been here for this, Li Mei thought, looking around the banquet hall. She would have been so much more accomplished, so welcoming, so elegant. But she is gone, it is partly my fault, and strangely I stand here, greeting guests, acting the hostess. Being her. And time goes on, and life continues, and grief turns into sorrow, and there are obligations to fulfill.

She paced through the room, smiling as well as she could, correcting a flower arrangement on the table near the entrance.

"Lovely party," Johnny Ma had said an hour before, winking at her. Li Mei suppressed a snarl. She could not remember having asked to deal with temperamental cooks. She did not recall expressing an ambition to run a restaurant. She had tried as politely as possible to decline the task of organizing this ridiculous banquet, not once but several times. If it was a disaster, it was only what Floating Ant and Johnny Ma deserved for pressuring her into managing this party.

She wasn't fooled by Johnny's flattery, either.

A thread was ravelling from one of the ties of her overgown. Surreptitiously she licked one finger and tried to smooth it back into place.

She prowled back to her place at the end of the high table, far from the exalted dignitaries, and close to the kitchen, so as to be able to intercept problems as they arose. Well, things seemed to be going smoothly so far. The exalted dignitaries were having a fine old time, to judge by the snorting pig sound of Emily Thompson's laughter, which punctuated Johnny's stories at fairly regular intervals. Li Mei allowed herself a small, dour smile. She had been right to seat Southside's heir next to the new Minister for the Interior. Two more good-natured, clever, thoroughly unscrupulous people it was hard to imagine. Thick as thieves, and didn't they deserve one another.

She did hope poor pathetic old Huang Ti didn't show up and make another scene as he had when the new government was sworn in without him. Mm. She'd have to tell the doormen to be alert.

A young woman came drifting over from the buffet and sat across the table in the chair Li Mei had specifically left empty to give her a better view of the hall. The interloper was vaguely familiar but Li Mei couldn't place her. Green blouse with a daring neckline and a slit skirt that she wore with easy familiarity. Emphasis on the easy. "Is there a problem?" Li Mei said frigidly.

"No, not at all! S'Delicious! Pretty nearly as good as what they laid on in the Southside, I'd say."

"Ah. Indeed. How very kind of you."

"The only thing I really miss from there would be the cabbage rolls. Oh, and they have these red things, these vegetables—oh, what were they called?"

"Beets."

"Yes! Beets! That's right. Most amazing things. So . . . passionate. Don't you think?"

Li Mei looked at her. "I am terribly sorry," she said, excruciatingly solicitous. "I don't believe I have you on my guest list."

The young woman tried to pick up a barbecued chicken's foot with her chopsticks. When it slipped for the third time she gave in and grabbed it with her fingers. "My name's Wire," she said between nibbles. The little trollop smiled winningly. "Raining said I could come."

"Ah," Li Mei said. "She did, did she?"

Johnny Ma walked behind her on his way to the buffet. He stopped and gave the trollop a second look. And a third. His smile was every bit as winning as hers. "Is Li Mei here giving you a hard time? She's a damp firecracker tonight."

"Not at all! We were just talking about beets."

Johnny spared Li Mei a merry glance. "I see. Well, be a good hostess, my dear girl. I almost think this young lady is here as my guest." The young lady in question examined the exceedingly dapper Minister for the Interior. She smiled archly back at him. "Yes. Now I am certain of it," Johnny said. "Perhaps, when we are done here, I could show you something of Hastings Street after dark?"

Really, it was too repulsive. If Johnny were a cat, he would be spraying the woman's chair legs.

"Have you ever been to one of our casinos?"

"Yuck. What a waste of a nice night. But I would very much enjoy a tour of the grounds. My one previous stay in Government House was a bit confined."

Li Mei could just see this Wire as a blackjack dealer. Or maybe a cocktail waitress.

"I can think of some charming views already," Johnny said. At least he had the grace not to look down her dress while he said it.

Li Mei watched him eel over to the buffet. She noticed that the page boy had overlooked a crooked flower arrangement on the head table. She wondered if she could have him flogged.

The dinner was a great success, especially for the hosts. Li Mei had not forgotten Winter's feasts of Scotch and beets. She extracted a terrible vengeance by alternating the Peking Duck and crispy crab and black cod with platters of steamed chickens' feet and bowls of rich broth, floating in which were succulent chunks of what she explained to Emily, half-way through her bowl, was boiled tendon.

When the food had been cleared away, Li Mei sought Claire out. She explained that Water Spider had not been present at the dinner, but had just now arrived at the front door and was wondering if the governess could spare an hour or two. He had promised himself he would introduce her to a cup of rather special tea, should the occasion arise.

Claire accepted with pleasure. Lacking Emily's muscular enjoyment of politics, these diplomatic functions left her bored to stupefaction.

Water Spider walked Claire back to his apartment.

There he made Ti Kuan Yi in a tiny pot of great beauty and took it out onto the balcony. The first serving he left for the gods. The rest of the fragrant gold-green tea he poured into two cups of exquisite porcelain, one embossed with a dragon and the other with a phoenix. "This is the tea they call the Iron Goddess of Mercy," he said. He gave the phoenix cup to Claire and they sat down on the balcony in the warm late summer night.

Claire took a sip and closed her eyes. The tea was the distant smell of grass burning; wind on the mountaintop; old grief remembered.

They drank together for a little time.

"I was sorry to hear about Jen," Claire said. "I came to like him."

Water Spider nodded. The Iron Goddess of Mercy opened in him, delicate with the scent of autumn and distant smoke. "He is something of a hero now. Cold comfort to his mother. You remember Pearl? I—the Government has provided her with funds to open a modest shop. Small reparation for a great loss." He sipped his tea. "Jen is a hero, and I am something of an embarrassment. Which is how it should be."

"You served your people."

"Did I? I am not so sure. Certainly that was not the way Huang Ti saw it."

"Oh, him. Anyone who takes him seriously isn't anyone you need to care about. Come to think of it, I didn't see him tonight. Was he ill?"

"Mm. No, Huang Ti is no longer a member of the Government. In fact, he is living at his mother's house. He has suffered some . . . reversals."

The look Claire gave Water Spider was skeptical in the extreme.

"He ran afoul of another colleague of mine," Water Spider said, in his most detached voice. "The former Minister for the South, since promoted to Minister for the Interior."

"Ah yes, Johnny Ma, isn't it? The one who always looks like he just drew an inside straight. Somehow I hadn't figured him for a political heavyweight."

"I never saw worse from Huang Ti than cutting off a man's hand. But Johnny Ma and I were junior officials together when his supervisor made the mistake of offering him an insult. Johnny took the trouble to ruin his business, buy his house, evict his parents, and get a child on his wife." Claire blinked. "Any Minister for the South must keep pace with the Double Monkey. He or she must be a person to be respected, or indeed feared. Never trusted."

"Are you then also dangerous, a man who was the Honorable Minister for Borders?"

"Deadly," Water Spider said. "That is the point of a meritocracy. But that was a long time ago. I have lost some of the edge arrogance provides, but have not yet discovered a replacement for it."

Claire could find no immediate reply. She sipped her tea.

"I wondered if you could tell me a little more about the Southside," Water Spider said, with unconvincing nonchalance. Claire looked at him narrowly. He was working extremely hard to maintain his habitual blandness.

"Why?"

He coughed. "Curiosity, largely." She looked at him. "And, actually, I have been toying with the idea of asking for the post of ambassador."

"You?" Claire said. "Living on the Southside?"

"Do you think I would be a poor ambassador?"

"No, well, I'm sure you'd make an—wait a minute. Surely someone from the Ministry of Foreign Affairs would be given that post?"

"Under normal circumstances, yes. But, although this is not yet public knowledge, I can tell you that there is soon to be an Emperor in Chinatown again, and I will have some leverage in that quarter.''

"An Emperor! Who?''

"My father,'' Water Spider said, with some satisfaction. "It was actually Winter who started me thinking in this direction. As soon as I did, the matter became obvious. Chinatown needs an Emperor. Too long have we sat with the red throne empty. But who to reconcile the different Powers? Who was aesthete enough to please the Lady, strong enough to satisfy the Dragon, devious enough to earn the respect of the Double Monkey? Who could clearly be seen as an heir of Wu Lei, the last to hold the Dragon Throne? Who else but the last of his knights? Who but the man who had wielded both sword and pen? Who better to lead Chinatown back into the daylight, as the magic's long dream draws to a close, than the one man among us who can remember a time before this world of ghosts and spirits?'' Water Spider paused. "I also thought it a suitable revenge, for what he had done to me.

"I surmise my honored father's accession will occur before midwinter. His rise will doubtless mean a senior post for Li Mei. So, at least one of my people I will not have utterly destroyed.''

"Good for Li Mei.'' Claire laughed. "I didn't get much chance to talk to her tonight. She looked like a cat trapped in a car wash. It was worth it just to watch her squirm, though.''

Water Spider drank the rest of his tea and took a deep breath. "As I said, I am something of an embarrassment here. That will only be more true when my father takes the throne. But I had one other motive for considering a move to the Southside.''

"Which was?''

From the pocket of his robe Water Spider pulled out a small jade box and studied it very intently, not meeting Claire's eyes. "Perhaps I could unfold that more fully at another time. In a few weeks, or months. For now, would you do me the honor of accepting this small, this unimportant . . . ?'' Running out of words, he held the box up and lifted the lid. Inside was a small green-gold ring set with a white diamond that gleamed like frost in sunlight.

Claire looked up in surprise. "Oh. I really don't think I could—"

"Take it. Please." Lifting the ring from the box he pressed it into the palm of her hand and folded her fingers over it.

Claire was just beginning to protest again when she stopped, the words turning to tears in her throat. At the touch of the diamond in her palm, the strangest sensation came over her, as if she had found something she thought lost forever. Something precious to her beyond all price. Memories flooded back into her. "It's my day," she whispered. "The one they took from me in the Garden. I—I don't know what to say."

"Then do not speak," he said.

Water Spider did become Ambassador to the Southside. There he and Claire were married. Some years later, Claire stood with their daughter in the snowy field of McKernan Elementary. It was Christmas Day. Most of the houses around them were empty; the good people of the Southside were in church, chanting the long, joyful Christmas mass.

But Claire had seen the sun burning bright and low in the sky and felt the sharpness in the air. She sneaked out with little Mei, who had no more enthusiasm for standing still and chanting in Slavonic for hours than any other five-year-old. Even if it was a little wicked, how glorious and open the skies and field, compared to a tiny dark church! How sharp the wind compared to clouds of incense; how much brighter the sun was than candles.

There were sun dogs in the sky, one, two, no four of them, dazzling and incorruptible. Arcs of brightness joined them. Little Mei clapped her hands and laughed and Claire picked her up and swung her around so the snow and sky went spinning and Mei laughed so hard she got the hiccups.

Claire put her daughter down and opened her arms to the cold and the snow and the whole world white and dazzling. "This is for you," she said.

CHAPTER 34

Many years later.

First, she laid down two color masses: blue-grey sky at the top of the canvas, pale green Forest beneath. The green was one of her favorite colors, pressed from iris blossoms and boiled with alum. Clothlets dipped and dried twenty times made good watercolor cakes. She wet her brush in gum water and took up the dried color, quickly building a few masses in the Forest; there the suggestion of a salal bush, here a hummock she would later clothe in cedar needles.

Butane candles hissed softly overhead. Once each year, in the spring, she stayed up through the night to do this. She hummed softly as she worked, occasionally sipping from a cup of blackberry tea. Tree trunks shadowed in brown and black; the hanging green-gold film of morning sunlight. The stillness of the wood, rendered in tiny, particular strokes of her 00 brush. An old-fashioned painting, this, without her current flash; not lit, slashed and smoldering with her beloved reds.

Nick she placed near the edge of the canvas, standing on a path in the morning. Waiting. Lines of frost in his dark hair. Overhead, unseen among the branches, a Steller's jay, just leaving her perch, black wings showing brilliant blue where the light touched them.

Nick, standing on the dark path. The bright bird in flight. Toward him? Away?

The long wood poured between them, like a river.

These were her parents.

Lark finished the painting and drank her tea. When dawn came, she walked out of Cedar House to a certain place in the Forest. She brought the painting with her. Here, in a little pit made of stones, she built a fire. Dried moss and cedar needles for kindling, small twigs on top in a careful pattern, then larger sticks and two useful logs. When the fire was ready she put the painting on top.

It was a beautiful morning, clear and dry. The huckleberry bushes had put out their fine lace of green leaf. Birds bustled, flitting overhead and airing their opinions. Lark found herself humming again.

Kneeling, she struck a long match and touched the kindling with it, here and here and here, and the match gave each time its gift of light. Dry orange moss hissed and burned. White flame skipped up a ladder of spruce and cedar needles, crackling. Lark blew softly on the fire. Bigger sticks caught. Light danced and heat trembled from the fire's red, red heart. Smoke began to pour around the edges of her painting. Dark stains flowered on its surface, spreading over the trees, and the jay, and her father on the path.

Then the canvas pulled apart, and fire came through it like a revelation.

Acknowledgments

As always, my profoundest gratitude to Christine, who was the first to name the heart of this book, and to Philip, who led me, over waffles at a Richmond pancake house, to the discovery of Chinatown's desires, and many other things. Heartfelt thanks to Susan Allison for making me do it all over from the beginning. Also, thanks to Sean Russell for many excellent suggestions, and for introducing me to David Hinton's incomparable translations of the poetry of Tu Fu. Tom Phinney, Maureen McHugh, Michael Stearns, Karin Fuog, and Bruce Rogers all weighed in with much-needed insight at crucial times. Linda Nagata did the same at tremendous speed at the eleventh hour. I owe them all.

This book is dedicated to the cities of Edmonton and Vancouver, and to my grandfather, A. G. Thornton.